# THE LORD'S
# TUSKS

## JEFFREY ULIN

Black Rose Writing | Texas

ISBN: 978-1-68513-068-8
PUBLISHED BY BLACK ROSE WRITING
www.blackrosewriting.com

Printed in the United States of America
Suggested Retail Price (SRP) $23.95

The Lord's Tusks is printed in Garamond Pro

*As a planet-friendly publisher, Black Rose Writing does its best to eliminate unnecessary waste to reduce paper usage and energy costs, while never compromising the reading experience. As a result, the final word count vs. page count may not meet common expectations.

*For Eve, Charlie, Teddy and all the dogs*

# THE LORD'S
# TUSKS

# PROLOGUE

*Middle of the Savanna, Kenya— 1965*

Colonoso's trilling bird call cut through the bush and froze the hunting party. The signal meant a predator was near. Richard Keeton placed complete trust in his guide's senses and scanned the landscape for movement. Unfortunately, the light was dimming with sunset only an hour away, meaning they would have to wait another day to sight their real target. Colonoso had been tracking a family of elephants who were likely meandering toward a nearby watering hole. Even though Richard's heart skipped with excitement, the predator was a nuisance. Richard was after ivory. There was nothing like the adrenaline, though, of bagging a leopard or lion, and Richard tried to calm his breathing while waiting for Colonoso's next note.

A quick whistling sound and three clicks from Colonoso's tongue caused Richard's eyes to shift to nine o'clock from their position. Almost imperceptible amidst willowy grasses, three female lions plodded forward in a straight line until the leader halted. Cocking their heads in unison, yellow eyes stared directly at Richard. Who was stalking whom? Richard checked his rifle, careful not to make any sudden movements. Nearby, a wildebeest restlessly shifted after catching the scent of the lions. The lead lioness pivoted her head toward the wildebeest as the Picasso-faced antelope strode into the bramble at the edge of the clearing. Game on.

The two trailing lions split off, circling left and right, disappearing into the shadow of the grasses as they slunk toward the wildebeest. Richard marveled at the choreography, the lead lion alert on her haunches, focused on the wildebeest's heading. Patiently waiting for her sisters to flush out their prey, she remained perfectly still, her outline revealed by the falling sun filtered through blowing grass in animated flashes. Richard considered a shot, but the lioness was too far away. He dared not edge closer, having lost bearings on the other two. He hoped Colonoso would chirp a new signal, freeing him to creep nearer before the lioness moved. Almost telepathically, a new call whistled, and Richard cocked his rifle in synch with the sound to mask the bolt's clank. Safe to advance, he began inching forward, gauging he should be within range in less than thirty seconds.

The lioness continued staring into the thicket where the wildebeest had fled, coiled to spring, unconcerned with Richard's approach. Another whistle and chirp cut through the quiet, causing the lioness to rotate her head and Richard to look sharply to his right. Less than fifty paces away, one of the other lions emerged from behind a thorn bush and then paused between Richard and her prey. Despite its shelter, the wildebeest was faintly visible to human and lion alike. Richard raised his rifle and pulled the trigger in one smooth motion, the bullet exploding into the lion. She was dead almost instantly, but rather than check whether his shot proved fatal, Richard had already spun and taken aim at the distant lioness. Another bang violated the sanctity of the savanna. This shot entered the lioness's hindquarters, knocking her down as she roared in pain. Knowing there was nothing more dangerous than a wounded lion, Richard reloaded and jogged straight toward her. Staggering to her feet and gnashing her teeth in defiance, the lioness fell with the next shot, a tragic victim of an unfair fight.

·    ·    ·    ·    ·

Back in camp Richard celebrated his double kill, downing a local beer and reliving each sequence leading up to the final shot. When the adrenaline waned after dinner, he retired to his tent and fiddled with the static on his radio until securing a news broadcast. Richard would struggle to sleep tonight without something to settle him. Boring news from home usually served as the perfect sedative. His whole body, though, snapped alert as he listened to the evening's headlines.

The anchor repeated, "It is with great sorrow we report that Her Majesty's Ambassador to the Republic of Kenya, Nigel Dunning, has died in a plane crash. The small airplane was reportedly returning to Nairobi from a conference on the eastern coast. Nigel Dunning was Britain's first ambassador to Kenya since the Republic, now a Dominion within the British Commonwealth, was granted its independence just a couple of years ago. It is expected that a memorial service will be held locally, attended by the former Governor of the East African Protectorate and Kenya's President, with a funeral to be held in London. There has yet to be a comment from the Royal Palace, but a spokesman from 10 Downing Street made the brief statement that 'Ambassador Dunning was a decorated servant of Great Britain, instrumental in establishing a smooth transition to independence in the East African Republic. This tragic news shocks us all. We express our deepest condolences to his family with whom the government will plan a funeral benefitting his stature and service to the Crown and country.'"

Absorbing the news, Richard ripped open his tent and bellowed to Colonoso, "Begin packing up everything. We leave in an hour. I need to be in Nairobi before morning."

"I thought we were setting out at dawn for the elephants?" Colonoso asked, his head slightly bowed.

"Shut up and do it! Plans have changed. I don't need to explain myself."

"Yes, Sir."

Richard returned to the radio, hoping to gain more information, his mind churning how he could turn Dunning's passing to his advantage. He had met him a few times at the Polo Club and other local gatherings, along with the ambassador's wife. Nigel was a decent enough fellow and had always treated Richard with more respect than often accorded second (or godforsaken third) sons of titled families. The news was bad, but Richard was not about to waste his time mourning. Instead, his mind turned to Nigel's wife, Julia, whom he reckoned was just bestowed with a title even worse than third son: young widow. She was a bit flighty, but good legs and deep bank accounts made up for personality defects. He wondered how she would deal with this turnabout, no longer the first lady of what until recently had been one of the empire's greatest colonies. How does one recover from such loss of status? What would this mean for local government? And more importantly, for Richard Keeton? By the time he reached Nairobi, a scheme was forming.

·     ·     ·     ·     ·

Richard waited almost an hour for the operator to put through a call to his solicitor in London. Finally, Henry Radcliffe joined the grainy end of the line: "Richard, nice to hear from you. I understand you're back in Kenya. Tracking down more of your peerage's faded glory? It's a shame you never met Lord Keeton."

"I've spent plenty of time with my brother. But for once, this call isn't about him. Or at least not directly."

"You know what I meant—not your brother, of course. Your grandfather. Anyway, I'm still working on that research. Bit delicate. What can I do for you?"

"Have you heard about Ambassador Dunning dying in a plane crash?"

"Of course. It's been front-page all over the papers. What a tragedy."

"Yes, it's horrible. And I've met his whole family. That's why I'm calling. I'd like to attend the funeral."

"Well, that's…very respectful. My condolences. I didn't know he was a friend of yours."

Hesitating a beat, "Yes, well, we weren't very close. But you know how it is. Small circle of sorts down here. And I thought it would be proper to attend. Important for us Brits with ties to Kenya to show solidarity."

"Cut the bullshit, Richard. I've represented multiple generations of Keetons and known you since you were a kid. Are you really asking me to procure an invitation to a funeral?"

"Well, Graham surely isn't going. And yes, that's exactly what I'm asking. Can you do it? Rumors are it's being held next weekend in Westminster Abbey."

"That's what I read here. And I'm guessing you think there may be an invitation posted to The Lord Keeton. One that you can borrow. Am I on the right track?"

"Guess you know me pretty well. Which means I shouldn't have to repeat myself. Can you do it?"

"I'll let you know tomorrow."

•     •     •     •     •

Traveling first class to London had been very expensive. However, Richard wanted to be well-rested and told Henry Radcliffe to charge everything to his brother. In Graham's invalid state, he would never know the difference. Nor would Graham have any idea that Richard was in town and attending the funeral at Westminster Abbey in his stead. It was an uncharacteristically bright day when Richard strode from a taxi toward the cathedral's central archway, his prematurely chalk-white hair gleaming. The square lines of his face looked chiseled straight from the Abbey's stone.

On his way into the nave of the great cathedral, Richard was surprised to bump into an old friend, Andrew Harrington. Andrew had bought a couple of glorious ivory tusks from one of Richard's recent hunts. After exchanging formalities about the tragedy befalling Nigel Dunning, Richard decided he might as well do a little business. "Andrew, I may be bumping up my supply a bit if you're interested."

Raising an eyebrow, "What, becoming a better shot or something, Richard?"

"No, just have some ideas to diversify my supply."

At that moment, the grieving widow, Julia Dunning, burst into tears, drawing everyone's attention to the front row. While glancing toward her torrent of sobs, Richard continued, "I have some ideas that may help cut through some of the bureaucracy, ease shipping."

"Fine, Richard. We can talk about it later. Not really the place, you know. My god, listen to that poor woman."

"Yes, of course. Later. And I have something special that might pique your fancy," ignoring Julia's wails and thinking about the lions from his recent hunt. Richard expected the heads would look splendid mounted on a wall; or perhaps, even better, Andrew would want the whole animals, stuffed head to tail! He was glad he had Colonoso properly skin them. Maybe he would have to think about diversifying from hunting elephants. No, ivory was becoming too profitable. Putting his thoughts aside, he said, "Let's sit," leading Andrew into a reserved pew, breaking protocol over assigned seating.

Once settled, Richard craned his neck, scanning the crowd before refocusing on his current prey. Julia Dunning was now quiet, sitting head down together with her two young children. Her son was staring ahead toward the coffin, but the motion of rubbing his eyes belied the boy's struggle to appear brave. Julia had an arm around her daughter, the long-legged girl clinging to her, the press of mourners hardly providing comfort to the girl's overwhelming grief. All Richard could recall about the girl was that she already had a reputation as an accomplished rider, able to hold her own at the Polo Club. Maybe talking about horses would be a good icebreaker. He would approach them later, perhaps dropping by their house, offering to help with anything that required looking after back in Nairobi. Maybe the little girl's horse needed attention. Richard made a mental note to call his solicitor as soon as the service ended to confirm where they were staying. He smiled, absorbed in his thoughts, oblivious to the choir's soaring hymn and the muffled cries coming from the girl in the front row. Yes, he thought, landing the widow of Her Majesty's ambassador would be a proper fit when the Lordship was his— not to mention the benefits of smoothing requests for hunting permits and rehabilitating his bank account.

Three years after the funeral, Julia Dunning was heading back to Kenya. This time, though, as Mrs. Richard Keeton. Dangling the prospect of becoming Lady Keeton turned out to be quite seductive.

# CHAPTER 1

*Nairobi, Kenya— 1980*

Guards bearing machine guns stood at the foot of the airplane's stairs while the queue of passengers methodically moved from checkpoint to checkpoint. Warned in advance about passport control, Michael Sandburg calmly took out his tourist visa, advising the officer he was staying at the Hilton. Trying to explain he would be moving to a tent in the middle of a game reserve would raise complications. He hoped to collect his working papers within a couple of days, and after a long trip a comfortable hotel bed offered multiple benefits. An expressionless guard stared at him through bloodshot eyes. Michael averted his gaze, pretending to be preoccupied with the young attendant who pounded his American passport and waved him into Africa.

Michael had sent his equipment ahead, leaving only the hassle of claiming two checked bags. They were already sitting on the ground next to the baggage carousel, primed for inspection, when he entered the room. He had hoped his contact would whisk him through with VIP treatment, but found himself alone walking toward the exit door. On the other side, a crowd of strangers jostling to stand at the front stared at the first passenger off the plane. Michael pulled a crinkled scrap of paper from his pocket, reading the name. Ron Easton was the agency fellow supposedly greeting him. Scores of people were shouting, but none directly to him.

Michael nervously scanned the crowd and put down his bags. The din of cab drivers preying on the latest arrivals swelled with each passenger emerging from customs. Michael squinted at a white sign with bright red lettering bobbing up and down amid the swarm. He fought his way through the masses, deploying his luggage as crude cudgels, and relaxed when able to make out the name: Michael Sandburg. The man holding the sign was still jumping about as Michael set both bags at his feet. "Hi, I'm Michael," he said, extending his hand.

The short black man put down his sign and grasped Michael's palm. "Jambo, Jambo," the traditional Swahili greeting: "Welcome to Africa."

"Thank you. You're not Ron Easton, are you?" Michael asked, expecting a craggy white man in boots and a safari suit.

"No. Mr. Easton was delayed and sent me to greet you. I'm Peter, your driver."

"Driver? OK, great. Nice to meet you. How do we get out of here?"

"Follow me."

A few minutes later, they were speeding through downtown. As the sun began to rise, the quiet streets gave the newcomer an unobstructed view of the government houses and city promenades. Michael yawned, the rush of excitement from his arrival now giving way to exhaustion.

The plan was for Peter to leave him at the Hilton to nap away the morning then pick him up at noon to meet Ron Easton. By the time Michael opened his eyes and peered out his hotel window, a sea of black men and women jammed the square below. Soon he was back in the car, moving again and still disoriented. It took Peter half an hour to honk his way through the crowds and would-be intersections before they began heading towards equatorial suburbia.

Along the only paved road climbing from the city plains to the lush, bucolic landscape stood the Nairobi Polo Club. The rectangular polo field bespoke order, wedged between the meandering road and sprawling bush. The faded blue clubhouse was a two-story-high wooden building fronting a stand of small bleachers. No more than fifty people could sit on the benches, the present crowd sparsely scattered on the wooden planks leading to the second-floor entrance. The second floor was dominated by a screened-in porch and a bar defined by a few tables and a broken television. The bar was where the real action took place. Players and spectators would gather, and with a full mug glance over the field to flit away the afternoon.

Though small, this oasis provided the few members a place to wallow in the colonial stench. The grounds begat nostalgia, naturally providing the perfect place for high tea and conversations sweetened with references to the Queen Mother. Michael grinned at the thought, straining to eavesdrop. He hoped it was only half the bastion of elitism he pictured. Nevertheless, he had expectations, and it seemed to take minimal effort to overhear the ballyhoos of what was happening back in various London royal boroughs.

Out on the field, another chukker began. Dust flew up as the horses contorted themselves, their masters swiping at a hard ball which half the time managed to strike the leg of a compatriot filly. The players skill levels ranged from mediocre to lousy. Except for one.

Finding Ron Easton sitting alone halfway up the bleachers, Michael managed to move past introductions and ask, "Who's that?" Ron gave Michael a smarmy, tobacco-stained smile. He had a paunch equally appealing. Ron's gaze courted shadows, and his receding hairline exposed red blotches. Michael shifted uncomfortably. The man came off as phony. Even Ron's clipped speech seemed strained as if his British accent was the result of practice instead of flowing naturally.

"That's our best player at the club, a two handicap, the stepdaughter of Richard Keeton, philanthropist, avid big game hunter, Lord—or rather soon to inherit a Lordship—take your pick. See him there in the red cap?"

"Yes. Did you say that's his daughter?"

"Stepdaughter."

"I guess that shouldn't surprise me. For some reason, I didn't realize women played the sport. Ashamed to admit it, but I had an outdated image of this place as a Colonial outpost, filled with men or even soldiers," Michael said.

"I know what you mean. Don't need to be embarrassed about being a chauvinist here, though. Local law lets each man take up to one hundred wives," Ron quipped with a straight face before breaking into another telling smile. Michael sheepishly returned the grin, grateful when Ron excused himself to refill his drink. It was exceedingly hot as usual, and everyone partook of the luxury of having ice nearby. The liquor was merely a filler.

Out on the field, mallets circled in a rhythm with the horses' strides. High speeds were reduced to slow motion as the swirling dust stayed suspended in the rising heat and cast a film over the field. Michael stared into the haze. The horses and riders were perhaps thirty yards off, filtered like a mirage. He took off his sunglasses for a moment and wiped his brow, dripping sweat onto the already stained bleachers. Michael made a mental note to buy sunscreen urgently, his pale white skin under assault. The sun was so bright he could not see without squinting, using his hand as a visor against the glare.

Replacing his glasses brought the match back into hazy view. One horseman broke free of the pack, gracefully lunging forward, bending down with the gallop and sending the ball forward with a fluid smack. The wind picked up, sucking a hat into the air. The rider's head freed, a wave of hair the color of melted butter untangled and shot back, echoing the mare's mane. Transfixed on this tandem, Michael watched the pony's urgent strides, its master, or in this case mistress, moving the ball ahead with an effortless pinwheel. The goal neared, and their distance from the chasing pack grew. A final stroke assured scoring, the natural motion propelling the ball straight through the center of the white goalposts.

Moments later, the timekeeper's bell clanked. The dust began to settle in the distance, and a new cloud trailed the riders into the clubhouse. Fighting the heat and sweat, Michael drew himself up and headed around back to the bathroom. Splashing water on his face and neck from the rusty sink, he arranged his hair with his fingers. He smiled into a tarnished mirror, tucking his shirt in as he moved. The left rear side was never successfully stuffed.

Researchers are seldom the fastidious type, and Michael was no exception. He only bothered shaving every other day. In the morning, he would usually run a comb through his thick reddish-blond hair, rarely picking it up again until waking the next day. Such are the advantages of good looks and dimples. Effortlessly presentable, he pulled his five-foot-eleven-inch lanky frame up the club steps.

Michael found Ron perched with a drink just inside the porch, gazing out through the screens at the dismounting players. Ron loosened his ascot, a piece of silly couture in the heat. "Quite a goal, huh, Michael? She made the field look like a bunch of old men. Hell, half probably are! I expect they're all telling her how they would have liked to show her something in their prime."

"What's her name?"

"Caroline. Caroline Dunning. She's a real beauty. She's got a fiancé back in England, though. Maybe one of us will get lucky, and they'll break up. Come on. I'll introduce you."

Michael let out a small snort before following. He soon paused, coming across Caroline Dunning with her back to him. Yearning for a clear view of her face, Michael settled for piecing together the shape of her smile. Her willowy figure was provocative, at least hints teasing past boots and the back of a riding jacket.

Lingering a few steps away, Michael nervously waited for Ron to make good on his promise of introductions. He momentarily froze, though, seeing that Ron had drifted into another conversation while Caroline and her stepfather, Richard Keeton, turned around to move toward the bar. Now directly in their path, Michael had little time to react, saying "Terrific goal!"

"Thank you," she and Richard Keeton both said at once. He smiled, removing his cap, while she shook her head and jokingly raised her mallet.

"I did pass it to you," Richard said through a magnetic grin.

Caroline turned back toward Michael and said, "He's jealous as usual. It was a great goal! Richard here owes everyone a drink, and I'm sure he would love to include you. Will you join us?"

"Sure, I'd love to." Then catching himself, he asked her father, "If that's OK with you, sir?" Richard nodded, telling them he would join them in a moment. He was keen to shed his boots and find a fresh shirt. Michael paused to watch Richard leave, caught in his orbit. Richard had that effect. Half a century seemed only to cast his hunter frame in bronze, his hair brilliantly white as if scoffing at such a muted color as grey.

Michael followed Caroline and the others into the bar, finding the courage to introduce himself. Suddenly conscious of not being a club member and striving to legitimize his presence, he told her he was Ron Easton's guest.

"Are you related to Ron?" Caroline asked, a flicker of discomfort passing through her eyes at the mention of Ron Easton's name.

"No. I'm here doing research on baboons, and Ron is my contact at the wildlife office. I actually just arrived and am supposed to be moving out to camp, well, I hope in the next few days. I'm not sure. I've got to sort out my permits and pick up some equipment they're holding for me at customs." Michael paused, hypnotized by the changes in his life, "I can't wait to get out into the open savanna—a lifelong dream really."

"You'll love it. The first time you come across one of the big five just sitting there, you'll wonder if it's real. No boundaries, no rules. Nature at its most primeval, the way it's supposed to be."

"Sounds romantic."

"Well—it is. No beating around the bush. Sorry for the bad pun," she blushed. "I've always been a bit smitten by the savanna. I wish I could just sit there with the sun baking on me, breathing in the scents on the wind as if I was one of the wild animals." Moving toward the bar she added, "Dare I admit my nose is more attuned to picking up changes in the air than hints of whatever is in a glass of wine? Anyway, usually when I get lost in those dreamscapes, wondering if I can sense a predator, reality hits, and I have to get back to work."

"I assume back in the city, then? Can I ask, what do you do?"

"Oh, I'm a vet. Or almost one. I just finished veterinary college and in my practicum of sorts. Focusing on horses and gaining some experience helping when wounded animals are spotted in the parks."

The notion of being a veterinarian in the wild was as foreign to Michael as the Polo Club grounds. This was no "I'll have a Coke and fries" set. Transfixed by her jade-green eyes, he could only begin to wonder what this beautiful aristocrat's life was like. Who was this woman managing to eviscerate the gentlemen set's bravado with her equestrian prowess, yet whose passions lie in saving her mount's undomesticated cousins? His musing was interrupted by an untimely hand on his shoulder. Ron had finally arrived to make good on his pledge.

"Caroline, how are you? I see you've met Michael already." Ron hesitated, sensing Caroline's easy comfort with the new American. "I hate to do this, but, Michael, we need to push on. I need to go over some things with you, and I'm afraid we're already behind schedule."

"Right now?"

"If you want your supplies for camp."

"All right," extending the words reluctantly while turning to Caroline. "I'll let you know how my first romance with the bush goes."

Radiant, she said, "You'll have to tell me about it."

"Perfect fodder for a lonely tent," Michael said before becoming self-conscious of his status, or in fact, the lack thereof. "Very nice meeting you," he said with an unconscious bow. He could sense Ron shifting with disapproval beside him. Michael extended his hand, and Caroline took it. He wished she had responded with a hug rather than her fingers, but either way, he found himself at ease in her presence. The waft of the match clinging to her boots and the warmth of her hand made such a wonderfully awkward mix that he paused just a beat before saying, "Well, if sick lion cubs bring you my direction, please track me down in camp. Give your nose a simple test picking me out from my troop of baboons."

"I'll keep a sniff out," she smiled.

When Caroline then turned her head to look around the bar, though, Michael's hopes of her actually stopping by deflated. He sensed he was just a novelty. Perhaps, but then she cocked her head back towards him with a puzzling glint in her eye. "Where's your camp? I'm sorry, did you say?"

"I'll be near Amboseli, by Kilimanjaro. I don't know anything more specific. Ron, do you have any idea?"

Even though Ron knew the vicinity of Michael's campsite, he offered, "Not directions, sorry. It's a huge reserve. And it's time we start going.

Caroline, a pleasure as always seeing you. Let's catch up another time. Oh, and I'm sure we have Michael's location back at the office."

· · · · ·

The two men left without seeing Richard Keeton again but found themselves face to face with him a couple of hours later, waiting in the wildlife funding office of Jack Whitehead. As Deputy Minister of Wildlife for the Kenyan government, Whitehead was the most influential man overseeing research and conservation projects. Tourism and hunting together comprised the soul of the bereft economy, and if the foreign granting agencies were snubbed, foreign funds not so mysteriously slowed to a trickle.

Ron Easton took a job under Whitehead about a year before, hoping to usurp power over the agency one day. His strategy was to remain obsequious, nodding to his boss's commands, leading Whitehead to misjudge his ambitions. When the right moment came—and he devoutly believed it would—he would be ready to pounce. His boss was not hungry enough to stay in power much longer.

Whitehead was a straight-arrow Brit who inherited seventeen million dollars from his father at age forty, moving to Africa putatively for his health. Suffering from emphysema, his doctors recommended the climate. He reckoned the equator's air to be ambrosia-laced, for beyond a bit of coughing and being moderately overweight Jack was otherwise in good shape. His wife, though, chastised him for enabling the pudginess overtaking his chin and rounding out his already wide face. After a few months in the African sun and gaining little traction in coaxing exercise that would help shed Jack's extra kilos, his wife began harping on him to find a pursuit to busy his days. Jack agreed, and decided on joining the wildlife agency— donating his way to the top. To his surprise, he enjoyed the job, becoming a champion of conservation commensurate with his position. Even with his newfound cause, it was amazing that he had met with success given his lack of rapport with the staff. Tending to look down on those needing to draw paychecks and intolerant of requests for facilitation payments, he often failed to see the yearnings of ordinary folks and employees with wanting morals.

Ron Easton had been playing the lackey for longer than he had planned, and while Whitehead's hubris rubbed off, his penchant for honesty had not. Ron constantly seethed at the bribes his boss would turn down—both from shameless climbers in the midst of corrupt government ranks and from wealthy aristocrats like Richard Keeton. For a while, he kept a mental tally of how much money he relinquished from refusals. He estimated his cuts should be at least ten percent, and as the number grew, he stopped himself from counting. Thinking about it was frustrating, and feigning pleasantries around his boss insulting. He tried skimming a little on the side but stopped when he sensed Whitehead was becoming suspicious. He was not making enough money to incur the risk. He consoled with the thought that one day he would have Whitehead's job and the money with it. It was only by looking to this future that Ron could absorb Jack's belittling attitude and scrupulous bargains.

While Ron rifled through files to prepare Michael's paperwork and Michael and Richard Keeton made awkward chit-chat, Whitehead pulled his Mercedes up to the building. His office was a two-room clutter of paper in a rickety white building once housing the French Embassy. Striding to the entrance, he saw the door ajar and heard two voices bantering in the waiting room.

Immediately recognizing Richard and extending his hand, he began, "Richard, good to see you. Sorry, I'm late. I just got rid of my driver a week ago and decided to give it a go myself. I'm not very good weaving about in traffic." Turning toward Michael, he asked, "I'm sorry, I don't believe we've met. Do you have an appointment?"

"I think so. I'm Michael Sandburg." Whitehead didn't show any sign of recognition, so Michael continued, "Ron Easton brought me over. He's arranging my permits and has been showing me around. I have a grant coordinated through this office."

"I see," nodding, trying to recall the request.

"Boston was supposed to have cabled everything. Ron's in the other room trying to locate the records so I can get my money and permits. I'm studying baboon behavior. I was told don't worry about my visa—just come as a tourist."

"Ah, yes," the matter now dawning. "The American lad. Nice to meet you," extending his hand. "Ron should be sorting your working papers. Could be a couple of days, though. These things are always slower than you expect. And you'll also need to wait a bit for your money. Sorry, I don't think it's cleared yet. Have you got enough to survive for a while?"

Stunned, Michael creaked, "Not really. I need to order a lot of supplies before heading out to my camp. And I'm already about broke given my travel costs and equipment I've shipped over..."

Keeton, sensing the growing tension, interrupted, "Jack, can't you help out the kid? He's just arrived. Not a very nice welcome to strand him."

"No, I suppose you're right." Turning to Michael, "I'll talk to Ron and see what we can do. One thing you'll have to get used to around here is being patient. Paperwork can move slowly."

A bit speechless, Michael was rescued by Richard coming to his defense again. "Michael, don't worry. I'm sure Ron's got the records. Jack, why don't you send a telegram and let him come in for the funds in a couple of days?" Richard shot a cursory glance at both men and, with approval in their gaze, said, "Michael, would you mind leaving us? Jack and I have some important business. Take a cab back to your hotel, and one of us will get in touch with you later today."

"Yes, don't worry," Jack said, eager to move past the bureaucratic snafu. "And we'll make sure to figure things out if you have to hole up a few days before heading out to your camp."

"Okay," Michael said, before looking at Richard. "Thanks for your help. I don't know what to say."

"Forget it. Go get washed up. You look exhausted."

As Michael left, Jack Whitehead called for an assistant to put on some tea, beckoning Ron to take a seat on a hardwood chair in the far corner. Richard took a chair across from Jack, cordially allowing the minister to drone on about his learning to drive. A fan above clanked, whirling around at a pace so slow that the individual blades failed to become a blur. Soon tea was served, and everyone sensed the socializing was over.

"So, Richard," Whitehead said, "What is it you really want from me?"

"Oh, I think you know."

"I want to hear it from your lips." He looked at Easton in the corner, adding, "Don't mind Ron. Someone else has to hear it to keep us both honest." Jack smiled as Ron silently acknowledged his role, raising his cup toward Whitehead in a toasting gesture, sitting back waiting for a juicy bribe to unfold.

"All right, cards on the table. You're aware I like to hunt and sell a few of the more choice trophies. A notorious exporter, or at least that's the way the rumors seem to portray me. The fact is that I love to hunt and I've accumulated a lot of debts on a family manor I'm trying to keep in England. It's my grandfather, Lord Harold Keeton's place. Anyway, I've decided to ship back more trophies to auction in England. It's all quite on the level. I don't understand why people in the ministry are so suspicious. They all get their cut, and if one of them double-crosses the other so that someone is cheated out of their share, I can't help it." Richard slyly omitted that his father had depleted the family's accounts, leaving insufficient funds for Richard to enjoy the proper life of a Lord when the title was finally his. Costs for his invalid brother's care further contributed to the estate's decline. Siphoning some of Julia's money allowed Richard to keep up a façade for the present. Trading ivory, though, was the key to restoring the fortune he coveted—even if that meant branching into illicit methods.

"Come on, Richard, I'm waiting for your pitch, not part one of a biography we already know. This needn't be a cathartic experience for us all."

Glaring back and in a more business-like tone, Keeton said, "The ports in Mombasa and the men at the airport have quadrupled my export taxes. They don't trust me to give them their cut, and I'm being blackmailed. I can get around a lot, but bottom line I need to ship out the goods. I'm in debt to people back home and can't meet these payments at the rates I'm being charged."

"Well, I'm sorry for you, but I still don't see what you want from me."

"A ministry stamp and a letter clearing the goods will stop those thieves from bleeding me at the ports. They'll understand their boss is taking his cut and that if it gets back to the right people, their cuts and jobs are over. They know who to go to for their share, and I'm just trying to set the system right again."

"Your request, Richard?" Whitehead's tone tilting from boredom to impatience.

"I want your help securing the papers. You control the inflow of research money and the people behind that carry clout with tourism and the government. I'm not trusted. You know that, and you also appreciate it's for that reason that I'm forced to come groveling to you. I'm prepared to give you five percent of the profits on everything you help me ease through the ports. Sterling, deposited in any bank you want: England, private Swiss accounts. If you prefer Kenyan shillings, I can try to work that out. But I don't think that alternative would be advantageous for either of us."

Fidgeting, Ron Easton could not bear the thought of Whitehead turning down this boon. He fought the urge to jump up and volunteer accepting on Jack's behalf, fixing his greedy eyes on his boss. Ron was distracted briefly by Richard casting a glance in his direction, Richard sensing Ron's enthusiasm.

Whitehead replied, "Well, here's my answer: yes and no. I'll help you by not having the present taxes doubled again and by not having the men at the ports block export of all your goods. For that, I'm perfectly willing to accept your five percent, and I would prefer it, as you so wisely guessed, in sterling. If you decide to turn down this most generous offer, don't expect to get anything cleared out of this region."

"I should have known better than to come here. What the hell are you doing in this job, anyway?" Shoving his chair out of the way, Richard stood to leave but paused noticing the look of shock, perhaps disappointment, on Ron Easton's face. Giving Ron an awkward nod goodbye, Richard turned away from Jack Whitehead and walked out.

With a smile as wide as the savanna, Ron Easton said, "God, Jack, I didn't know you had it in you. Do you really think you'll get the money?"

Whitehead had not been focusing on his assistant, and upon digesting the words said, "You really are stupid. I just don't want to get involved."

·　　·　　·　　·　　·

Outside, Alijah, a native Richard Keeton was sponsoring for his own benefit, rested in Keeton's rover, dozing with one of his long arms dangling out the rolled down window. He woke as the door slammed to the chorus of curses. Alijah knew better than to speak and sat listening to the familiar words whose tones, if not every nuance, he had quickly learned.

"That's it," Keeton ordered. "It's time you lived up to what we've been planning. Tomorrow, we're going to the bank, then for a little ride."

Thanks to Richard greasing his path, Alijah rose through the tourism ministry's bureaucratic ranks following his graduation from school. He spoke British English and could civilly converse with the most polished officials and expatriates. Alijah was smart, good-looking, charming, and as arrogant as the day Keeton first met him. Most importantly, he had honed his God-given gift of manipulation. He mercilessly hurtled above the rest of his peers, forging ahead to become a respected and envied member of the ministry.

The toughest of assignments were funneled to him in the hope of discrediting or embarrassing the brash upstart. The schemes never worked. Consistently mastering the task, Alijah made his doubting supervisors appear as the foolish ones. By saving men rungs above his immediate boss from embarrassments, curing ticking disasters that were their ultimate responsibility, he guarded against reprisals from a mere manager. Appreciative senior ministers took notice, and he began leapfrogging to the top. Being too clever, though, can create its own limits, even danger. Others feared him, and in an on-the-take bureaucracy that engenders insecurity and talk of suspension.

Keeton grasped it was time Alijah moved elsewhere, a natural progression of his plan; the next step was already in motion, a conspirator unwittingly waiting. He relaxed a bit at the wheel, the consummation of his plan slowly unfolding.

The next morning, Richard drove to the bank with Alijah, instructing him to wait in the car while he grabbed a briefcase from the back of the Jeep. Sauntering into the branch, Richard emerged half an hour later to lay his enabling money on the seat. For most of his life, the sight would have been meaningless, but now Alijah's eyes opened wide as Keeton opened the case and allowed him to peer inside. It was more cash than he could fathom.

Slightly nervous about his pending recruiting pitch, Keeton sped toward Langata, Nairobi's suburban enclave for transplants like himself. En route, Keeton described more of his fruitless meeting with Whitehead to Alijah, embellishing his part and highlighting how he walked out after the absurd threat. It was remarkable for a titled white man to confide such a meeting to a native, especially when Keeton deemed Alijah beholden to his largesse; however uncustomary, Keeton reconciled candor may be the best course in maintaining Alijah's confidence and loyalty. The former tribesman was vital to his scheme and not easily fooled.

Climbing through the hills and passing the timeless colonial mansions framed by bougainvillea and other colorful flowers, Keeton announced, "Alijah, today you are going to become an important man in the service of your government. But before that happens, we need to visit an unimportant man and convince him of his importance in running this country. I don't want you to say a thing. I may not even have you come inside. In fact, until I call you, don't stray from the car."

"What am I going to do?"

"Patience. Wait until everything is set."

"Where are we going?"

At the question, Keeton sharply turned onto a dirt road and stopped. There was a gate about twenty yards ahead and protruding from an overhanging branch a sign: "Easton."

They proceeded through, the dirt road yielding to gravel, tires crunching on pebbles announcing their approach. Alijah strained to spy the brick mansion set back more than a hundred yards from the opening in the brush. Vibrant purple and yellow flowers brightened the swatch cut in the otherwise green forest. Accustomed to the privilege of visiting countless such estates, Keeton took for granted the beauty of sculpted bushes and landscapes. Alijah, unfamiliar with grand manors, inhaled the fragrances and vista, a newcomer to manicured opulence, rolling down his window for an unobstructed view. Save for once visiting Richard's house, Alijah had never been on such grounds. Keeton eased up to the house, finer gravel defining the circular driveway, a class-defining threshold.

This house symbolized why so many men of his creed ventured to the dark continent. What could top the lavishness of an English mansion and the vibrancy of the African flora—and at a fraction of the cost? Rolling to a stop and climbing out of the car, a sudden shriek broke the tranquility of the ride through a latter-day Kipling poem.

Two salivating Dobermans bounded toward them from the house, and after pausing to raise a leg by the car and stare down Richard Keeton, continued to where Alijah was standing next to his open door. Immediately, the dogs started to pounce. The quicker of the two gnashed his teeth, tearing at Alijah's calf, his pack-mate, eager to join in the frenzy, tugging on his pant leg. Richard Keeton sprinted over and grabbed one of the dogs; between the two men yelling and Alijah's furious wrestling to climb back into the car, the dogs backed off.

Ron Easton and one of his houseboys, rushing outside upon hearing the screams, began calling back their dogs. Surprised but intrigued to see Richard, Ron stuck out his hand, "Richard, what a pleasant surprise. I'm sorry for the disturbance. Will your man be all right?"

"I don't know," Keeton answered, looking back into the car where Alijah was tying a tourniquet around his leg. Recoiling at the sight of the blood-stained seat, Richard wanted to force him to get out of the car but refrained.

Easton motioned for a couple of staff to come help Alijah before turning to Keeton. "Don't worry. I'll have one of my houseboys wash and bandage it. He'll be fine. Not the first nibble we've bound up. Come on in. I was just going to pour another drink. You've rescued me from turning to tea."

As they walked towards the house, Keeton turned back, his eyes meeting those of his grimacing protégé. Not knowing what to say, he half-heartedly waved before turning back toward the house.

"Ron," began Keeton, "What went on? Do you have them trained to attack? I don't understand why they bypassed me. But I'm glad. You sure he'll be okay?"

"Oh, he'll be fine. I'm sure, just a minor flesh wound. They'll throw some alcohol on it to sterilize the area. Might hurt like hell, so don't worry if you hear a bit of a shriek. And you needn't worry. You're white, after all. That's the problem. I didn't mean to train them this way. It's just a bit of a phenomenon. They can sense the difference."

Suddenly, it hit Keeton: "Racist dogs?"

"Ah huh," a bit too positively.

"I've heard about something like that but thought it was a joke. It's actually true?"

"They've never gone after a white man, and your servant is our fourth victim. I wish I'd known you were coming. I could have warned you and sent someone outside to meet your car. If they see me or I introduce them to a black man, then they're as friendly as a regular old Doberman." With that quip, he laughed and opened the door, beckoning Richard to step inside. For the second time in a few minutes, Richard was left frozen, contemplating how much Ron cultivated the behavior before walking forward.

A colossal oak foyer with a grand staircase spiraling up to distant halls gave way to a corridor decorated with hunting pictures. Confounded by the stately walls, Keeton asked, "Is this your family place or..."

"You like it? I'm renting it. I've got an option to buy it. If I can just turn my finances around a bit, I think I'll take it. I don't make much money here. Anyway, a salary isn't the answer."

"Well, yes. And I can relate. It takes more than a job to rehabilitate the old accounts," Richard chuckled, trying to pass off the remark.

"Oh, I didn't mean to be impolite. It's just that I moved for the same reason most of us are here. I have an estate back in Essex, but the upkeep's brutal. Started to have to sell off bits. Here I can be king again! Well, not quite. No pending peerage like you. But as you see, I still live quite well. The one thing I forgot to calculate is how expensive it is to leave. I like to get away and travel in style, so I decided to start working part-time for Whitehead. Easy hours, some pounds, some parties. Anyway, he thinks I'm just a sniveling fool. He's turned native on us, always championing the reserves. I don't suppose you came to march for conservation?"

"No, not exactly," Keeton said, now aware of Ron Easton's intoxicated state. No matter, Ron's forthrightness, while disarming, lay bare his motives. He had assumed Ron Easton was merely another bureaucrat who might be tempted to dirty his hands. However, Richard began wondering if he could leverage Easton, a seemingly kindred spirit in trying to restore the glory of ancestral lands and fortunes, in bigger ways. Ron's frustrations might just tempt Ron to dabble in extracurricular pursuits beyond accepting the average bribe. Enduring Jack Whitehead's servile treatment clearly smarted, and associating with Richard would elevate Ron's social status. Though Ron was tolerated among the right people, absent a titled pedigree Easton had no free pass. Failing to exercise scripted manners and doing little to remedy his odious physical appearance further compounded Ron's social quagmire. Whether Ron was exactly the bumbling underling Whitehead thought or a clumsy social climber trying to assimilate at the Polo Club hardly mattered. Either would do if his signals of discontent, avarice and ethical flexibility were accurate. Richard could even look past those tobacco-yellowed teeth.

A young black woman wearing a dress more expensive than a maid could ever afford caught Richard's attention. She walked past the room, taking only a quick peek before disappearing. Curious about the pretty young woman, he innocently put the question to Ron, learning she did some work around the house. Richard sat back smiling, now appreciating why Ron kept to himself outside of the club. Yes, it was about manners and assimilation, just not in the prescribed order.

Wasting little time, leaning forward, Richard began, "Ron, wish this was a pleasure visit, but I came here with a proposition for you. Took a chance you'd be home, knocking off early end of the week. Anyway, I wasn't very pleased with our meeting yesterday, as you might have guessed. This is between the two of us. If I can speak bluntly, Jack is out of this arrangement."

"Well, that's fine with me. I wasn't exactly pleased with that conversation either. How can I help?"

"It involves a native I've been, well, how do I say it. Sponsoring. I've paid for his education, and he's progressed up through the ranks at the Wildlife Ministry and now doing a rotation over at tourism. I want him promoted to head or assistant head of the anti-poaching unit for the government. He speaks flawless English, is dedicated, and is smart. I thought you might be able to lobby a word with the right people. Push the system along a bit."

"I'd be stepping on some big toes, you know. Why should I stick my neck out for someone I don't know?" Easton stood and refilled his glass. "What are you really after anyway, Richard? Why have you turned into such a benefactor? You're a hunter and not such an honest one."

"Reputations can be easily slandered—as you know. Fact is, I am one of the more successful and soon to be one of the richest." More confident than when he arrived that he could use Ron to accelerate his plans, Richard said, "Wait here a minute. I have something I meant to bring inside. I left it in the car amidst the commotion."

Sluggish to react from too many drinks, Ron gave an acknowledging shrug, happily remaining in the study close to his decanter. Richard Keeton swiftly walked back through the alcove and out the front door. Immediately the two dogs ran up to him, barking. Sensing they were reacting to his fear, he tried to relax. He picked up a stick to play tug of war with one of them before hurling it for both to chase. Dashing to the car as soon as they ran off, he peered in, looking for Alijah. No one was there, and after calling out Alijah's name, he grabbed his briefcase, picking up another diversionary stick to toss before jogging back to the house.

Striding back to the study, Richard set his case on the brass table, then opened it to reveal several neatly stacked bundles.

"Three thousand now, and three more on the promotion."

"I don't get it?"

"We all have our motives. Just assume it's better kept a secret. You're not doing anything terribly underhanded. What do you say?"

"Of course, I'll do it. But I wish you'd tell me more or cut me in on what you're doing. You can trust me. If you're willing to let me do this, you've already decided I won't turn on you."

Richard smiled, his instincts validated. Ron's reaction was more than he could have prayed for upon leaving the bank. And yet, Richard was parading down a slippery slope and needed to proceed with caution. Fingering a bundle of the bills, Richard said, "When I walked in here, I was hoping you'd say something like that. But you...we, need to be patient. Maybe within the month if you succeed pushing this promotion through. Everything hinges on that. With Alijah in that post, he'll be in a position to take cuts from poachers in return for letting them off. Then, with your help, we can also procure licenses and customs clearances free of bribes to smuggle out whatever I want. They're going to hunt anyway. We aren't going to change the inevitable, so all we're doing is instilling order. And our bonus for bringing more predictability — prices going the way they are right now — we're looking at thousands, maybe millions of pounds. I've been waiting for this morning. I have a lot of the buyers, shipping routes figured out, people at the other ports. But Alijah's the key. With him head of the anti-poaching division, we can't miss. And if you'll go along, well, what better cover than the Wildlife Office? I could have everything pass through you while I work in the background."

Ron beamed, "When do I start?"

"Secure that promotion first. Without that, I'm just another hunter, shipping my trophies to collectors who don't have the courage or fortitude to pull the trigger themselves." Richard handed over a rough biography of Alijah he manipulated, hoping it might expedite the process.

"Alijah? Nice name, good credentials. I can probably do it," Ron smirked. "You know, we've been watching the poaching situation closely for the last few months—more audacious raids than we've seen before. If you can organize this thing, I don't think you appreciate just how big you're talking. You're going to have to seek more help than me."

"Well, just force this promotion through, and if 'business' starts growing, then I'll deal with it... I don't want you recruiting." Emphasizing his words, "I trust you will not discuss our enterprise with anyone. Including that woman that walked by. You need to be more careful from now on. Okay?" Richard stood up, formally extending his hand. The bargain concluded, he said, "Let's go outside. I want you to meet Alijah."

Taken aback at Richard's presumptuous move in keeping Alijah in the wings, Ron sighed, "He's here?"

"Oh yes. Your dog bit him."

Within one week, Kenya had the youngest assistant wildlife minister in its short independent history.

# CHAPTER 2

*Bungalow on the Outskirts of the Savanna— Kenya*

Richard sat on the porch in his favorite sloped wooden chair, arms crossed, listening to monkeys chattering in the bush. He had supervised the rocking chair's cutting and even pounded in a nail or two. Craftsmen came in only one class back home, but in what Richard liked to call the wild, he indulged in a thwack to the ebony. Still, he kept his craftsman's mark secret, innocuously asking guests what they thought of his splendid furniture. Designed by Keeton, made by hand. An artistic guild held back not by talent but by the mores of vanity.

A hunting party planned to depart at sunrise, and as the sun rose toward its pinnacle, there remained no sign of Alijah. True, it would be possible to set out with English rifles and tongues, but a guide assured trophies. Local guides were invaluable; a truth repeatedly confirmed when collecting ivory was only a hobby. Now, Richard thought of the orders and his dependence on his native partner. He squinted into the distance, aware that this time he could not afford to lose his guide.

His first guide in Africa, Colonoso, was supposed to meet him on a similar morning years before but disappeared without explanation. Richard never met a better tracker, and as he rocked himself a twinge of hope that he might reappear interrupted his growing impatience with Alijah. Colonoso was a Wakamba, schooled in the secrets of the bushmen. Every scent and every bush uttered clues which his people hoarded as a birthright. With straight bamboo arrows, deftly barbed at their tips, and poisoned with the resin of an inconspicuous root, Colonoso always killed more animals than Richard managed to fell with his rifle.

Keeton remembered sending word to Colonoso twice but heard nothing until the float of a rumor that he died from the black tick. There was no source of confirmation, nor any doubt that one of a plethora of diseases could have stricken him. Cholera and malaria were often touted as the white man's nemesis venturing into the area; the real danger, though, lay in the diseases known only to a few parasitologists in distant laboratories. Worms, ticks, mosquitoes, and water could bear dreadful tentacles of death and mutilation, all working their hideous alchemy beyond the grasp of the human eye.

Richard liked to imagine himself immune, always trying to suppress the itchy tension of each new cut or rash. Without luck, his denial would surely court mortality. Tranquil surroundings served as dangerous traps lulling foreigners into a false sense of safety. A hunter losing his guardian sense of anxiety too often saw life come to a halt. A snake camouflaged as a dormant log or some animal without the instinct to respect the food chain's natural order would win. Parasites struck men of bad luck or carelessness. It was always so easy to wash off the week's crust in an inviting waterhole.

Richard stood up from his chair and, leaning against a wooden post supporting the porch, stared out into the savanna, wondering what snared Colonoso and whether he would ever again see the crafty Wakamba. Colonoso had baptized him into the lore of Africa, and Richard reminisced over their hunts, thinking back to when he managed to shoot two lions. They had been necessarily close, and as much as he resented being dependent on a tribesman, he could not repress the pain. The windswept grasses had a way of knitting friendships, conjuring the sense of a master plan to remind man of his distinct character while treading so close to his past.

Keeton tugged at his shirt collar in the sweltering heat. Alijah was now two hours late, and Richard began to speculate, morbid thoughts flashing through his mind. He recalled their first meeting. "Go find me a new guide," he had commanded a houseboy who rushed off to recruit a replacement for Colonoso. Natives in fringe areas, aware of the white man, always had a few relatives willing to work on the sole recommendation of the lore. Then, of course, there was money, that strange commodity more flexible and enticing than barter goods. A meeting with a Maasai named Mwobyu was soon arranged at a game lodge bar. The tragedy of drunken warriors at tourist lodge bars was just one of the woeful ramifications of juxtaposing government game parks next to tribal life. Men living close to these package tour outposts would wander in and drink as much as they could afford. A warrior bedecked with native paints posing for a camera-happy tourist could collect sufficient tips for an afternoon binge.

To holiday-goers, the money was well spent. A snapshot without consent—and consent was never coming except from the drunken men and women prostituting themselves at the lodges—would likely spark the hurling of a spear. Nobody wants to die with five feet of steel skewering them, and it was a rare Maasai who understood a camera well enough to realize their soul was not being stolen. Richard left his camera behind.

Seeing him coming, Mwobyu stood up, shaky even at the early hour. Lanky at six feet three, the woebegone warrior smiled, revealing the jumble of teeth and spaces defining his mouth. Keeton had met countless Maasai but stopped, quixotically examining Mwobyu's ears. Maasai pierce their earlobes with a thorn at a very early age and progressively widen the hole with larger pieces. At the extremes were those with lobes dangling so low that they could fold them back up over the ear. What distinguished Mwobyu, though, were his earrings, not his ears. Usually, feathers or beads would decorate the dangling flesh, but Mwobyu, his lobes sporting a modest hole, wore a Kodak film canister in one ear and a toilet paper dowel in the other. Keeton sported a broad smile, containing himself as best he could, condescendingly introducing himself.

"I hear you have a younger brother who just completed initiation."

"Yes, Galo. The finest warrior born in our village. Many eagles," Mwobyu slurred with pride.

Keeton nodded, replying, "Mzuri," the Swahili word generically used to indicate praise. Knowing the skills needed to fell birds with the rongu, a throwing club whittled down to a knot at the top and a thin handle a stretched ruler long, he continued, "I understand he may want a job."

"Yes. He hear that white man with smoke kill Ndovu (elephant) even when charging."

Keeton's eyes glistened, sensing that he had come upon a warrior filled with the requisite intrigue. He would need to pay him next to nothing, perhaps five or ten pounds a month. Arranging a meeting, Keeton bought Mwobyu two drinks as a token of his commitment. He was cocksure the Maasi would follow through; if they consummated a bargain, Mwobyu would boast ongoing ties to the white man and, more importantly, free drinks.

Two weeks later, Galo and a slightly younger Maasai unexpectedly appeared in front of Richard Keeton's porch. Keeton momentarily recoiled, unsure how to judge Galo's appearance. His dangling earlobes and arrow-shaped cheekbones gave his face the impression of stretching all the way toward the back of his skull; a hawkish nose flattened out at the nostrils, carving an anchor above his smile. His eyes hid in their sockets, making Richard feel as if he spoke to nothing more than a pair of lids. Failing to accent any particular feature, bright yellow paint dashed across his forehead, a collar of plastic beads less garishly hanging from his neck. Somehow, though, this awkward jumble of features meshed warmly.

In a quaking voice, Galo stepped forward, introducing himself. Before he could continue, though, Keeton interrupted, able to speak pidgin Swahili.

"I've been waiting for you. I need a guide and a good hunter. Stand there." Keeton leapt off the second step and walked away from the two men toward a tree about twenty-five yards away. Taking a knife from its sheath on his belt, he plunged it into the bark and turned back towards the house. Addressing Galo again, he motioned for him to throw at the knife.

Expressionless, Galo nodded his head and turned toward the tree. He raised his spear and looked back at Keeton, who blankly sat on the front step, feet stretching out on the ground—Richard's bored and incredulous look sparking a challenge. Muttering something in a dialect unknown to

Keeton, Galo pivoted and, in elegant silence, fired the spear with the deftness of an arrow. Almost instantly, the sound of metal rang out as the knife clanged to the ground, striking a rock.

Ignoring the feat, continuing to stare at Galo, Richard asked his friend's name and whether he wanted to give it a try too. Although he asked in Swahili, and before Galo opened his mouth, the younger of the two stepped forward, answering in English, "My name is Alijah, brother of Galo, brother of Mwobyu." Alijah was tall, with the same arrow-sharp cheekbones of Galo framing a more handsome face than his professed brother. Keeton considered whether they were actually biological brothers or, more likely, kinsmen who, coming from the same clan or village, called themselves brothers. The answer, though, was of less interest to Keeton than the manner in which Alijah spoke. Wrinkling his forehead, Richard scrutinized the enigmatic adolescent.

"I suppose you want a job too?" Keeton challenged, now knowing that Alijah, but not Galo, could understand him.

"How much?" Alijah responded with a big grin.

Keeton could not contain a laugh, pulling himself to his feet. His hands were dirty, but he nevertheless ran them through his hair. It remained an idiosyncratic habit that neither the maids nor his mother could stop. Sun in his face, his khaki shirt stained, Keeton reeled through his mind before finally looking Alijah in the eye.

Smirking, Keeton asked, "How old are you?"

"I am younger brother of Galo. I passed my initiation in..."

Keeton cut him off, "Never mind." He should have known it was a stupid question. "Probably still in your teens," he muttered to himself; trying to pinpoint the age more closely would only prove futile. Alijah looked more the athlete than Galo, muscled long arms hanging from an imposing trunk, but paraded without the reputation. "Let's see what you can do, huh?" as he picked up his knife and strolled to the same distant tree that Galo had just so gallantly pierced. "Okay, let's go," he beckoned him. For some reason, the sassy nature of the younger Maasai intrigued him. Keeton was taking this challenge as a game, enjoying it, daring the cocky brother.

Alijah centered himself, looking down and scratching at the dirt in front of him with his spear. Suddenly, like a bull bolting from its stall, he sent the spear hurling, screaming a haunting pitch into the distance. He struck the tree; Keeton had expected no less. However, he missed the knife. Alijah's thrust traced about two yards high. Galo's reputation remained intact.

"Ah, I hit!" bragged Alijah.

"Your brother was much closer, and I only need one guide," Keeton scoffed. He was sufficiently impressed with the toss but enjoyed taunting him. "Maybe next time. Where did you learn to speak English so well?"

"The white man, they come and teach me the Bible. I studied very hard." Alijah now spoke in his native dialect, apparently embarrassed at the questioning about his speech.

Galo interrupted, "The white man said he was the fastest learner they ever have. They teach him to make design and to understand."

Alijah began to write his name in the dust, and Keeton grasped that Galo was trying to tell him that the missionaries taught him how to read and write. He had never encountered nor heard of a tribesman so schooled. His first thought had been to hire Alijah as a houseboy, but now he began formulating a crazier notion.

"Alijah, how would you like to go to the university?"

Keeton knew he had the workings of a brilliant plan, smugly conveying he was delighted they had come. He would enroll Alijah at university in Nairobi and hire Galo to serve as his guide. He would pay Galo a mere few pounds for his efforts. The salary sounded generous to Galo until Keeton explained that Alijah's expenses would be coming out of the total. Still, it was adequate. Neither would have agreed simply for money. The lodge's elixir was still a relative unknown, and unlike Mwobyu, money was not integral to their lives. Curiosity overwhelmed them. While few among their tribe entertained similar yearnings, those enticed by the mystique of a distant world would never turn down such an opportunity.

Just when Richard began musing about what would happen if his most recent investment disappeared like Colonoso, Alijah's jeep came barreling toward the house. On occasion, Richard would still employ Galo too, but Alijah was equally adept as a tracker; Alijah's inferiority in wielding a spear next to his brother mattered little given his new expertise with guns.

Richard ranted, "Where the hell have you been! You're almost two hours late."

"I had to come from the village. You know the roads."

"Well, come on, let's go. I've got to have two sets of tusks by this weekend. I don't have anything left over in storage. We're going to have to figure out a way to get you a plane so we can ramp up already."

"I'm supposed to get a plane?"

"You'll at least need to convince people at the ministry you need access to one."

"How am I a going to do that?"

"How else? Money. Let's go. We'll figure it out when we get back. I'm going to need the tusks to pay this time."

• • • • •

Michael mused how to salvage the afternoon as he continued to wait for his permits. Fortunately, Jack Whitehead had managed to find him cheaper accommodations and arranged a small advance on funds. He finally received notice he could collect his gear at customs the next morning. Maybe things would start moving. Bored and anxious to leave the city, he was in no mood for shopping, and the politics of visiting with virtually anybody he knew in town seemed little more appealing. The one person he thought about calling was Caroline Dunning, the alluring veterinarian from the Polo Club. He could picture her perfectly. "Why not," he thought, picking up the hotel phone. As he went to place the call, though, he hesitated thinking about Richard Keeton answering instead, suddenly less sure of dialing. What was he thinking! The stepdaughter of a Lord, a vet and engaged no less. He was literally outclassed.

By dinner, he had put Caroline out of his mind and sat anxiously listening to Hugo Bennett describe Michael's future home. He would be taking over Hugo and Susan Bennett's camp. For the first week there, he would overlap with Susan while Hugo remained behind in the city, completing the paperwork for the couple's departure home. Susan presumably was winding up their research and would have some spare time to orient Michael to the area.

"You'll leave soon for camp to meet Susan," Hugo explained, "and then after about a week, she'll come back to Nairobi. I'm sorry I can't show you around too. It's just impossible to make arrangements for turning in our car and getting all the travel plans set while taking down camp. So, we decided to split it up this time. I came into town instead of Susan because everyone around here's edgy about letting a woman sign papers and all. Not a very liberated lot."

"I'm not surprised from what I've seen so far," Michael nodded. "Is she safe out there alone? You're not worried?"

"Nah, she's all right. She can take care of herself better than I can. The men don't listen to me half the time anyway. Susan has a way with the natives. They love her. And she seems a bit infatuated with them."

Michael soon thanked Hugo for his advice, frustrated that he was still listening to other people's stories rather than experiencing camp himself. The next morning, he entered the customs package room at the Nairobi airport to collect his equipment, checking a near-final box on his pre-departure list. Michael had shipped two rifles, a box of tranquilizer pellets, and assorted tracking gadgets ahead to the wildlife office. Customs officers were habitually loath to allow weapons into the country, and Michael had been advised to circumvent conventional channels by shipping his guns separately. Ever fearful of coups, the military-beholden government carefully monitored the movement of arms into the country and imposed severe sanctions on violators.

It was a crime to possess firearms without a permit, and those well connected enough to possess permits could lose them for the most minor infraction. Not surprisingly, the rules tightened even more snugly around foreigners' weapons, which tended to be more sophisticated than the local staple of older Russian-made fare. Michael's university contacts back in the states finessed his permits but proved powerless when coping with the practicalities on distant shores. High-powered guns with sights focusing to pinpoint accuracy within one hundred yards could practically take over the country if coupled with a few walkie-talkies. Michael assumed his substandard rifles should pose no such threat, nor should hand radio gear —necessary for any researcher alone in the jungle—prove suspicious. However, neither the air of legitimacy nor the absence of accomplices could change the customs officials' predilection for labeling him a potential subversive. He was cast with shackles of suspicion just for bringing moderately new equipment into a land of musty muskets.

Michael had asked Ron if he should accompany him, but Ron prevaricated that tagging along would not help because officials would undoubtedly want to question Michael alone. The presence of another foreigner, likewise possessing hunting permits and rifles, would only complicate the matter. Everything ought to proceed routinely, Ron pledging to call ahead. So, armed with Ron's weak assurances and a letter from Jack Whitehead, replete with a ministry stamp and seal, Michael strode into the office.

After suffering through endless checks of his paperwork and condemning stares, Michael resorted to following Ron's other advice. If all else fails, make a donation; or, as Ron put it, offer a facilitation payment. Like bribing a maitre d' in Las Vegas or an apartment broker in New York, the indignant feeling of paying for what should be coming free clung to Michael only until he walked away free of the bureaucratic hassle. He had his guns, and lest he accidentally shoot a warden, he could probably keep them.

Permit delays further postponed Michael's departure a few more days, and it was nearly two weeks before he finally managed to depart for camp and start his baboon research. Michael had checked his equipment more times than he could count and was itching to leave. So far, little had gone to plan since arriving.

Peter, the same driver from the airport that had picked him up, was guiding him on the route; a second car joined the convoy, and would bring Peter back so that Michael could keep the rover in camp. Jolts from the craggy road leading to the game park grounds kept him alert. Finally, arriving at the outskirts of the reserve, they turned onto another dirt road, replete with jagged rocks and unexpected potholes. To Michael, every turn was challenging, and every movement seemed ominous. There was no reason to fear anything, but the very fact of being in game park grounds caused him to imagine being surrounded by lurking animals. No eyes, though, shone back against headlights streaking through the darkness. The high beams faded into the unknown, the mysterious space that surely held creatures he had only seen stuffed or behind bars.

·　　·　　·　　·　　·

Alijah's training pilot, Jordan, shouted, "Take your hands off!" as Alijah reluctantly slid his hands away from the Cessna's steering column. For close to an hour, Alijah had been touching every instrument and trying to wriggle free of his seat as the Tiger Cub plane cruised a few hundred yards above the savanna. Richard Keeton once futilely described an airplane to him but could not overcome the Maasai's incredulity. Alijah had no prior notion of cars or planes. While he adapted to riding in a car, the concept of flying with the eagles in a closed metal craft remained baffling.

Alijah cried out like a little boy riding his first Ferris wheel, reveling as the plane swooped down to give them a better glimpse of a herd of elephants spotted through his binoculars. This was supposed to be a lesson; however, the trainee would stand for nothing less than a chauffeured tour of the sky. In two hours, they covered more ground than he had walked his whole life in the bush. His country spread below, yet he could barely recognize anything from this vantage. The pilot passed over a reserve and a river that Alijah had walked past perhaps a thousand times. It all appeared unfamiliar and dazzling.

Mount Kilimanjaro towered in the distance, the only easily recognizable landmark, the timeless twenty-thousand-foot rock that, unlike the rest of the landscape, failed to become any less dominating from Alijah's new perspective. It still blocked the horizon, looming against the blue sky, a landmark overlooking several tribes who linked their separate beings to its lore yet never knew of each other. Alijah stared at the glistening snow unevenly capping its top, mesmerized, sensing another unlocked sensation within his grasp.

Descending too rapidly, the pilot, Jordan, yanked the plane up, creating a jolt. The sudden climb brought Alijah back to his senses. Grasping his binoculars, he scanned the horizon, searching for the herd. He had lost them, looking in every direction and unable to lock onto a familiar road or hillock. Then he looked straight down and yelled, "There. Ndovu!"

Below them thundered a massive herd of elephants. Difficult to count from the distance, Alijah guessed the number to be between thirty and fifty. He focused more intently through the glasses, a task which, strange in itself, he had not fully mastered. Alijah adjusted his face to the sockets, pushing the binoculars flush against the cockpit window.

Dust flew, and even the pilot could see the group stampeding away toward a break in the bushes. "They must be making a terrible noise," Jordan said, safe in their insulated bubble, unable to sniff the dust or feel the quiver of the earth. As they continued flying in a lazy circle above this activity, Alijah asked, "Did the plane frighten them off?"

"Oh, no. We could if we wanted to. It's easy to swoop down close and make them run. But we're far away. Maybe the noise bothered them, but we're still very far. I don't think we scared them this time."

Still glued to his binoculars, Alijah noticed several stationary elephants in the area where some of the dust was clearing. He pointed down, commenting to Jordan, "Look, they're standing still. Very brave!"

Jordan brought the plane in closer, thinking the rest of the elephants were scared by something. The cockpit fell silent when they drew near enough to see at least four elephants lying motionless on the ground. Passing over the spot, their plane cast an ominous shadow, dwarfing that of the vultures. Although the imagery of big wings sported by the Cessna was comparatively new to Africa, the intruders in their puffing machine seamlessly blended into the macabre scene. One of the creatures had such a gaping hole in its side, spilling over with blood, that neither man reached the point of musing about the beasts taking a rest or naturally meeting their fate.

"Poachers," Jordan murmured, Alijah throwing him a stony glance, his eyes dilating with expectation.

"I want to go down. Did you hear me! Down! Down! Now!"

"We can't. There's no place to land."

"First lesson yesterday, you told me in case of emergency we land on the road."

"Yes, but that's crazy. We don't land on roads unless there's no choice."

"There's no choice. Land on the road past those bushes, or I'm firing you when we get back!"

Alijah did not yet wield such clout, but he was already an important man with significant contacts across government departments. Jordan, used to taking orders and outranked, was afraid. Alijah had a vigorous temper and a dominating reputation, constantly forcing the targets of his ire to yield. Fearing Alijah might go beyond his threat and kill him if he did not attempt to kill them both by landing on the road, Jordan pointed the plane's nose down. Any sane man would have braced himself for the landing; Alijah, though, leaned forward scanning for more elephants until the thrust of the plane hitting the rocky path threw him back against his seat.

Jordan whooped in celebration as the plane careened along, swerving its way to a crawl, miraculously avoiding cartwheels. Jordan genuflected, making a trapezoid as the result of not fully grasping the missionaries' lessons. Alijah shot him an annoyed look, opened his door, hopped out, and beckoned Jordan to follow. They had landed on a road of sorts bordering a grove of bushes, thick savanna grasses on the other side.

Walking in high elephant grass is always dangerous, but Alijah was a native with an instinct for safety. Defying the hazard of straying too close to a hidden animal or snake, he marched confidently through the knee-high stalks, divining the only significant danger rest with the poachers. A route through the bramble teased a shorter path but appeared impenetrable without a machete; safer to trek out in the open. Traversing through unchartered brush, even the most astute Maasai could wake a sleeping buffalo around a corner or rouse some cat lying in the shade. The open savanna was dangerous but always the best option. Jordan, mouthing another prayer, followed cautiously several yards behind.

The area proved much larger by foot than it had appeared from the air, and Alijah strode through his lesson in perspectives with every step. The two knew the direction of the carcasses but no manageable shortcut to finding them. After about fifteen minutes, they reached the edge of the brush, making their way to the other side. They could see a line of trees ahead of them, recognizing the stand as their last hurdle. With their goal in sight, the duo moved faster. Jordan began to forget his timidity, hurrying forward, stride for stride with Alijah.

Finally reaching the far side, they burst through the thin line of trees, frustratingly finding nothing but open scrubby ground for as far as they could see. Alijah threw up his arm in disgust and scratched at the dirt with his foot. Neither elephants nor poachers were visible. On the threshold of despair, Jordan cried out, pointing to the air. There, circling above, buzzed vultures. Those harbingers of death would show them the way.

The vultures drifted roughly two hundred yards away, and naively the two men kept their focus on the telltales fluttering in the sky. The sudden sound of a shot sent them scurrying for cover, but none could be found. Within minutes, the poachers surrounded Jordan and Alijah, each carrying a rifle pointed at them.

Both men froze. Alijah threw his hands up. He was intimately familiar with guns and their range, having learned to shoot with Richard. He cursed coming unarmed for his airplane lesson. Jordan learned how to fly planes in the Kenyan air force and was only too well aware of their predicament.

"Both of you. Raise your arms!" shouted a voice.

Alijah muttered to Jordan who copied Alijah's position.

Keeping his rifle trained on them, a white man clad in khaki and donning a wide-brimmed safari hat approached. Seeing Alijah and Jordan unarmed and complying with his order, the man motioned them to lower their arms.

"Do you speak English?" he asked, not knowing if they had understood his commands or had reacted to his gestures and shouts.

"Yes," Alijah responded. "I do. My pilot doesn't understand much."

"What's your name—and your pilot's?"

"I'm Alijah. This is my pilot, Jordan. I was taking a lesson for a bit of fun when we spotted the elephants," Alijah began, his tone brash. While still a novice at the ministry, he handled himself like a consummate professional. Jordan gave him an awkward stare, amazed at how coolly and convincingly he was trying to take charge. Alijah continued: "We don't want to cause any problems. We didn't even know there were people down here. We just saw a group of elephants on the ground. We thought they might be sick."

"They're sick all right," the poacher laughed. "I should spread the disease around to the two of you." He turned around to confer with one of his mates who stepped forward to observe the captives, his men all roaring at their boss's crude joke.

Jordan turned to Alijah, whispering, "They're going to kill us."

Alijah looked at Jordan, debating their next move, sensing the prediction was probably true. Time to gamble.

"Sir, I know this may sound odd, but I can help you," Alijah boasted, inducing the two men to cease talking and look astonishingly at the English-speaking intruder. "I am a government official. If you happen to be hunting elephants without, how can I put it, proper permits, then I can help make arrangements. Ensure you don't have any trouble."

Blake Roberts, the poachers' leader who first barked orders, took a step closer while leveling his gun, "I'm not sure what you're talking about, but I'll let you finish your sentence."

Jordan listened, petrified, not able to follow the conversation. He rarely sweat and was befuddled how to respond to beads of perspiration oiling his face. Keeping his arms to his side while staring at Alijah, he waited for his minister to speak, trusting him for little justifiable reason. Jordan was as amazed as the white men at Alijah's bravado.

Alijah cleared his throat, haughtily continuing, "I have important friends who can help you sell your goods or help you get the right documents to make smuggling them out easy. Either one or both."

"And you expect me to trust you?" Roberts laughed. "I don't know who you really are. But if you get out of here alive, you're gonna turn us in. I would."

"I can't give you anything but my promise. Take one of us or our plane as security." He then boldly translated for Jordan part of what he had said.

Jordan's and Robert's mouths both gaped open in reaction. Blake Roberts' smile, though, shone in stark contrast to Jordan's hanging jaw.

Jordan feared he was being used as bait, but then wondered whether Alijah was making up options, stalling to figure a way out of their predicament. Unlike Alijah, Jordan did not have the courage to bluff. He stood cowering, the line between heroism and stupidity dangerously fuzzy; hopefully Alijah appreciated that balance and they would survive to tell the tale. Paralyzed what to do or say, Jordan remained mute.

"An interesting proposition... have your friend stay where he is. Come over here and talk to a few other people. One more thing. If you have any desire to live through the night, you better cut the bullshit. What the hell do you really do for the government?" Blake motioned him forward, fingering his rifle.

Collecting himself and taking several short breaths, his gamble reaching its limits, Alijah hesitantly confessed, "I work in the government's anti-poaching division." Leaving out his rank, he said, "I really was taking a flying lesson, and we accidentally found you."

The poacher laughed out loud again. "Damn good beginners' luck! I think you must be telling me the truth 'cause nobody'd be stupid enough to tell me what you just did." Blake, with his prisoner in tow, approached his ruffian comrades. Alijah could smell their foul waft of liquor and sweat. Blake Roberts lit a cigarette, summarizing the situation and curtly introducing Alijah to them.

Alijah continued his life-saving pitch: "We can help each other. If you give me a few tusks, I can claim to have made a big catch. I can even get you money. I have friends who will buy the tusks. If you help me look good, I'll have the power to hand you all the licenses you want. I'll be able to sort out official clearance at the airport or the port in Mombasa. All the papers for export, influence all the inspectors. Add a little cash, and they'll look the other way. You can smuggle anything out you want. You'll never be nervous about being caught. I may need more money to convince everyone. You can either give me the money, or I'll deduct it from your share after selling."

Dismayed, Blake Roberts said, "How do I know you won't just confiscate the goods and then turn us in? You could bribe one of your friends at the port to keep half the goods for yourself, sell them for a profit and convict us with the rest of the cache."

"I could do that. There's no way to stop it."

"Stop wasting my time. You're lucky to be standing here this long."

Alijah said, "I didn't say I'd do it! We both know the risks. I'd owe you a favor, and it would help me. If I tricked you, I'd only end up with one load of ivory. I can already find that. I want more, and I'm betting maybe you do too. You think I got where I am being an honest soldier? How could I have a plane at my age! Keep my pilot and the plane. I'll claim it broke down, he stayed with it, and I found a ride back. They won't expect to see the plane back for a couple of weeks. I'll need the plane back eventually, or I'll be fired. You give me the plane back, and I'll give you the money for the tusks, or the licenses, whatever you want. Name your price. I'm not the one with the fucking gun." Alijah rarely swore, but this seemed like an appropriate moment to break the decorum adopted from his British tutors.

"And I have one more idea, but can I have a word in private?" Alijah asked, looking over at both Jordan and then Blake's men, his eyes making it clear the request was for Blake's ears only. Blake motioned for him to walk with him, keeping the gun trained on Alijah's side, before Alijah continued, now almost in a whisper. "It would also help if you handed over one of your guides. It would just be temporary, but showing I've captured a native poacher would be quite a coup." Roberts looked at Alijah skeptically, the two walking and talking well out of earshot. Jordan, still scared for his life, wondering what this crazy minister could be saying, watched Alijah gesticulating from afar. A trickle of warm piss embarrassingly ran down his thigh.

"You know, for some reason," Roberts said, pausing to stomp out his cigarette, "I like you. You must be up to something or you wouldn't have a plane and speak English. Of course, you could just be trying to get away and sacrifice your friend, but that doesn't hurt me too much. And I'm comfortable that you don't know who I am or how to ever find me again." He eyed Alijah carefully. "You seem selfish enough offering up your friend that I think if you can get away with this once and make some money, you'll want to get away with it again. If I agree, I don't want your friend to know what's going on."

"He will never know," Alijah promised. "You fly with me and drop me off somewhere I can catch a bus or hitchhike back into the city. Then in one or two weeks, we meet as discussed. You bring the ivory and the guide. When I sell the goods, I'll bring you your money, and take my plane back. I'll take care of Jordan. He's more likely to turn me in than you if we do this. Let me deal with that."

Roberts weighed the risks, intrigued by how a contact in the wildlife ministry could provide him cover and a legitimate way to sell his cache. If he let Alijah go, this maybe-minister could come after him with an army. But how would they be able to find him? He could take the plane and pilot and simply disappear. He could use the week to think about it, perhaps check out Alijah's credentials, and continue with the rendezvous. Or, he could fly across the border and, as they do in the movies, into the sunset. It was wonderful having leverage. Guns had a way of changing the perspective. He wondered why Alijah would propose such a scheme, but cocking his rifle, the reasons lay evident. Roberts said, "If you trick me, no plane, no friend. I'm coming after you." Moving the gun's bolt, he shot just over Alijah's head.

Invigorated by the rifle's kick, Roberts gloated, listening to the blast of his intentions carry across the endless expanse. He stood unquestionably in charge. While some of the men mumbled a few words, none seriously challenged him. Most importantly, no one dared object to the bargain struck; of course, keeping a couple of the select details to himself helped.

Still skeptical, yet happy with the turn of events and his odds, Roberts invited Alijah to join him and survey their catch. The initial barrage of shots had long since passed, and the vultures were now back hovering. Only Alijah had been frightened by the latest crack.

· · · · ·

In Richard Keeton's bedroom, his clock struck seven o'clock in the morning. He turned over ignoring the houseboy knocking on his door. The strength of the rap increased, the young man boxing with the panels. Julia Keeton woke first, shaking her husband into the new day. Hearing the annoying thuds, he lumbered out of bed, grabbing a smoking jacket strewn over a chair by the dresser. He did not bother thinking to ask who beckoned before pulling open his bedroom door.

On seeing his houseboy at the threshold and realizing Julia was watching from under the sheets, he grumbled and asked the meaning of the intrusion. Jomno, shaking in anticipation of the conflict, tried to explain. When he told him that Alijah waited downstairs, Richard's eyes widened from their dawn slits. Something was wrong. He had instructed Alijah never to come to his house in the daytime; being seen together was too risky, not to mention improper etiquette.

Richard poked his head back into his bedroom to assure Julia that everything was copacetic before traipsing to the stairs. He held onto the banister during his descent, still waking and a bit wobbly. At the base of the steps, he came eye-to-eye with his native protégé.

"Come," he said, walking toward his library and, once inside, shut the door. Alijah did not allow him the time to sit before racing into the tale of his capture and the promises made. Keeton listened intently without interrupting, scratching at his morning's growth and nodding his head, encouraging Alijah to complete the story. Alijah spat every detail, animating the nuances with flailing hands and flashing eyes. At first, Keeton thought something had finally scared his wunderkind, but as the story unfolded, he saw differently. Alijah radiated exhilaration, emboldened by the challenge. In the most tenacious of entrepreneurs, a thirst for success stings until the most unthinkable goal is surpassed. Competitiveness must be stoked, not diluted when it turns from a bureaucratic sport to the dark side of the law. When there is no dark side of the law because the law is in the actor's hand, there is no slaking the drive. As Alijah finished his discourse, Richard smiled slightly, letting the silence punctuate his approval.

It took two hours and lots of coffee to calculate their plan. They were layering careful traps, disguising them, and then smugly sitting back, ready to later spring free their coils. Alijah left, and for the first time, Keeton shook his hand. Keeton knew how dearly they needed each other. Still, he placed a call to Ron Easton. Two was too small a number.

· · · · ·

At a remote airstrip near the port of Mombasa, Richard Keeton and Alijah greeted a truckload of tusks. Two men leaped out of the front seat, pointing rifles as the partners lifted their black and white arms in unison. Seeing them unarmed, the poachers lowered their weapons, shouting greetings. Instantly, Alijah strode forward, introducing Keeton as Sir Richard Appledorn, an important wildlife exporter stocking zoos around the world. The moment called for selective honesty. He consciously slurred Richard's last name, ensuring it was unrecognizable. Blake Roberts watched from a distance, judging like Richard there was more to lose than gain from exposure.

Under tarps covering the back of the pickup truck lay fourteen ivory tusks. The agreement had been previously struck, peaceful consummation the only unknown. Alijah's booty this time remained modest: he thought it a gesture of good faith. Initially, the poachers held all the leverage.

Alijah kept four tusks plus a captured Wata hunter. He would claim to have caught a group of poachers, wounding some in a confrontation and then taking one captive. Poachers came in all colors and nationalities, but local tribesmen provided expedient scapegoats. The Wata tracker was his cunning private request to Blake Roberts.

The Wata, native to the Tsavo region of East Africa, carried a notorious reputation as poachers. A small and stocky hunter-gatherer lot, some disparagingly referred to the skilled hunters as "Waliangulu" or tortoise eaters. Knowing little about them, Alijah presumed this captive an excellent hunter. Poisoning their arrows with acokanthera resins (a local shrub), the Wata specialized in striking elephants. A good strike to the ribcage from twenty-five paces could crumble a mature elephant in minutes; a less precise prick of the arrowhead could bring days of tracking.

They had not bothered to validate this particular pygmy archer's skill. Undoubtedly, though, the man was an adept elephant hunter. Ivory is a key component in the brideprice a Wata male must gather to take a wife. The skill of hunting elephants is culturally linked to crossing over the threshold of manhood. The disoriented Wata must have been twenty-five to thirty years old; no one in Nairobi would mistake him for less than a poacher once the label was ruthlessly affixed.

Keeton asked Alijah if the Wata would suffice. Suspecting so, he nevertheless wanted assurance. Because Alijah grew up a hunter, Richard presumed he instinctively bonded to his quivered brethren. However, to the Maasai or Wakamba, a rival tribe inspired no greater bond than the alien whites or the railroad worker Indians. The instinct to bond by skin against a common enemy is not natural except where it has already been tried. Kenya and Tanzania bred no Zulu nation, and the British could placidly sit back sipping tea. Divide and conquer proved all too easy a strategy when all that remained was conquering. As for the splintered tribes, loyalty became the paramount virtue. To have an identity meant to cling to frayed roots. For Alijah's purposes, though, little of the captured tracker's background mattered: he would sell this Wata to the devil.

Attention now turned toward the ivory, the cache to be presented and sold along with other booty at government auction. Of course, the records could be altered. Kenya would never miss them. In fact, Keeton struck upon the notion that mixing his own poached goods with items confiscated by the government, sitting around gathering dust in storage for eventual sale, might make the perfect cocktail for laundering. In fact, it could dramatically boost sales. He gazed at the tusks, bearing the smugness of a bartender trying to hide a secret ingredient, scheming how best to add his loot to government ivory and confident no one would question the particular blend. He would have to question Alijah regarding the practicality and who oversaw the government storage facilities.

As for the poachers, Alijah gave them a choice. He could auction their share, inconspicuously at the public auction at Juba Zoo, or he could provide papers enabling Roberts and gang to ship them free of tax and suspicion.

Extra hunting licenses were handed over anyway as a token of friendship. The poachers enthusiastically took the licenses, requesting Alijah auction their tusks locally on one condition: they wanted sterling. This was beyond Alijah's power, and he turned to Keeton. Richard nodded. He did not want to speak or be recognized, hiding his face by wearing a wide hat and dark sunglasses. He divulged nothing to remember him by but the alias he had agreed with Alijah; even then, it had been uttered just once and briskly.

Keeton motioned for Alijah and the captured Wata to move the tusks to their lorry, walking off to fetch the truck and maintain his distance. One at a time, they heaved the seventy-five to one-hundred-pound gleaming white tusks onto the back. Tension reverberated with each thud on the pile, but the transfer finished calmly. The poachers knew Alijah's name and address for the future. Blake Roberts verified Alijah's identity before allowing this hand-over. Punctuating the risk of any double-cross, Roberts made sure to ask whether they should stop by Alijah's office, noting the exact address and even the name of his boss. Roberts would contact him in two weeks for the sterling. Alijah could have his plane the next day, his pilot with the cash.

Several tusks and one prisoner richer, Keeton and Alijah found themselves alone again in the clearing.

.     .     .     .     .

The Indian Ocean seemed like a far-off place even while there. Fish paraded like aquarium prizes amidst shimmering turquoise waters. Fisherman knew not of sonar. Nets and spears were in vogue. If the shore were populated with tourists, everyone would have been sweating. But it was just the German lechers chasing after the black women who were sweating. If anyone of note ever chose to vacation there, sleazy magazines the world round would have a holiday. Richard Keeton, though, was not very famous. He was merely a petty aristocrat clinging to the trappings of a more renowned past. He had come for market. The ocean was neither a soothing tub nor an avenue to adventure. It represented an economic channel by which he could ship exotic trinkets to scavenging collectors too provincial to grasp the true value of their pricey acquisitions.

So, Richard Keeton, avid hunter, slick trophy peddler, and now poacher, walked into an ivory auction for the first time. Juba Zoo in the Southern Sudan might have been the region's hottest ivory market, but Mombasa hovered at worst a close second. For years government ivory was sold at public auctions in this Kenyan seaport. Mixing with salt from the ocean, the stench of corruption wafted over the marketplace. Images of Casablanca walked the streets.

Theoretically, only government ivory was up for auction. Lots of formalities, though, theoretically took place within the port. Alijah bribed one of the men cataloging the stock to include his cache and pay him the money. This was Alijah and Keeton's first auction, and they had debated whether to try a flat bribe or offer a percentage of the sale. A bribe of a few Kenya shillings was apt to be simpler and more profitable.

The price of ivory had recently gone wild. A couple of years earlier, a pair of seventy-five to one-hundred-pound tusks fetched a little over £100. Now the same sale could clear a profit of £1000, and soon dealers would earn a multiple of that. No one knew precisely the reason; just that shortly after 1970, ivory's price more than doubled and then continued its upward spiral, a new commodity on the market. Traders now flocked to auctions, the sea of natives mixing with white would-be barons. Some schemed to ship their prizes abroad for a quick profit; these were the majority. Keeton considered sending a shipment along but remained jittery over Jack Whitehead. Alijah and Ron would soon have sufficient clout to pass through trophies. He would ship the next cache.

Mombasa was a long way from anywhere, and Richard fretted about how to build a trustworthy network. Selling the few tusks would make them enough money to bribe a sufficient number of people to solidify Alijah's move up the ranks. His scheme at customs and the ministry was about to pay off, making the future look engaging. Richard Keeton, nevertheless, winced at the thought of lost profits from selling now rather than shipping later. Hiding his anguish beneath a poker face, he begrudgingly stepped up onto an overturned crate to watch the proceedings above the rest. He refrained from taking any visible part.

Alijah lurked backstage, keeping an eye on the treasures. As a black man with a government beret, he was blessed by claiming respect while moving as an inconspicuous onlooker. The auction began late, just after 11:00 am. Even in shadow from the brim of his hat, Keeton's face seethed perspiration from the blistering rays. His white hair was matted with sweat. How the auctioneer could hear over the din, he never knew. A couple hours later, the square stood quiet, and he was thankfully several hundred pounds of ivory lighter. As feared, the auctioneers blackmailed them into conceding a percentage cut. Richard and Alijah took the remaining share, acquiescing. Threats were apt to be futile. They were succeeding in their crucial goal, though: developing contacts in the ivory market. If Alijah could maintain his pace, sales and exports would run through the port regularly.

Richard Keeton spent all his life hunting for skins and wall trophies, earning just enough profit to finance the trips and make it fun. Now there was the promise of a denied fortune at his feet. One sale and one accidental capture netted thousands of pounds sterling. That was the figure he would earn for his shillings on Nairobi's black market—or nearly ten thousand dollars if he deemed the dollar more secure.

A pervasive black market yielded forty to fifty percent higher exchange rates than legitimate methods, but was risky. Many third-world countries function exclusively on the black market, and changing money can be done anywhere and with anyone. Walk into a bank in any number of cities, and the teller may close down the branch and move the transaction to the street; even after his cut, the yield may be twenty-five percent higher. But in Kenya, like many developing countries, the government was trying to keep strict control over the money supply, counting every dollar flowing in and out and maintaining receipts for exchanges at the airport. Richard Keeton had enough savvy to avoid the scrutiny of the tourists' wallet but also enough common sense to move carefully on the figurative and literal black markets. Of course, he did not fear prison but rather the money he would lose. Rumors had it the police sometimes took a fifty percent cut!

When Alijah handed the money to Keeton, they stared at each other silently. Both knew the other was contemplating whether Keeton believed Alijah was passing along all the money. In fact, he transferred everything. Trust energized through their gaze. Keeton forgot about race. Alijah forgot his growing greed. They had known each other several years now, but in their high-stakes moves through the government and the markets, time passed slowly. Even routine smuggling passes slowly. Keeton wondered whether for those on top who were well-protected with immunity close-by, the anxiety waned. Still, his face remained calm, a cool assurance bolstering Alijah's radiant confidence. Taking the money from Alijah, Keeton's eyes flickered. This time he would forego any extra share.

Ron Easton soon gloated as Keeton counted out the money into his palm. A system filled with snags had found a place for him. It would be a cozy triumvirate.

•     •     •     •     •

Alijah was staring at the wall in his ministry office when someone brought him in a folded note. The curious scrap, a dirty piece of paper stuck together with some type of gum or tobacco resin, read, "Your deadline passed yesterday. At 6:00 this evening, you may have to learn how to fly yourself. Be in the dining room of the Hilton with the money."

Within one hour, Keeton and Easton were pouring over the same words. Both knew the poachers that trapped Alijah would eventually come to collect. Keeton had set aside their money from the ivory auction, hoping they would call soon. Roberts and his crew still had Alijah's plane, and Alijah would soon need to explain its whereabouts. He had been able to stall for a bit more time, exposing the Wata hunter they had taken captive and the hoard of recovered ivory in the press. Given the theatrics, even the president heard rumors of Alijah's deed. There was no stopping his rise now. Later, in a less than magnanimous gesture, Alijah bribed a guard to let the Wata go free. A trial heralded little significance once the government boasted an appearance of working. Alijah ignored that the forsaken Wata had never been out of the bush and stood little chance against the city. No one would pause to learn his fate.

"We were waiting to hear from you," Alijah began the evening, extending his hand to Blake Roberts, the leader of the poachers who still held Alijah's pilot captive.

"We contacted you twice," Blake replied, "but you never answered. You left us little choice."

Shaking his head, Richard Keeton said, "We never received a message. I don't know what you're talking about."

Blake Roberts, agitated, demanded, "Let's sit."

Richard Keeton shot a glance to Ron Easton, who accompanied him, as they followed Blake Roberts to a reserved table in the back of the restaurant. Richard was still posing as Richard Appledorn, but could no longer disguise his appearance. Ron was more exposed. Working in the ministry, he was forced to give his true name. They had agreed Ron should sit in the background and keep his mouth shut—which knowing about Alijah's capture and escape he was happy to do.

Richard debated whether a message had been sent to Alijah, which he never received, or whether Blake was bluffing. It only mattered yesterday. "We didn't have any trouble selling at auction," Keeton began. Roberts continued glaring at him until Richard reached into his blazer's bulging pocket, calmly pulling out an envelope.

"I think this is about what we had agreed upon," laying the unsealed packet on top of Roberts' silverware.

"You'll have the balance when I have my plane back," Alijah cut in.

Richard and Alijah furtively glanced at each other, waiting for the next move. Richard agreed with Alijah's initial gambit that it was worth the risk to befriend this group and act as middlemen. When Alijah became adept at trapping men like Roberts, they could even take cuts for letting them roam freely.

For a moment, no one spoke, Roberts looking back and forth among the men, his mouth turning up into a slight grin. Richard Keeton sat back, assuming the dignified posture with which he had been bred. For this relationship to have a chance, they must trust each other. Of course, suspicion would always reign, but it was important there was at least a gesture of trust. Roberts could always come back, threatening any of them. Hence, Keeton stared at the envelope, curious how Roberts would proceed. Not surprisingly, Roberts parted the seal and counted the bills to confirm the amount was correct. He gave Alijah a slight nod, and with that Richard and Alijah relaxed, relatively sure the plane would now be returned. After being paid the second sum, there would be less incentive to keep it. Roberts and his men might be poachers, but Keeton was betting that they would seriously ponder Alijah's stature and had little desire to add the label of international fugitives. The relationship was too thin to call for a war. As for Jordan, he would be freed with the plane; Alijah would tell him he had sold the gang's ivory as a ransom for his release. Jordan would keep his mouth quiet, immensely relieved, and likely awed that Alijah escaped from the poachers' clutches and managed to capture their tracker.

The moment passed quickly. One hour later, everyone was drunk and finishing their fish. It was superb fish, freshly flown in from the Indian Ocean. Two hours later, none of the men could recall what they had eaten. Such is the power of bulging pockets.

# CHAPTER 3

*Two Weeks Earlier— In the Savanna Spreading Beneath Mt. Kilimanjaro*
Basking in the morning sunlight, chirping birds urged the land-bound creatures below to rise or face waking to the midday heat. Michael Sandburg pulled on his khaki trousers and "Celtics World Champions" t-shirt, poking his head out through the tent's zipper and squinting through his first encounter with camp. Hugo Bennett's depiction of the area as small was technically correct but jaded; describing the area as mundane was inexcusable. Rich green bush enclosed an irregular dirt courtyard shaded by a sprawling canopy of limbs. Monkeys jumped above, scampering toward the smell of food until chased off by the cook. Coloring-book birds flitted about the lower branches and through tangled limbs. He could see an eagle circling above the trees.

"Good morning," Michael called out, several sets of eyes turning toward his stooped body trying to free itself from the shackles of mosquito netting. "This place is beautiful."

"Yeah, it's too bad you slept so long," Susan Bennett said. "There were some beautiful views of the mountain this morning. By this time, it usually clouds over. Don't worry. You'll get your share of views."

"I'm sure I will. What time is it anyway?"

Susan laughed, "Lesson one, time goes by daylight, and you can always see it fading. The days go quickly because it gets dark incredibly early. No city, no lights. It feels like midnight hours early. Eat, read and go to sleep. You'll begin to get used to 5:30 a.m. Even like it."

"We'll see. I'm glad I've managed to postpone the pleasure for at least one day."

Michael was now up and in full stride toward the picnic table. His witching hour arrival in camp had postponed proper introductions, and Michael took his first good glimpse of Susan Bennett. She was older than Michael had expected, but carried herself with youthful swagger, billowing blondish-brown hair tickling her shoulders. The sandy, almost gritty hair seemed appropriate for the setting, as well as her freckled, deeply tanned face. Wearing khaki shorts and a loose-fitting sweatshirt, Susan could have been a model for adventure travel.

Desperately scared of being alone, Michael was relieved to find Susan easy-going, and not too bothered by his delayed arrival. For the past days, he fought to wipe the image of Caroline from his mind. He even dared to contemplate dropping in on Richard Keeton before leaving town in the hope of bumping into her again. Maybe an animal nearby would be found ill, and she would unexpectedly drop by. Michael, however, chided himself for such selfish thoughts; he would never wish an innocent creature harm. Instead, he fret about the isolated months ahead.

"Here's some coffee," Susan said, handing him a steaming cup. "The food's not great, but with some sugar, the oatmeal isn't bad. We have some bread, too, if you'd like some toast."

"Thanks. I think I'll just stick with the coffee. My whole system's still a bit off." As Michael uttered the words, he could feel his stomach churn. That did not bother him. It was a bout with the runs that he hoped to escape. "So, what's the agenda for the day?"

"Well, I'm winding down our research. We're just making sure all our notes are in order and that we have the numbers and pictures we'll need to put our study together. The giraffes aren't doing anything interesting now. We really don't need to watch them too closely anymore. If you'd like, I can drive you around the area so you can reacquaint yourself."

"I'd like that. I think you may have misunderstood. I've never been here before."

In fact, Michael shook his head, amazed he was there at all. The complications delaying him in Nairobi days longer had cost him more money than planned, his financial worries now plaguing him in camp. He hoped he could afford a cook.

"Oh." Susan sounded surprised. "Then let's plan on taking a ride in a bit. You'll love it."

Two days later, just shy of 6:00 a.m., Michael finally saw Killy. That was Susan's name for Mt. Kilimanjaro. The snow-capped volcano, looming over the landscape like a backdrop enveloping a movie set, mesmerized its most recent visitor. For perhaps ages, tourists, tribesmen, and authors came to gaze at the inspiring sight in their natural quest to understand the majesty of nature that Africa so tirelessly exhibits.

Kilimanjaro cuts across cultural lines and conjures up an indelible message. Michael now knew what Hemingway knew. He wondered when he returned to the classroom whether he could possibly impart even a fraction of the knowledge Hemingway shared. The excitement of the daily safaris, which in Africa means a journey of any kind, kindled a boyhood enthusiasm that he made no effort to contain.

That afternoon taking a game drive, Michael's attention was averted from the animals and vistas to studying Susan. Leaning out the window of the rover, basking in the rush of air, her hair blew wildly. It was hot, and this man-made breeze was a luxury beyond the grasp of natives used to beating trails barefoot. The mid-afternoon sun pounded away, and as Michael intensified his gaze on the flow of Susan's hair, he began to worry about how he would cope when she left.

"So, are you going to miss it?" Michael asked, eager to strike up a conversation.

"The second I step on the plane."

"You're not lonely out here? Don't get bored? I keep worrying about that...I guess you've got Hugo, though. There's a guy who's supposed to be sharing camp with me. He's coming in a couple of weeks."

"Who?" Susan asked.

"Tad Olson. He's doing some elephant study. A biologist out of the University of Washington. I guess he's been here before."

"Sure, I've met Tad. He's a nice guy. I'm sure the two of you'll get along."

"I hope so. We've talked on the phone a couple of times. I'm just a bit timid about being out here by myself."

"Don't worry about it," she sighed, already awash with nostalgia. "It gets pretty romantic out here at night, though. If you have a girlfriend, I can guarantee you'll want to get her out here."

"Not much chance. I broke up with someone over moving here. Things weren't working out, and I knew I'd be going away."

Michael realized his story seemed cliché. It was only a coincidence that it was true. He opted not to say anything more.

"Well, why don't we head over to one of the lodges. I can at least introduce you to a couple of other expatriates so I won't feel like I'm stranding you out here. You up for a drink?"

"Sure, I'd appreciate that."

The game lodge was the most important and only social spot within two hours. Khaki-clad tourists gawked at the animals in the distance while locals sat at the bar and made fun of the tourists.

Tribesmen straying to this fringe of civilization frequently imbibed the local elixir and set the stage for their brethren to stumble down the same path as the Eskimo and aborigine. Michael quickly gathered that spears of men who had been gallant warriors in their youth became mere crutches to those lured away, selling their souls to the snapshots of tourists.

At a corner table on the deck overlooking the marsh below where a few zebras were grazing, Susan and Michael sipped color-infused spirits. Susan shook her head and began pontificating on the plight of the indigenous tribes. Michael relaxed into the burn of the cocktail, listening to Susan drone on about the strangeness of the place and the emptiness of the area around them. After a rambling sentence about alcoholism in the tribes, she winked at Michael, and ordered another round.

Her attention turned to an elegant Maasai leaning against the counter. He shifted his burden, propping up his gangly frame with a walking stick. "Isn't he gorgeous," she said. "A once noble warrior, probably has killed a lion with his own hands—strength of three men from home, muscles like rope from living off the land. Raw power. Honed instinct that makes us talk of courage, but really we'd cower in his place."

Michael looked more closely, devoid of the same seduction, confused by Susan's tone. He wondered if they were examining the same man. Characteristic of his people, the woebegone warrior was lanky, perhaps six feet four. His closely cropped hair framed a head sporting sharp features and traditional ear loops. This was Michael's first glimpse of thorn-widened ears, and he gawked at the extraordinary sight. One small loop dangled something he could only identify as plastic, a dowel of sorts discarded as trash by a tourist, while the rest folded back up over the ear so that the skin would not flop back and forth.

As Susan continued to gush over the warrior's prowess, condemning the failure of her ilk to acculturate the natives in a meaningful way to the encroaching world, her eyes coveted this lanky man draped in a blanket and equipped with his walking stick and spear. Maasai warriors are tall, handsome figures, equally elegant fixtures of the landscape as are the graceful animals around them. Susan had always found these men striking, and as she sat finishing her drink, Michael slowed his speech and, too conspicuously for his comfort, fixed his attention on the warrior. He silently asked forgiveness, knowing he was not peering into, lest stealing, any part of someone's soul. When the man toppled over from perhaps one too many sips, Michael shook his head, opting to spare Susan his own opinion.

After dinner, back in camp, the alcohol from the lodge hampered Michael's ability to read. Awkward sounds in the bushes further made it difficult for him to sleep. Alert to every crackle, Michael thought he heard rustling and voices from near Susan's tent. Susan had given the men working in camp the weekend off, forcing Michael to rise and investigate himself. Straining to translate every sound, Michael struggled to identify the shuffling in the bushes behind his tent. Michael softly called out to Susan, checking if she was safely in her tent. By the time he reached her, she was already sitting up and pointing a flashlight at him. Awake, she assured him it was nothing.

Apologizing for disturbing her, he paused, hearing more stirring in the bushes and pointing his flashlight in that direction. An authority of three days, he deduced, "It doesn't sound like an animal."

"I couldn't agree more," Susan said, assuring him that he was suffering from the inevitable paranoia of the first days. "Would you like to come inside? I'm not that tired."

Michael could not resist Susan's sympathetic tone, eager for the invitation. A jungle tent is as introspective a place as it is lonely. Michael would gladly duck inside Susan's tarp solely for the warmth and security of another person. That he found her captivating tempted him beyond good judgment. The thought of Hugo hardly entered his mind. They talked lying down beside each other on an air mattress until Michael suddenly stopped in mid-sentence. Susan stared up at the tent's apex, perhaps sensing a shadow, straining to identify the same rustling that she had dismissed as Michael's anxious baptism to jungle life. Torn between fear and a primal desire to roll over and smother her view, Michael inhaled deeply, trying to center himself.

He pivoted onto his back, similarly staring up towards the top of the tent. Imagining whether they were being stalked, childishly humming "lions and tigers and bears" in his head, he puzzled over the strange rustling just footsteps away. There was still enough ambient light to color the canvas and remind him that the stars were shielded. A cloud passed by. At least he thought he saw one, rubbing his eyes, closing them again and turning toward Susan, breathing in her scent as if he was on the prowl. Maybe he was. She seemed to have closed her eyes, though, rendering any urge moot.

Without warning, the silhouette that had blackened the tent ripped open the mosquito netting and stood beneath the awning in a stance that bespoke judgment. Susan sat up as Michael let loose an awkward grunt, mumbling "what the hell," unconsciously kicking her in a spasm of fright. She had dozed off, and her sleepy reaction was to turn toward Michael, her eyes clearing enough to gather an impression of his face. Michael, though, was staring directly at the silent, brooding figure imposing on the sanctity of their hiding place.

When Susan widened her gaze to follow Michael's eyes, she exclaimed, "Gamala!"

Thrashing back the canvas with his arm, Gamala began yelling in his native dialect. The tent was shaking from his grasping the netting. Gamala kicked at the edge of the tent, weakening the posts and trying to rip the stakes free before turning from the presumed couple to the emptiness around. Susan tried to assuage his temper, yelling at him to stop, but her words failed to quell the tirade. Michael sat baffled. He was unable to understand the Swahili exchange and too frightened to utter anything if he had. Finally, he turned to Susan, shaking her arm, "What are you saying? What!"

"He doesn't understand. He's screaming at you... he doesn't understand. He's completely crazy," she spat back, pushing him away, pleading with Gamala.

"What about me?" Michael pressed.

Susan turned back toward Michael with a look of disbelief that credited Michael with all the insight of a naive schoolboy. "What do you fucking think? You're in my tent. He thinks I'm sleeping with you," she screamed at him. "I'm trying to explain, but he doesn't understand. Gamala accepts Hugo. That's all right. But he won't accept my having two other men. I explained the difference in our systems—forget it. He's possessive, irrational. I should have known better. And now even Hugo," she paused.

"What about Hugo?"

"Forget about Hugo. If Gamala really thinks we're sleeping together he'll take it as a challenge. I think he might kill you if I can't talk him down. You've got to get away. Run when he backs off."

Before finishing her words, she cut a hole in the back of the tent and began to slither through. Gamala saw her and moved around toward the side of the tent. Michael hesitated only in his mind, for as soon as the tent entrance was freed, he bolted through, not stopping until he reached his tent. He struggled, chasing outlines in the dark. Frantic, he managed to toss everything into disarray before grasping another flashlight. Seconds later, he jammed a Swiss Army knife into his shorts, realizing the foolishness, though in a frenzy not seizing on a better idea. Michael's mind then flashed to his rifle. It was in his car and unloaded!

After also grabbing his keys, Michael rushed out of the tent, flailing his flashlight beam into the darkness trying to find Susan. Only a moment ago he had heard them arguing, but now he turned toward Susan's sobbing. The beam locked on her body, huddled on the ground. She was scraped up and in pain. Taking a few steps toward her, he suddenly remembered Gamala and froze. Michael was confident Gamala must be somewhere close. He imagined Gamala staring at him, hyped with fury, about to unleash his hatred and pierce his target. Susan's crying interrupted him again. For some reason that he could not fully comprehend, Michael turned away from Susan, angry, his fright disappearing. He spun around, screaming out to Gamala, recklessly challenging him to come forward.

Michael's newfound resolve began to crumble, however, upon seeing a clutched spear glistening in the light cast by the fire. He began to back up, stammering, "No," tripping before catching himself. Susan screamed, and Michael simultaneously lunged toward her. Gamala launched his spear, and it was only the tricks of the darkness and Michael's fortuitous move that caused the javelin to miss its target.

Michael scrambled over towards Susan, staring at her, petrified. They could not hear Gamala, but in the silence, they knew they were still being stalked. Susan whispered, "The car," and they quickly fled.

Michael sprinted forward, propelled almost magically by adrenaline to his car. Susan split off to her rover, just a few paces away. "Give me the light! Hurry!" she pleaded, unwittingly giving away their position.

"What are you doing!" he yelled back as he joined her and saw her rummaging through the open trunk.

Susan grabbed the light: "Here, open the case!"

"Let's get out of here! What the hell are you doing!" Michael answered his own question: the moment he finished his ranting, he found himself holding a small sub-machine gun. It was the first time he had ever seen an Uzi, the famed Israeli machine gun that had become the weapon of choice for elite forces. Designed by a former Israeli army captain, Uziel Gal, the 9mm gun was light at under 10 pounds but could fire at a clip of hundreds of rounds a minute. Almost reverently, he held it to his hip, ready to fire. "What are you, some fucking mercenary!"

Michael's eyes followed the beam of light that Susan directed back toward the campfire. Their time had run out. They looked up, seeing Gamala running toward the fire and gathering another spear from in front of the ashes. The guards always left spares by the fire in case an animal strayed into camp, and they needed to find a weapon quickly. If only it had been a lion causing the commotion, and she was reaching for the spear. Instead, Susan screamed at the top of her lungs—the next attack so close that both she and Michael already pictured the spear hurling through the air at them. There was too little time to escape.

Staring at death in the form of a five-foot steel lance, Michael let loose his gun, its bursts drowning their shrieks. He dropped it in shock, the hot cartridge nestling in the sand as quickly as the spear fell harmlessly against the ground. The echoes of their hysterical yells lingered; soon, the cries were replaced by the clatter of the monkeys and the swirl of birds that instinctively understood the meaning of the sounds.

While Susan remained frozen next to the gun, Michael stood up and slowly walked over toward the bleeding warrior. Gamala lay dead, riddled with gangland bullets without so much as ever knowing anything about life on the streets. The miscalculation of quiet, Rousseau-painted life in the wild hung in the air while smoke from the campfire drifted over the lifeless body of a lover mistaken yet still knowingly jilted across cultures. Michael began to talk but then realized Susan was balled up on the ground sobbing. He stared helplessly at her body-hugging arms, her fingers digging into flesh like a falcon whose talons will not release after snagging its prey.

Slowly, he moved over and sat behind her on the ground, wrapping his arms around her, forming a limbed circle, rocking back and forth. They were a wave on the dirt. Michael was in shock but also acutely aware that he was happy to be alive as he watched flies gather on the body in the distance. They needed a plan. He needed a plan. He fought to push the emotions away, the sickening weight of killing a man, of knowing that right then, his life was forever changed. Conscious that Susan's emotions were no less fragile and yet naively unaware of the greater burden of watching a loved one slain, Michael's self-preservation instinct took control. He was now just a beast in the wild, albeit with a slightly larger brain, comprehending his fate. Again, he pushed away the ramifications, instincts pounding at him to move on and deal with the kill. The king of the jungle would rejoice; the stronger gladiator won, Darwinian battling at its most brutal. What the hell was he thinking?

After a few minutes, Michael broke the haunting silence, asking, "What do we do now? Someone may have heard the shots. We can't just stay here."

"What?" Susan muttered, awakening from her cocoon and struggling to her feet.

"The body. We can't just leave him there. We have to do something..." Pausing, "Do we give him a kind of funeral or something?" trying not to sound too callous, realizing they were lovers, but desperately wanting to keep his distance from the topic.

"Do we really need to talk about this now?"

"Yes, we do. Right now!" Michael snapped. "I just shot him. No, killed him! I'm not waiting around to try to explain what happened. You think people will understand. Native with a spear and me with a machine gun? Fuck."

"Oh, so now this is about you," her tone slathering him with guilt. "He was my friend. He was my," her voice trailed off as if unable to finish the sentence aloud. Susan had secrets she was coming to realize were best buried as well.

"I know," Michael softened, "I'm sorry. We just have to deal with what happened and... protect ourselves. He's dead; I killed him. I can't take any of that back. We should dig a grave, say a prayer... I don't know. But we have to bury him and get out of here. I don't know what his traditions are...were." Michael's mind wandered to his anthropology readings, books on tribal totems and taboos. He wondered if anyone before him had struggled with the types of taboos he was witnessing.

"You're right," Susan brought him back, resigned. "We should bury him."

"OK," then looking over at Gamala and mulling over the literal dead weight, he continued, "How? I mean, how do we do it? He must weigh a couple of hundred pounds. We can't do it right here, in the middle of camp. We don't want someone discovering him."

"I don't know. Jesus. You figure it out."

Michael considered, "Maybe we can drag him, build a little sled of wood or something," as he became necessarily pragmatic. He looked over at a barrel used for storing drinking water, an idea emerging. "Help me over here. I think I know how we can move him."

His emotions numb, and as if he had done this a thousand times, Michael dragged the body. Stretching the limits of his strength, he stuffed it into an empty barrel that days before held clean drinking water from the lodge. Somehow, the two of them gathered the energy to tilt the barrel onto the back lip of his jeep, wriggling and rolling it up into the back. When they were done, he was so enervated he fought the urge to blackout.

Within an hour, they drove to the edge of a nearby gully, rolled out the barrel, and in near silence buried the body in a shallow grave. Scavengers were sure to finish their work. Susan lingered over the fresh dirt, saying a final prayer. After taking a few wildflowers and laying them across the turned earth hiding Gamala and their mutual shame, she simply nodded and climbed back into the passenger seat of the jeep.

Soon back at camp, the chirp of crickets and regular rustling from the bush served as a score to the tapestry of stars, as if this were just another evening and nothing unusual had happened. For those beasts of lesser cognition roaming nearby, not much, in fact, had.

"What will you do?" Susan asked, fighting the post-adrenaline rush, eager to rid herself of the residue and stigma of their cover-up.

"I don't know. I just want to get the hell out of here. What about the gun?"

"I'll leave it here for you. I won't need it anymore."

Michael was confused, mustering only a cough, "What?"

"Don't worry, no one will know. I'll tell Hugo something about the gun. He got it for protection against the poachers. We flew here through Tel Aviv, and a friend who married a girl in the military there managed to smuggle it over as a favor. I guess it was a big deal, and he always kept it hidden. His ace in the hole, he called it. Always afraid of stumbling into a rogue group. Damn poachers are better equipped than the military. 'Better them dead than us,' he used to say. But we never did run into any. Well, actually, we did run across a couple but never had to use the gun. Guess they're more interested in leopard skins than our giraffes." In mock resignation, she said, "Anyway, Hugo's not going to need it anymore," as her sentence dropped off.

They each craved being alone, intuitively realizing there was little more to say. Whether they would joust with their consciences or be able to suppress their now shared history would be for another day, perhaps even a psychiatrist's couch. Ramblings and speculations, catharsis, be damned; it was time to go.

A hyena cackled, and after a few minutes, they embraced goodbye. Five minutes later, neither of them could remember what they had said. Nauseated from the stains and odor of blood, Michael was paralyzed, stymied by silence, and unable to spit out the profound speech circulating in his head. Struggling to sum up his emotions, he realized any words were hollow. They barely knew each other. Only time would answer whether that would make it easier. In most ways, yes. Michael would come to question whether it was all real. It hardly seemed so. He pressed the pedal, and with Susan standing in the distance, he drove off.

While scrub bushes and a thin layer of baked dirt shielded Gamala's mangled body from the ubiquitous vultures circling above, Michael sped down the isolated dirt road leading out of the reserve. Susan bid him her silence, but what she might reveal did not trouble him. If fear alone failed to silence the tongue which had kissed too many men of too many races, then the chagrin of admitting her affair and being fought over in a perceived love triangle would unquestionably mute a confession. Hugo would never know his wife yielded to a tribesman who had never before known the warmth of a tent. Michael shook his head. He prayed the rest of the world would share in that ignorance.

After passing the mandatory checkpoint at the game park's fringe, Michael relaxed, shedding his burden. He hoped the nightmare would remain contained within the boundaries of the refuge. While the guard checked his papers, he struggled to appear natural. Everything was in order; he was at least beyond the grounds.

With the car surging ahead on the barely chartered dirt road, Michael shook with the momentum of flight. The emotional strain from the joy of an unmapped escape tore at the psyche of the suburban-bred biology student turned murderer. Memories and guts flashed through his mind as the maelstrom in his stomach grew more violent. He skid the rover to a stop, flinging open the door and stumbling a few feet into the open savanna. Clutching his stomach, he lurched forward and retched until there was nothing left to expel.

The splatter of vomit on his pants coupled with its stench roused him to his predicament. He realized he had to muster his senses to salvage his research, and more importantly, his life. Exhausted, he cleansed his pants and hands with dirt then dragged himself back into the driver's seat. Slowly, he started back down the road toward Nairobi. He supposed he could have stayed in camp, but instinct told him to flee. At least for now.

●　　●　　●　　●　　●

Thoughts during the remaining drive back cast the surreal fragments of a nightmare. Michael's mind yearned to take a different path, but stuck scrambling images of machine guns and spears. He intended to meet with Ron Easton's boss, Jack Whitehead, at the end of the week about future tranches of grant money; he tried convincing himself he was merely traveling early. He would need more funds soon anyway. This trip alone to the city would probably cost a couple of hundred dollars in petrol. Obsessing over the cost of filling his tank, he muttered "Those fucking Arabs" while recalling the picture of a sheik smirking on the cover of the International Herald Tribune. OPEC was going for the jugular, and as they tightened their grasp, the consortium's actions spiking prices touched people and places far beyond their immediate concern. Michael imagined the gas tank blowing up, charring Gamala's body, the stench of smoke like that steaming from the Uzi's barrel.

Paranoia induced by fleeing fed other fears. His thoughts veered toward the cost of a flight out of the country should his shooting prowess become a matter of public discussion. Three more hours, he forecast, glancing down at the dashboard. The instruments were dusty, and as he brushed aside the film, grit clung to his moist fingers. Through the wiped streak, he glimpsed how fast he was going. Somehow years of studying science failed to make the numbers comprehensible. He tried progressing through the calculations in his mind. One point six kilometers to a mile. No, that was wrong. Again, he changed his mind. Ninety-eight kilometers divided by 1.6. Yes, pleading to no one in particular, that must be it. He was staring at the dashboard, no numbers making sense. Michael dragged his arm across his brow. His forehead was the only clean part of his body or clothing left.

He wriggled in his seat and sighed, stepping on the gas pedal as hard as he could. He never completed his division. There were new numbers now, the metric figures still failing to click. It was like play speed: incomprehensible to grasp ninety-two in the dirt. He did not have to understand, though, for all that mattered was to keep moving.

The last reading was 120 something before new film covered the dial. Perhaps now it was two hours to Nairobi. Susan had told him to stop gauging everything in terms of time. It was hopeless. There was day and night, and if it was night and he was in camp, then there was kerosene to go along with the stars. If Michael sped, then the headlights would continue cutting through the dark. That was assuming his gas held out. "Fuck OPEC," he cursed at the hidden speedometer and the falling gas gauge. He tried the other forearm, only to remember that it was filthy. The caked dirt felt slimy as it slid across his brow. He was almost away.

•　　•　　•　　•　　•

Michael holed up in Nairobi, wandering the streets alone for a day before venturing into Jack Whitehead's office to discuss his future funds. Thankfully everything was on track; if not, he must have appeared so pathetic that Jack was graciously accommodating. Whitehead even invited him to an embassy party, telling him Ron and everyone in town would be there. Michael blankly listened, longing to be alone again. Jack told him to get some sleep, a welcome thought as he plodded back out into the sun.

Having drained too many shillings at the hotel bar the night before trying to obliterate the memory of murdering a stranger, Michael now aimlessly wandered back toward his hideout. He looked at the Hotel Diplomat, contemplating why he had chosen this spot, one of the only respectable places in town. Beyond the bar, the answer was uncomplicated: clean rooms, credit cards, decent food, and a notch above humdrum. The guest book swelled with Indian names. He pondered if that bespoke of four stars. He debated if he was desperate enough to extend his stay and put everything on credit; the bill would go back to the states, and the fact his payments would become delinquent was unlikely to reach Nairobi within the season. Michael could not imagine them validating cards. They would never know. It was only American Express he had to fear. Without that credit card, though, he might not be able to afford a flight out. That was unless he surreptitiously dipped into his local grant money and converted the shillings back into dollars. He was tired from pivoting between the grey lines of contingencies and last resorts.

"Fuck, they'll never trace Gamala to me," he mumbled, striding up the steps. The smell from the kitchen followed him up the stairs to his room on the third floor. He tested the water and examined the locks. A creaky double bed took up most of the space. The only other piece of furniture was a small desk along the wall beside the door. A window by the desk's edge looked out onto an alley; another window on the far side of the bed was open, causing a thin drape to flap around in the hot wind. The sound of cars and crowds in the street still invaded even after latching the shutters.

He was lucky he had met Richard Keeton and started off on good terms with Jack Whitehead. At least he had his money. Many of the white expats had been friendly to him. Michael seemed automatically included in their clique. He shook his head. Unsure whom he could truly trust, he resolved to be cautions and keep some distance; best not to cling like a leech to this privileged set, sucking on their goodwill, and growing too much in their debt. One thing for certain: he would not be calling Hugo Bennett.

In the midst of these thoughts, Michael looked down at his pants and noticed a small bloodstain on the left thigh. He had not seen the blood before, and despite the smudge's insignificance to the innocent onlooker he was too paranoid to keep wearing the trousers. His body tensed, and after ripping them off and pacing back and forth across the room, he called the front desk. He asked if there was a laundry service, praying his inquiry sounded routine. To his relief, someone would come up to his room and fetch them immediately.

A man soon knocked at the door, and Michael opened it a crack, handing him all his clothes and repeating the Swahili word for "quick." Naked, he sat on the edge of the bed. Seeing himself in the mirror on the far wall, he had to laugh.

# CHAPTER 4

*Nairobi, Kenya*

Michael felt conspicuously white. He was hyper-aware of his pale skin when walking down a street in Nairobi amidst hundreds of black men and women. Before arriving in Africa, Michael wondered whether being the only white man around might make him feel strange. Would bystanders stare at him? To a degree it was inevitable, Michael self-consciously stuck in a frame, a living camera of eyes recording his contrasting attributes. Striving to ignore the gawkers, he tried focusing on the commotion of daily life. There were ample distractions: invalids on a corner, children begging for money, a man in the perfect suit, an old man in an alley working on his next carving, a strikingly tall Maasai woman with austere features and rubber band ear lobes.

Michael would notice a white man or woman in a sea of black bodies, as would anyone. Playing a game, when locking eyes with another Caucasian he would run through a profiling checklist. Were they native white Africans, tourists, or expatriate workers like himself? Whatever he speculated, Michael never perceived a bond the way some people describe like experiences. There was no sense of brotherhood. He would not single out that lone white pedestrian among the other hundred people on the street to ask for directions. That is why he felt so self-conscious when a white British woman, whose name he could not quite remember, picked him out of the crowd to ask directions.

Later that evening, after succumbing to Jack Whitehead's invitation to attend a party at the British Embassy, Michael stiffened when his eyes came to rest on the woman who had earlier singled him out on the street. To his horror, her eyes once again met his, and she was striding his way. There were no black men or women in the room.

"Geoffrey," she called to her husband, "this is the gentleman who helped me catch a cab back to the hotel." While her husband nodded dutifully, Audrey John-Robb-John continued, re-introducing herself.

"I'm sorry, did you say Robb-John?" Michael asked while shaking Geoffrey's hand.

"John-Robb-John," Geoffrey quipped.

"John-Robb, ah, my apologies."

"No, still don't have it. John-Robb-John."

"Geoffrey," Audrey interrupted, "Michael helped spirit me away from all those natives. It's not safe to be out on the streets alone, you know. I thought I would take a walk and all of a sudden found myself, well, completely alone in the street."

"But there were hundreds of people," Michael protested.

"Well, yes, there were the blacks."

Before Audrey could continue, Ron Easton walked up, sunburned blotchy as ever, handing Michael a beer. "Ever have a Tusker?" Ron asked, then turning to the John-Robb-Johns. "Geoffrey, Audrey, good to see you. I see you've met Michael, our American. Would you mind excusing us a minute? I need a word with Michael."

"No, of course, Ron," Geoffrey nodded, relieved to be free of Michael. The John-Robb-Johns would not likely pick Michael out of the crowd in this room again.

Michael relaxed as they turned away, glad to be rid of the prejudiced twat. Ron, sporting a hideous lavender ascot, now had his attention. Asking himself how much worse can this get, he pushed Ron, "Are those friends of yours?"

"Oh, not good friends. It's a small community. Geoffrey's a renowned heart surgeon. Came down here a couple of months ago to train people at the hospital with some new equipment. They're probably heading home soon. Did you know they can do open heart surgery here?"

"What else?" Michael scoffed. "Can they cure malaria, though? That's the issue. Millions of dollars to save a few people when most of the population can't get their babies inoculated."

"I've got my hands full with wildlife grants. Don't ask me about the politics of medicine."

"Well, his wife's a piece of work, and I didn't get the sense he was much better. Pretty elitist, prejudiced, I could do on," Michael spat between chugs of his Tusker.

"Yeah, you tend to find that in the Brits who come down here for a touch of colonialism. The natives, second-generation Africans, are better. Just ignore it. Anyway, how are you faring? I was surprised to hear you were back in town so soon."

Michael shook his head. "It's a long story. And just thinking about it reminds me I need another drink. Can I get you anything?"

"No, I'll wait here."

What Michael craved most was to be left alone. He assumed he would not know anyone except Jack Whitehead and Ron, and had come thinking it would be therapeutic to go out. Perhaps it would help snap him back to the person he had known just a few weeks before. Snap out of it, he chided—it was an embassy party, for god's sake! When would he ever have another chance to wander anonymously amidst the paparazzi? The world of diplomats is as seductive as the world of royalty. It would take more than a cloak of self-pity to miss a potential cross-breeding of the two. The room was abuzz with obsequious tanned Christians playing into the hands of those pompous enough to listen or those too bored to do anything else. Ascots on the Equator. What next, Michael pondered, turning the scene into another game. The man with the double-breasted blazer bearing a coat of arms on a pocket must be a Lord or a Sir. With him suffered Lady Teeth, for the whole time Michael watched, she seemed frozen in a smile, not changing her clench even when forcing a trill laugh.

The pomp, even crusty pomp, proved invigorating. Michael considered what part he could play. Should he introduce himself to Lady Teeth as a spy, or perhaps a junior state department official? A new Tusker in hand, he toyed with the idea, leaning now toward an arms dealer. He had a machine gun to offer, after all. He did not have the nerve. She might take him for the murderer he had become.

Threading his way back toward Ron Easton, Michael gently slapped his leg, urging himself to stop fantasizing lest he find himself in even more trouble. Michael believed in streaks, and this did not have the makings of a good roll. He had come to research baboons, and within the month, he had bribed a customs agent and killed a man; now, he found himself trying to fit in hobnobbing with diplomats. Wisdom and maturity usually come with years, but events can expedite the process. Michael had jarring wisdom. He had the type of wisdom recruits have hammered into them on a battlefield. For him, this was a battlefield, or at least as close as he dared venture.

Michael barely avoided serving in Vietnam and had hoped to have more time to grow up. He dreamed that in Africa perhaps he could escape and delay the crush of maturity. With one shot, he killed those dreams and Gamala. Michael took a deep breath, trying to center himself and just enjoy the party. He was instantly rewarded as across the room he spotted Caroline Dunning—a small community indeed, he thought, shaking his head, and smiling at his turn of luck. Maybe the streak was flipping. Abandoning Ron, his recent revelations were reflected in the confidence of his stride. For the moment, he forgot the trepidation of being revealed a suspect, walking heart first toward her. He had the grit of life on his side.

She was as striking as the first time he met her, her willowy legs this time in non-riding boots. Caroline also stood out as one of the few guests his age in the room; he relished the companionship of someone he hoped would understand him. The streak's balance hung heavily.

In her own way, Caroline was also very much alone. No less a small community for her, there were scant days when a dimpled and rugged academic with a melting smile came to call. Yes, she was spoken for, but she also relished the attention. Caroline immediately recognized Michael, leaving her conversation to meet him halfway.

"I thought you were heading out to your camp? What are you doing here?" she began.

"I did. But I didn't know what I was getting into and had to come back for a few things. I'm only here a couple of more days."

"Me too," Caroline said, hoisting her Tusker. She had been raised in Kenya and knew how to drink with the men, whether judged proper or not.

"Well, we'll have to get together soon, then."

"I'm engaged, you know," jolting Michael's plan of attack.

Feigning ignorance but acutely aware of her status from Ron Easton's lamenting, he stammered, "Oh, I didn't know...Is he here?"

"No. Back in England."

"Good. Then you're free." Michael continued with a pleading stare, "Come on, I don't know anybody here."

"Then let me introduce you to some people."

"That's not what I meant."

"I know. But you still ought to get to know some people here," she said, taking him by the arm.

Michael had a date, or at least a new friend, by the time he finally rejoined Ron. Perhaps his luck was turning. Better not flaunt his advantage, though, as he recognized Ron was seething with jealousy. Michael had noticed Ron watching them flirt, but did not know about Ron's earlier failures trying to court Caroline—nor about his dreaming of trying again. In a perverse twist, Ron similarly tempered his instincts, allowing Michael to bask in Caroline's presence. Though he began scheming how to sabotage Michael's chances, he hesitated when remembering Richard Keeton was also at the party. For Ron, that promised a relationship of equal fantasy, and for now, he would wait. He was weary of waiting, but unlike Michael, he gathered in the swell of a good streak. He resolved not to jeopardize the payoff.

There were simpler ways to get even. As Michael approached, Ron moved across the room and drew Michael right back into a conversation with the John-Robb-Johns. Michael never managed speaking to a lord or diplomat — only people who claimed to know them.

•     •     •     •     •

Around the same time Michael entered the embassy affair, Alijah drove up to a different party at the University. This was his first trip back since graduating; he could not help reflecting on his life's progression. The changes were hardly as dramatic as those following his and Galo's initial meeting with Richard Keeton. After leaving his village, Alijah had worked as a houseboy for Richard, becoming accustomed to the so-called modern world. He ceased decorating his face with tribal paints, discarded his beads, and no longer stuffed his dangling earlobes with random accessories. In tandem with transforming his appearance, Alijah began polishing his English and developing reading skills that had barely scratched the surface in the bush. After a couple of years, he was finally ready and moved to the university, slightly older than the average city-dweller matriculating but more worldly than any know-it-all proud of their college prep. Since then, challenges felt less startling; Alijah adapted to navigating Richard's scripted path, maturing with his career and approaching life with a spirit of adventure.

He had dreamed of driving a car and now was driving his very own vehicle up to campus. He had experienced modern wonders he could not possibly explain back in the village. Life was no longer predictable, and as Alijah meandered through, he kept wanting more of whatever he was exposed to without quite understanding why or where he was going.

Alijah was intelligent and curious as a student, one of the types everyone knew would succeed. The problem was in defining success. The wildlife and tourism ministries meant little to him except for the trappings. The benevolent potential, and the value of his job, was as distant from him as the city had been when he was a boy. Richard Keeton had placed him there after a stint as some bureaucrat's assistant, and Alijah was now playing in the spoils of his benefactor's scheme.

Alijah was hardly unique in his feelings. The gulf between tribal life and the city remained so great it seemed almost incomprehensible to live. Both worlds held wealth at the top; only in the communally protective tribe, though, was there also wealth at the bottom. Alijah, like so many others, grasped at material possessions as a security blanket, blinding him from where he came and shielding him from where he could fall.

He was spoiled by success and the appreciation of having bridged two worlds. Walking into the party on the university campus, he reflected on how differently he perceived his stature. Many of his new friends had grown up pampered with privilege; few, however, were similarly pulled by what seemed like an alien past. Unlike Alijah, most university students were the progeny of government bureaucrats, professionals of various degrees, and successful merchants. They had grown up expecting to go to university, greedily thinking about how they could maintain the fat from whence they came.

The man feted by tonight's fundraiser grew up torn by many of the same pressures of the encroaching modern world. Abo Daniel Oguru was recently named a general after leading a vicious and decisive attack to quell a neighboring bully's ambitions. Oguru was now poised to live a comfortable life in the military, far from his tribal roots. Rumor had it that his clan were once cannibals, but there was no proof; nevertheless, such rumors do one no disservice in battle.

A university coach that believed Oguru's father, a giant of a man, had Olympic potential, brought the General's dad to the city years ago. "The strongest man he had ever seen," the coach always said. He set school records and may have become one of the greats, but eggs of some parasite cost him a big toe, and he was no longer world-class. From the day of the amputation on, he labored as an assistant, bringing his family to the city, hoping they would lead a more prosperous life. Tonight, his dreams were coming true. His oldest son, initiated as a great warrior in the bush, later joined the Kenyan army and achieved the glory of a general's rank. The old coach, who once dreamed of Olympic gold, now championed raising a scholarship fund in old man Oguru's name based on the strength of his son's success. Oguru's father was happy, only wishing his son and former coach could understand that.

Abo Oguruo, though, was a bitter man who succeeded in battle by unleashing his frustration. He fixated on the fact that his father toiled long hours and they were poor. They had been ripped from their roots where he could have grown to be a king, only to wind up near the bottom. From self-sufficiency to dependency in a generation. No, in less than a generation! In front of his eyes—this defined his upbringing!

These typified the men brought together in the university's melting pot, in the tribal melting pot that had become independent Kenya. So much hope and despair and confusion and ambition that anything proved possible. How ironic that surrounding the physical laboratories breathed a living laboratory in much greater need of testing before the results went public. Alijah, one of the laboratory's prime specimens, entered the party largely oblivious to the scale of the forces molding his life.

Alijah was concerned with the immediate, and after leaving his car and walking into the reception, he scanned the room. He was not looking for a transformed tribesman, or a general, or even a scholar. He just wanted to meet a pretty girl.

Alijah married Tza in his village but had been forced to leave her behind for his new life. He loved her. It hurt him so deeply to think of Tza and his son Kiku that he stopped visiting. Kiku would soon be old enough for initiation, inevitably pulling Alijah back. He would buy him the finest spear a warrior had ever held and enough cattle to make Tza the wealthiest woman in the tribe. Could he still manage to live both lives if he thrived in the city? Should he give Kiku the same choice? Shuttling back and forth; he wondered if it was possible.

Alijah's wondering stopped when Abo Oguru entered the room, and everyone stared at the towering young man. Nearly six-eight, he dwarfed everyone there, his mere presence intimidating. After brief applause, the guests returned to their prior banter, and Alijah again began scouting the room. His eyes fell upon Sara, a woman with somewhat plain features but whose shapely hips and elegant style made her stand out. She radiated in a group that was talking, or rather listening, to General Oguru. Alijah quickly gathered that most of the disciples were merely being polite, perhaps even eager to be rescued. He moved into the circle, pretending to be interested, awaiting an opportunity.

"I think the Indians are a real threat, and the Muslims too," Oguru droned on with his prejudice. How ironic that later in life, among these same groups he scorned, he would find some of his most critical allies. The minorities would ultimately commiserate and bond over this type of treatment.

"Have you been to the new mosque in Nairobi?" Alijah interrupted, causing quite a commotion, and to his delight, also gaining Sara's attention.

"No, why do you ask?"

"How can you preach of a threat then?"

"It's enough that they're here, running businesses, taking jobs away from natives."

"They seem peaceful enough to me, General. But what do I know? I work in the wildlife ministry patrolling parks. Danger to me is a rhino in heat!"

Several of those gathered laughed, and Alijah walked away, confident in having made an impression and hoping that Sara or a friend may follow. Game parks are a sexy topic, and Alijah was cocky enough to assume some of the group would splinter off to hear him pontificate. He was right. Moments later, while walking toward the bar for a drink, Sara came over to him.

"Pretty brave to challenge the guest of honor," she began, relieving him of the pressure of an opening line.

"Well, it's their family's moment of fame, and it's gone to the General's head. He's just an angry man who probably doesn't enjoy life. He's in the right profession!"

"And who are you to judge, sitting in a cozy job looking at animals all day?" Sara responded in a tone more teasing than challenging.

"I'm Alijah. And you?"

"Sara. Nice to meet you, Alijah," pausing on his name. "Like the prophet?"

"Not quite. And what about you, what do you do?"

"Must I do anything?"

"No, I just assumed," acting somewhat surprised.

"I'm just kidding. I'm a teacher. I graduated from the University last year. You look familiar. Did you go here?"

"Yes, yes I did," Alijah said, both migrating to a couch. They continued to talk passionately, jabbing at each other, enjoying the challenge. They probably would have talked through the night had the old coach not interrupted the party announcing the grand prize contest.

The evening pledged to raise money, and in return, they had organized a couple of prizes to attract patrons. The grand prize was a motorcycle that Alijah coveted, and he excused himself from Sara to participate. The party organizers had planned to conduct a race, with the fastest man to win the bike. However, the plans changed when realizing that not everyone wore appropriate shoes, and many of the men protested running it barefoot.

Only Olympic events seemed fitting, and someone suggested a javelin. At the announcement, Alijah's heart raced. He had a chance. He had an excellent chance. Few of the men were tribesman, and though not as accurate as Galo with a spear, he was tall and strong and among the best from his village. He wanted to impress Sara and patiently waited his turn, trading with a couple of others so that he could go last.

A crowd gathered, tolerating the man in the lead bragging, eyeing the motorcycle. He would not lose to this final bureaucrat. Alijah smugly stepped up to the line. He closed his eyes, drawing back a few steps and thinking back to his youth and throwing the spear for Richard Keeton. He raised the shaft over his shoulder, bolted forward, and yelled something in his tribal dialect that few could understand. The javelin shot into the air, screeching to what seemed like twice the distance as the next best throw, plunging into the ground so far away there was no need to measure.

As the group applauded and crowded around the winner, Alijah searched for Sara, beaming a broad smile as she approached.

Unfortunately, not only Sara approached. The old coach and Abo Oguru also drew near. The General wanted to join the competition. He would now throw last.

Alijah stood aside, concerned, not gloating like the prior leader. Given his brawn, the general might be able to throw the weapon out of the field. Abo drew back, let out a groan, and arced the javelin into the sky. He clearly would have won if it had sailed straighter, but he threw the toy spear so high that it took seemingly forever to come down. When it fell to earth, it was near Alijah's spear, but the winner remained unclear from their vantage.

Alijah marched out to check the mark, with Oguru following behind and gesturing for everyone to wait. The two men, proud and unyielding, strode in silence. When they reached the spears, it was evident Alijah had won by about a length, but he did not say a word, looking up at the General.

"General, it looks like you've won," Alijah slowly spoke.

"Thank you," Oguru accepted. "I miss it. I know you do too."

The two men walked back, Alijah proclaiming the General had won. The two former tribesmen appreciated what the other had endured to reach this point. There was respect in their gaze and strength in their hearts. Jarring wisdom. Oguru announced his disqualification as the guest of honor; despite his toss, the motorcycle would go to Alijah. Alijah nodded gratefully, wishing him good luck. Men like them needed it.

Sara waited by the motorcycle, and Alijah soon joined her. "Want a ride?"

"Sure, you can give me a ride home," she toyed with an inviting smile and settled those marvelous hips on the bike.

•　　•　　•　　•　　•

The last thing Michael expected in Nairobi was meeting another woman. Alone and reticent about approaching those who imagined him a very different person than he had recently become, he sensed Caroline might empathize with his plight. Maybe only a woman would understand;

perhaps only a complete outsider could offer guidance. What made him think a stranger would understand — and not judge him to be exactly what his story made him appear— remained a worry he suppressed until this instant.

He tried rationalizing why he succumbed to attending the embassy party. The more challenging question to fathom was why he asked Caroline Dunning to dinner, knowing she was engaged and leaving within the week. The truth lay in a mishmash of reasons, most, of course, without solid logic. Outwardly, she was beautiful, engaging, and as close to pure society as he had ever come. She was also a contemporary and willing to listen. Michael inwardly sought a confessor, and whether anything else made sense or not, he intuitively chose her. Though he might deny it, and without the benefit of much-needed psychiatric counseling (who exactly do you seek after murdering someone?), he craved companionship. The lack of distractions, when alone, kept launching his thoughts down a path as unnerving as it was dark.

Now walking through town to meet her after work and take her to dinner, Michael cursed ever picking up the phone. He squinted at his scrawled directions on the back of a street map he had ripped from a safari pamphlet. Looking across Mama Ngina Street, he stared at a movie theater's marquee: "James Bond in Goldfinger." A movie promised a decent alternative. He could keep quiet, not even having to face her. He hoped she would be interested in the film; there was little choice, as another movie theater might be no closer than a plane flight away.

He judged the street he was seeking should be about three more blocks away. It was difficult to discern from the map. The grid was the type he hated, only labeling the major streets and leaving the rest to the imagination. He was looking for Kenyatta Avenue and then a tiny road off the main boulevard. Kenyatta itself stood out, among the grandest streets in Nairobi. Michael remembered it as soon as he reached the busy intersection. Divided in the middle and lined with palm trees, the avenue had all the stately trappings of a street bearing a President's name. Jomo Kenyatta had led Kenya over the threshold of independence, and though a vain gesture, Michael thought him at least worth a street's name.

At every corner, vendors sold carvings and native beads, but Michael looked up when a particular peddler walked up to him, uttering, "Antique." The man held the same carving of an eight-inch high elephant with fake ivory tusks he had seen a thousand times just that morning. He no longer afforded these hucksters the respect of a "No." Michael walked on, flashing his open palm as the international "Stop" sign, shaking his head from side to side. He toyed with turning onto one of the side alleys to watch the men carving their figures, the fresh mahogany destined to be an antique when carried a block away.

He reached into his pocket for the crinkled directions before turning the corner, reconfirming his heading. The street was crowded with people, and after pushing his way forward, making way for a legless invalid walking on his hands, he reached his destination. It was an art gallery, which doubled as a shop. The showroom was refreshingly empty; the woman who first greeted him did not appreciate his sentiments. After asking for Caroline, the assistant encouraged him to peruse the showroom while she went upstairs to find her. The gallery's theme seemed to be random, displaying works ranging from modern art and safari photographs to ebony carvings and African masks.

Michael pegged the masks as interesting souvenirs, possibly unique gifts to ship home. He wanted to send something to his brother JJ but deferred to procrastination. While examining one with a repulsive expression, the mouth contorted in a sneer, and the eyes and forehead streaked with a disturbing mix of color, Caroline snuck up behind him, tapping him on the shoulder.

"What are you looking at?"

"Hi! I was just looking at this mask. You know, something spooky and native to send home."

"Well, I hate to tell you, but that isn't native."

"What do you mean?"

"There are hardly any native East African masks. They almost all come from tribes in West Africa. All those masks you see the tourists carrying home from the stands are made in the back alleys."

"So why do you have these?"

"To satisfy tourists wanting to take home a genuine mask," Caroline said, smiling. "They are African, after all."

"Well, I think I'll pass. On the mask, I mean. I'll have to give the rest of the gallery a better inspection."

"I'd show you around, but you'd have no incentive to come back," Caroline said as she delved into her pocketbook for a cigarette. "I'm dying to get out of here."

"Why are you here, by the way?" Michael questioned, now wondering why they met at a gallery. "Aren't you working at an animal clinic, doing something like an internship? I don't know what they call it for vets."

"Yes. I'm working at the clinic most of the time. I want to specialize in equines."

"Horses?"

"Yes. But I'm just starting out, so have to deal with whatever comes up. If any of the horses at the Polo Club need care, though, I'm on call. Anyway, I came over here to help a friend whose family owns the place. I've been trying to find a time to stop by before heading to England. I've taken some photos out in the bush that they tried to sell. But no luck. I now admit I'm better at cutting than snapping." She paused, a bit melancholy at the loss of one dream, even if fulfilled by her new budding career. "Anyway, let's go. I hate being cooped up inside. I don't know if you have your heart set on a specific place, but I know this new restaurant that I think you'll love."

Michael considered the movie but held back. "An idea or two, but what were you thinking about?"

"The Horn & Hoof."

Michael thanked God there was nothing in his mouth as he choked on a laugh.

"You're kidding, aren't you?"

"You'll just have to believe me until we get there. It's only about a fifteen-minute drive from the edge of town. Toward Nairobi Park."

"OK, sounds great," then apologizing that they first needed to catch a taxi to fetch his car.

Michael's doubt lingered until he saw the sign reading "Horn & Hoof" protruding over the gate to the gravel parking lot. Conceding the score, he hopped out of the rover, walking around to open Caroline's door, only to find her shutting it herself. Dusk arrived during their ride, and now that the stars were peeking through, the temperature dropped. Caroline was familiar with the tricks of evening and not-so-warm African nights. Michael, however, had fallen prey to the popular myths regarding the heat. Nairobi in winter could become cold, and, as he massaged his goosebumps, he eyed Caroline's sweater. She laughed seeing him shiver. "You're exposing yourself as a newcomer. Nairobi is at a much higher altitude than your camp."

A covered wooden walkway opened into a courtyard filled with tables and small pits of warming fire. The main dining room, with its famous venison buffet in the center, stood a few paces in the distance. Instantly, a maitre d', sporting all his teeth, trotted up and welcomed them: "Good evening. Two for dinner. Inside or out?"

Simultaneously, Caroline said, "Outside," and Michael said, "Inside." The man looked bemused.

"Too cold?" Caroline asked.

"Oh no. I don't care. Outside is fine."

"Why don't we sit at that table over there by the fire," pointing to one of several small tables clustered around a glowing open-pit blaze. Michael gestured to the waiter who led the way as the two took their seats. Michael nudged his chair as close to the flames as possible, just short of singing his rump.

By the time dinner arrived, the fire had blushed both their faces, cherub cheeks already reddened from the local ale. The mixed venison plate nicely balanced the taste of the alcohol but failed to counter its punch. Michael seemed genuinely happy. He was seduced by Caroline's lilting voice, her accent a mix of posh British and clipped Kenyan, and enchanted by her blowing blond hair, which flickered off the light cast by the fire. Her green eyes threatened to put things over the top.

"So, you study baboons," she said, giggling. "Didn't you ever think about something a bit more, I don't know, social?"

"No, I always wanted to live with baboons, even as a little boy. What do you think?" he joked.

"That you had one of those calendars of African wildlife hanging up in your kitchen. For some reason, which I can't fathom at the moment, you didn't focus on the lions or elephants like everyone else and became infatuated with monkeys, or maybe even an actual baboon. Did it have a yellow baboon?" Caroline played along. "Hymadreus or jaundice—which one? Let's not underestimate the importance to humankind of those animal calendars."

"Okay, enough," Michael capitulated. "I have no good defense for the baboons, but they are a close relative of sorts, and research into behavior, sociobiology, even genetic linkage is hot right now. Studying relatedness, behavior, family hierarchy is, believe it or not, kind of groundbreaking. So, it's kind of interesting, and not unimportantly is sexy and attracts grant money. And with grant money and research comes academic opportunity and respect. A lot of people in the sociobiology field feel that if you combine it with evolutionary biology, you'll have wave two of the Origin of Species." Michael shook his head and briefly closed his eyes, his belief in the subject touching an emotional chord. "We're onto something special about understanding our behavior. I actually have a coveted position. Make fun of it or not. I might look at a troop out in the bush, but I'm doing something bigger than helping out a couple of baboons."

"So, you think my saving just an animal or two is...a waste of time?" Caroline asked, an edge to her tone.

"No, no. Sorry, I didn't mean to imply anything like that. I'm in awe of vets and people who devote their lives to helping animals. Really, I mean it."

"Okay. So we're on the same side." She hoisted her glass in conciliation. "I understand the fondness for a species. I grew up riding horses and am still pretty passionate about them. So, no big surprise I've decided to specialize in horses, maybe even racehorses. It's great being able to start focusing on them at the clinic. Sorry if I'm repeating myself."

"No, not at all. And, I'm not surprised. I was pretty awed by your Polo skills the other day, by the way. You were far and away the best rider out there."

"Thanks," Caroline blushed slightly. "Helps starting to ride so early— the hardest part was convincing them to let a girl play. Maybe I've always been up for a challenge. In veterinary school, I wasn't satisfied with just studying horses. Growing up close to the savanna, I also wanted to focus on the large animals. So many vets take care of cats and dogs, but out here in Africa, there aren't enough specialists for the big cats and all. And now, with poaching on the rise, there are more emergencies than ever. I'm about to start spending some time at a rescue clinic helping animals hurt out in the wild."

"Wow. That sounds amazing—sad as the reason is you'll be there. Guess the name rescue clinic says it all. It's unconscionable. I mean about the poaching. I'm sort of embarrassed to admit it, but I guess I haven't thought much about poachers or what happens to an animal that's injured and gets away. I'll say one thing: saving a life sounds a lot more noble than my writing up genetic research on a bunch of dumb baboons." Chastising himself, aware how naive he had been, his statement stung as a feeble admission. Cloistered in Ivy academia, he had labeled his pursuit to be pioneering; and yet, now out in the real world, exposed to the brutal forces of nature, including man-made ones in the form of poachers hunting the last of majestic beasts, he felt humbled. While he delved into theories around wild animals, Caroline was on the front lines of fighting extinction one calamity at a time. After only a few weeks in Africa, he was absorbing the perspective of a lifetime.

"Michael, are you okay?" Caroline asked, interrupting Michael's introspection.

"Sorry, yes. I was just thinking about what you do. It's just so, I don't know, almost heroic. As part of my thesis, I'm thinking about making a documentary about my troop. But someone should really make a documentary about you and what you're doing to rescue animals in the field."

Caroline paused to sip her drink, taking in the compliment, but also thinking it unduly flattering. She had grown up in Africa, and her path felt natural. There was no particular calling or nobility to it. The animals, the land, the people were symbiotic. To help a wounded elephant was merely acting responsibly. She had a deep sense of empathy for animals, knit from taking care of her horses from before she could remember, which had come to extend to hoofed sufferers of any stripe. Of course, she was proud of what she did, but did not grow up with the god complex that bred arrogance into too many doctors. Hailing from the aristocracy, she was never pushed by her parents to tear up the world in some social climbing mania to prove herself. That freedom bestowed by wealth, coupled with the luxury of growing up in the bounty of the savanna, paradoxically imbued Caroline with a natural humbleness.

More remarkably, she strove to be an equal, sensing her generation's liberation from the shackles of women being subservient in the pedigree of British society. Effortlessly becoming the best rider as a child and later taking pride in being the best on the polo field, why not be a doctor or veterinarian too? Primogeniture may have propelled the kingdom for millennia, but soon there would be women prime ministers and ambassadors, and Caroline assumed it her birthright to pursue what interested her, regardless of whether that fit debutante expectations.

And what interested her, not surprisingly given her upbringing, were animals. She loved them, especially horses, and wanted to be a vet. It wasn't bravery or even a noble pursuit. Funny this slightly scruffy, sexy lad from America should think her heroic. And yet, quite flattering. Now it was her turn to be introspective, the conversation having gone quiet, as Michael roused her from these musings.

"Hey, what did I say?"

"Oh, sorry. I think it's the alcohol. I'm flattered you think what I'm doing is so…not sure what the word is, heroic or filmworthy. Whatever, that's a bit over the top. I'm just doing what I love, and am lucky I've been able to explore what I want—especially as a woman, which isn't a given in my social circles. It's funny, though, Edward didn't think much of my going to vet school."

"That's your fiancé?"

"Yeah. He's okay with it, but doesn't understand why I want to work so hard when I don't have to. And I don't think either of us thought what I'm doing is heroic. That's what vets are trained to do: help animals. Just a tragic twist here when the animals need help because of people. But it isn't always that way. Lots of reasons they may be in need. Anyway, I'm rambling, and as you can probably tell, I'm getting a wee bit drunk. I think we better go soon, or neither of us will be able to drive back."

"OK. Just a couple more," he said, as she playfully nudged him and told the passing waiter to bring one more round with the bill. Michael desperately needed to drink, though he had managed to dissociate why he craved each glass from the fun of the conversation.

As they locked arms to help each other reach the rover, he thought of nothing but the warmth of their bodies fueled by the drinks. He drove mechanically, his headlights piercing the unlit road leading back to town and Caroline's house in Langata. Caroline lived in one of two modest guesthouses on Richard Keeton's compound. On arriving, she offered a nightcap, having to raise her voice above the chatter of crickets and an assortment of shuffling in the surrounding thicket. Michael willingly accepted. He ignored the fact that he had no idea how to find his way back, further overlooking that downing another drink probably rendered him even more unfit to drive.

"You know it's a pretty closed community around here. I'm happy to see a new face," Caroline began talking while mixing drinks at her small bar. "I haven't drunk or laughed like that in months. And I guess I won't again too! God, I can't believe what I'm about to do."

Her words fell on dizzy ears, Michael collapsing on the couch and staring at the thatched ceiling above. The intricate weavings were a drunk's delight, twisting in never-ending patterns and undulating toward a peak. He managed to sit up when she brought him a rum and something, faithfully sipping without inquiring into details. The alcohol burned in his throat as she sat down beside him. He attempted to say something witty about the thatching, but her eye contact rendered him mute, and he put down his drink. Unfortunately, he lay the glass horizontally on the woven rug, not noticing the liquid seeping onto the floor, while he reached out for Caroline. She paused, enjoying the flirting; however, solidly betrothed Caroline pulled back. Realizing he was crossing a line, even in his state, Michael looked away and back up toward the ceiling, fighting a jumble of urges.

In silence, he started to daydream, following the ceiling's weavings as if traveling through a maze. The maze took him through the bush and eventually to his camp's clearing. Michael began rambling, just incoherently enough that Caroline wondered whether his meandering story was true or but a dream. If Michael realized he was confessing, he would undoubtedly shake the spell; however, his subconscious led the way. The alcohol was breaking down his walls of shame, urging him on, knitting a bond of false comfort. Shielding his deeds within the privacy of his conscience threatened his equilibrium. He sensed, though, that he could divulge the truth in the confines of this protective estate. Oddly, this gazebo of thatching wrapped him in a cocoon of calm even while reminding him of staring up at the apex of a tent that had so tortuously failed to provide shelter. He was a murderer, and he could not hide in a maze forever; eventually, he would escape, even if he could not yet unravel the configuration of his own prison. Once his confession began it was as if the dam burst and events began pouring out—not melodramatically, but in a dispassionate retelling. Michael was unwittingly narrating his own documentary, the BBC host asking us all what we would have done—one week in an ivory tower, the next in lawless nature about to be impaled by a spear that seemed an anachronism in the modern world. While self-defense may be righteous, its malignant product lives on in guilt and nightmares, and self-therapy was proving no match for self-defense.

Caroline listened bewildered. She sat back, somewhat dazed, while Michael recounted the tumultuous evening of the week before. He was sitting up, furtively glancing between her and the ceiling, glassy-eyed. Methodically, his narration set the scene, describing the awful sequence of events. His fist clenched when he came to the shot. Michael ran his fingers through his thick reddish-blond hair, then rubbed his already bloodshot eyes, the image of Gamala's bloody body seared into his memory. When he finished with the details, he looked up, speechless, searching for what he feared were hollow, justifying words.

"I had to do it...I can't report it. I have no idea why I'm telling you."

"I wouldn't even know who to tell," Caroline offered, the tone sympathetic yet shy of the absolution Michael so desperately craved.

"Maybe having told someone, I can forget it. I'm sorry. I don't mean to burden you."

"What are you going to do?" she asked, not merely to be polite but genuinely wondering.

"All I wanted to do all week was get on a plane, but I didn't. I can't tell you why, but I want to stay." Michael paused and, in a moment of lucidity, added: "I really appreciate your listening. I wouldn't blame you if you'd thrown me out ten minutes ago."

"I was the one who invited you back." Caroline sighed, "Look, I'm exhausted and still tipsy enough that if you're lucky, I won't remember most of this tomorrow. And if I do, we can talk about it. I don't know what the right answer is. And obviously, you don't either. But I doubt it's going in and confessing to the police." Pausing, neither of them wanting to talk anymore, she broke the stalemate, "I'll get you a blanket, and you can sleep on the couch here. The bed's a mess, and you're so drunk that, oh, never mind. Okay?"

Michael nodded, happy to have her go and be left alone. Within minutes, his exhausted body molded itself awkwardly into the couch's contours, one leg propped up over the end. In her bedroom, steps away, Caroline lay on her back, eyes open, staring at the labyrinth of thatching. Twice she raised herself and walked to the edge of the couch, quietly returning after seeing Michael peacefully sleeping.

She debated moving to the other house, but worried about him, she could not leave him alone. For her, sleep was alien. She had toyed with the notion of a last fling, a silly escapade out of some far-fetched movie—and instead was burdened with a cathartic outpouring. Would she have done the same thing? Her mind reeled. Probably, and she certainly thought no less of him for it, taking the story at face value. In fact, the more she spun the sequence, the more she began to admire his courage and even stoicism. How had he managed to keep the secret! Her thoughts were a jumble, emotions so different from what she expected. Horror, sympathy, confusion, and now a craving to hold him. Would he even want that? In an odd way, he had spurned her. But so had royalty and rugby players. Those adolescent games were different; her mind churned, her body flushed. She was engaged! Again, what was she thinking?!

Control yourself, girl, she pleaded, struggling with the maelstrom of emotions wrought from Michael's festering wound. His plea for help, inadvertent or not, sowed trust that she recognized could otherwise take years. Left to its own devices, such a trust might never mature. British reserve could hold back that level of intimacy for a lifetime, even generations. Why was she being drawn closer when she should be revolted and pushing away? Damn him. Breakdowns should not be contagious like yawns. She desperately wanted to fall asleep. Finally, tortured from being witness to a tragedy barely in the past, her thoughts briefly turned to nightmares. As it always does, the night passed.

She rose with the sun and resumed her normal routine. After finishing breakfast at the Keeton mansion's main house, she peeked in to check on him. "Hi, Michael. How are you feeling?"

"I've been better, but not this week," he groaned, the burden of a physical and emotional hangover giving him no relief.

Despite the nightmares, Caroline had managed to sleep and fared much better. She was not keen to relive the evening, though, nor was she certain where her emotions tugged, deciding distance to be her most prudent option. "Well, look, I've got to run some errands. I'm leaving in a couple of days and have a lot of things to tie up. Richard's having breakfast out on the patio. I told him we had dinner, and you stayed in the guesthouse. Take a shower and get something to eat. You'll feel better. I should be back soon. If you have to leave before I return, give me a call, I'll be around. And don't worry about last night. We British can bury secrets deeper than an Orwellian coalmine. And out in the bush, secrets are carried away on the winds."

Michael looked up, dazed. Weakly nodding, he gingerly pulling himself up. "Thanks, I'll … I'll call," he said, not knowing what to add, fuzzy about the details of what he had said after coming back to the compound. He needed to be alone — again. Minutes later, the cold shower staggered him, shocking his body back to life. His head kept pounding, though, a wicked hangover unrelenting, driving him to gulp a handful of aspirin mercifully left in the bathroom. At least he hoped it was aspirin. If they were malaria pills, they probably would not have made him feel any worse.

After dressing, he staggered outside. Michael held his hand up against the morning's brilliant sun, fighting the glare that thankfully brought renewing energy. Enveloped in the brightness, he made his way to his car in search of sunglasses. Even after donning the glasses, he shielded his eyes as he made his way back across the vast lawn toward the Tudor and brick mansion. Michael kept blinking as he approached, the image ahead more likely a storybook scene. At a trough in front of the stables, a giraffe bent over taking a drink. The giraffe looked uncomfortable, cocked over as stiff as a tilted tripod, its neck and legs straight and bent to what seemed almost impossible angles. From a distance, the animal appeared large, not daunting, but as Michael drew near, it sensed his approach, standing up freakishly tall to look at him. Michael looked like an ant next to this gentle giant, a perspective that would humble even Goliath.

If the giraffe packed more brain and less bulk and thought like a predator, it would snicker at this easy prey. Michael was foolishly weaving forward, his hair tangled in the morning breeze, gawking. He was wearing the same wrinkled clothes he first put on to greet Caroline at the gallery; it was no surprise the giraffe caught his scent.

Engrossed in the odd encounter, Michael failed to recognize the danger he was courting. Giraffes are fairly docile, but they have a mean kick and are no keener on being approached than their shorter and teethier comrades. Richard Keeton looked up when he heard the animal stir. Quickly registering the predicament, Richard jumped up, whistling and flailing his arms to chase off the giraffe. The animal wanted none of Richard's antics, loping into the distance, pausing at the edge of the clearing in front of the house to look back, as if to nod goodbye before disappearing from view.

"Good morning," Richard hailed from above on the patio as Michael struggled to climb the few steps to the house. Looking like he was straight out of a Town & Country brochure, he continued, "We've been keeping breakfast warm, figured you'd finally get up before noon."

"Good morning. Had a little bit too much to drink last night. Guess I'm still not thinking very clearly. Thanks."

"Oh, don't worry about it. It's quite a sight. We've had lots of guests walk right up to the giraffes and forget what they're doing. Gigi wouldn't harm anyone."

"Gigi?"

"Yeah, she was an orphan, and we rescued her. Comes back and visits every now and then. I've never fancied hunting giraffe."

A maid brought Michael's breakfast out on a tray. Unsure whether he could hold down the food, he began feeling better after the first couple of bites.

"So, Caroline tells me you're a Harvard lad, that true?"

"Yes, sir."

"No need for the formalities."

"Thanks. Yeah, undergraduate and graduate. I'm working on some research to finish my Ph.D. and then hope to get an assistant professorship. Studying baboons. Hope you don't hunt them either."

"Nah, but someone ought to. Pesky creatures. Got a hell of a mean set of teeth."

"Yeah, I wasn't too thrilled the first time one chased me in camp."

"You have protection out there?" Richard probed.

"I've got a couple of rifles for emergencies, if that's what you mean."

"Good. "

"I had a heck of a time bringing them through customs. A friend bought me all the gizmos as a gift, but I don't know how to use most of the stuff." Michael paused and pictured the machine gun but kept quiet. "I hope it all rusts away without ever being used."

"Well, don't ever let that happen. I'll buy the lot off you if it comes to that. Impossible to find good rifles around here anymore."

"Well, I'm here to study the animals, not shoot them. I could never do that."

"You never know. Let me know if you ever want to join us on a hunt. You may surprise yourself."

Michael thought about answering but nodded noncommittedly at the invitation. Past time to steer the conversation in a different direction. After a half-hour chatting about the Polo Club, Richard's house, and the type of trees in the distance, he regained enough energy to leave. Richard slapped him on the back, and he set off. Despite all the odds, he apparently made a decent impression. Maybe that would help with Caroline. Caroline! Oh my god, he remembered. What did I say last evening? He tried replaying the conversation in his head as he swung his car onto the dirt road leading from the Keeton estate.

Chagrin set in, causing Michael to clench his fists around the steering wheel. While driving back to his hotel, he let every challenging car pass him, mechanically at the wheel but mentally disconnected. At first, what happened between them seemed trivial compared to the horror that he had broken down and confessed a trio of sins: a murder, an escape, a cover-up. He wondered why he accepted her invitation for a night cap in the first instance; and, like the evening before, cursed his commitment to calling her. Perhaps he could leave a message feigning illness or claim a disturbance at camp forced him to leave. There was, regrettably, no plausible excuse. He needed a measure of resolution, and once arriving back at the hotel picked up the phone.

"Hello," the woman at the veterinary clinic answered.

"Is Caroline there?"

"Hold on. I'll have to check. I think she just went out. May I ask who's calling?"

"Michael Sandburg."

"Oh, yes, she left a message for you. She thought you might try her. She'll be back at her house later this afternoon. You can ring her there or stop by. She'll be packing. Whatever you wish."

Michael recognized he had no choice. He had made a fool of himself last night—or at least he assumed so. He could not recollect every detail after they drove home from the Horn & Hoof. He remembered talking about camp and vaguely telling how he pulled the trigger; no need to recall anything more. If he hoped for rehabilitation, let alone being comfortable with Richard Keeton's help, he could not leave their discussion a mystery. Or could he? In a couple of days, he would be back in the field charting baboons, and she would be long gone in England. Nature has a way of restoring its balance.

· · · · ·

A resolve never to be a quitter, augmented by a dose of fear, tipped the scales. More defining, Michael wanted to see Caroline again, rationalizing be damned. Hence, freshly clothed, Michael headed toward the suburbs and the Keeton estate for the second time in less than twenty-four hours. When arriving, though, he hesitated, suddenly aware of his impetuousness and lack of strategy. Maybe her message had been polite trappings: did she actually expect him to stop by? It was virtually her last day at home! Of course not, he thought, self-flagellating, fumbling for his next move.

Nevertheless, forging ahead like a precocious schoolboy, he walked around the side of the house, uncertain what he was looking for, spying for a sign, hoping for inspiration. Michael pressed against a knotted tree, leaning around the trunk just far enough to cop a view. He was soon rewarded.

Caroline strode into view and as quickly right back out before Michael could conceive a passable gesture. He kicked at the tree in disgust. He gathered up a twig, snapping it in pieces, throwing little bits of bark at trees and bushes, eventually storming his way around to the front of a house. There would be no pebble against the window scene. The doorknocker thudded when the pulp of his fist smacked against the great oaken gate. Michael hoped Richard would not answer. Michael would struggle mightily to explain his reappearance.

Soon Caroline stood in the doorway, a bit surprised to see Michael, yet poised and smiling. Michael fidgeted, swaying from side to side, gradually becoming more at ease as she asked him in, failing to slam the door on his creaking ego. Michael anxiously glanced about the parlor, fearing Richard would emerge from behind another oaken panel to turn him to salt. His rotating neck did all the talking.

Perceiving his unease, she began, "Don't worry, Richard's out hunting. You look awful, by the way." They sat down in the library, elegantly bound tomes pressing in on them from all angles. Michael looked at the ladder on wheels perched against the far wall before yanking himself up from his slouch, "I guess I do. I've had better weeks."

"So, I hear you had brunch with Richard after all."

"Yeah, we had a pleasant chat. He even rescued me from being kicked by a giraffe. Long story... Unbelievable actually... Look, I hope I'm not intruding. I just felt, well, awkward about last night, what I said.... I thought about waiting around, but I was still in my old clothes and figured I'd go to the hotel, take a shower. I called and got the message you left at the clinic and decided to risk taking you up on your offer to drop by."

"It's fine. I understand. Really. And I'm glad you showered," she said, trying to lighten the mood.

Not ready to joke, Michael said, "I must have sounded pretty crazy last night. Whatever I can do to redeem myself. I don't know; I was trying to sort out some of the things I said on the drive over here. I know this is awkward, but just how far did I go?"

"Oh, I'd say pretty far."

"Christ. That's what I feared," holding out his hands in a gesture of conciliation and welcoming: "Friends?"

"Yes, yes, of course. Look, Michael. I'm not sure what to say either. I admire your courage, what you had to do. I'm sorry for everything you've been through. Really. The story is unbelievable, awful, at least from the version I was able to put together. And it sounds like you didn't have much choice. You can't beat yourself up too much for defending yourself. Anyway, it's going to take you a while to process everything—well, last night, that's obvious... What do you want me to say? You want forgiveness? Fine. But I don't think I'm the one that can give that to you."

"I'm not asking for that—anything really. I just wanted to apologize for last night. It's my problem, and I shouldn't have brought you into it. So that's it. I'm sorry, and thank you. For listening and now forgetting," he paused. "It would be easy to pack up and go. Believe me, I've wrestled with that. But I've decided to go back to camp. I don't want to just disappear. And I wanted to say goodbye in person." He looked into her eyes. Those jade green eyes. He could not read her mood clearly, but neither turned away for a few moments. "So, as I was saying, I'm off to camp. I've got to face up to myself and make a go of it again out there. I feel like I've aged twenty years the last few days. Maybe I'll end up with the life expectancy of a baboon. I didn't plan on joining the troop, just watching a bit," he said, trying to joke and find calmer ground. "I don't know. Hopefully, things will turn around, and I'll come out better for it. That's what I've got to think. I'm not used to this. Back home, I was the superstar. The research post everyone wanted. It's gone crazy."

Michael stood up, gazing down at Carolyn. She had stretched out supine on a couch, like a Renaissance Venus, a benign smile glossing her lips. Her long legs hung over the sofa's edge, the dust-caked soles of her bare feet teasing against the needlepoint pillow lying beneath them on the floor. He so wished he had confessed earlier and with someone else. But he did feel better, even comfortable.

"Do you think we'll ever see each other again?" he asked. "God, how will you ever bring yourself to listen to me?"

"Church holds no exclusive right on confessions," she smiled, sitting up and holding her hands palms up. "Sorry, I don't mean to joke about it. Don't worry, of course we'll see each other again. And about last night, I have no motive to tell anyone. I'm not even angry if that makes you feel any better. As I said, I feel sorry for you. And a little awkward. These aren't the most normal of circumstances. I was just enjoying being swept off my feet a bit, figured it might be the last time, you know. Look, this is all getting too philosophical. You want to help me pack?"

"Sounds good," he said, relieved, also wondering what the hell she meant. Did he have a shot? Had he blown it? Dinner started so great, laughing like old friends, even an actual date perhaps. But she was engaged, and he just confessed to murder! Jesus. All-time worst timing. "Forget it…try to act normal," he mumbled to himself, following Caroline out of the room. "Hey, did I tell you Richard invited me hunting. I guess I'll just pass."

"Oh, go ahead and go hunting. Don't worry about me and what he thinks if that's what's troubling you. We're close in some ways, others not so. Stepchildren and stepfathers share little in common beyond a bond to a woman who can't understand why they don't love each other as much as she thinks she loves them. He's very nice to me, though, and has been a kind surrogate father. Maybe someday we won't patronize each other."

"I'm sorry."

"Oh, don't be. You Americans just don't grasp the formalities of the English family. Drink plenty of tea out in the bush! You won't be able to resist."

Caroline missed Michael's actual intention, but he decided not to press the point. He hardly wanted to discuss hunting further today. Caroline exuded just enough tomboy lacquer she probably liked it. After a couple of hours packing, they shared a quick embrace, and he retreated, trudging across the lawn and through the trees to his car. It took only five minutes before the emotion of leaving hit him. He stared out at the road and the thick brush on either side, driveways intermittently appearing, breaking the illusion of infinite dense greenery. He marked each turn, a castaway on land. The road would always tug at him. Allowing he foolishly squandered any chance with Caroline, however remote, Michael drove forward, wistfully staring toward the forest's vanishing point.

# CHAPTER 5

*London, England – Several Weeks Later*

Andrew Harrington was an old friend of Richard's from the Royal Naturalist's Club. An alcoholic by trade, Harrington sobered up enough every weekend to fox hunt. Ironically, he looked a bit like a fox, his closely cropped red beard covering a pointy face. Habitually, he toddled back to one of his clubs to drink and discuss the chase for another week. Richard Keeton knew little about Andrew Harrington's personal life other than, like the rest of the club patrons, he reeked rich. Besides an unemployment level nearing one hundred percent, wealth was the common denominator among the members. Men of Richard Keeton's class contributed little to the British GNP, and those dabbling at life through a tumbler with Andrew Harrington siphoned off the gains left from generations past.

While perhaps no longer a star contributor to society, Harrington was still among Keeton's most reliable customers. Richard knew he could count on a willing buyer in Harrington back home for whatever beast he hunted. Only the taxidermist stood between them. In fact, Andrew had bought the pair of lion sisters Richard shot just before learning of Nigel Dunning's death. Since that day the two men had sat together in Westminster Abby, Richard laying the groundwork to hunt Julia, Keeton had lost count of his sales. It must have been at least fifty. He always wondered what Andrew did with them. When inquiring, he was invariably instructed to focus on shooting; a market will be there. They initially met at the club, and hearing that Richard loved to hunt in Africa, Andrew began asking questions. Two scotches later, he placed an order.

Keeton never pushed the inquiry further, feeling uncomfortable when his hunting practices crossed paths with his naturalist society's membership. Hypocrisy never much bothered Richard except when staring him in the face. Either Andrew lacked scruples or engaged in something he deemed best to leave a mystery. So, Keeton simply hunted. Meanwhile, Andrew, with his tedious and false sanctimony, stealthily acted as a broker for even richer men willing to turn a blind eye to the source of their mounts. Such was Richard Keeton's rationalization. What mattered were Andrew Harrington's renowned contacts. Chatting with a drink in one's hand for months at a time will build a few friendships, and schmoozing at exclusive clubs will guarantee a lifetime of privileges.

Begrudging the need for a personal trip, even when asking for a favor from an acquaintance he had not seen in a year, Richard Keeton taxied over to the club. He had called ahead to confirm Andrew sat on his throne, learning Andrew was busy pontificating. It was a small place, and by Richard's arrival in the early afternoon, they found themselves alone.

"Andrew, how are you? It's been quite a while, you 'ol lush."

"Guess you know me too well! So, what brings you back to London? Seems like I was just having a drink with you, discussing the last big kill."

"My stepdaughter, Caroline, is getting married. Julia's all excited. You'd think we're London high society or something. I've got to remind her we live in the bush."

"Well, congratulations." Shifting a bit uncomfortably, "Quite a turn of events after seeing her as a little girl weeping at Nigel's funeral. Anyway, she's all grown up—glad to see she's happy now, and about to turn society heads. Ravishing woman, daughter of Her Majesty's ambassador. Does she become a Lady when you get the title, or out of succession line as a stepdaughter? Suppose I'll have to start subscribing to the tabloids."

"God, I hope the tabloids don't get a hold of this. They'll bloody the whole thing, start digging up stories about old Lord Harold Keeton."

"The great white hunter!"

"No, that's me," Richard chuckled, touching his hair for effect. "I better be careful what I say, or I really will be in the tabloids! And no, I don't think she gets any title." Pausing, "Look, Andrew, I need to ask you a favor."

"Go ahead."

"I have a Dutch painting I want to have auctioned at Sotheby's this weekend. It's a minor Hals. One of the few things Lord Keeton willed to me directly that isn't tied up with Graham. He had a thing for the Dutch. I guess tied to my grandmother being part Dutch. From Leiden. I've only been there once years ago. It's a charming town, with some nice canals, not too far from Amsterdam. Can't remember if Hals was from there or just visited." He shrugged. "Doesn't matter. Tiny country, and getting a provenance out of there after the war was hopeless. Damn Nazis looted everything, and you'd have to go basement to basement to figure these things out. Anyway, I don't have it listed, and I don't have any connections at the auction house. I'm going back to Kenya next week, and I want to get this taken care of before returning home. Do you know anyone who can help me out?"

Becoming quite adept at cover stories, Richard had rehearsed a plausible excuse why he planned to sell the heirloom. He had dipped a little too deeply into Julia's bank accounts and needed to restore the balances before anything was discovered. Richard lied to preempt any questioning as to his motives: "It was going to be a wedding gift, but I could really use the cash. Accounts still tied up with Graham, and I don't like going to the solicitors for favors."

"Consider it done. You realize, of course, that you might not get as high a bid as you want. Money is tight around here lately, and you'll have no press announcing the sale. The big fish after a painting like that probably won't be aware. Sorry Richard, but I have to ask, you do have the paperwork confirming your right to sell? A bit touchy with Graham and all, and I'm sure the auction houses will want to confirm."

Bristling at the implication of a clouded title due to his older brother's mere technical authority, "Yes, yes, the invalid Lord. Graham still has the peerage, but in name only. He's not doing too well, and one day it will be mine. And, of course, I have all the paperwork. Notarized by my solicitors at Sandton Radcliffe & Parks. Even had old Henry Radcliffe double-check. Don't worry. And, as I said, this is mine directly, nothing to do with Graham."

"Good, good. If I'm not prying too much, what do you mean exactly by he's not doing too well."

"The doctors say he's in a gradual decline. He'll never regain his faculties, and I'm his appointed conservator. They don't expect him to live another five years. I used to go, but now I just don't see the point. I can't speak to him, he doesn't recognize me, and I feel awkward going over there." In response to Andrew's raised eyebrows, he added, "Yes, I think about the title passing to me as soon as he dies. There, I said it. Wouldn't you? I'm not a monster for stating the obvious. I'm entitled to the Lordship, and it's frustrating to wait for no good reason. I make sure he's taken care of, so nothing to feel guilty about."

"What a shame. Shame," was all Andrew could muster. He deemed it best to turn the conversation back to the painting. "Well, for the painting, as long as you have the documentation together, I don't see any problem. People are bound to understand your wanting to sell off an item or two while you're waiting to inherit the estate. The whole situation isn't exactly a secret. Not too much whispering while you're away in Africa, but everyone is aware. In fact, most people respect your discretion. Wouldn't do to be around here hovering. Not in very good taste and all. May be a bit of a discount if local buyers feel it's disrespectful to Graham, thinking he's involved, but I don't expect that to be a factor. Plus, most of the buyers these days are foreign, and they could care less." Andrew's thoughts continued that any sentimentality for a drooling Lord, especially in the face of a rightful heir eager to get on with things, was a sentiment better suited for days of Victorian formality. Perhaps that may be perceived as hypocritical standing under racks of leather-bound tomes, but he was a progressive. At least he liked to think so. He had, after all, spearheaded the committee's relaxation on wearing the club tie on weekends.

"Good," Richard interrupted his vainglorious thoughts. "Just let me know if they think the price will be significantly off."

"Hard to guess," Andrew's thoughts privately churning what angle there may be in this for him, especially if Richard was finally close to inheriting his Lordship. "The markets have gone crazy from the Arabs. Taxes have been gnawing at me for years, and now some of my holdings have become prickly. I don't even think I have the cash right now to bid on your next catch. I can still act for others, of course."

Keeton had set the meeting to evaluate Andrew as a potential partner. He judged him trustworthy from their past dealings and liked that they knew relatively little about each other outside of their business. Anonymity provided a valuable cushion so long as there remained steadfast dedication to their pursuits. His original tactic was to pry into Andrew's finances just enough to understand the landscape before approaching him about acquiring larger shipments. Now, realizing Andrew was already a middleman, he touted carpe diem. With luck, the parties buying the trophies he sold initially to Andrew would serve as an ideal distribution network. His mind reeled.

"Andrew, I have a proposition for you."

"Will this be as easy as the last request?"

"Maybe easier. How would you like to make money from my hunting rather than buying from me?"

"Well, that doesn't sound too different from what I've always done. You don't think I have thirty heads hanging in my house, do you?" he chuckled.

His hunches confirmed, Richard continued less cautiously.

"How does more ivory sound to you?"

"Always plenty of interest out there. Can never find enough," Andrew said, turning his back and walking toward the bar to refill his drink. Upon returning to their table, he stared at Richard, who remained calm. He took a sip, deciding to test him. "You know the seriousness of what we're discussing. I can handle it, won't cock it up. I wonder whether you can. I presume you're new at this. I also presume that you're so sure of success that you feel you can't turn the opportunity down. That's how it always starts."

"Presume what you want. I don't see a need for either of us to know more details than necessary. I'll tell you my connection because you'll need a story on your end. I have a deal in Kenya with a friend in one of the government ministries. There've been terrible droughts, and hundreds, probably thousands, of elephants have died from natural causes. On routine inspections, game wardens, wildlife officials—I really don't know who—collect the tusks and bring them back to Nairobi where they're kept in a warehouse. There are lots of rhino horns too. Some are sold and brought to Mombasa for auction. The numbers can be altered, and often, are never counted. I can take as many from this supply as I want, and I don't even have to do any work. More elephants are dying every day from the drought than I could ever shoot. The only problem is getting them out, but that's my problem."

"I have no place to sell them," Richard continued after a brief pause, "and I'm assuming that you do. If they're best shipped elsewhere, like Hong Kong, that can be arranged. I just need someone to ship them to. You're the first person I thought about; now I'm wondering if you know someone in the Orient."

Andrew Harrington drew back in his chair, slowly taking another sip of his drink. He wrinkled up his forehead, itching his wiry beard just below the chin, accentuating his feral look. Keeton anxiously awaited a response. He had put all his cards down, managing to lie only about how he was acquiring the ivory. Andrew could confirm a severe drought and that many elephants were reported dying from the heat. It was even true that the government confiscated some of these tusks and auctioned them off for their own account. But the warehouses and access to some enormous supply were pure fabrications. Perhaps it could be true. That was what made the story so compelling. He had not bothered backfilling any details until concocting the tale on his way over to meet Andrew. Richard first contemplated the feasibility of such a scheme after the Mombasa ivory auction. He must now push Alijah about the idea when returning. The delicacy of the subject foreclosed any more immediate investigation.

"Richard," Andrew said, "you've got a partner." He extended his hand, firmly grasping Richard's in return and smiling widely. Such emotion was uncharacteristic of both men and effusive for the setting, but the deal warranted celebration. "I know you won't believe me, but the

Naturalist society provides more outlets for the goods than we'll ever need. I want to look into the Arabs and Orient, though. In fact, I have an interesting idea. Perhaps even a way to kill two birds with one stone, and you can meet a prospect at the auction. Just show up Saturday at Sotheby's, and your painting will be coming up. I'll let you know before then if I can set up a meeting there."

The smiles puncturing the formalities of the gentlemen's discourse signaled the conversation's significance. This was more than a tale of the hunt. Richard Keeton confidently strode out to a taxi, and Andrew Harrington took rare initiative in setting down his drink and leaving to place some telephone calls. The elk over the fireplace failed to stir, and the bartender lumbered away from his taps to wipe the now empty table.

How many times had Harringtons so plotted, and how many times had men tried to redirect the world while sipping on scotch? Keeton shook his head in the cab, realizing he was now privy to the inner circle—a circle heretofore denied him as merely a third son. How easy it was to scheme and compromise, sensing his destiny within grasp. If he only knew what the ugly future foretold.

•　　•　　•　　•　　•

Andrew began making arrangements for Richard to meet a Saudi businessman at the weekend auction. The challenge lay in orchestrating the introduction. Both Andrew and Richard agreed the rendezvous should be as inconspicuous as possible. Any conversation in public could draw attention, especially with the hordes of professional gossips flocking to Sotheby's. Andrew struck upon a brilliant idea: an undisclosed owner should sell the painting. That would also preempt unseemly whisperings about Lord Graham, and most serious buyers would trust the auction house to deliver an unimpeachable provenance with the sales documents.

When the painting came to the floor, Saudi millionaire Mansour Mohamed Nebavi would open the bidding. Richard would follow, raising the price; Nebavi even told Andrew that he might buy it as a goodwill gesture before seriously negotiating with Richard if he liked the work. On

Saturday, the two men anxiously sat amidst the crowd, scanning faces in hopes of recognizing each other before the charade began. Richard thought he spotted Nebavi, but the bidding was begun by a bearded middle-eastern gentleman in a three-piece suit rather than the white-robed sheik he had been watching. Richard's mistake, though, was hardly in vain. The white-robed sheik ended up buying the painting.

When the session neared a close, Nebavi stood up, nodding his head to Richard, who, moments later, rose and joined him outside in the hall. Richard, wary of snitches, began, "Too bad, huh. I see we both lost out on that oil."

Mansour said, "Yes, it was a beautiful work. I can't understand why the owner wanted to sell it unless he desperately needed cash."

"It's hard to tell with these things," Richard cautiously responded, following Nebavi until they navigated to a corner table in a nearby hotel brasserie. No longer afraid to speak and hoping to keep their talk short, he said, "Andrew Harrington tells me you might be interested in a partnership. Has he explained the terms?"

"Yes, but I'm afraid that I'm not personally interested. I agreed to meet you because I have a cousin in the petroleum business who's been involved in supervising oil workers and production throughout the Mideast. The last time I talked to him, he reminded me of an old friend of our family's in North Yemen who may be in the market for, how should I say, your product."

Richard's eyes lit up. North Yemen was rumored to be one of the world's largest markets for rhinoceros horns. A solid contact there heralded a greater boon than he ever anticipated. If they could strike a deal, he would need to scale up his operations immediately. Composing himself so as not to appear overanxious, Richard asked, "Are you willing to share the name of your contact?"

"Yes, but it won't do you much good without my introduction. Relations in the region are all important, you know. The person you want to meet is Ahmed Al-Hassari. I met him once in Jeddah, but he deals often with my cousin. I'll have my cousin telex him tonight and let him know that you'll be in touch. I don't want to know details about what you're selling… And, I think it may be best if you were, let's say, economical with that information as far as Andrew is concerned as well. That way, I can stay out of trouble if things don't work out."

"Why are you doing this for me?" Richard asked, his suspicions aroused by the paradox that the conversation was going so well.

Mansour laughed. "I didn't say we were uninterested in the price. My cousin and I still need to eat." Turning serious, almost harsh, he then admonished, "I really don't care about you. We'll probably never meet again. This man has helped my family out, and it's an easy way to repay a debt in case I ever need a favor from him again. He'll be delighted to hear from you. If there's a little in it for me, all the better. You won't have to deal with me directly. My cousin will make sure I'm taken care of if you deal with Ahmed. And, of course, we need to deal with our mutual friend Mr. Harrington."

"Sheik Nebavi, I think we understand each other perfectly. And I thank you for your introduction. May I simply ask you one favor?" Richard decided to risk a further step. "Could you provide me the names of one or two other potential buyers from North Yemen, so I can appear like I know what I'm doing and offering him a fair deal."

"You mean so you can negotiate a better price for yourself."

"It all depends on how you phrase it."

"I think I can accommodate you." Mansour snickered, letting out a full laugh as he twisted his pen and scribbled some names and Ahmed's phone number on a napkin. The names he gave Richard were wholly made up but sounded common enough to be plausible. No reason to compromise his cousin or Ahmed; yet selfishly, if Richard could indeed strike a good deal, he would benefit from Andrew's largess. While he would never fully trust Andrew Harrington, one reason he liked doing business with the British was he knew Andrew would steal a bit less from him than what his cousin would take. As he said, he needed to eat.

"I'd say I'll have to find Andrew and let him know how things work out, but I suspect you'll keep him informed." Mansour did not want to implicate his own arrangement. "Please send him regards and let him know I had to leave for Morocco and didn't have time to call. He won't mind, now that my little debt is repaid," he said, covering his tracks, a little disinformation never hurting.

Richard raised an eyebrow, wondering what Nebavi meant, but let it pass, wanting to move on quickly, hoping he would not have to deal with him further. Both men smiled and shook hands, not fully appreciating each other's motives, yet quietly smug that the introduction may prove more rewarding than the other suspected. Richard let Nebavi leave first and then followed, hailing a taxi to join Julia for dinner.

•     •     •     •     •

Brimming with confidence, Richard Keeton cabled Alijah to meet him for dinner the night he returned to Nairobi. He also wrote, "Get busy," there would be little time to celebrate. Alijah read the missive suspiciously; Richard had never deigned to invite him to his table. He knew Richard planned to be in England for a while but was not privy to the whole of his plans or any specific deals. He only knew that Caroline was getting married and that her nuptials provided a convenient excuse to accelerate their operations.

The next step was up to Richard. Keeton always choreographed, expecting his cast to execute without question. But Alijah now questioned. Ironically, by virtue of holding the position that Richard helped purchase, Alijah possessed sufficient clout to raise his voice. In a week, he even had an appointment to meet President Nazuto. A tribesman at heart in a city populated by workers and British, Alijah struggled for identity as his power swelled.

He had been dating Sara ever since that evening he took her home on the motorcycle. She represented the perfect class, someone who could help him fulfill his new identity. A university-trained teacher whose father managed Coca-Cola's bottling plant in Kenya, she grew up with relative wealth and a world of expectations. Her sophistication helped Alijah forget his naked youth.

At first, he worried she was so worldly he could not credibly hope to win her permanent fancy. After dating, though, her experiences became shared adventures, her travels and perspectives sinking in through osmosis. The more she let him in, the more he explored next levels, experiential intimacy a corollary to sexual desire. Alijah was also not beyond purchasing his way out of perceived inferiority. He took Sara to the most expensive restaurants in town, brought her to an embassy party attended by President Nazuto, and flew her to the coast in his plane. As he grew fonder of the person rather than her type, Sara similarly began looking beyond his flashy image and warrior physique. All that remained was breaking the news to her that he was already married.

Reading the cable from Richard and thinking about Caroline's wedding caused him to think about Tza, his tribal wife, the woman who had beckoned him at a ceremonial dance years ago. It had been a while since Alijah visited home from the city; during his last trip, he was also surprised to learn she was carrying another child. Her pregnancy merely accentuated how he had become trapped between his warrior kin and motor-wielding friends.

He recalled years ago when all the newly initiated warriors traveled to a distant village and sat watching the women gyrate. Tradition called for them to choose a man, but the wind would have the last word on obligations. He went along, never grasping the lifelong implications of the trip. Tza spotted him during her dance, glancing conspicuously at him every time the circle swayed his direction. The girls were moving in a circle, sometimes holding hands, sometimes breaking free into the center spotlight cast by the fire. They sang lasciviously, and the men around them clapped and laughed. Alijah had seen her too. Drawn to her first, he was transfixed. He did not know why, just naturally returning the gaze from her inviting almond-shaped eyes. When she came toward the group to make her choice, he instinctively rose, almost before she extended her hand, tempting him. Soon she led him to the grasses where they kissed and lay together, ignoring taboos and blessings. Youthful indiscretion and raging hormones have a knack for superseding cultural boundaries. She was his first. Nine months later, he celebrated becoming a father, and now Kiku had grown, ready for initiation. All these years later they were expecting another.

Alijah sighed, thinking of when he brought Tza to Nairobi. He had tried futilely to usher her into this other world. She had not coped well with the city and Alijah's educated friends. Even he became embarrassed. He fought off being ashamed of her, chastising his friends who joked about women from out in the villages. A city-tribal snobbery pervaded, with the city elite looking down on the village nomads, ashamed of where they came from and hoping to cut clean from their past. Men with toilets looked down on their own fathers because they still pissed in the grass.

Alijah passionately wanted Tza to fit in and cursed Richard Keeton's name when she pleaded to go back to her true home. He knew it was best. Some were born to adapt, but not Tza. She liked the bath, but she could never wear shoes. Alijah bought her a radiophone so he could call her. Except when she returned to their village, the men forbade her from using it. They were scared of the voices, warning her it contained evil spirits. She tried explaining how it worked, but they refused to listen. One day it disappeared, and she knew better than to hunt for the culprit. It had been stolen by a bloodline. Turning his attention back to the present, Alijah tore up the cable, frustrated by the pressures in his life. He would have to double down to satisfy Richard's new promise of trophies.

His reward would be pure cash, his ticket to continuing to impress Sara. Perhaps he would splurge and buy cattle for Tza and Kiku. He was not sure; he never knew what to do for them and could not entirely cut himself off from his roots. That might have been possible if he lived a continent away, but not when he regularly flew over their land, wondering if he should provide Kiku the same chance Richard Keeton had granted him. That presented a haunting quandary: Kiku was becoming old enough that he would be tormented by the same dilemmas tugging at Alijah. Alijah would attend his son's initiation, lying to Sara about his destination and hoping fate would make the choice for him.

•　　•　　•　　•　　•

London was at least a second home to Caroline, if not a first. Both her parents and her stepfather were British subjects, but the luck of conception in Hampstead and birth in Nairobi afforded her the luxury of playing chameleon with how she portrayed her roots. She was certainly old enough now to clarify her citizenship, but the mere fact of delay indicated her love of the equator. A white native African she would remain while keeping Her Majesty's passport and the memory of her Ambassador father. Her lineage conferred a peculiar status she infrequently dwelled on and which rarely caused her conflicts. Good-hearted but admittedly sheltered, reading a headline about South Africa, she barely paused to consider the issue of race.

Stories from South Africa constantly filled the papers, but inexplicably to the oppressed the news tilted more toward economics than politics. The diamond market was going berserk, prices spiraling upward to record highs. The London gold market closely shadowed the rise of the sister gem until it proved impossible to distinguish which commodity tugged at the other's price. Few focused on the implications for ivory. Gold traded consistently between $100 and $200 an ounce until the price jumped above the value predicted by the most extreme forecasters. When $800 an ounce passed, even Caroline succumbed to the pressures prompting less patient sellers to part with jewelry at $500 an ounce. She had a beautiful gold necklace given to her by her father she would never consider parting with, but a watch never worn, no use in the bush, and with no sentimental ties fetched an irresistible price.

Caroline trembled walking into the jeweler who purchased her watch a week earlier. When she left for London a few weeks before, the last thing she would have dreamed about was selling her engagement ring. Now it was gone, not a product of the OPEC shocks inflating the gem's value, but a symbol of a bitter separation.

She had been studying at the Sorbonne and met Edward when he came to visit his sister on holiday from Oxford. They fell in love for lack of anything else in common—other than mutual sexual attraction. Caroline was the biology whiz and gadabout society girl, befriending peers before inquiring past their names. Edward, in contrast, was a snob; he shunned an entire class of people, who in turn disliked his set. Raised with accouterments and aspirations that breed arrogance, an exception was one thing he never strove to be. He planned to step into his father's business, his present schooling first a social function and second a training ground preparing him to run his family estate. If Edward's skill in economics only rivaled his charm, there might have been hope for the business. The life of the club, though, made him a full-fledged playboy, Caroline's distance enabling his philandering. Her innocently waiting jungles away allowed him to prey on unsuspecting women without fear of being caught. Edward boasted to his friends about having the best of both worlds. He also comfortably lied to his dates, feigning loneliness and lamenting his failure to find someone he could love. With his boyish good looks and mop of toe head blond hair, Edward seemed to have little problem seducing willing participants.

The night before Caroline's trip to the jewelers, his world hummed perfection. Any warning at all of her early arrival and the marriage would still be set. Spontaneity was one of Caroline's greatest gifts, but now she wondered whether to curse or praise God for impulsively flying to London a week early as a surprise. It did not matter that Edward cared little for the naked brunette riding the body he swore was sentimentally detached. He was equally undressed, and no barrage of apologies could alter his exposure. The marriage was off. Caroline grew bitter as Edward's apologies turned toward criticism: "You're not such a virgin yourself, you know!" he unleashed his frustration.

"God, it was so fucking crude! All I can think of is your face as she clung to you like a pogo stick!"

"And what if I had surprised you in Africa? Are you telling me you've never thought about an affair?"

"Thinking, yeah," she paused, becoming philosophical, her mind flashing back to Michael. "We all have standards. Doesn't matter how you want to cut it, you broke all the lines."

"It really isn't what it looks like," he pleaded, realizing his tactics had placed him in a worse position, if that could be possible.

"Right, that makes a lot of sense! You know, it's for the best anyway. I just needed a good excuse." As she walked away, she realized she meant every word. They had never been well suited, just attracted, a crush that had gone too far. Neither had been mature enough to admit that. Caroline suddenly found herself in London without anything to do or anyone to see. She had not contacted old friends because she had hoped to spend a quiet week with Edward. It had been several months since they had seen each other.

Now she hesitated contacting any of her friends or relatives, except one. Her best friend from secondary school remained her closest friend. There is something particularly sentimental about just growing up, for the bonds of the past seem ever dear despite whatever divergence of personalities age may bring. Caroline craved that old security and headed toward Elizabeth's house.

They had gone to France for university together and traveled across the continent two summers in a row. Elizabeth was now a teacher living in a flat between Sloane Square and Harrods. What seemed to be the only friendly face in the world burst into a wide smile as Caroline paid her second unexpected visit of the week.

Elizabeth Hennessy was a plain twenty-five-year-old schoolteacher who looked the part. She wore her straight brown hair in a pageboy cut with bangs that drifted too near her eyebrows. Bred in the misty English countryside, she possessed the natural ruddy complexion that cosmetic companies so abhor. Five eight and zaftig, she enveloped her old friend in a hug.

When Caroline stepped back, she scrutinized Elizabeth, curious how she had changed over the last two years. She appraised her surrender to a settled look. Signs of bags under her eyes puffed faintly visible where once there was only a gleam. Appearing glamorous had never claimed priority, but she now yielded to the impulse of looking the way her body was inclined. Caroline smiled, thinking that at least she still wore jewelry.

Creeping to the living room, she was careful not to wake the newborn baby sleeping in a crib standing haphazardly in the middle of the otherwise planned furniture. Caroline had forgotten about the child until arriving, nervously plumbing her memory for the announcement and phone call. Finally, the name came back to her. She could cease worrying that she would call little Emma, Alice or Albert. She cheered how lucky the baby was: a mother so caring that she constantly bordered on maudlin, a prosperous and smart father stepping into his father's barrister's practice. The sense of family was overwhelming.

"Caroline, what are you doing here?"

"The wedding is off," she said, seeing no need to prolong the story.

Once unburdened, her composure crumbled and Caroline burst into tears. For two hours, the two sat as Caroline recounted what happened, sparing no details, crying over the dreams she had come to believe.

Trust had been irrevocably shattered. Edward spun half-truths, pleading that affairs were mere lapses. Yes, he claimed he still loved her, but that was mere manipulation. Edward was a master at twisting her to believe whatever story he lay at her feet. There were many things she could compromise; honesty in a spouse, however, was not subject to bargaining. When she finished, Liz simply nodded. She knew her friend spoke from the heart—rationalizing would be shelved for a different time. Caroline had come to confess, baring naked emotions, arriving at a painful but obvious choice.

For the next week, the baby's room-to-be became Caroline's, and the proud parents went sleepless. Caroline's stay defined an imposition devoid of guilt. She did not want to be alone, and they did not want her anywhere else. Half the days she puttered around the house; the rest she spent browsing amidst the London stores. Nairobi commerce had its limitations, and the variety began to cheer her mood. At some point, though, she acknowledged her retail therapy would have to end, and she should move elsewhere.

It was awful having no plans and no commitments. That freedom would bring a nice bid from many. The option of spontaneity, though, remained grim to a lonely woman who had looked forward to the security of fixing her place. Of course, that was not really her personality, but it was what her mother Julia taught her, and what for the time being she convinced herself she could accept.

On the seventh evening of her stay, Elizabeth's husband brought home a friend, Clive St. Something or Other, to meet Caroline. After Liz berated him for bringing Caroline a date so soon, he explained that his friend owned a publishing house that could offer Caroline a fun job. Their products included a line of calendars, and Elizabeth's husband had talked St. Clive into offering Caroline an opportunity to take photographs: England or Africa, her choice. Liz had always raved about Caroline's eye. They even had one of her pictures of two lion cubs hanging in the foyer.

Silly Liz, Caroline thought. They had joked about becoming artists at university, but that felt long ago, and Caroline was now officially a veterinarian. Where would she find the time gallivanting to take photos? It was at that moment she realized she should run over to the Royal Veterinary College and see her old advisor. They would have a job for her, and she could complete some research. Perhaps work on horses after all and put off studying the more exotic species until her life settled. And ride. She missed riding and would find a stable, maybe even take one of the horses from the Salisbury estate. It offered the perfect solution: a chance to get away, start again, all while continuing what she loved. Could it be time to trade on being a Keeton and a Dunning?

Her pedigree in this town was more than racing studs could aspire to and a card she had always been reluctant to play. Her heart yearned for Africa, not London society. And yet, she would be swooned over at Ascot. There would hardly be a polo player her equal, a woman of her beauty who uniquely understood a mare inside and out. Would-be suitors would grovel at her feet. Research and work by day, riding in the evenings and weekends, and a bit of teasing whenever she desired to make herself available. The beginnings of a plan started to form. She could even begin to see herself happy.

Over port, she politely thanked Clive St. Something or Other (why bother to remember his name?) for his offer, but she was too busy professionally to take on anything else right now. She had a meeting at the Royal Veterinary College in the morning, she reminded Liz, whose faint smile veiled her surprise. No matter that she did not actually have an appointment; it was all about the going, not the formality of scheduling. A Keeton, and a Dunning, and a vet. Maybe she was ambitious after all. Oh, what poor Clive, or Edward for that matter, would never taste. The burn of the port warmed her, and for tonight, she would let the comfort of privilege lift her over the barrier of depression.

· · · · ·

Disaster struck swiftly a couple of mornings later. Julia and Richard Keeton had arrived in London expecting the wedding to take place on the date they helped plan. They called Edward only to learn their daughter had left and the ceremony was canceled. They went to sleep confused, knowing there would be no sleep until they could locate Caroline and learn the truth. When morning finally came, the weary couple had the additional displeasure of reading about the separation in the paper. It turned out Clive St. Something or Other proved good for something when Caroline followed up dinner by asking for a favor. She never feared for her reputation and found no guilt in denying Edward the chance to move on unblemished.

Seated across from a single gentleman in their hotel's coffee shop and looking out across the street to Kensington Gardens, Richard Keeton noticed a picture that resembled Caroline. The man across from Richard and Julia read one of those tabloids that Richard himself sneeringly eschewed; as the page flipped, the shocking image floated past. Richard excused himself from the table, glancing at the paper's name, and proceeded to the lobby to buy a copy. He flipped through the pages walking back to the table. Precisely when he reached his seat, he stopped turning. His eyes riveted to the page, Richard grasped his chair in such a violent gesture that the table shook.

Julia became hysterical when he placed the article before her. In bold print, across the top of the page and beside a picture of Edward and Caroline scowling at each other, a headline read: "Sex Scandal Jilts Royal Wedding Plans." Always a socially conscious woman, Julia asked, "Are we really considered royalty?"

Richard grimaced, "No. If a piece of trash like this finds out a girl is from a Lord's family and the groom is related to whomever, they can't resist. It makes great gossip even if no one is actually royalty or if the story is completely false. It's because of old Lord Harold Keeton."

"But if we're royalty, and we're related to the people here, I think we should have at least made the front page," she said in a tone just serious enough to outrage Richard. He tore the paper from her hands.

"This is absolute rubbish! A slow news day, and they denigrate my name. At least it wasn't on the front page!" Grateful they had not dredged up anything about Graham again, Richard turned the paper to the front, suddenly curious as to what glossed the cover. Not unexpectedly, the headline contained the four-letter word so bandied about London these days: OPEC.

Richard turned his thoughts to Graham. Why couldn't he die already? His poor brother, that most dreaded and hated of beasts to younger brothers like Richard, who was entitled to inherit great Lord Harold's title by dint of squirming out into the world a year or two quicker. Oh, he had not resented him growing up; in fact, he revered him. The resentment had grown in the years after Graham's car crash. Graham was a dashing university student on that fateful day when his MGB convertible swerved to avoid a rabbit, and he found himself wrapped around an oak tree. His girlfriend was miraculously thrown free and suffered only ugly bruises. Richard had long wondered whether it would have been merciful if Graham had died rather than be left an invalid, slowly declining over the years with no hope of regaining his faculties, let alone his bowel control.

He could barely utter the phrase, Lord Graham, for it lacked the linked dignity it should rightly convey. There was no chance Graham would father an heir, and so it remained a cruel matter of time while Richard waited to take up the title. Of course, Richard had asked their family lawyer Henry Radcliffe to research if there were a manner to expedite the grant. Unfortunately, though, the letter's patent creating the original hereditary peerage included the customary vesting to heirs-male of the body. The stuffy opinion from Sandton Radcliffe & Parks advised any amendment would require an act of parliament; that, especially with the taint of his current extracurricular pursuits if rumor ever spread, was hardly an option. Resigned to biding his time, he resolved to do whatever it may take to secure the means to live as befits the position, ensuring that he would not live the life of a Lord in name only when he was finally invested. The estates, the grandeur, and the esteem of Lord Harold would be renewed, with a new flourish that would ensure the Keeton dynasty well into the 21st century. Richard smiled for the first time today, looking at Julia, his first stepping stone to his rightful place: widow of Britain's Ambassador to Kenya, predictably looking to one-up being Mrs. Ambassador to being addressed as Lady Keeton. No wonder she hardly noticed his occasional burrowing into her funds to sow his future position—even if hidden poaching profits now largely tempered the need. This was scarcely the first English marriage of mutual convenience. Family and fortune, hurrah!

At lunch, that highly touted family was united and fully informed. Somber looks and curt comments about the food set a tone more upbeat than Caroline had expected. She thankfully would not be driven into tears.

"I don't understand why you came," Caroline began.

"Why wouldn't we come to your wedding?" her flighty mother replied.

"I mean once you knew it was off."

"We didn't know," Richard said. "We just found out last night when we called Edward to talk to you."

Caroline put her hand over her eyes: "I sent two telegrams: one to the house and the other to the clinic to forward. Then I called and left a message at the house. I tried at least half a dozen times. And Jomno! I talked to him at the house, and he promised me he would tell you I called and to call me. It was an emergency. Nothing? He didn't say anything?"

"We had no idea," Richard said, now worried whether Alijah received his message.

"I don't think Jomno really understands English very well."

"I kept asking him if he understood. And he kept answering yes."

"Well, anyway, here we are," Julia said. Somehow her words brilliantly summed up the day.

# CHAPTER 6

*Nairobi, Kenya*

Alijah's outwardly charmed life was actually quite complicated. The government's newest superstar was upset, even stymied, when Richard called on his return to Kenya from Caroline's aborted wedding. Why did no one consult him before finalizing the deal with Andrew Harrington? Did the parties they were courting honestly not want to negotiate with black men? After Richard dared to suggest that slight, Alijah challenged why they wanted to do business in Africa? Richard's quip that they wanted to make money rang hollow.

"That's the way it is." Keeton said, "I advise you to stop questioning everything I'm doing. Look, come over, we'll discuss it."

"I'll meet you as planned," Alijah gruffly conceded, still a newbie to an ecosystem lingering with colonial arrogance.

Alijah was too drained from his personal problems to fight with Richard. Ever greedy for a bigger cut, he had already borrowed money, anticipating greater loot from deals like those with Harrington. He bought a house in a Nairobi suburb; now, he was pricing a new Mercedes. Alijah had decided to make Sara his second wife, reconciled to the fact Tza would never conform to his new lifestyle. The fact Tza was with child made the decision more difficult, but hardly changed his mind.

Even in a polygamous society, though, marrying a city-educated woman posed problems. Anyone outside the tribal atmosphere might not accept the union. At a more practical, perhaps selfish level, he would need much more money to support any spouse fitting into his increasingly lavish lifestyle. Whatever the drawbacks, Alijah made up his mind to marry again.

"Of course," Sara beamed. "I hope you know what you're getting into!"

"I do!"

Alijah suppressed, "You don't, you don't." He had still not been able to bring himself to tell her about Tza and Kiku.

"When?"

"Whenever you want."

"I want a big wedding!"

Carried away by her enthusiasm, Alijah had not focused on the details. His attention was only on Sara, relishing the idea of marrying her without thinking through ceremonial trappings. They laughed together. She exuded poise, even in the company of the President, burnishing Alijah's image. He did not need much more. The details! Did etiquette require him to invite Richard Keeton to the ceremony? His gut told him he should, but Richard's latest remarks made Alijah wonder. That promised to be one of the more straightforward matters. His most significant problem remained that Sara wanted to meet his family. That, to Alijah, represented an impossibility. And which family? His mother? How could he introduce her to his wife and nearly grown son?

He resolved to lead separate lives. Sara would have all the accouterments symbolic of prestige and would share most of his life. If she knew, would she find it difficult, bedecked in gowns, to avoid competition with a bare-breasted illiterate? If no, the absence of jealousy would cruelly shield her from noticing the tribal link which Alijah and Tza shared so dearly. Sara was doomed to become a display piece far from his heart's core, no matter what he wanted to feel.

Alijah trekked out to Tza's village—his village!—shortly before the ceremony to break the news. Her pregnancy bloated, and he knew the elders gossiped about the disgrace of marrying while she labored with their child. Taking another wife at this moment would mock custom; supposedly bad luck for the unborn child. Alijah dismissed the superstition and told the village elders about how he needed a wife in the city to conform to the white mores and cocktails.

They nodded disapprovingly and enviously. Only rich men had two wives, and no one in living memory at Alijah's age had ever married twice. Richard told him that it is the rich men who set the rules. As Alijah received the elders' blessings, he smiled at the fulfillment of the prophecy. Sometimes he even fancied marrying a few more times so that he could have a wife in each city he routinely visited. None of it would happen, though, with empty trucks. He realized he must break the news to Tza and return to Nairobi by the following evening.

He ducked into the mud hut, seeing her weeping. She wore a wide collar of colorful beads spiraling out in concentric circles from her long regal neck. Crafted to convey beauty, the pattern also spoke to her status in the tribe. Now, the beads seemed to ripple with her tears.

"Is it true?" she whispered.

"Yes, I'm sorry," Alijah said genuinely. "You were in the city. You saw my life. What choice do I have?"

"More than me."

"That seems to be my greatest problem." Knowing she could not fully comprehend his burdens, he said, "You will always be my first wife."

"And see you every few moons. What about Kiku and the baby?"

"Nothing's changed. I'm coming for Kiku's initiation. I'm giving him twenty cattle. He'll be the richest warrior in the village!"

"Did you know he went to raid the Somalis? They killed six men and took thirty cattle. He led the raid. There's talk he may be the next chief. He throws like Galo and thinks like you."

"Is he here?"

"No. He'll be back in a few days. He's on the journey to the mountain to prepare for initiation."

"Ah."

Alijah looked at Tza and let her eyes melt the tension he carried with him. Alijah was home. He slept peacefully in the dung hut, cuddled next to the stomach full of his child. In the morning, he awoke to flies crawling on his face. It was time to leave, for Sara and a bed.

·   ·   ·   ·   ·

The operator told Richard his call to Andrew Harrington would be connected shortly. Since their last conversation, Keeton had flown to North Yemen, meeting with Ahmed al-Hassari, the man referred by Andrew's Saudi contact in England. During his advance research, Richard confirmed that North Yemen ingloriously ranked among the largest illegal importers of rhinoceros horns, and consequently, they also paid the steepest prices. Yemeni men coming of age often used the horns for jambiyas, extravagant ceremonial daggers with curved blades and handles carved from the horns, symbolizing wealth and rank. Another effect of surging oil prices, newfound prosperity in the Yemen capital drove up the price of rhino horns; handles made from the prized commodity conveying status, a kind of Rolex of daggers to be proudly displayed tucked in one's belt. After an initial outreach, and Ahmed's confirming his willingness to meet, Richard telexed that he would be visiting his country for a few days. Unsure about local protocol, Richard took the initiative to play host, inviting Ahmed to dinner.

Richard, receiving a return telex from Ahmed confirming he would be quite welcome, boarded a plane the next day. On arrival at the airport, a driver unexpectedly waited to whisk him to Ahmed's house: he would be the guest after all. They feasted with Ahmed's family that evening, meeting alone for the first time the following morning. By the next sunrise, he was airborne on his way back to Nairobi, a richer man to be. The going price in dollars promised to be between twenty and thirty thousand dollars per horn depending on the horn's weight and size. Ahmed agreed to buy up to seventy-five, Keeton extracting twenty-five thousand apiece, leveraging his presumed supply chain. Ahmed would resell them at a respectable profit, acting on a local monopoly with such a large supply. He tried to bargain Keeton down at a discount for such a large number, but Richard remained unmoved, dropping the names of a few others in the country he claimed were interested. Mansour's tips, though their randomness should have doomed Richard, nevertheless proved invaluable. After the second name, which Richard so dreadfully mispronounced that he unknowingly intimated an actual rival, Ahmed grew concerned and virtually stopped haggling. The price was set. For the moment, Richard seemed to have a horseshoe up his ass.

The horns would be shipped out of Mombasa on a steamer bounded for Mecca. They would travel up the East African coast and then head through the Gulf of Aden, docking at Djibouti rather than Aden if there appeared to be any trouble making it through the straights. Once on the Red Sea, the ship would dock at Luhaiya in Yemen to unload the cargo. Ahmed would pick up the smuggled horns at the port and then transport them by truck, protected by armed men, to near Sana'a where he lived. Given the current and seemingly endless turbulence in the region, they decided it was safer to take this route than to smuggle them aboard a tanker bound for the Persian Gulf and subsequently ship the horns across Saudi Arabia. If the cargo made it safely through the Persian Gulf, it risked being lost somewhere crossing the desert.

Ahmed wanted seventy-five horns, but Richard only had a few in his inventory. To his surprise, Alijah informed him they recently acquired ten more, bringing the total to sixteen. Richard decided he would ship that number and send a second shipment later, thinking it prudent not to send everything at once. How he could source nearly fifty additional horns— an enormous number for a mature organization—would be Alijah's problem. Richard sent a telegram to Ahmed naming the ship and, using an agreed code, notifying him of a shipment of sixteen baskets. The balance would follow later in cargo known just to the two of them. Only that morning, he received a response, acknowledging the message and confirming half the payment would be made upon arrival of the first shipment.

Richard Keeton grinned. In a week, he would have a quarter of a million dollars of horns out to sea but would be paid almost one million dollars. The money would be deposited to an agreed Swiss bank account he had established in anticipation of completing the deal. Until Ahmed received the second shipment, however, he would not touch the money. Richard remained superstitious. He also decided to be selective in what he told Andrew. He would describe the first shipment of almost twenty horns. Yes, he would tell him twenty, a generous round number not to be questioned; if he managed to fulfill the balance, that would remain between him and Ahmed. No one would ever believe a shipment of seventy-five horns anyway. If anyone challenged the number later, he would deny it on his honor. He just prayed that Ahmed would make good on stealing more from his cousin than he would from Andrew. Too much greed could rouse unnecessary suspicions, and no need to prompt Andrew to start digging into details. He hoped never to meet Mr. Nebavi again.

Keen to close the business loop confirming yet a different shipment, Richard continued to wait for his call to London to be connected. Harrington finally answered: "Richard, good to hear you made it back safely. Did you stop off in Morocco on the way home?"

"Oh yes," Keeton lied.

"Good. Look, I'll keep this short and discreet. I'd like all the baskets you can ship, after all. If I can't sell them immediately, I'll sort a way to keep them myself and open up a little shop or something."

"Wonderful," Richard answered. "Do you have the shipping information straight?"

"Yes. They're being shipped to Hong Kong. From then on, you'll deal directly with Roland Weathers over there."

"Yes, that's good enough for now. What about payment? Are you sure you understand the terms? I really don't want to talk about them over the phone. If you see any problems, let me know."

"Don't worry. There won't be any need. If you can't trust me on this one, you're not going to be able to trust anyone."

"That's not much comfort, Andrew... No offense, but this isn't much of a trusting type of business. Anyway, it's Roland I've got to trust now, not you."

"Yes. Unfortunately, after this, we may need to pause for a while. I hope that isn't a problem."

"Is that a statement or a bit of advice for me, Andrew?"

"No. No warning. Just getting a bit conservative with age."

"Okay. I'll be in touch. Buy a round for everybody at the club on me, will you?"

"Sure thing. Bye, Richard."

Keeton hung up, the order for one hundred tusks placed. God knew what Andrew would do with all of them, he thought; at least the huge number should satiate Andrew and keep him off the scent of his second load of horns. Maybe the size was why Andrew signaled slowing down purchases. Richard had agreed to take the risk of price fluctuations. The market seemed more unpredictable than ever. Only a year before, a pair of seventy to eight-pound tusks would fetch just over one hundred pounds, and now the same set of piano keys would fetch ten times that price. Depending on the dollar to pound exchange rate, that meant each set of tusks could clear him between $2,500 and $2,750. If everything went as planned, this shipment ought to net him over one hundred thousand dollars. The tusks were not as profitable as the horns, but he agreed with Ron to expand their market and diversify shipments. Good business practice abhorred depending on only one client. A hundred thousand dollars was still a damn good loot, Keeton relished, hanging up the phone. Tax-free too, he laughed out loud.

.     .     .     .     .

Alijah came over before dinner to meet privately with Richard. Both men belied composure. The money shuffled too closely now to let some accident or go-between steal their success. Keeton was distrustful of Alijah's pending meeting with the President. Richard could see Alijah double-crossing him and watched for twinges of hesitating loyalty. Alijah had no notion of stealing from Richard, but he did entertain thoughts of cutting others out. He had no sure plan yet, keeping his ideas to himself for the moment.

"I still don't understand how you're so sure we'll get the money," Alijah pressed.

"You mean Ahmed and Roland? You're worried they might not pay?"

"Yes. Why do you trust them?"

"I guess I've been more worried about the ship captains and everyone in-between than the people I know."

"I don't trust all those people in-between either," Alijah said, thinking of his son Kiku and whether he should leave him in the bush or train him to be his most trusted mole.

"Look, Alijah, here's what I've worked out. We crate the tusks and horns in large boxes and claim they're ebony carvings. The weight will be a bit off, but at least they'll be heavy. If we say we're sending baskets or rugs or something, the weight difference will cause suspicion and make everything more difficult. Whoever you and Ron sort out at the port in Mombasa will make sure the crates get on board and are invoiced on the freighter as carvings. I don't think you should have much trouble with the documents."

"No," Alijah smiled. "That's why you have me in this job, right? My government colleagues?"

"Yes," Richard grinned again, thinking back to when he first arranged to move Alijah into the ministry. "At the receiving end, Roland and Ahmed will pick up the cargo, so they'll arrange to have the boxes unloaded and get them past any inspections. I'm not worried there. That part should be the easiest step. We're dealing with some real rogues. I feel good about that!"

"What about ports on the way?" Alijah asked.

"Well, there isn't much we can do. If you have any men you can trust, I guess we could send them along for the voyage to keep an eye on everything. The trouble is if anyone knows that much about it, I think they'll be tempted to sell the ivory en route and take off. I've thought about sending Ron with the horns because they're so valuable."

"But that would mean Ron would try to claim a full share," Alijah blurted.

"Of course, what are you saying?"

"Well, I don't see what Ron's doing for us anymore. I don't see why we need to cut him in. At least not as a full partner."

"Because if we don't, do you really think he's going to keep his mouth shut to protect us? He knows too much. If we start turning on each other now, this whole thing is gonna kill us. Besides, he provides additional cover for us at the wildlife ministry, eye on a different division. Plus, he can falsify and procure licenses."

"But you don't have to do anything special to protect me. I'm at the agency! I'm almost a cabinet member! You don't think I can get all the documents we need? All you're doing is protecting yourself. I want my cut. I may even want another. But at least I want a say in the next one. I don't buy this cover."

Keeton sheepishly looked up, a bit stunned. "We'll keep him, let's say, a bit less involved if you want, but I don't think it's a good idea. Okay? It's not like we're in this alone and can change the rules for the hell of it. If anything, we need the granting side of the ministry too, and he can help forge export stamps and proper licenses. That's not something the anti-poaching division issues. Best damn cover in the world. I'd like to find a way to get him promoted. It's Jack Whitehead's god damn ethics that are causing us problems."

Alijah smiled for the first time, savoring his small victory. Maybe Richard was right, but for the moment he basked in the sense of equality. It had taken him years to learn the only way to pierce the belligerent ego of an Englishman was not to parade their errors but rather subtly enlighten them as to how to follow a path of higher returns. His studies taught how men like Keeton conquered the world only to grow up and then give it away. Curiously, some found themselves giving back too much; there even seemed less land to go around. Keeton would soon have his share back. Alijah understood Keeton coveted that redemption more than the money itself. He wanted a return to the life that his grandfather knew in the flesh, that he had only glimpsed in pictures.

Alijah's dream world consisted of something different, something more modest. He was as content with Tza in his village as when sipping local beer with Richard. He craved both, without one ever touching the other save through his design. When in Nairobi, he longed for space; when with his tribe, he noticed the eye diseases he was blinded to growing up. He assumed that his mother's eyes naturally blotted red. That flies were not meant to crawl inside them when she slept among the cattle forged a tragedy he could no longer bear. He would go home and tell a sister to wipe her baby's eyes since the baby had grown too weary to flick the flies aside herself.

The tourists found his brethren fascinating. To them, they represented bold creatures with spears who knew a self-sufficiency they could only lust after with a desire devoid of enabling courage. It was not possible to disassociate the nobility of the chase from the danger of the snakes below foot. Tourists vicariously followed the hunt of a native through jaded eyes. Excitement brought risk that those gawking from afar would never tempt. That grounded the fascination. They clutched at flirting with mortality, survival pared down to stalking game where dying of thirst was a conceivable outcome. The people they watched, that they shook their heads so pitifully for from their cars, really did perish from those diseases. How could people live so constantly close to the edge and seem so happy? If they only knew.

Any jealousy of the chase, of the sufficiency of the freedom, was tempered by these thoughts. Come play safari for the day. Watch me shoot the big bad lion and bring its teeth home to mama. Pity these brave souls risking a week of their lives hoping to get just close enough to danger to conjure a real scare. Only then would they absorb living and touching that part of life starting each native's day. Tea waited benignly in the cupboard at home. They would never thirst nor sweat under a sun so strong as to dream of a pinch of water being left in a root and spend the morning digging in prayer.

Rich is better, the proverb goes, joked his teachers. You can always adapt to a better way of life. No one wants to be disease-ridden. The amenities of modern life are not hard to accept. Even a toilet can be seductive in its own way. Alijah shook his head in disgust as he left the study. Whoever invented porcelain never invented it for him. His kinship rest closer to the maker of wood. Bare-assed on a wooden splinter, there was at least enough pain to keep one's senses low to the ground. If you fell, you fell; there was little gradual or mysterious about the method or course. He knew no word in the bush for slippery.

•    •    •    •    •

Richard paused to appease a momentary jitter that Alijah stirred. He thought he perfectly worked out security for the payments. When loading ships in Mombasa, or if Alijah secured a vessel in a minor port, he would have his customs invoices stamped. The documents would be dated and sealed properly, but the contents falsely described. He would then have Ron fly, or perhaps even fly himself, to Switzerland with the papers. Initially, he planned to send them on but then changed his mind worrying about the possibility of his airmail instead being diverted to sea. Richard could stay in Switzerland, but there seemed little point. Better to keep hidden. He would remain safer mingling with as few people as feasible.

When on his last trip, he met with Jacques Frankel, a childhood friend and son of an old friend of his father's, who lived in Lugano and flourished among the banking set. Richard always thought it was fortunate Jacques was the scion of wealthy bankers, as otherwise his thin frame and beak-like nose might peg him as an undertaker. Jacques had agreed to assist Richard in setting up an account and transferring the documents into the bank's possession. When the banks had the papers, they would then send out a notice to both Roland Weathers in Hong Kong and Ahmed al-Hassari in Yemen. The message would not be sent directly to them but rather to a designated correspondent bank in their respective countries. As soon as the banks contacted the parties, they then had two weeks to deposit the agreed upon sums with their local correspondent banks, who would then transfer the funds on to Zurich, or perhaps Jacques' quieter branch in Zug. The banks would post a guarantee so that the funds would be deemed automatically transferred as soon as the money hit the Swiss banks. The transaction would thus only take one day to clear.

As soon as the money alighted into Jacques' control, he would wire Richard in Nairobi. This was merely a formality they had agreed upon, assuring Richard the simple peace of mind that the first stage of the transfer was complete. The Swiss bank, working through Jacques as its representative, would then hand over the invoices in their possession to Ahmed and Roland or to any representative they sent.

The bank could not refuse invoices automatically due on presentation of the money. Any delay in deposit, though, would allow the bank to retain the invoices. Should something trigger that scenario, Richard would have to fly to Switzerland to reclaim the invoices and then personally claim the shipment.

Andrew was working on a backup to avoid any trouble claiming the goods in Hong Kong if the deal went sour. Richard struggled conniving a plan B in Yemen if the money failed to materialize. That would be a problem. It posed a problem, though, only in a non-payment contingency; he fully expected Ahmed to live up to his bargain. Further, Richard remained keen to keep Andrew away from his now prized Yemenis connection and limit his involvement to Hong Kong.

Ah, there lingered one last catch, he remembered. Even though the money would be transferred to Jacques and the invoices handed over in return, ninety percent of the money would be put in a bank trust untouchable without one additional document.

Richard needed to secure a receipt confirming the transfer of goods in order to release the funds. The agreement required either a customs invoice upon delivery of the goods or a photograph of the crates being taken off the boat in the respective ports; either would suffice to release the money. This device was necessary since neither party would approve access to funds until they were certain that the goods were delivered. As soon as goods landed in port, everything would be released and, in theory, the deal would be consummated.

As soon as the bank released the money to Richard, Jacques would destroy the transaction documents, including all temporary bank records and files. The funds would be transferred immediately to Richard's account, and Jacques would receive fifty thousand dollars in Swiss francs for his work. All documents, shipping receipts, and invoices would be destroyed at the other end as well. All records kept through correspondent banks would cease to exist.

Richard knew telling Alijah details regarding the financial complexities, and the banks' pivotal role, would make him nervous. He breathed relief that their conversation had conveniently terminated. That was the most disquieting part of the sale. For no good reason, he trusted both Roland and Ahmed to pay because he believed they wanted the goods. They awaited a tidy profit, too, the gain solely dependent upon his delivering. In some ways, he was doing them a favor. The banks, though, could screw everything up. They demanded the goods as collateral while in transit. If someone found out the discrepancy between the money deposited and the cargo's nature—listed as ebony carvings—then trouble could develop. He had been assured this element could be finessed in small print and be undetected. Nevertheless, Keeton stroked his ivory hair in discomfort.

He decided upon the banks because the only common denominator among three untrustworthy parties was a trustworthy party. The banks ultimately held all the cards and would be accepted by everyone. No one received their goods without the bank's invoices, and Richard could not steal away his money without delivery of goods and proof to the bank. It all seemed so simple and legal. The only potential disaster was a wreck at sea, an unlikely event—or so he hoped. If they were stolen, he felt assured of help to track the goods down. He was far from the only one with an interest.

•　　•　　•　　•　　•

Alijah sat quietly outside the President's office, caressing his jacket to feel its stuffed inside pocket. He had met the President several times before, but this would be the first time they alone filled a room. It was already one hour past the scheduled appointment time. Alijah stood up again to pace the hall. Every time he rose, the two guards at either end of the room snapped to attention and watched him. From his outside pocket, he pulled a handkerchief and dabbed his brow. As he looked at the handkerchief, he muttered "stupid English" and tucked it back into place.

Alijah rose through the government ranks too quickly to appreciate an honor so great as a chat with the dictator in chief. As soon as he tried to out-throw his brother Galo in front of Richard Keeton, he stepped into a world overzealous to embrace him. Being schooled at the university first set him apart. Being befriended by the British elite gave him the contacts that but a handful of his brethren possessed. Catapulting to the wildlife ministry's top echelons made him one of the most powerful men in the country at thirty. By local standards, he was rich. By any means, he sat comfortably.

Money proved the most crucial element in Alijah's ascent. Without Richard Keeton as a benefactor, he would never have attended university, and without higher education, his shrewd skills of manipulation would never have been let loose to con the world. He was charming, bright, and aggressive, but money bought him his present status. Ironically, his success came without sufficient appreciation of what money is and how you get it. Alijah treated currency like a toy: you want a plane, a job, a friend, a wife, just hand over whatever it will take. That most folks in the city had no money was a concept which he never fully grasped. The work ethic masqueraded as a subset of greed.

A man poked his head out the door at the end of the glittering hall. "The President will see you now," the sporty aid told him, closing the door behind him and disappearing. Alijah stepped towards the chamber. In fact, he walked a fine line, knowing rumors held Nazuto to be an arrogant dictator, an imposing figure emboldened by the daily fear of coups. At the moment Alijah reached for the handle, the door flew away from him. There stood the President.

"Alijah! I was just coming to see what was keeping you. Come in. I read your note, but I didn't understand what you want."

Before Alijah could respond, the President turned around and moved towards a couch against a wall across from his desk. Watching Nazuto sit, Alijah could not help comparing the balding man with the portrait below which he rest. Without hesitating, Alijah reached into his pocket and snatched out a Kenyan bill, holding it up to see yet another pose by his leader. The likeness on the currency downplayed Nazuto's thick black glasses and slightly swollen face.

"I think I like the shilling better," Alijah quipped.

Nazuto leaned back and laughed, gesturing for Alijah to sit. Gathering in the trappings of success suspended from all corners of the office, Alijah took his place and said, "Thank you for granting me this audience."

Again, Nazuto laughed. "You'd have me a King. I could declare it, you know!... Look, I've had some of my men report to me on you. You control too much now for us to be so unacquainted. I'll let you keep your job for now—just remember who's on top," Nazuto smiled again and noticed Alijah shift a bit in his chair. Alijah had not come with any intention of discussing his job, no prior fear his fiefdom may be in jeopardy. But Nazuto knew all that.

The revelation that he prospered as a crony of Nazuto's and that he fortuitously maintained his rank without being a close friend was all Alijah's. Without a word, the meeting had already taken on greater importance. His actions were now so risky that Alijah wondered what made him request a meeting.

"I don't know how to begin," Alijah started, "so I think I'll be blunt. I need to work closely with the Wildlife Agency's funding arms, especially with the private conservation agencies. All those people bringing in money..." He cleared his throat. "The problem is Jack Whitehead. He treats me as if I were still carrying a spear. Never listens to what I say. How am I supposed to help supervise the anti-poaching blokes and work with the wardens when I have no power over the people funding everything from the outside?"

Nazuto scowled at Alijah, trying to figure out what he really sought. No one ever criticized Whitehead except for being honest. Whitehead had his enemies, but even the President knew who he was and the resources Nazuto permitted him to control. Nazuto glanced back at Alijah, watching the youngster cross and uncross his legs. The President squinted and leaned forward as closely to Alijah as his reach would permit. Spit from his first words sprinkled Alijah's face as he challenged, "I don't see what they have to do with each other. You're trying to stop poachers and Whitehead's trying to report back to the BBC what a wonderful job you're doing." Nazuto leaned back, allowing Alijah the chance to wipe his face. A foul mix of moistures clung to the youngster's hand.

"Mr. President, I don't think you understand. I enforce the rules about where the British hunt and Whitehead's men do their studies. We're not always on the same side. It isn't that simple, and I didn't come here to have you tell me it was."

Nazuto's eyes widened, and just as Alijah sensed he was about to stand up and rant about his insolence, Alijah tossed a packet from chair to couch. The President puffed out a sigh, exaggerating the breath so that it would ring loud and his feelings made clear. He picked the envelope up from his lap and did not look up until he had finished counting every shilling. In dollars, it would have counted just under ten thousand.

"Do you think I can be bought so easily?" his voice seemed to reverberate in the room.

With a slight smirk, the innocence of which could not go unnoticed, Alijah softly responded, "How am I supposed to know what to give you? It's my first time at this, and it's more money than I've ever had. How much more would you like? I have a very rich friend."

"How much more would I like? Are you joking?"

"I'm not joking. My career's hanging on your answer."

"I suppose it is," Nazuto said, making the moment seem to take hours. "You know, you're quite good at this. For a moment there, I was almost taking pity on you. Let's suppose your job does depend on this. What would you propose next?"

"I don't think I can give you anything more for nothing. Any more, and you fire Whitehead. And, I get to pick his replacement."

"Fire Jack Whitehead?" Nazuto said a bit bemused. "And, replacing him, who do you have in mind?"

"Ron Easton."

"Sounds familiar. Who is he? Can't quite place him."

"Whitehead's top assistant."

Silence. Nazuto stood up, took off his glasses and paced to the far side of the room, keeping his back to Alijah. Alijah could see him chomping on a cuticle in the reflection of his portrait. When he finally turned around, Alijah had joined him standing, but only Nazuto was standing still.

"Firing Whitehead will cause hell, you know. He's well respected, well known...Twenty-five thousand more and I'll see about it."

Seizing the opportunity and sensing twenty-five posited a reasonable number, not twenty-five thousand more (silently wondering whether Richard would kill him for going so high), Alijah proposed, "Fifteen thousand more. I think that would be fair. I know I said I have a rich friend, but I don't think I can get more than that. Plus, that would make it twenty-five thousand in all."

Nazuto tossed his head back a bit and laughed. Whitehead had boosted the reputation of the game reserves, but why not profit a bit given the increase in tourism? His hand clasped Alijah's as the men locked in an almost romantic gaze. Their different ages and motives made each curiously envious of the other. Fingers locking generations, a bond pulled more tightly than the grasp. They were brothers, intrigued by the same wonders, lusting after the same goals. Both saw their country for what it was, not what it had been or could be. No dreamers here. Dreams only come to those who sleep easy. These were the type of men who slept with their eyes wide open. Their hands sprung apart, and Ron Easton finally had his dream.

·　　·　　·　　·　　·

Michael Sandburg sat across the table from Ron Easton pleading his case. The balance of his grant money, though insufficient, had come through, and all the papers to prove it were splayed on newly promoted Minister Easton's cluttered desk. The jumble also contained multiple clippings about Ron's taking over Jack Whitehead's job. Michael assumed the display was purposeful, designed to show off Easton's ascension to the post. Ron cast a smug grin while watching Michael's eyes graze over the headlines from different papers. Ron could care less if his tactics lacked subtlety; in fact, he had worked hard to seed some of the bigger stories. It was time people paid him proper deference.

Michael sat upright in the hard wood chair, stretching his arm out to reveal an elbow through what purported to be a sleeve. Stubble curled from his face like weeds. Before the meeting Ron had considered whether there was an angle to cultivate and profit from this American connection. He still harbored a bit of envy topped with resentment at how Caroline Dunning had seemingly been charmed. Well, this lad had no realistic chance with her, Ron mused, and if he thought he did then a word with Richard was in order. He would enjoy watching when that fantasy burst if, despite the odds, it ever began to progress. Poor sod, no idea what he was in for on that front either.

The favor Ron would ask for today was quite benign, but would at least help his partner while also keeping Michael under watch. Alijah had decided that his son, Kiku, should learn to speak English. They talked about sending him to school at the university or mission, following in the steps of his father. Alijah, though, was not sure he wanted Kiku exposed to the city and the gulf from which he might never return. Thus, they set upon the scheme to place Kiku as Michael's guide.

Kiku would learn English and would have time to refine his hunting skills. He would capitalize on the opportunity to learn the customs of the white man. With luck, he might even befriend the park warden and provide them tips on patrols. For Michael's part, he needed a guide and sentry, and they assumed it would be an innocuous request.

They were right. Michael eagerly agreed, and Ron reached for his pen. With the stroke of his signature, Michael's money was authorized and would soon be wired to a local Nairobi bank from the agency's account. The dance over, Ron having punctuated his status and leverage, Ron looked at Michael, pondering the researcher's plight. It was damn tough for white guys with no money, Easton thought, uncharacteristically offering to advance him part of his next payment. Perhaps that might help keep the researcher in his debt.

Michael grabbed the receipt, thanking Easton and promising to return the favor. He told him to stop by camp anytime and then offered to buy him a drink. Easton demurred and declined. He had already taken the advantage. Besides, they hailed from different classes. Whites stuck together after hours, but certain lines had to be drawn. First strike, Michael was an American in a town distinctly British. Second strike, he was young and merely on the way up. A twenty-eight-year-old Leaky family member would have presented an exceptional case. Finally, his appearance hardly blended with the double-breasted class. Living amidst squalor commanded all the more reason to dress properly. To look as though one fit in Nairobi's alleys signaled a social faux pas beyond recovery. Ron tugged at his ascot and took another draw on his cigarette, unwittingly coating his smile with a bit more tar.

.    .    .    .    .

The beginning of every month drew Alijah to the warehouse that Ron Easton rented and supervised. When he arrived, their converted tanker truck already sat backed up against the rear door. The driver, Omondi, was waiting for Alijah to open the barn-style door so the truck could pull inside. The converted tanker truck had worked magnificently.

Since its modification, the truck had hauled rhinoceros horns and tusks in the false walls, back and forth between the warehouse in Nairobi and boats in Mombasa. The goods were heavy enough that shipping them by sea was the only practical option.

Both Alijah and Richard were convinced the truck represented the safest method of moving the items to the coast. Ron Easton argued the railroad was more efficient and cheaper, but Keeton was reluctant to let the goods out of their sight. He argued this might cost them a bit more, but at least everything remained totally under their control until in the hold of the freighters. They maintained a warehouse in Mombasa where the goods would be crated for shipment abroad. There appeared little danger of theft or detection at any point.

The only potential complication concerning them was the truck itself. Should it break down en route, they would have a real problem. The solution? Equip the driver with a radio. If trouble developed, they would come and rescue him with a lorry; they would load everything in the back of the truck and cover it with canvas, hoping to avoid discovery. As one further safeguard, Ron hired the warehouse mechanic, Omondi, who originally sold him the old truck. Ron never fully trusted him but did feel

Omondi knew as much about fixing the truck as anyone else if it broke down in transit.

Their goal was that near the beginning of every month, and the first day if they could arrange it, Alijah would supervise the truck's loading and send it off to Mombasa. This would give them a few extra days if anything went wrong, for ships taking the poached goods to the far and middle east theoretically left sometime in the middle of each month. Because they knew the ships would not run efficiently, Alijah, Richard, and Ron unanimously agreed to run their shipments punctually. That way the shippers knew they could depend on them for a load and would invariably contact their warehouse in Mombasa when ready to leave. They would always send whatever they had when a boat was set to sail and orders were on hand. Of course, whether Alijah knew the captain or the cargo line was an important factor. His job required collecting the papers from Ron, having all the licenses and permits ready, bribing the right dock workers and mates to ensure they did not compromise their baskets, and paying off the captain to ensure quiet delivery of the goods.

Alijah sat watching the truck being loaded and hollered in disgust. The warehouse in Mombasa was already thin, and now they did not have enough goods to fill the truck. A less-than-full truck scarcely heralded economic disaster: each shipment tended to net at least one hundred thousand dollars. Nevertheless, their overhead managed to keep growing. They had to maintain two warehouses and the truck as well as pay dockworkers, customs officials, ship personnel, Omondi, and two guards for the warehouse. At the other end, there was Jacques in Switzerland taking a cut and intermediaries such as Roland Weathers in Hong Kong.

Finally, Alijah felt compelled to grease Nazuto with money periodically, even when there appeared little reason to do so. They all believed it was essential to foster that relationship in case trouble ever developed. They never divulged their smuggling to Nazuto, though they suspected he knew. Alijah paid him for little favors and, after a while, almost out of custom. Alijah's authority continued to grow, and with it, Nazuto's confidence in him. When Nazuto wanted a second opinion, he would often solicit Alijah's advice on an informal basis. He knew a candid point of view would be rifled back, valuing Alijah's brash instincts.

Such closeness to the President was remarkable, for only a handful of people even knew where he lived. Ever fearful of coups, he maintained several houses and moved amongst them as if playing a shell game. At any moment, he could be anywhere. Few insiders knew his precise schedule. Alijah might not have been able to count himself among this elite group; nevertheless, he circulated among a still select few who could find out which house he slept in by placing one call. This power was held in the strictest confidence because the President's whereabouts was a topic not taken lightly.

One day, Ron Easton had been driving through town when Nazuto's motorcade passed through. At first, there appeared an auspicious policeman on a corner pretending to watch the traffic. Minutes later, men in military uniforms stood guard, watching the cars pass from every corner in sight. Just after the crowd of military grew conspicuous, cars were stopped, and the motorcade breezed past. Across the street, a tour bus emptied so the passengers could sneak a glimpse of the President.

That proved precisely the wrong thing to do, as the soon to be chagrined driver learned. One of the passengers raised his camera when the limousine passed, clicking off a couple of pictures of the stealthy pageantry. A Mercedes quickly pulled up to the bus and a man in a green uniform, bearing a rifle whose nozzle dwarfed the tourist's zoom lens, demanded every camera. Methodically, he ripped the film out of each, exposing it all and tossing the frames to the ground. He left the man who had brazenly focused on the cars for last and threw his camera to the ground, smashing it with his foot. A warning followed that this never took place and repercussions would result. Jarring wisdom.

·     ·     ·     ·     ·

Access to the President, though, did not fill trucks. When the next month's shipment was light, Alijah reached for the phone. "Ron, we've got to make a run. I'm over at the warehouse and we're short again. I'll fly over to Tsavo. Can you arrange for a truck to be ready over there?

"Sure. How big, how many men?"

"Just a normal lorry. I'll take Omondi, and that's it. Omondi can drive and fix anything, plus he's not a bad shot."

"Okay. I'll get on it. When do you need it? Tomorrow morning?"

"No, right now. We can be there by noon and hopefully find enough animals to send off everything tomorrow morning. If not, we can stay over at the lodge and go out again in the morning. We're not that short. I'm sure that will do it."

"Jesus, you could have given me a little more notice."

"I thought you were the greediest one of all of us. You want to send the truck off half-empty?"

"All right. You know my weak spot. Do you want me to call Richard?"

"Already did, but he's tied up. Anyway, he prefers hunting when it's going to be a few days and we're planning a big run."

"Okay. I haven't talked to him in a bit. I can't believe we have this thing running so we hardly need to get together anymore."

"Except to get paid, you mean."

"Of course." Thinking about the money, Ron's mind tacked to covering his tracks. He had not finished filing the paperwork for the truck they bought from Omondi Aguru and now considered whether he should delay. If they were ever caught, then the documents would reflect Omondi as the owner. "Why not," he said to himself, smiling.

Soon Alijah and Omondi were airborne, Omondi no wiser and Alijah recklessly at the controls. Alijah's lessons from Jordan were far from complete, but he demonstrated quick aptitude and now had enough experience with take-offs and landings to put a fright into his passengers while not quite posing an outright danger. Safety in the skies is a relative proposition with small winged craft in the savanna. Alijah did little to raise that bar, yet he was smart enough not to fly in bad weather. Navigation was the complication; so long as he could pick out landmarks and enjoy clear skies, he managed to find his way. He loved to swoop down, overwhelmed by the panorama. Omondi was more focused on his stomach, fonder of land speed records and begging Alijah to keep low and forget the forays into the ravines. This was the first time Alijah was forced to make a trip in a few weeks. As supervisor of the county's anti-poaching force, he had been able to build up a steady clientele. Once he would catch someone, he made arrangements for a percentage of their slaughter. Depending on the person, that could be as high as fifty percent or as low as ten.

Most poachers eagerly accepted his propositions. It all worked simply. Alijah first gave them a choice of accepting his terms or a prison sentence. He kept pictures of Nazuto and two generals on his wall, proudly telling his prospective clients that he considered the courts and review a matter of finesse. If they thought they might prefer to continue reaping huge profits rather than withering away in a dank cell without a chance of release, they might consider his offer. He kept the terms reasonable, knowing they would accept. He usually allowed them to keep most of what they collected and promised his services in return for what he called his meager cut. Licenses for a legal front could easily be procured, as well as pre-approved customs invoices for their shipments. It presented a nice package deal. If they ever double-crossed him, he promised to make scapegoats out of them, prosecuting them for poaching. He would even welcome their disloyalty, for he needed to flog a poacher occasionally to demonstrate his fidelity to the job.

Alijah infrequently had to bear arms himself, at least lately. His deals were working quite smoothly except for one group tempted by his arrogance. Although they had come up with a tremendous catch in the first two months after being caught and blackmailed, they decided Alijah did not pose the threat he proclaimed. Through a snitch, he learned they were shipping ivory out of Malindi to avoid inspections at Mombasa's main port. By coincidence, one of Alijah's men had gone up the coast on a weekend, running into a cousin who asked if he wanted to make a few extra shillings loading ivory. The man wrote down the name and told Alijah when he came by for an inspection, thinking there might be even more money in it for him. Indeed: Alijah let him keep five percent of the cache when and if he caught this poacher.

Only a matter of weeks passed before he tracked down "the Tanzanian rogue." He knew what their plane looked like and had feelers out at every major airstrip in the region—a wildlife APB. When the plane was reported near the border, and Alijah learned they were camping near Masai Mara game park, he took off instantly. No one tipped them off that Alijah was coming because everyone was either working for him or on his private payroll. Ambushing them in their tent, accompanied by three "deputies," he quickly tied all their hands. Casually, Alijah then asked their leader, a man named Eli with a bloated belly and a thin head, to step forward. He wanted to make an impact on the men around him and chose his words carefully.

"Do you remember when we had our little chat a few weeks ago?"

"How could I forget?"

"I don't know. I never double-cross anyone who doesn't double-cross me. It keeps me alive. It gives me friends. It makes me rich. It's going to kill you."

Without hesitating, he pulled out a gun and placed it to Eli's head. Alijah continued, "You're a disgrace, a wanker. A tortoise eater. We play by the rules so things don't get out of hand. I spend half my life kicking people like you so there's enough left for the rest of us." Rarely swearing, having become accustomed to British etiquette, he made an exception to emphasize his point. "You're a dung-eater, a greedy piece of shit." Alijah backed off briefly. As Eli sighed a breath of relief, Alijah pointed the gun towards the ground and shot him in the foot. Eli toppled to the ground screaming, and Alijah motioned to his men to pick him up. With his deputies holding the traitor, Alijah raised the gun, pressing it against Eli's forehead. Slowly, he moved the muzzle down and placed it against Eli's groin. Eli screamed in pain and terror. Alijah looked down, shooting the ground just next to Eli's other foot, and walked away. He called over one of his assistants and told him, "Wrap up his foot I don't want him to die."

Alijah put the three men on trial for poaching in Nairobi and assured they were all found guilty. It would have been easy enough for them to bribe their way out had he not been sure to equal the ante to keep them in. He was not the type who enjoyed watching his back. They would rot for years. Eli would likely never see the savanna again, where even if he wanted to run, he no longer could.

Alijah had successfully solidified his position. In the government, he was hyped as a poaching enforcer extraordinaire, ridding the country of the fear of slaughter. The local papers detailed how he caught the latest gang and how much ivory the government recovered. The people in the streets knew not to cross him and, more importantly, that he would come through for them if they delivered the piano keys.

Alijah himself felt little guilt. He would tell Nazuto that these people were scum, raiding their country of its most valuable resource and knowing every moment exactly what they perpetrated. They represented bad press and dirty money. These people had the most sophisticated planes, automatic rifles, and state-of-the-art tracking equipment. Their entire operations were structured to garner illegal riches while thwarting the ability of men like Alijah to catch them.

Unfortunately, Alijah had been on a tear setting examples, whipping scapegoats at the expense of his own cut. Cementing his cover by proving the government would not tolerate poachers, he had neglected keeping proper watch over his rogue network. With the market going crazy, his suppliers were looking for ways to keep more themselves. Even once principled hunters now shot everything, focusing cash in their sights. Meanwhile, legitimate license requests skyrocketed one hundredfold, adding competition and pushing some poachers into more remote areas. The upshot was Alijah's truck waited half full again, and that would not help pay off his lavish wedding to Sara nor secure his partners an early retirement.

•　　•　　•　　•　　•

Alijah's mind turned to Sara, wondering if he had made a mistake finally telling her about his past. She had nearly backed out of the wedding when learning about Tza and Kiku. "Another family? You're married?" she had said, looking revolted. Alijah had surrendered to the likelihood she would inevitably learn about them and decided better to take the pain now than risk an untimely discovery. He had begged Sara to understand, not to harbor jealousy, swearing there was nothing to worry about. His village roots were too frayed to reel him back, his life now occupied with government administration instead of spears and traditions. It was as if his former self was dead, and in many ways, that was true.

Sara had naturally stormed out, threatening to cancel the wedding. Alijah had hoped Sara's anger would blow over, and she would accept his tribal family was a consequence of his roots and not a betrayal of her. He knew no other way to rehabilitate himself. After a few days, Sara did return, still smarting yet willing to talk. Ultimately, they agreed to treat his relationship with Tza like a divorce —just one, like a Catholic separation, that would never be completed.

At least that is what Sara thought and Alijah feigned. Alijah would never fully cut himself off from Tza and his tribe. Sara could not comprehend that where he grew up having multiple wives was an honor, not something to hide. More challenging, Alijah loved Tza. She and Kiku were his family, too, and that bond gave him a type of grounding even if he was willing to deny them in educated Nairobi circles. Alijah was perfectly fine, however, keeping his distance and compartmentalizing Tza's receding role in his life; in fact, that arrangement already reflected reality. As for Sara, he better fill-up that truck to fund his ongoing penance. Maintaining two families, and one with burgeoning material expectations, did not come cheap.

· · · · ·

Alijah and Omondi kept cruising at the lowest of altitudes, nearly clipping trees when particularly curious about a spot. Although Alijah's renewed focus and scare tactics had successfully boosted supply, occasional runs were still necessary; consequently, he found himself on this last-minute foray to properly stock their truck. This was not a business Alijah, Richard and Ron could fully delegate. Soon they spotted the river and flew along it until they came to a marshy pan. When Omondi spotted several elephants bathing, they brought the plane down. There was no landing strip, but also no obstacles. The adjacent parched savanna stretched beyond where they could see. They only needed to select an approach angle, not an exact spot to touch down or stop.

Rifles in hand, they jumped from the cockpit, about one hundred fifty yards upwind from the marsh. No sign indicated that the animals had detected them. As they came over the slight rise, they found themselves virtually eye level with gray bulk. Four elephants stood below them, immersed in a thick muddy swamp, one drinking from water pooling at the fringe. The two men stood on the level ground just above the edge of the water, feeling perfectly safe. There was little chance the elephants could jump the few feet up the incline from where they bathed. The modern mastodons would have to wade out and ford several more yards before the rise tapered off enough to provide a ramp up. Why they wandered so far into the swamp and bathed in such a vulnerable position puzzled both men.

Elephants are very intelligent animals, and Alijah well knew that when staring them in the eye—a huge eye encased in majestic gray folds—an elephant can then communicate back. There is a soulful sadness in their gaze, as if speaking to the bulk they carry, a true weight on the world, pounding meaning into the ground with each heavy step. Myths often refer to the eye of birds or a third eye. The elephant's eye is worthy of equal wonder, much overlooked in its supposed ordinariness when compared to the playground hose of a trunk or the splendor of tusks piercing the vanguard of their march. An elephant's eye can feel as large as a human's face. With that unique visage and blinking of its wise and aged folds, an elephant beckons. If you could read their minds, they would likely admit staring at you, piercing your thoughts much deeper than a camera is supposed to penetrate a believer's soul. Decades of plodding, literally tons of weight on their backs, the burden of carrying knowledge across the grasses. How can an animal heavier than a pickup truck be so gentle? How can their sad, wise stare express such depth? Alijah remembered a poem from his childhood: *Look into an elephant's eye and let the beast speak back. How much they have seen in their lives! Oh, silly humans, thinking you are so wise, that you can see with your eyes. You do not carry the same weight of history, the slow movement of time. Oh, silly humans.*

Alijah shook the poem from his head, chiding himself that this was no time to be sentimental. Together with Omondi he stared into the eyes of these gentle beasts, neighbors who had trod the history of this land. Typically, thirty paces from an elephant is too close with a rifle; here, they could walk up and almost pet each one, gazing more closely into their eyes than should otherwise be safe. The closest elephant blinked and turned away, as if sensing these men did not appreciate their toil. Disparaging the meek onlookers before taking water in his trunk, the natural hose slunk back, the elephant spouted cooling black muck over his torso. Mimicking a fountain, the elephant bull snorted and grunted in the delight of his shower. Omandi moved close to peer at the wrinkled folds of the trunk on the old bull male. Its ears flapped as his trunk curled down towards the water to drink. Quickly the bull whipped his trunk out of the water and turned towards Omondi, blasting him with guck.

Alijah dashed away and then fell to the ground in hysterics. Omondi was dripping wet and swore at the top of his lungs while wiping mud from his arms and ringing out his hair. Soon shots rang out from the savanna. They shot to wound but not kill since retrieving the tusks from the swamp would be impossible. Each animal thrashed around before stampeding out to its death. Following a rifle blast straight to its heart, the old bull's eye closed slowly for the last time. The tragedy was unspeakable, and perhaps that is what the eye spoke with its final shudder. Alijah and Omondi surveyed their handiwork, but unlike the wise elephant in the poem, clearly they could not see.

Within minutes the vultures started their circles. With so much blood around, Alijah and Omondi knew they must work fast. It was impossible to predict what may arrive to scavenge. Forty-five minutes later, eight tusks, or four pairs, lay separately from the trunks that used to caress them. The process of severing the tusks was gruesome, akin to extracting a fifty-pound wisdom tooth at its root with but a hacksaw. Omondi measured one pair, still tipped with blood, that Alijah reckoned would fetch a particularly high price. The tusks stood much taller than either man, curling at the tips like a crochet hook. The men loaded four into the plane and strapped the others onto racks on the outside that Alijah had designed and mounted. The weight kept them down a long time, but the runway stretched as far as their fuel could take them, and finally, the plane arced aloft. The truck would be full enough.

Within hours of their arrival, Omondi took off towards Mombasa with the cache. As usual, crates would be waiting in the warehouse along with straw for packing and fake stamps for appearance. In a beaten knapsack, Omondi carried a new set of forged customs inspection invoices. He would bring two sets back to Alijah once stamped at the port. One would be presented to the bank for payment, which in turn would send it on to the buyer's bank before the arrival of the goods. They reserved the other as an extra copy should anything go wrong.

Richard insisted on passing everything through the bank for the appearance of propriety. Ron thought it stupid to create public records of the transactions, but acquiesced. The banks elevated their credibility with buyers they never saw. Alijah agreed with Ron; he always wanted cash at the port and had difficulty comprehending bank accounts and securities.

.     .     .     .     .

Driving over bumpy terrain to follow his baboon troop as they marched through the savanna, Michael Sandburg smothered the butt of his last American cigarette, tuning his battered Panasonic to radio Moscow. Radio Free Europe never seemed to come in, and as he moved the dial back and forth to refine the voice that only a desperate ear could follow, he looked up, scanning the emptiness around him. In the middle of the hot savanna randomly marked by sprawling acacia trees, Michael fought the tension of feeling at home and looking out of place. An anachronism defined.

While he knew his presence presented an intrusion, the voice from the box unabashedly bellowed the manifesto of communism. The jargon of Marxist dogma translates uncomfortably into printed pages and even less eloquently into spoken words. The propaganda rang through the static, and Michael chuckled, embarrassed for the speaker. To those schooled to find security in capitalism, the propaganda of communist pitchmen sounds ludicrous.

Kiku sat beside him, enchanted with the talking box. Alijah's son had his father's quick mind and was fast mastering the English language. The radio tested all capacities. Kiku was asked to accept the barely conceivable notion that men further away than he had ever ventured talked through this contraption. At the same time, he strained to comprehend the words without the reinforcement of watching the speaker's lips form the syllables.

Michael assumed that Kiku, through his father, knew more of the world beyond than was in fact the case. Perhaps he made that leap because Kiku, with his long limbs and arrow-shaped cheekbones, reminded him so much of Alijah. Michael had been testy when Kiku questioned him about the most basic items but had recently embraced the daily onslaught of queries. He now found Kiku's innocence refreshing, especially as compared to the know-it-all British who otherwise controlled his movements. On reflection, a radio truly is amazing. Wonderment twinkled in Kiku's eyes as he struggled to absorb first the sentences and then their even stranger meanings.

"The ways of capitalism have secured the aristocrats and suppressed the tribesmen and peasant farmers who work so hard in vain to join the new world..." the radio blared. How many takes did they need to tape these shows without laughing, Michael wondered. That the message could be sincere would be inconceivable if there hid less truth to the poverty and suppression the narrator lamented.

Kiku interrupted the manifesto: "Capitalism? I don't understand."

"I suppose you don't. It's not easy to explain. Most people in the world live under one of two great beliefs. The first is capitalism. That's what Britain and the United States believe. It's complicated, but what it really means is that you put your trust in people rather than the government. The land, tools, most things are owned and controlled by people who trade and try to become wealthy through their trade. Those who succeed are wealthy like your chief. Those who are poor traders serve the others. The system is supposed to be set up so that anyone can become anything.

I could become a great chief or end up serving someone like your father, Alijah. The government is basically there to keep order and settle arguments."

Kiku's attention fell riveted on Michael. This was one of the most fascinating things he had ever heard. He questioned whether he understood, still transfixed. His mind jumped to the cattle Alijah promised him for initiation. But he had no intention of trading them. He wondered how he might name them and how rich he would be. He next imagined his goat herd growing so large he could celebrate drinking limitless gourds of blood.

"The man talking on the radio believes something different. Russia and many African governments believe in communism. They think the government should own and control everything. People can work for the government and the government will take care of the people. That's about it. Except, each thinks they're right and that the other's beliefs will lead to the downfall of their own countries."

"Who's right?" Kiku asked.

"The capitalists, of course. Unless your Ph.D. advisor is a Marxist anthropologist."

"I don't understand."

"Neither do I, really. Come on, let's listen a little more."

"The United States gives you money to lull you into believing that their system works and that it can eliminate the poverty that so many Kenyans suffer through each day. Their promises are lies. They have homeless in their decaying cities, and their prisons swell beyond capacity. Their rich and selfish leaders care not for the peasant, for the worker who loves and toils for his country. Democracy is but a charade, for the leaders hypnotize the people into believing that they act in their interests. No! Do not trust them. They inspire the passion of greed, fostered by their capitalist system of defeating friends and neighbors in the quest for material luxuries. They lull their people to sleep talking of these things everyone can someday obtain, but their materialist lust obscures the lack of compassion for the ordinary worker. False dreams lead the unwary into the fold. The communist party..."

Still trying to keep an eye on his baboon troop in the distance, Michael snapped off the radio. The broadcast was becoming an unwelcome distraction. What always began as amusement again inspired anger. Michael yearned for a good slug at the party broadcaster. Even if the diatribe was true, the distortions remained so great the thought of natives listening to this man, and believing what he preached, was revolting. Radio Free Europe always felt manipulative, blatantly using lame techniques that made the US look as lowly as the Russians in disseminating propaganda. Slowly his opinion wavered; something had to be done to counter the slurs.

Michael's disgust blinded him to the fact that almost all the population was too poor to buy a radio. Worse still, those with money tended to be people like himself who listened either out of curiosity or amusement. The ripples of radio waves surged across the plains in hopes of educating people living in a world of the past. Invisible to all and reaching only a small percentage, the intrusion was but one of many subtle tentacles the developed world stretched into the unspoiled grasses.

Michael turned to Kiku and said, "You know, where I come from, a wealthy man is one who can afford a house surrounded by trees that is so private he can't be seen or bothered by his neighbors. Here Kiku, the wealthiest men are those without anything, the tribesmen that never know there are people like me who know they are there, watching them."

Sometimes when Michael began pontificating like this, Kiku just walked away. The more white men Kiku met, the crazier he thought them to be. Alijah had cautioned his son to be wary, that no matter how helpful Michael may be, he was still a foreigner and apt to be driven by motives that would be challenging to appreciate. Also testing the relationship, their pairing was set up for mutual advantage, not grounded in one man independently reaching out seeking friendship. No matter how much Kiku and Michael exchanged ideas, at essence they were boss and aide, or teacher and student. Neither thought too much about that asymmetry, yet race and class and wealth and opportunity cast barriers. If they could scale the chasms of such cultural differences then genuine friendship may await, but more likely these formational divides could hold back trust.

Fewer differences can spur men that may otherwise be friends to become enemies.

Only time would settle their relationship, yet Michael felt a bit troubled by how easily Kiku seemed persuaded by the radio. In an attempt to open Kiku's eyes, had he instead allowed an estranging seed to grow? Michael sensed this but never tried to alter their banter. He truly believed it to be best that way. The bond of simply being could transcend the cultural gaps which, if indoctrinated, would most likely make them foes.

"I think I'll be a communist," Kiku boasted, understanding enough of the radio message to become an instant sympathizer.

"Jesus Christ. The shit propaganda actually works," Michael lamented, more to the air than directly to Kiku. "Whatever you want. The way things are around here, you'll get a chance to fight for whatever side you want. We'll tune in to the capitalist rebuttal tomorrow."

"What is rebuttal?"

"Never mind. Maybe we'll talk about it more later in camp. I think I'll drop you off first and then run over to the lodge to see if I've got any mail. You can get a fire going early. Before then, let's get closer to the baboons. I still have to finish making notes for today."

Soon the sun began to sink and Michael's baboon troop began its daily journey back across the savanna to the trees where they bunked every night. The life of a baboon could be so boring. Every day, Michael followed his troop out into the grasses, charting their food, fights, and sex lives. They would eat, frolic, and hump, and the next day they would eat, frolic, and hump. Then at night, they would come back to their trees, show their incisors and howl a bit to scare off the monkeys who took over their territory during the day. Before falling asleep, maybe they would play a bit more or hump again.

After a week or two of studying them, Michael had named each member and constructed the dominance hierarchy. With more money, he could follow additional troops and perhaps complete some research of merit. A few radio collars and videotape equipment would assure him tenure. Perhaps his ordinary observations would be good enough. Primate behavior was a hot topic, and hundreds of students back in the states vied for a field position like his. He snickered at their jealousy as he wiped the sweat from his brow while packing away his notes before heading back to camp. He pulled out his binoculars, taking one last look for the day. They were humping again. The students in Cambridge were jealous of the wrong lot. Researchers sit around all day charting food intake and the frequency of shits. The baboons were the ones playing in the grass and having sex all day.

Later, when Michael drove back into camp after stopping at the lodge, he saw the natives working for him, including Kiku, tossing pebbles at two helpless monkeys they had caught and kept in a makeshift cage. These monkeys persisted in stealing their food, and after every maneuver short of killing them, Michael decided to trap a couple and put them in a cage. Once they calmed down, he would move them to some distant area. The staff reveled in pelting the poor screeching creatures. Kiku, in particular, seemed to be enjoying today's moment of torture.

Michael railed at his campmates before to stop this hideous practice, but he had largely given up, yielding to the native mores. Watching Kiku celebrate a hit, though, strained Michael's new level of tolerance. Michael had come to feel responsible for Kiku, entrusted with the young man's education of sorts. Kiku was destined to be a chief or government official. Alijah could dictate either but still waffled on his choice. It was odd looking among the men and acknowledging that this one protégé should be so special. To be fair, Michael should have started a small English school and taught them all. But who was talking about fairness? Michael dolefully watched the monkeys hug each other in fear against the back of the cage.

Many natives had little appreciation for their animals and absolutely no sense of conservation. The tribesmen respected the wildlife, growing up with stories that reinforced the mystery and beauty of the ecosystem they knew they did not dominate. But absent telling stories, especially if they had not been raised as hunters, the lack of respect for native species they deemed pests was startling. To some, these animals existed for their amusement. Even revered creatures were not always safe. Hitting an elephant with a rock between the eyes to make him trumpet was as natural as hopscotch.

Conservation was not a word easily translated into a native tongue. Until the current moment in history, no need existed. The animals roamed so abundantly that the notion of game parks seemed absurd. Enlightened visitors, lamenting how the reserves evolved, acknowledge that game parks are no more than natural habitats usurped from the tribes by rules less civil than eminent domain. That the government was composed of former tribesmen who, in spirit, liked to retain their indigenous identity made the contradiction more bitter on analysis.

"Hey, stop that, leave those monkeys alone," Michael hollered, unable to bear the sight a second longer. His bellow roused Tad Olson, who emerged from his tent upon hearing Michael's command, only to see the pelting in its full glory. Tad was studying elephants and had been sharing camp with Michael for the months that passed since Michael left both Nairobi and Caroline. Tad found the natives' attitude toward the monkeys amusing, thinking the damn creatures deserved every welt the way they kept trying to steal food. African raccoons, he called them. The concept that torturing raccoons was equally cruel never filtered into his thoughts.

"Yeah, stop that," Tad joined in, authority missing from his voice. Michael knew Tad was putting on a show for him but appreciated the gesture anyway. Michael could never bean a monkey to pass the time, at least he told himself. He always managed to control his actions, stopping temptation before starting down the conciliatory slope of rationalizing why this or that exception would do no harm. In the process, he rarely crossed thresholds that would allow a guilty conscience to develop. Tormented by the thought that he might delight in landing a pebble against a furry skull, and even more fearful of dredging up memories of killing Gamala, he never dared himself to try.

After a brief nap, Michael lumbered from his tent toward the campfire. Tad fiddled making soup, but his body kept disappearing between the light cast by the fire and the lanterns. He recalled Susan Bennett telling him that when the sun sets in the bush, it quickly feels like the middle of the night; no lights, and nothing distinguishes 7:30 from 4:00 but anticipation. They sat very alone. The blackness pulsed so dark that Michael still flinched at each crackle in the air.

"Hey, I stopped at the lodge today and picked up some mail. You got a letter from Kathy," Michael called out loudly as if his voice would scare off anything in his path until he reached the light.

"Thanks. You know, she's great. I'm so lazy. All I have is free time, and I don't write half as much as she does. We know it's no big deal living here. It isn't really dangerous. But people back home, God, you'd think we were surviving the odds every day. Snakes, scorpions, wild animals. I exaggerate when I go home. I tell grand stories, but she worries about me an awful lot as a result."

"I don't know. I wouldn't take the safety for granted either. I'm scared shitless every night when I go to take a whiz behind my tent before going to sleep. Ever since I walked back there one night and saw that leopard..."

"You mean you thought you saw that leopard."

"Fuck you, Tad. I saw a leopard."

"Okay. You saw a leopard. I piss in the same place every night. Any animal that wants to come near that spot, I want to see! Let me have that letter."

Tad had already eaten, and while Michael ladled out some soup, Tad partook of the native weeds and read his letter. Every night he would sit by the fire and enculture himself.

Michael now pulled out his own letter, having nervously stuffed it away earlier. It was from Susan Bennett. Michael continuously struggled to keep her out of his mind but still flinched when a gun went off or a spear was raised (or tonight, when the sun set). He could never bring himself to write, fearing that Hugo or someone else would intercept the missive. He had not had any contact since that dreadful evening, and as Michael secluded himself in his tent, his hands shook. He ripped open the envelope, mustering courage to read what he hoped was not the stirrings of a confession:

*Dear Michael,*

*I'm sure you're surprised to hear from me, but I hope this letter will bring you some relief too. It's not easy carrying a secret such as ours. I wish I had a chance to get to know you better, so I could perhaps help you cope. My intuition tells me you carry a heavier burden than me and cannot move on so easily without the hint of a shadow. Hopefully I'm wrong. I trust you've never uttered a word to anyone, and if it brings any solace, you can count on my discretion to do the same. At times, I've been tempted to talk to Hugo, but I have held back.*

*My research was well received and I was offered a few different teaching posts. Hugo and I of course wanted to be together and right now the only place to take us both on for tenure is the University of Wisconsin. So, come winter, it looks like I'll be doing a lot of cross-country skiing. I feel a bit like I'm going home because I'm originally from Michigan. Hugo's from New York and isn't as happy, but c'est la vie.*

*I wondered for a while whether you would stick it out in Africa and called your department office to see if they had any word from you. They referred me to a Professor Barton who told me he had a couple of letters and that you were getting along fine. That's how I knew where to write. Don't worry. I didn't say anything to him. I told him you'd originally taken over my camp and that I wanted to contact my old cook. We chatted a bit and he asked me about my research. No suspicion at all. Anyway, from the conversation, he didn't seem to have any hint of trouble, nor suspect that I was a kind of distant alibi, and I take it then that you're doing okay and have put everything in the past.*

*I hope we can talk sometime. I don't know when you plan to be back in the states, but whenever it is, please let me know. I don't think I'll be back in Africa for at least a year, and I assume you'll be back, at least for a visit, before then.*

*Good luck. I hope you don't blame me for what happened. You know I could never have anticipated what…well you know. I was just letting things take their natural course, perhaps I got carried away with the fantasy. I don't know. And then I think of it as another natural course taking its way. Violent perhaps, but raw natural emotions. I think if Will Shakespeare had lived in the bush he could easily imagine more sordid tragedies than we could have ever witnessed. Think of it all as an adventure. What else can we do? Happy surviving, kiddo. Hope you are doing well, and your research is thriving.*

*All my best,*
*Susan*

Michael crumpled up the letter into one hand and lay back on his sleeping bag, blankly staring up at the tent. His mind reeled. The trauma of reading the letter slowly subsided and the chill of night began entering his thoughts. He pulled himself up, listening to the shrill sounds of nocturnal prowlers seeking refuge by the campfire, and left his tent to warm by the flames. Tad stared into the distance and, without a sound, passed his reed pipe to Michael. A couple of drags and he too was staring, but into the burning letter atop the fire.

Flickering away, casting a protective spotlight, this bounded their circle of safety. No animal would dare stray there. No animal would *want* to stray there dangled the truer sentiment. Common sense suggested that animals instinctively would shy away from anything foreign. Wary, they huddled by their alien fire, sheltered in the flames, vigilant not to walk beyond the periphery to the latrine.

In the bushes, which appeared thick by daylight, puffed lions. At least a couple, perhaps a whole pride, Michael guessed. The researchers were expecting a roar but were about to learn the significance of the puffing through the glassy stare of their resident warrior. Kiku sat rigidly on the log by the fire, reaching down to the ground, checking to ensure that his spear lay at hand. They were quiet as Kiku looked at them, coolly uttering, "Simba." The pupil had become the teacher. Michael now realized that a couple of the men had joined them.

"You mean lions? I thought they roared?" Michael said.

"That simba, Haummmppff," Kiku puffed the sound perfectly.

"Are they hunting?" Michael asked, his nerves taut. To some, he may have appeared a veteran of the bush, but these were still unfamiliar sounds, new frights to someone raised continents away. His ear had become attuned to a multiple of chirps and thumps; and yet, the puffing of a lion tested, evoking a primal shiver no matter how hard he built up rational layers of defense.

"No, they're content. They're far away," Kiku said dismissively.

Michael reckoned that a strange comment, for the noise sounded so close that Michael almost expected the breath from the puffing to blow past. Beyond the bushes, perhaps one hundred yards away, lay a dirt road. He drew a picture in the dirt for Kiku, who gave a confirming nod, muttering, "Simba, Simba."

Quietly Kiku stood up, undaunted, walking away from the firelight, leaving Michael and Tad alone. Michael shot to his feet, heart beating, only to see Kiku smiling at him as he strode back, his hands wrapped about a huge decayed log which, like lead, dropped upon the waning fire. Cinders flew about, and everyone shielded their eyes. The red specks danced, flickers of firelight highlighting the hues in Michael's reddish-blond stubble, casting that warm circle of safety.

"Simba doesn't like fire?" Michael asked in a pleading tone.

"No. Simba like fire. He's curious. Sometimes it even attracts him."

Michael turned ashen. There was no point in faking bravery, no one around to impress. His supposed sanctuary was actually a spotlight, illuminating the only area for miles as if to say, "Come, here's dinner." A loud roar cracked through the air sending everyone to their feet. The roar was not what he had been expecting, somehow very different from the majestic beauty ushering in the next MGM classic. More than anything, it reverberated louder, dominating the landscape. People become accustomed to sounds from zoos and shrieks from soundtracks, but at the moment this sound bellowed, there was an instant awareness that here preyed a lion, a hungry, cold, methodical beast. Michael shook and stared pathetically at Kiku, a plea for reassurance on his suburban face. Why had he returned to this desecrated place?

"He's far away," Kiku muttered, laying down his spear and resuming his position straddling the log. "Four, I think, by the road. Just sounds loud. They're close before when go 'umppf.' That's the male, he moving away."

Just as he finished, another roar echoed through camp, this one coming from a different direction, causing Michael and Kiku simultaneously to pivot toward the south.

Kiku stirred the fire and said, "Nyingi simba," watching Michael to make sure he understood. Chuckling, he kept repeating, "Nyingi, Simba," drawing three, then four, then five lines in the dirt, shrugging his shoulders indicating he was not sure how many lions were out there. Kiku poked at the fire and repositioned the new log, its belly now in the heat of the fire.

Michael, terrified at the thought of so many lions, twisted his head about, eventually staring back at his calm guard. Kiku continued, "Simba is full. Happy. So he roars. Like your beating communists."

"Not quite," Michael snorted, the tension momentarily broken. "You mean he makes all that sound and puffs when he's done hunting? He's just resting?"

"Even I knew that, moron," Tad said, grinning, rejoining the conversation.

Kiku laughed and stirred the fire.

From great relief, Michael was suddenly overcome with panic. All had been fine with the roaring: the lions puffed, happy. But now, they had stopped—dead silence. A silence took over, more terrible than the roaring had just been. His heart beat faster as he transfixed his eyes on the flickering embers. The fire had caused the log to smoke, and on top, an entire army of ants was scurrying out. How long had this log served as a peaceful home before being turned into this incinerator? He stared at the hundreds of black legs running along the log, watching them bunch at the end one to two feet off the ground, knowing the path back brought certain death. They had no choice but to jump, and that they did. One at a time, in clusters, even with a ladder made from sister bodies.

The sense of survival was fantastic, these stupid little creatures scrambling out of their now flaming log, leaping to the safety of the ground as their only escape. Now a column of ants moved from the ground, disappearing from the light of the fire into the scrub beyond. A vanguard warning the lions? Michael shook his head at how ridiculous his thoughts had become.

Suddenly, Michael stopped being a passive observer, shaking his leg and standing quickly. One battalion had begun the climb up his leg, and as he shook free of these pesky predators, another roar cracked the air. Shaking his leg one direction and turning his head the other way to try to place the sound, Michael hopped a couple of steps to keep his balance. Tad slapped Kiku on the thigh and laughed, pointing to their acrobatic friend.

"I don't know if you're cut out for this life," Tad snickered. "What do you say about retiring to the luxury of our tents? I had mine soundproofed today."

"Give me that reed!" Michael inhaled, going through the whole smoke himself.

·     ·     ·     ·     ·

By the time Michael woke the next morning, his troop had set off without him, and only after an hour's search did he find them humping in the grass.

Once again, he found himself charting numbers of copulations neatly into his notebook so that one day a book on mating strategies would include a footnote to the baboon mating observation study by Michael Sandberg. He pondered whether posterity through a citation on microfiche in the Library of Congress was truly his goal. Surely not, but he needed to publish to earn enough money to study and do what he really desired.

Was that the truth, he questioned himself? With more money, he would probably just videotape baboons humping and show the clips as a macabre gesture at a bawdy bachelor party. No, the money was important. With money, he could hurdle the tedious tasks performed out of necessity and reach a plateau where research was tailored to one's passion without compromise. That represented a natural yearning, regardless of one's profession. A film director dreams of commanding a final cut, possessing total creative control over their masterpiece and not kowtowing to hack studio executives and profit-hungry financiers. Why should research or any vision be so different? In the end, it signified freedom, freedom to direct the course of one's research, freedom to explore and plumb tangents that only the director could sense would lead to revelation. Discovery, proving the yet undocumented, was not so different than building a fantasy, as both required a master's guidance. Tamper too much, and the result would be off course or diluted; but allow the master his or her vision, unfettered of enablers' interests or economic choices that could taint the master's direction, and presto the unknown may be breached. Maybe this captured what Michael wanted. At the moment, he did not know. The simplicity and promise tantalized, yet the isolation was becoming intolerable.

Back in camp, Tad was teaching their cook how to use a slingshot. At the moment Michael drove into camp, the novice succeeded in striking his first monkey between the eyes. Muttering, "This is too much," Michael floored the jeep into a 180-degree turn, leaving the camp entrance in a cloud. Disobeying all park rules of safety, he sped along dirt roads, hoping no animals would stray into his path before reaching the game lodge. Reckless driving was still morally justifiable over the slingshot. Animals should have the instinct to run, he thought.

• • • • •

While devouring the international papers in the lodge's foyer, eager for what he viewed as unfiltered news from British or US sources, Michael noticed that the game warden of Amboseli Park, James Oejo, sat at a table on the balcony overlooking a watering hole. James was a large man, six-two or three and easily over two hundred pounds—perhaps from the waist up. Power from the post contributed to more than his girth, James' swollen ego justifying his running the park as a personal fiefdom. James knew the tourists kept the place running, though, and did an admirable job of enforcing the rules. At least publicly, he preached against the evils of poachers. Whatever the truth, the local lore held him to be well-intentioned but a tad arbitrary. He had been known to revoke camping licenses randomly. Most assumed that was his way of keeping the whole lot honest.

Michael sidled his way over to James, surrendering to local politics and debating how best to secure the warden's attention. In the end, he simply asked if he could buy him a drink. James, contemplatively looking out at the watering hole, smiled in acceptance and invited him to sit. Reconciled to the fact that he would have to join, Michael internally cursed his judgement, second thoughts hovering. Conversations lately courted trouble, and the better call would be to keep to himself. While buying James drinks might massage park privileges, budgetary and moral constraints weighed against the gesture. It was challenging to not do the wrong thing in the face of an egotistical boss. Still, James had always been chummy with him, perhaps enjoying the novelty of an American versus what he viewed as the pretentious British set.

"Catch any lately, James?" Michael asked, thinking he would let James gloat over his latest exploits ridding the park of loiters and hunters.

"Women, you mean!" James retorted with a devilish grin.

"No, poachers, you gigolo. Aren't two wives enough? We only get one back home, and I'm not even doing that well here."

"That's because you're a polite guest in my country and leave them all to me! Poachers, now, I haven't had a good couple of weeks. We had reports of some sneaking across from Tanzania and taking a couple of elephants, but I couldn't find them. They're sneaky little barbarians. I'll shoot every one of them on sight when I catch them. It's just too hard. Lately, I mean these guys with their planes and rifles swooping in for a kill and disappearing long before we discover it. I don't stand a chance."

"Has it always been this bad? The poaching, I mean," Michael pressed.

"Oh no. This is new. I don't know why, but the game department has been swamped with so many licenses that they lose half of them. It doesn't matter; people go out and hunt anyway. I can't expect to stop it all…except when they have the audacity to come into the game park— because they know there are so many animals here. It's the one area we have to stop them. The tourists leave, and I can't sit around and have drinks with you like this. Anyway, I will never accept the shooting. I love the animals. They're Kenya. That's why you come here."

Michael knew the answers but raised the questions because he knew it would let James run off a sermon. The drinks were now dry. "Let me fill the glasses," he proposed, at once escaping the table and appeasing the warden. In only a few months, Michael had become an expert in the game. He had to be.

# CHAPTER 7

*Nairobi, Kenya*

Ron Easton cocked his head back, sitting smugly in the barber's stiff wood chair while soaking his right hand in a finger bowl. He was not a terribly brave man, so when the straight blade closed in on his cheek, he closed his eyes. A warm towel soon caressed his stubble-free face, now ruddy cheeks blending with his natural blotch of sun rash. The barber knew better than to linger with a mirror, sending him on his way with a splash of cologne. Ron dashed out to his rover after leaving his usual meager tip, pausing at the door to peer into his side mirror. He rubbed his skin hard to gather in that fleeting scent of cleanliness. The old man always crafted a fine shave, no bristles.

Climbing inside, he smiled into the rear-view mirror, holding the gaze long enough for a few vain thoughts to pass. Ron judged himself good-looking, ignoring the shadows and blotches infiltrating his face. He compiled a mental and extraordinarily biased mug book: five-ten, thirty-eight years old, blue eyes, brown-though-sadly-receding hair. New head of the wildlife agency, a true man of the world—and now becoming rich! Providence suggested he could finally catch Caroline's eye at this evening's fundraiser.

Later that afternoon, while fumbling with his tuxedo studs, Ron received a notice confirming crates departed on a tanker heading for Hong Kong, and corresponding invoices were presented to the bank for payment. He smiled, calling to Nwebe, his Somali girlfriend. He had lived with her for a year, only contemplating casting her aside when fantasizing over women the likes of Caroline. Nwebe was the daughter of one of his former houseboys. Her father had worked for him ever since he moved onto the estate, and he first entertained a dalliance when she visited, needing a temporary place to stay.

She was still shy of twenty then and had since grown into a striking woman. Curvy with luminescent skin, she would be quite a prize for a different sort of man. She walked with the poise of a woman carrying a basket on her head while only carrying her straightened long black hair. Ron watched her hair wriggle free from its barrette as she stooped down to pick up the stud he fumbled to the floor.

Ron picked the paper up off his bureau, folding it back for her to see. On the inside page read, "Easton to Host African Fundraiser." "Tomorrow, my picture's going to be on the front page!"

"You see in advance?" Nwebe asked, indulging Ron's penchant for story stretching.

"Of course," he said, omitting how he had worked to ingratiate himself with the editor. Ron reasoned a little promotion flaunting was in order. "The party's the biggest night of the year. Show biz! A couple of American movie stars are on the organization's board of directors, and they're in town for this fundraiser. I may tag along on safari this week. I need to see how long they're staying."

"I don't know what you're talking about."

"Do you remember when I made you go to that movie in town, where they turned out all the lights?" Ron paternalistically asked, looking at her to ensure her answer of "yes" was sincere. He wanted her to experience a movie theatre; however, he refused to accompany her for fear of being seen together in public. Nwebe pleaded with him, begging him to enter secretly, moving once it grew dark to sit beside her. He had been tempted, but declined.

"Yes, I remember. The people from that movie. They be there?" her English still rough.

"No. These people are famous from TV. That's like a movie in your home." He paused to think whether she had ever watched television, remembering a long conversation after she had gone to the movie. "One of the men there is a talk show host. One of the biggest celebrities in the world. The other is an actress. A beautiful woman. Neither was in the movie."

Ron slid the last stud through the French cuff, which never seemed to cease folding, before knotting his bow tie. Accustomed to attending these affairs, he perfected the origami-like twisting of the silk. He kissed Nwebe, holding her for a moment to comfort her from yet another lonely night. "I'm sorry you can't come. I'll probably be back late. Don't wait up for me."

Ron did not bother telling her it promised to be virtually an all-white affair. That outcome was not intentional, of course, or so he deceived himself into thinking. In truth, he had paid little attention, inviting his clique from the Polo Club and relishing his opportunity to mix with the stars. Selfishly, this was only his night to feel equal.

The next morning Nwebe came in with breakfast. As Ron sat up, thanking her, wiping his eyes, she turned around and headed for the other room. When he called her to come back, she strutted in proudly displaying the front page. Ron and some man she had never seen before beamed, their arms around the woman she hoped was the actress. Ron wished it had not been the actress. He never got his arms around Caroline. At least the editor had come through for him. Above the photograph with Ron the headline read: "Celebrity Bash Raises £20,000 for Wildlife."

·　　·　　·　　·　　·

"Hello, Michael!" Warden James Oejo called out, barreling into Michael's camp, his Jeep kicking up a trail of dust. After chatting at the lodge, Michael had told him to stop by anytime. This morning, apparently, James was taking him up on the offer. It was still early, that time of day when James exuded energy, his girth not yet wearing him down, anxious to roam with the animals on patrol. James looked around, gathering in the routine of camp life. Kiku snored rhythmically, having stayed up on watch most of the evening. Tad and Michael were preparing to head their separate directions for the day. In parallel, the baboons, already done with their morning grooming, started to march off into the savanna.

"Warden, this is a pleasant surprise. What are you doing here?" Michael greeted him.

"Thought I'd stop by, see where you head out every day. There aren't many people living in the park; I mean outside the lodges. I was hoping you could show me what's been going on in this section, if you don't mind. I'm not too busy today."

"Sure. Why don't we take my jeep," Michael offered. "I'm kinda used to the terrain. You don't mind being chauffeured, do you?"

"I was waiting for you to ask."

After an obligatory exchange of greetings with Tad, Michael and James set off searching for his baboons. They found them foraging in the open savanna, not far from camp. The troop had come to trust Michael, and he could approach without much threat of attack. James, though, posed a problem. The baboon Michael named Thor flashed his fangs, forcing the spectators to retreat to the car.

They sat for nearly thirty minutes, handing Michael's binoculars back and forth, watching nothing but a couple of young baboons annoy the elders who were perfectly content basking in the sun. To a researcher, or probably to anyone who came bearing binoculars, the precocious taunting by the adolescent baboons was enchanting. This defined the type of charming behavior that causes men to speculate on their origins and revel in nature's simplicity. To James, however, a native that found the common baboon no more than a pest, the boredom proved overwhelming. He coaxed Michael into moving on for a drive through the surroundings.

Making their way toward a deep ravine, they heard some animals nearby and turned to see what stirred the commotion. A hundred yards further, their car scared off whatever scavenger had groaned, leaving them alone with two fresh elephant carcasses. The animals had been huge, but it was difficult to tell looking at the bloodied heads, tusks hacked off, lying in a tangled heap. Flies buzzed everywhere, and the stench was beginning to spread.

"Jesus," Michael muttered, turning off the engine. "I've never seen anything like…"

"It's all very familiar," James lamented, his voice noting that despite the common sight, he had not acquiesced to the inevitability of the slaughter. "Fucking bastards! They've been here within the last couple of hours."

"What? You think they're still nearby?"

"I don't know." Looking around, he said, "Over there," pointing to vultures circling in the distance, perhaps signaling another kill.

Michael started the rover again, jolting forward toward a thicket and the vultures' shadow. In a few minutes, they found another butchered elephant. While gasping at the sight, the elephant suddenly moved, struggling to stand without even knowing a foot had been severed. Poachers often cut off feet and lined them to be used as planters or wastebaskets.

Michael shook with the notion that the elephant might think them its killers. In an act of mercy, James put yet another shot into its hide. The poachers had cut off the tusks, moving on after the herd, not bothering to put the victim out of its pain. A fifty-year-old bull that could shake the earth and that had spent its docile life munching grasses and tree limbs closed its eyes for the last time. The elephant was not the only creature around in pain.

Michael screamed in anger until James admonished, "Quiet! They may be nearby. I don't know. Maybe near some water. Probably were trying to herd them there where they're boxed in. Come on!"

Michael started the car, driving with abandon across the plateau, pausing at a crest where they could look down past the thicket to the swampy muck. The river runoff from the mountain slowly drained into the looming desert, forming a long marsh before it dried. It spread across dangerous ground, hiding animals and only approachable on foot.

James grabbed Michael's binoculars, spying something on the edge of the marsh. If they approached from the north, they would be downwind with the cover of trees. Swinging around, Michael cut the engine, creeping nearer, able to roll down the hill toward the edge of where reeds marked the beginning of damp soil; continuing any further risked losing traction.

James heard a rustling in the bushes behind them and trained his binoculars in the noise's direction. In the distance, he saw a baby elephant, but this youngster had only three gray legs; its fourth was streaked red, bleeding no doubt from stray bullets. There exists no reason to kill a youngster without tusks. James swore bitterly, his eyes tracking what appeared to be yet another orphan. Before he could begin thinking about a rescue, James heard the echo of a shot and instinctively ducked. His own survival quickly took priority—calling in help for the baby elephant would have to wait. Hopefully, it was a flesh wound and looked worse than a graze. Still, the sight of the blood fueled his rage: these poachers crossed the wrong man.

"Do you have a gun?" James barked, loading his rifle.

"Are you crazy? You expect me to go after these guys with you?"

"Yes! What do you want me to do? Report it? Turn in a damn investigation report to myself!"

"You want my help, you swear you'll never mention what you're about to see."

"Fine."

"I mean it!"

"All right!" James cried, the veins in his neck bulging, trying to contain his fury, the frightened eyes of the baby elephant seared in his memory.

Michael moved to the trunk, pulling out Susan's relinquished Uzi. He kept it after killing Gamala, deciding on his return to camp he would be foolish to give it away. It gave him an edge, and if he learned nothing else since arriving, it was that he needed an edge and more. Unlike Susan, though, he tended not to keep the gun loaded, now methodically sticking in the clip.

"I told you," he said, countering James' shocked look.

"Are you a fucking poacher too!"

"No, it's been handed down from researcher to researcher in my camp. I didn't want it but was convinced it's dangerous out here. They were right. You promised," Michael spoke sternly.

"Arrogant white men. Come here claiming to do research and back yourself up with a submachine gun to stop a baboon. Let's go. Follow me and keep quiet."

Michael and James crept along the marsh's soggy border until they saw the brush spike out, creating a small clearing with solid land protruding. A truck and a jeep were parked, spaced well apart, and both sitting empty.

"Let's get closer, within range," James whispered. They'll be back any minute."

"Why don't we shoot out the tires?"

"Good idea, but they'll hear it."

"So what?" Michael said. "You want to wait while they're in there killing god knows how many elephants or whatever? You go over and get in the jeep. Once you're inside for cover, shoot out the tires on the truck. Then get down. I'll cover you. Or shoot the tires first then run for the jeep."

"Now you're the crazy one. Why should I risk that?"

"Because you're the fucking warden," Michael spat, losing his temper, swearing for emphasis since he needed to keep his voice down. "I was sitting watching my baboons, writing in my lab book. You're the one that wanted to come over here."

"Well, mate," shaking his head in resignation. "I hope you know how to use that."

"Don't worry."

"Yeah," Jame thinly smiled.

Michael squatted in the last of the thicket's brush as James ran toward the jeep. In the adrenaline rush of the moment, he reached the car before Michael had any chance to think twice. No reassessing of plans—seconds later, James' gun blast twice. The truck slumped. James dove into the jeep, crouching out of sight. Michael's heart beat faster. Jarring wisdom.

Three men emerged from a finger of the marsh hidden by brush, heading cautiously toward the vehicles. Two approached bearing rifles. The other man dragged a tusk, leaving it on the ground when they drew closer. Staying down in the car, and as soon as he could hear them approach, James called in Swahili for them to freeze. The poachers paused, uncertain where the voice came from. One pointed toward the jeep, his comrades in tandem raising their rifles.

James risked raising his head to peer out. The poachers immediately saw him and fired. James ducked down, releasing a quick shot back out the door. It was a wild shot, meant more to scare and stave off the attack than escalate the fight. He was pinned down and, remarkably, now fighting for his life rather than the elephants. While both sides hesitated, Michael stood up, triangulating aim from a different direction, yelling for them to drop their weapons. Unfortunately, he did not speak in Swahili, his vocabulary limited to simple greetings. They turned toward him without understanding a word. One of the poachers shot, but his hasty triggering sprayed far off the mark, his target still relatively far away and moving. Michael, who had zigzagged before dropping to the ground, now poked out of the bramble, opening up his gun and showering them with fire. He hit them all, two of the men killed instantly. The third fell wounded, shrieking. James jumped out of the car, rushing to take him prisoner before he could reload, the afternoon's carnage complete.

Almost unconsciously, Michael turned his gun toward the sky in thanks, the staccato rhythm of the nearly-exhausted clip still ringing in his ears. He then eased his jackhammer forearm down in exhaustion, the savanna suddenly quiet. Michael looked at James, who was shoving the poacher in the back, marching him toward the jeep; he would commandeer the vehicle, taking it temporarily to Michael's camp. In the distance, rested the dropped tusk. A visceral hatred boiled within Michael. The surviving poacher was lucky Michael had lowered his weapon; otherwise, the poacher might never make it to stand trial. Would he dare mete out savanna justice? James looked over at Michael, reading his thoughts.

"Remember," Michael said, slinging his gun back over his shoulder, "You promised not to say anything."

"Don't worry. I wish I had ten of you," James's tone wistful. "Let's go. I need to call this in and get some help for that baby. I hope we're in time."

Enervated, Michael nodded, climbing into his car and silently steering back toward camp. He passed by the troop of baboons, still frolicking in the savanna, slowly making their way back home, oblivious to the powers shaping their future world. Michael looked at them play and longed for the ease of their routine. He wondered if they understood their own mortality. He wondered if they wondered.

· · · · ·

James took the poacher in his jeep from Michael's camp, heading to the park's administrative headquarters. They agreed to meet at the end of the day for a drink at the lodge. It was a tough call who should buy. James owed Michael his life, but in a way, Michael owed James his courage. He felt oddly proud. This was not a crusade, yet he felt himself forging ahead buoyed by a purpose. More than the beginning of a streak, this marked the type of turning point he knew he would look back upon even while it was happening. This was crazy. He needed to ward off insane impulses to act again, hunting down others—and for the moment, stay silent. No matter what he thought of himself, no matter what he wanted to be, he remained an outsider, a mere socio-biologist charting the copulatory frequency of baboons. Maybe so, but he would not stand by and wait for the baboons to be the only ones left.

Later at the lodge, James and Michael celebrated, brothers in arms. After a few drinks, though, the verbal back-slapping ebbed, and they were more reflective than boisterous when they noticed Alijah entering the bar. Michael had met him a couple of times with Richard and another when he visited Kiku in camp. James was savvy enough to heed his reputation, striving to build a decent working relationship, knowing it would prove helpful having Alijah as an ally. Despite his efforts, silently, he doubted his overtures would mature into friendship. They were on the same team, yet teammates in his profession tended to be wary of each other. In fact, James had told Michael he did not fully trust Alijah, even going as far as to intimate he thought Alijah was a bit of a fraud— grandstanding about his captures and exploits instead of helping James fund desperately needed teams to patrol the parks properly.

Michael was unsure what to think, his own dealings with Alijah tinged with a bit of mystery. Michael recalled Alijah asking him to keep his relationship with Kiku, along with Michael's role in teaching his son, between the two of them. Alijah specifically cautioned him to keep the relationship quiet in public and never give rise to a hint in the city. Michael respected Alijah's requests, even if he did not fully understand the reasons, but complications abounded. This afternoon, in particular, he was not eager to play the polite game. What was Alijah protecting Kiku, or himself, from? Michael made up his mind to exchange greetings and head home. The last thing he needed was more drama. The day seemed an eternity.

James, in contrast, was thrilled at his political opportunity. Though senior in age, James was junior in rank, respectfully standing to put on a show. How auspicious! Given a world of contacts and perks, James smiled on his good fortune for Alijah to walk in on this triumphant afternoon. Today, he would be the one doing the boasting. Maybe his unexpected success would finally convince Alijah to fund more teams.

"Are you gonna tell him what happened?" Michael asked.

"I have to," downplaying his hand.

"Be selective. I don't exactly have a license to shoot people."

James would not hide their heroics, of course. As soon as Michael left, James would embellish their feats. Michael suspected the same, futilely trying to dismiss his worries. How could he be in trouble? He had been enlisted and probably saved the warden's life. He was a hero! Whatever transgressions he may have committed were far outweighed by the outcome. Such ethics are practiced by dictators and utilitarians alike: Michael had an entire spectrum on his side.

Alijah extended his hand, warmly greeting Michael. In a sense, Michael served as a tangible bridge to his other life. Ever cautious to keep his world's separate, though, and believing knowledge about his family could prove a liability in the wrong hands, he took Michael's arm, escorting him to a spot beyond James' earshot. Only then did Alijah eagerly ask about Kiku's well-being.

"He's picking up English quickly," Michael reported, proud to play the mentor, watching Alijah beam. "I'm not sure how much I can teach him, though. Have you thought about sending him to school? Maybe one of the missionary schools for some of the basics. He could even go to university. He's a bright kid."

"I've thought about it. He has his initiation soon. He could be a chief. Or he could work for me."

"I meant to tell you, he's shown a real interest in politics."

"Very good! Maybe he should join the army! I want to hear more. Just a little bit now."

Michael walked Alijah to the bar, continuing to laud Kiku's progress. Alijah listened patiently, promising to visit, wondering whether Kiku would soon be tempted like he had been. He wanted to provide him the choice without bearing responsibility for gifting him the dilemma of choice. The fact that he could influence that choice mysteriously channeled a dark power; for his son's sake, he vowed to keep his distance. The malignant knowledge Alijah acquired from the so-called civilized world should be kept at bay. If Kiku wanted to leave for the city, Alijah would have his own dilemmas to resolve.

Looking around, not wanting to create gossip by pulling Michael aside for too long, Alijah said, "Let's not strand poor James," emphasizing James's name as he steered Michael back towards the warden. James smiled on hearing his name, playing the obsequious colleague holding the table. Rejoining the warden, Alijah slapped Michael on the back, offering him a chair, pleased with what he heard. Michael, though, uncomfortable with his surrogate role in Alijah's presence and needing no more conflicts after the day's drama, excused himself: "I think I'll leave you to catch up on business. I'm going to attend to some serious drinking."

"Bye, and thank you," James said, sincere in his words but eager for the privacy to recount their adventure. Little did he know Alijah was in cahoots with the poachers; nor could he have imagined Alijah would chastise him for his good deeds. In a few minutes, James would be ordered to stick to his job managing the reserve and let Alijah and his team deal with any poachers. Oblivious that he was about to be blindsided, James could hardly contain himself when Alijah finally sat, and Michael turned to leave.

Walking away and, good to his word gathering another drink, Michael found a quiet table, easing himself down. He craved alcohol, or more specifically its numbing glow, and sipped while scanning the room, gathering in the dusk commotion of tourists recounting the lion of the day. Looking over at James and Alijah, Michael was overcome with a sense of isolation, wallowing in feeling out of place. There was an intense loneliness to killing a man. He left his drink and dragged himself out, wanting simply to get away—again.

•     •     •     •     •

Driving away from the lodge, Michael passed assorted park outposts, the last of which pitched a makeshift convalescent area for rescued animals. Usually a handful of animals were there being weaned back to health before being introduced back into the wild. Secretly, he always feared coming across one of us his troop here if some accident—if a predator's claws could be considered an accident—were to befall them. He was becoming quite attached, a voyeur inexplicably coming to think of himself as extended family, benevolently wanting to watch over the troop and shield them from the very dangers that bespoke of their freedom. Michael shook his head at the irony.

Drawing closer, Michael noticed quite a bit of commotion and slowed his jeep to a crawl. Several cars were scattered outside, and people were shouting from inside the rescue center. Through the slats of a makeshift corral, he could spy a group of people huddled around what appeared to be a large animal on the ground. Michael turned off his ignition, his curiosity pulling him toward the scene for a closer view. At the edge of the fence, he froze: the baby elephant they had seen shot in the bush lay on a wooden sled.

Warden James must have successfully radioed in the location, and a rescue team probably tranquilized the baby before bringing it here. It, he thought—I don't even know whether that's a boy or girl, bile rising in his throat as he pictured the butchered scene of what happened to this poor kid's parents. Michael took some solace in not seeing any blood, finally smiling, thinking that something good had come of the afternoon. The group around the sled was starting to disperse, claps of camaraderie ringing out, relief and joy evident in their faces. It seemed a mirage when one of them turned, and his eyes came to rest on Caroline Dunning, the one woman he had fallen in love with after fifteen minutes.

She had not yet spotted him. In the few precious inconspicuous seconds he had left, he turned away, mustering his energy and thinking of what to say. Perhaps it signaled a streak after all. He ducked into the clinic's men's room, trying to splash away the grit of the day. Soon he swaggered back outside, taking a vector that would hopefully force him to bump into her, sparking an innocent, yet not so innocent, rendezvous. Why so much scheming, he thought to himself? I can shoot a man but don't have the courage to walk right up to her?

In real time, his moment of insecurity and admonition lingered only a few seconds. Not long after Michael emerged, starting back toward his car, his eyes and Caroline's locked.

"It's good to see you," he began as if running into her marked the most natural thing in the world. "Is she alright?" he asked, looking toward the sleeping baby.

"Yes, and it's a he. We got to him just in time. I can't believe someone would shoot a baby elephant," shaking her head in disgust. Her mind then snapped back toward Michael, and she said, "What are you doing here?"

"Well, if you can believe it, I actually rescued him. I was in my camp with the warden, and when we were driving back here, we came across a group of poachers and spotted this orphan. James Oejo radioed it in. And from the looks of things, they must have called you. Looks like you're a hero, saved his life."

"Maybe both of us," Caroline nodded.

Michael opened his arms, his exhaustion now becoming apparent. In the gesture, weariness from the ever-growing improbability of the day made his arms feel like fifty-pound weights. Caroline stepped forward into Michael's hug, accepting the accolades and letting the relief of saving the baby elephant wash over her. In the dawning that they had unknowingly teamed to save this life, he did not have time to debate how she would respond, and her squeeze brought both relief and hope.

He tried to compute how long it had been since she left for London. He fumbled at the calculation; so much had happened to him, in such a brief span, time seemed somewhat irrelevant. Then he remembered her marriage, and in a reflex, let go.

"Wait, what are you doing back here? It hasn't been that long has it? I thought you were getting married and then staying in England a while?" Glancing at her hand, he added, "And where's the ring? Or do you have to take it off for surgery and all?"

Knackered from the grueling task of rescuing the elephant—she has just cleaned the wound, extracted some stray shrapnel, and performed a skin graft that she was not yet expert enough to be attempting alone—she toyed with her fingers, similarly at odds with reconciling the passage of time. "It's a long story."

"Are you staying at the lodge?" he asked gingerly, sensing her melancholy tone and that he had unwittingly intruded into a private area. "How about dinner and you can tell me about it? I'd be happy to cook, but I don't have anything other than cabbage in camp right now. And I'm guessing we've both been around enough rotten smells for today."

Giving in to a smile, she nodded, "Sure. Today's no less crazy than when I last saw you…. What is it, Michael, carnage just follow you?" she managed to kid, back out of her haze.

"Not funny, but also not wrong," he paused. "Just a couple more people killed today," he said deadpan, sure she did not know the truth. The lunacy!

"Still modest," she continued to mock him. "Well, it must be good for you. You look well. A bath may be in order," she chuckled.

"What do you expect spending all my time in the sun with baboons?" Michael said, pouting exaggeratedly. "I'll head back and take a shower. How about we meet back at the lodge?"

"Sounds great. Eight o'clock?"

"Well, I don't have a watch. How about I call your room when I get here? You never answered—I assume you are staying at the lodge?"

"Yes. And I definitely need a shower myself, and a nap." Caroline reflexively raised her arm toward her nose, catching a horrid waft of whatever results from a dab of blood mixed with sweat and elephant guts. Waving to him, she jogged to say goodbye to one of her veterinary colleagues. The pair walked arm in arm toward the clinic, the euphoria of success and the bliss of moving on almost maudlin in the illumination cast by the falling sun.

· · · · ·

While Caroline relaxed in the lodge's modern shower, Michael began to heat water over the fire. With primitive pulleys, he hoisted a bag of water over a tree branch, periodically yanking on the cord to keep the warm trickle flowing. Despite its awkwardness, the device worked rather efficiently. Michael had a hot shower, a feat even the game lodge could only inconsistently duplicate. Water was a premium resource, and such showers accordingly rare. Normally, the toils of transporting the jugs justified use for cooking and drinking. Every couple of days, he would indulge in a shave and perhaps every week or two the mechanics of a Robinson Crusoe shower.

Today certainly warranted a shower. Invigorated by being clean for the first time in more than a week, Michael headed back to the lodge. How his motivation had changed from when he barreled up to the parking lot a few hours before! No longer a newcomer to the continent, he knew better than trying to place a call from the desk. Occasionally the phone at the lodge would work, but the radiophone at the joint game and police barracks next door was more reliable. Or, truly back to basics, he could simply knock. At what he reckoned must be close to 8:00, he crisply rapped on Caroline's door.

When she appeared, Michael stood besotted by the lines of her dress. A white sundress caressing her darkly tanned body held his not-so-subtle gaze. Somehow, he was surprised to see her out of beaten khakis and a t-shirt. Only hours before, they were mutually disheveled, lucky not to be covered in blood. Caroline's effortless style contrasted with Michael's garish sports coat. The need to dress up infrequently arose by the equator, but following the embassy party, Michael had decided to buy a linen safari jacket imported from Bangkok to Nairobi, donning it tonight for the first time. The jacket looked horrible, but he walked like a millionaire.

Michael told Caroline she looked beautiful. He spoke without agenda, utterly sincere, his tone disarming. Flattered and suddenly a bit self-conscious, Caroline led the way toward the lodge's restaurant, her tanned cheeks disguising a slight blush. Michael followed, too smitten to notice he had not been asked inside her room.

At dinner, demons soon surfaced. "Why did you stay?" Caroline asked. "I thought after what you'd been through, it was pretty likely you'd pack your bags. You know, put everything behind you, like a bad dream."

"I don't have a great answer. I thought about it—a lot. I kept coming back to the fact I wouldn't finish my research and would have to start over again. I didn't have any easy options, and in the end thought I'd be running, maybe even haunted a bit, whatever I did. So, I decided I'd stick it out for a few months and see how I felt."

"And I guess my running into you means it's going well. Or you would have given up by now."

"I don't know about given up. But yeah. I'm over the worst, sleeping again, and have largely put it behind me," Michael said, almost pleading, unable to bury all the fears when juxtaposing the events of his day. His mind tracked back to when in a drunken confessional, he had borne his soul to her. That seemed like a lifetime ago, but comfort dangled in knowing, for once, he did not have to spin a tale. She knew the truth and still sat across from him having dinner, as if any of this were normal.

His life had become a surreal epic, murder to murder, justification to justification, each act a little easier than the last, a twinge of pride overtaking fear and doubt. Michael found himself traversing the psychiatrist's slippery slope, with moral conundrums fading in the distance, his having summited the rationalized high ground. Was this how criminals felt? Or perhaps an addict, the high trumping how you got there? My god, he shot someone today (again!), and now reclined sipping wine and ordering venison carpaccio. It was not like he spent the afternoon meandering through a mall shopping for shampoo and a new belt. Perhaps more stunning, he was not hiding or being sought; and if pursued, the officers would more likely beg him to recount his tale or put him on a pedestal for bravery. He had to change the subject lest he continue wallowing in the murk of defining morality.

"Enough about me. What about you? I didn't expect to find you here either. Last I saw you, you were off to get married, embark on some research at the Royal Veterinary College, if I recall. You were a bit evasive before. Not trying to pry, but whatever you feel okay sharing."

Suddenly it became Caroline's turn to face demons, wondering whether opening up would have a cathartic effect or sound self-pitying. While not privy to Michael's full deeds and horrors, she sensed a deep pain and worried that whatever her woes, they would sound trivial. And yet, she had been quite shaken too, now struggling to put the lack of living to script behind her, for the first time carving a truly independent path. She had been wrestling with her future for weeks, burying herself in work and research in part to escape, but also genuinely enjoying her trade. It was no longer an aside, an "Oh, by the way, I'm a vet too" placeholder.

Yielding to the question, she replied, "Simply, the marriage is off. When I went back to England, I learned my fiancé hadn't been faithful— and that pretty much is the beginning and end of the story. I walked away, spent a fabulous time working on a horse farm, training and treating racehorses, even managed to combine it with some research at the Veterinary College. I may go back to that—I loved it—but I also missed it here and just thought I'd come back for a bit more local training. Can't exactly save a baby elephant in South Ken."

"Wow, I'm sorry."

"Oh, don't be. I've moved on. Freer and happier than I've been in a long time."

Freer and happier, Michael pondered her line. What the hell did that mean? He lived less inhibited than he could have imagined, unshackled even from societal rules of sorts, consciously privileged to be living in the wild as if teleported to the days of great explorers. Yet, in other ways, he was hiding. Michael shook off the maelstrom of conflict, smiling. "Congratulations then. I think I know something of picking oneself up from a shock and moving on. It's a bit like being reborn, just without the religious stuff. And with the perspective, you see what you truly want, chasing things for yourself, not out of obligations."

With equal recognition that the tone had turned too serious, they both pushed for a new equilibrium, craving a rush to normalcy. Eventually, the conversation began jumping from topic to topic, and mercifully, silence never cast its awkward shadow. Exhausted from the day, Michael had worried whether he could be himself, especially whether he could avert another cathartic lapse. After their initial parries, his anxieties melted away, Caroline's presence the perfect salve. Freely challenging each other's opinions and joking with ease, they laughed in torrents. Caroline even told embarrassing stories about shopping in England after fifteen straight months in Kenya. He pictured her savaging the shelves. With the discussion finally nearing a lull, Michael asked a question he wished he could take back; he did not intend to stir the serious overtones it convulsed.

"Were you jealous of your friends living in London, leading a normal life?" Michael asked.

From Caroline's delayed response, the answer hung at least partially clear. She was torn, but no less than he. Michael felt guilty for asking the question, berating himself after just probing why she returned, the topic still acutely sensitive. Searching for a relief valve, he said, "You know, in camp, I think about going home all the time. There's always that urge, but for some reason I never give in to it. I don't know why. Maybe I'm jealous of my friends back home. Hot showers every night and finally making some money. Seems like everyone's buying a house, and I'm trying to understand baboon grunts."

"Well, I wouldn't be so dejected over it. There's nothing to spend money on here anyway. Besides, who do you think is more jealous? You or some guy working in an office until late at night thinking about his friend who drives around in a jeep all day watching animals and topping it off with a Tusker?"

"You know, you're right. I don't know why I'm sulking. If I wanted to move back, I'd be there now. I'm sure the same's true for you. And how many guys could I kill at home and get away with it?" he toyed, cocking his finger and thumb like a gun.

"Come on, just sounds like you're lonely or bored to me. You've been rationalizing your whole life since we sat down." Caroline sensed her remark made Michael uncomfortable, but she spoke only of what lay too suppressed for him to bring up on his own. They did not know each other well yet sensed the other's thoughts. Eerily, they had both lost their fathers in plane crashes; though under very different circumstances, and continents and risks apart. Maybe that tragic bond, coupled with sudden upheavals in their personal lives, created a similar prism through which they now more cautiously analyzed their steps. Perhaps they shared a fervor to grasp life despite setbacks quite rudely throwing lives off course. Both off balance like never before, searching as if in an eye test straining for perfect calibration where all would be clear, there rumbled a growing intuition. Maybe balance was not achieved alone. Why was it so hard to accept the good fortune in front of them, discarding the fear this may be just a rebound? The world is too littered with regrets of those who failed to act for want of perfect timing. Though he could not articulate the thought, Michael kinetically sensed the jungle-inspired chance to break free of appearances and protocols and for once follow instinct.

After pausing, Michael acknowledged Caroline's diagnosis that he was wallowing in rationalizations: "Yeah. I can't deny that." Then summoning courage, he asked, "Why don't you come back with me to camp? You can get away and use the time to write up your notes about saving that orphan. I assume you have to turn in some form of report. I see all the big game every day, and who knows, maybe we'll find another animal in need. More likely out there than in the city," he said, knowing his argument stretched thin.

"I've already got plans to go back to Nairobi the day after tomorrow and am booked for a safari tomorrow. But if you're planning to come to Nairobi..." The invitation hung in the air.

"I think I've heard that before." Undaunted and perhaps finding surprising resolve in being a near fugitive with little more to lose, Michael said, "Come on, you can be more honest than that. If you don't want to see me, just tell me. I hate the slow no. I was forced to forget about you and wrote you off to a London marriage. Now you appear out of the blue and are disappearing as suddenly tomorrow. Take a chance. What do you have to lose?"

"Michael, I just don't know. Part of me would really like to say yes, escape for a couple of days, but I can't do it on a whim. I'm still sorting out a lot in my personal life," she said, somewhat weakly, not having dated seriously since calling off the wedding.

"Well, please think about it. Door's always open. Or maybe better, the tent flap." He snorted just shy of a chuckle.

"Okay, I promise." She smiled, reflexively batting her green eyes, sending the type of signal Michael hoped to recognize when chronicling the mating rituals of his troop. How similar the games.

Michael slowly walked Caroline back to her room, this time conscious of whether she would invite him inside. The clues Caroline let slip initially bode poorly, yet he sensed her wrestling with her feelings. Confident she would not reject him but petrified to make the first move, the short walk took forever. If he failed to take the initiative, he would never know. When she unlocked the door and turned toward him, he slid his hands onto her shoulders, kissing her before she could speak a word. In the morning, an extra party was added to the safari.

# CHAPTER 8

*Alijah's Tribal Village- Kenya*

Approaching the circle of huts with Kiku, Michael's mind wandered far away, thinking only of Caroline. Today, Michael was an honored guest. Few white men had ever witnessed the initiation ceremony. His feet stuck in the muck lining the center of the village. The sun was slowly hardening the dung like mortar, burning away the odor. Boys ran about carefree, stopping to piss when the urge came. Michael lifted his boot from a moistened spot back onto the baked dung. He could only smell Caroline's perfume. If she was thinking of him back in Nairobi, he was glad Caroline was oblivious to his scent.

Kiku ushered Michael toward the far side of the circle, the whole village now gathered. Ever since Michael had known him, Kiku's hair had been long and braided, sometimes even plaited with red mud in ceremonial elegance. For initiation, he had been shaved bald. His head and face smeared in rust-toned paint, Kiku indeed looked older, ready to cross the threshold into manhood. Everyone in the village beamed with pride.

"This is my mother, Tza," Kiku said, switching between English and Swahili.

Michael nodded, saying "Jambo" while marveling at her magnificent almond-shaped eyes and following spirals of colorful beads tapering up her long neck. His immediate impression was of a tribal Cleopatra.

Tza kept her tongue still, thinking how much she distrusted this man and how much her son praised him. None of it made sense. She met many white men living in Nairobi with Alijah, but that interlude faded long ago. Almost a dream. A bad dream. There had been lots of bad dreams after she lost her new baby in a miscarriage. She managed not to dwell on it, losing the fetus a part of nature just as the pregnancy; and yet, she was tormented at night, perhaps a sign of wrestling with Kiku growing up and departing, the void of a child, of family close, now not to be filled.

She eventually asked Kiku a few questions, Michael straining to listen. Staccato clicks masked her accent, everything a jumble. He recognized his name, and then Kiku left them. She turned to address him, knowing a bit of English from her time in the city.

"You are a friend of Alijah's?"

"Yes. He asked me to teach Kiku English."

"Why?"

"I don't know. Many people speak my language—even you have learned some. I'm sure he believes it will be an advantage to him," Michael's answer rang hollow. He always assumed teaching Kiku English was a good idea, the natural step. Now he asked himself why. Had it been selfish? Wrong? No, it was necessary. The English tongues of the city were encroaching. It would give Kiku a better chance. Tza couldn't grasp that future. Michael had to believe learning was the better course. He was no longer thinking of Caroline.

"You speak our language?" Tza asked.

"A little," switching to Swahili. "Kiku has been very helpful."

"Is he going away?"

"I don't understand," Michael answered, back in English, fully understanding.

"Are you taking him with you?"

"It's up to Kiku. I don't know. I don't even know if Alijah knows. But I'll do as he wishes. It's not in my power. Do you understand?"

"Yes. You will leave him here. Today he becomes a man. He will be our chief."

Michael nodded, absorbing the gist of her admonition. He looked across the camp, Tza gazing toward Kiku quarreling with the other warriors. Michael could barely pick him out of the group of freshly bald men.

"They don't trust him because of you. Maybe after initiation he will be taken back. Go. You have already taken Alijah. Go!"

"Tell him I will always be his friend."

Tza nodded, and Michael slightly bowed. He moved toward the back, behind the elders, squatting on the ground to collect his thoughts. The music had started, and drums pounded his head. Faster and faster they beat, the boys-cum-men dancing themselves into a frenzy. A toothless man passed Michael a pipe, and he drew in a long breath. Next came a gourd, and he drank without hesitation.

He was not sure how long he had been dancing in a circle when amidst the sway, he sensed Tza's gaze. He squinted through the smoke and bodies. He felt dizzy, but no matter. He was flying. He could fall to the ground forever. He morphed into an eagle, soaring, his arms feathers. How long had he been leaping? The carnage of the butchered elephants below made him sick as he flew away, screeching with the wind. The shaman shook something in his face, then leapt away. The drums beat on. He lay on the ground, wet in the dung. Writhing, he slithered a snake. Hissing. The men were singing. The song somehow familiar. The roar of a lion mixed with the human scales. Bodies crashed to the ground rhythmically. The ground became a drum, being beat with sticks of legs. Pounding. Surging up, reverberating, then beat down again. Another surge, and Michael soared. The last beat knocked him out.

Michael woke up cold and alone. Tens of men lay quietly on the ground, contorted in the shapes in which they had fallen. His head was exploding. He wondered how long he could stand. When his sputtering stirred one of the men near him, Michael wobbled toward the village entrance. He watched the sun slowly rising, beautifully red on the horizon, a reflection of his eyes. A giraffe nibbled at a tree by his jeep and then loped away. Its silhouette against the rising sun froze Michael. It cast the most beautiful sight he had ever seen. The dreamscape burst when the throbbing came back. He climbed into his jeep and started back toward camp.

Michael thought about driving straight to Nairobi. He had told Caroline to expect him in a few days. A buzzing plane interrupted his planning. Warden James on patrol. Shit, he thought, remembering his promise. He saw the plane landing in the distance and changed direction to rendezvous with James. His mind was finally clearing. He had a water bottle in the car and drained it, trying to dilute the potion still surging through him. The morning chill lingered stubbornly, and he quivered from the water he spilled down his shirt.

Mist clung to the ground, and the careening car scared the dawn's animals off like fleeting shadows. A group of impalas sprung into the bushes, the image crystallizing the Africa of Michael's dreams. He cut his engine to watch, his path unexpectedly bringing him near a small pool— the morning watering hole. The wildebeest lowered their already depressed heads to drink next to the impalas. In the distant fog, three giraffes bent awkwardly for a drink.

Out of the corner of his eye, Michael saw a lion spring from the grasses, streaking full speed toward the helpless wildebeest. It closed the gap in mere breaths, eager to inhale death. The female lion sunk its teeth into the wildebeest, tearing at the animal's neck, both animals kicking and pulling with vicious power. Birds took to the sky in panic. The other animals fled in full gait, their hoofs kicking up clouds of dust replacing the rising mist. The commotion and hoots were tremendous. Michael grabbed his binoculars, watching a herd of elephants stampede off in the distance.

When he found the lioness again, it had ripped apart its prey. A bloody piece of meat stuck in her teeth. The lioness licked her mouth, circling the carcass and looking for scavengers. She bit into the wildebeest's neck and began dragging it off, searching for a quiet place to hide the prize and let her pride share in the wealth. When she plodded out of sight, Michael decided to follow, driving ten minutes around to a rise above the far side of the water, above the ground just trampled by the frightened elephants.

The savanna whispered again, grasses blowing gently, and from distant high ground, downwind, Michael watched the lion devour her catch. He stared mesmerized, able to imagine the smack of her jowls, though too far away to hear above the breeze.

Without warning, a shotgun blast echoed across the savanna, and Michael spun to search the ground below. Through his binoculars, he saw the plane in the distance. It was not James Oejo. A hundred yards away from the plane, three men marched toward a fallen rhinoceros that had been on its way to drink. It lay slumped on the ground, awaiting the machete to hack off its grand horn.

The animal courageously staggered to its feet, suddenly out of a daze. In great pain and enraged, it ran frantically. Straight toward Michael it charged, growing larger in his binoculars, but still more than a safe distance away. The men were chasing at full speed but losing ground. One of them stopped and took aim. Another shot shook the savanna, a group of monkeys hollering in the distant trees.

Michael paused to consider whether there could be any explanation other than poachers. Could it be a government trap and rescue unit? Could the animal be wounded, the shots trying to tranquilize it and help? No, he was pretty sure he recognized the rifles. These guns were not spewing benign projectiles. There appeared nothing benevolent about this chase. Once, he had accompanied Alijah on a training run, gathering in the cadence of men trying to dart innocent targets. They choreographed a different type of coordination, unhurried and studious, trying to coax their quarry into understanding they came as friends; there would be no killing, no targeting them as prey. By contrast, men approaching with slaughter in their eyes proved easy to spot. It was as if the whole ground stank.

The poacher's shot missed, and the rhino kept charging, now veering away from Michael, running along the base of the hill. The men kept coming too. Michael wiped his brow, wondering if this was another hallucination. What a morning! He felt nauseous but kept his eyes to the binoculars, following the rhino disappearing in and out of the grasses in the rolling hillside, then moving to find the men chasing forward. They appeared to be growing weary. It seemed they had lost the chase. They neared the edge of the hill where Michael hid, and he wondered whether to approach them. He was hidden in the fog, which shifted just enough to reveal their chase. In a few minutes, it would lift, and they might be able to spy his jeep.

He turned his gaze back toward the rhino. The grasses waft a thick screen, and the terrain dipped into shallow valleys where he looked down on the acacia tops. Scanning from left to right. Nothing. Back and forth; again, nothing. Back along the ridge. The rhino charged back at full speed! It was heading directly toward the men, but they could not see him. In a minute, the rhino would crest the rise, coming into full view. It would be an easy shot! Certain death! The rhino's head shook madly while it ran. A tank in the grass. Michael thrust a clip into his gun, released the safety, and crept down the hill, resting against a tree for balance. His head still throbbed, and the Uzi seemed to weigh more than he could bear. How could it happen again? "Why fucking me!" he mouthed. If he was going to shoot, he would need to take dead aim. Men like these were not easily scared off, and as soon as Michael pulled his trigger he would become their next target. There was no longer any doubt in his mind these were poachers: it was illegal to hunt rhinos. More than that, he had seen the machete.

The rhino came onto the rise, and Michael let go, spraying the poachers with bullets. They all fell, and as Michael dropped the gun to his side, he saw the rhino heading straight toward them. One was alive but unable to move. In a moment, he would be trampled to death. When the rhino neared, though, it veered off in a different direction, uninterested in the man. A nearsighted beast, it had not even seen the men until almost running them over. Michael wished it had.

With one of the poachers still writhing in pain, and the others likely dead, Michael debated his next move. He was no medic, plus it was impossible to tell if others may be lurking. He decided it best to drive back to the park and report everything to Warden James. The sun heralded midday before he found James Oejo and recounted the carnage. Stunned, yet cautiously buoyant, the Warden immediately dispatched a team to investigate and tend to any wounded. Another week would pass before Alijah boasted in the paper of killing Blake Roberts' gang. Alijah's association had continued profitably, but he never managed to forget their first encounter and shed no tears at their fate. He often thought about vengeance: how fortunate to have it carried out without having to dirty himself and how convenient to claim a victory. The relationship had now fulfilled its poisoned destiny, full circle.

True heroes, though, are hard to hide, and slowly the news about Michael began to leak around the park. It was time to head back to Nairobi for a while. Beyond his latest encounter, when he spoke to James the Warden continued to lament how not enough was being done to protect the animals. This time, though, James did not stop at venting his frustrations about Alijah. James was planning to launch a small, secretive anti-poaching unit of his own and floated the idea that Michael should join—even lead it. Michael wondered if that promised to be his calling. He could not explain how or why he had encountered and triumphed over another group of poachers. The timing, and his reactions, defied logic. The socio-biologist, schooled in reactions and predictability, grappled with the unpredictability of his own life.

Michael's radio picked up the Voice of America. He wondered if Kiku was listening. He hoped not. Bristling at the thought of Tza's warning, he stowed away his gun, wrapping it safely, and headed toward the city. The notion of becoming a vigilante hunting down poachers intrigued him. I just killed three more men, he reflected. It seemed impossible. No more, he silently vowed, fighting the urge but knowing it was a losing battle. He wanted to give James his gun but acknowledged the futility of his wish. Destiny plucked him to be the animals' protector, laws of man be damned. Maybe he should double down, even go to Ron Easton for a reward. No, better yet, Alijah, and give James the money to fund a team. How could this be a one-person job? He would lobby for the right to kill poachers. His head still hurt like hell. Michael passed a deserted Maasai camp off the road—they had moved further away from the city. Would Kiku's village pick up and relocate someday? He could still hear the drumming.

Caroline had invited Michael to stay at their guesthouse, and at midnight she was looking out her bedroom window in that direction. She missed camping in the bush where there were no clocks chiming that threshold marking a new day. She saw no lights, and laid back down fully dressed. Kicking off her shoes, flinging them to far corners, she closed her eyes; they refused to obey, not yielding to sleep, fitfully adjusting to the night. The gray room gradually grew brighter, and she could now make out the outline of her dresser and the Renoir poster above it. Actual light would reveal a rosy-cheeked girl whirling in a dance step, a man's face slighted by the perspective highlighting her smile.

The room pulsed almost bright enough now to study the girl, and Caroline punched at her pillow, plunging her face deep into the feathers. Moments later, she flopped over, facing the ceiling. Her pulse raced, the room suffocating. She threw off her dress, laying back down. It seemed bright as day. Only a few minutes had ticked into tomorrow.

Once more, she tried closing her eyes and, recognizing she would fail, jumped up and pulled her dress back on. She dismissed any attempt to button the back and glided down the staircase, stepping outside and gently closing the back door. One of the dogs barked at the noise, and she whispered his name, letting him know who slunk. The moonlight cast enough of a glow to illuminate the path to the guesthouse. Just as she approached, she stepped on a thorn, exclaiming in pain.

A flashlight lit her from the doorway. Michael stood bare-chested, his trousers unbuttoned.

"Ouch," Caroline grimaced, plucking the thorn from the ball of her left foot. "I can't believe I've got to sneak around like this in my own house."

"Well, your mother," he began before he swallowed the rest of his sentence. Despite the tumultuous events of recent days, Michael had constantly thought of Caroline. How could he be head over heels? Falling in love with a beautiful woman of a different class (no titled!) and country was borderline crazy; indeed, no more rational than events confounding the balance of his life. Still, he could not deny his feelings. Dwelling on the odds of their relationship continuing, looking to cushion any fall, Michael tried convincing himself he was simply lonely. Loneliness and convenience lay the cornerstone of enough other romances. If only he could deny Caroline on these grounds, he could walk away and avoid the inevitable pain. Once again, he was fighting the urge to escape.

Caroline's arrival melted Michael's insecurities. Squeezing her closer, he remembered how much he yearned to be with her. He wanted to suspend time just holding her, closing his eyes, and drifting. His body relaxed. No more energy would be wasted erecting barriers to soften rejection. This was not merely opportunistic nor escapist. Michael throbbed commitment. With the power of a revelation, Michael finally accepted his good fortune.

Caroline found herself struggling with similar emotions. What she tried to dismiss as an impulse, a remedy for loneliness, even a cliché rebound, had become more than she wanted. More frightening, it now kindled more than she understood. Whether trying to coax a buffer to provide some distance or rationalize away her feelings, her denials burst. She too was falling in love. Like Michael, she fought to push back, only to plunge forward helplessly. Finally giving in, it was the most glorious feeling she had ever experienced.

Their embrace no longer warding off the night's chill, they moved inside where Caroline lit a candle, walking its halo to the bed. She acknowledged the recklessness of lighting a flame in a thatched building, but she wanted to see him. She canvassed his scratched and bruised body—skin tattooed with miniature red zippers, twisted into painful shapes, testifying to life in the bush. Before the night ended, she kissed every one and more. When they woke, Michael joked Caroline should marry him, and they should run away to a continent where nobody knew them. How about the jungles of Brazil? Brazil no, but she knew if they continued and he posed the question properly, she would say yes.

The emotions of her fiasco in England cut raw, but the adoration of being so desperately wanted and cared about countered, making her tingle. She felt safe curling up in Michael's grasp, relishing the warmth.

He was the only person for whom she let her guard fully down, secure enough to act with playful immaturity.

Michael longed for the moment to similarly relax his barriers, confiding the whole truth about his guns and scratches. James had convinced him to go on another mission, the thorn bush providing their only cover. Though reluctant to admit it, he looked forward to taking the war to the poachers. Christ, he was almost itching to shoot another gang. Maybe he should simply trust Caroline and discuss an invitation James was lobbying him to accept.

That next night over dinner, Michael decided to open up. Selectively. He was still uncomfortable discussing all the details; even going back and forth in his own mind, he could hardly fathom everything that had happened. "Can I talk to you about something serious?"

"Of course."

"When I shot those poachers with the warden, it wasn't the only time. I've run across others out in the bush. They've got to be stopped. It's unconscionable what they do to the animals."

"No disagreement here. I think you know that. Protecting animals sort of goes hand in hand with being a vet. But I'm not following. How many times have you run into poachers?"

"That's not the point. Come on, I've shot people," skirting any description of his most recent escapade. The details would come out soon enough. "Some would say that's unconscionable too…There's a fine line. Well, maybe not a fine line."

"Michael, it was self-defense. You're too hard on yourself. What were you supposed to do?"

"Self-defense of who? Me or the animals?"

"Does it matter? Michael, what's this really all about?"

He caught himself before launching into a diatribe about the ethics of hunting generally; no reason to start questioning Richard's going after big game for sport and thrust family into the debate. It was the wanton killing for profit that he wanted to help James thwart. To Michael, the poachers' actions were simply criminal. He would leave sport and permits for another day.

"Oddly, I'm not struggling as much with what I've done as what to do next. James wants me to help train an anti-poaching unit. Actually, a bit of a clandestine unit. Seems Alijah's berated him for some of our actions, saying he's upstaging him. Stick to his job as Warden. But James doesn't trust Alijah, thinks he might be up to something. And doesn't really see him taking it to the poachers. Says everything he does is for show. I don't know. Guess natural friction within a bureaucracy. Anyway, James is going to try a new approach. Rather than monitor, they'll be more proactive. And with James, that means no limits, do whatever's necessary. Hunt them down if he has to. The way he put it to me, hell if he's going to wait around for those assholes to come into the park and kill his animals. And, he wants me to be a part. Actually, he'd love me to lead it."

Caroline's eyes widened, "What? Do you really want to get involved with all that? You'd be right in the middle of political crossfire. And gunfire. It all sounds pretty dangerous." Realizing Michael was stepping out on a limb to confide in her, seeking support as much as candor, she blew out her cheeks before softening her tone. "Hmm. It's complicated, tricky. You'd be crossing a lot of lines. But also, it's quite an endorsement asking you…" After taking a deep breath, she continued, "You've clearly been thinking about it, and the risks are obvious, so I'm not going to beat you over the head. I guess the real question is, do you want to do it? I assume you're leaning that way or wouldn't have brought it up."

"I think so. I mean, I want to help. I'm not inclined to lead anything, and obviously don't want to get shot at. I'm still here for my research. But I believe in what James is building, not just sitting back—and I understand we may need to work outside the lines to get the job done." Michael looked at Caroline pleadingly, willing to break the rules yet somehow not quite okay labeling the unit's actions vigilantism. "I'm okay with the risks. Going forward, I just don't want to be in the spotlight. Everything's happened so quickly. I got caught in the bush, confronting poachers in the act, and did what anyone would do. I think."

"Not anyone, Michael," letting the words sit. "Look, if this is what you want, I'll support you. I'm not sure if that's what you wanted to hear. But there it is—and I mean it, I'm not being bullied into agreeing. The reality is people have already heard about what you did. It's not like you're still in the shadows, even if you want to be. Now it's a choice not a reaction. Do you want to help or not?"

"It's not that simple."

"Out in the bush, it is. That's Africa. No time to ponder academic what if's. If you're looking for encouragement, not just support, then I think you should accept." Taking his hand, "I'd be proud of you. Just promise me you'll be careful. Really careful."

Michael looked at Caroline, wondering if he would be acting to cement winning her heart or to save the animals. Maybe both. Not unlike the dilemma of whether he had acted in self-defense or to protect the animals. Why did he crave straight lines? Couldn't he simply be happy if goals aligned? Not if a little killing was sprinkled in the mix.

"Really careful," Michael pledged.

•　　•　　•　　•　　•

Still wrestling with the implications, yet emboldened by Caroline's encouragement, Michael drove with Warden James for his first training session with the James's new anti-poaching unit. James had vowed to act under the radar, keeping this group largely off-the-books. He had authority to police the parks, but not go out and shoot poachers willy-nilly. Most of the time he could pass their patrols off as routine. When they took down poachers, though, he would need to control chatter. Equally important, if they captured anyone, he would have to turn the poachers over to someone he could trust—and who could quietly deal with them while disguising the unit's bolder motives. Not keen for Alijah to get wind of his exploits, James was still working on finding men he could absolutely trust. It would not be easy.

"We're really going to do this?" Michael asked.

"Of course. I'm already doing this. My job," James chuckled. "Did you think I was joking? And you're here, right?"

Sighing, "Right. But this isn't what I signed up for. I came to study baboons."

"Which you keep reminding me. But let me remind you: you're still studying baboons. I'm not changing your career. I want you to keep your fancy degrees—they help my pitch. And let me remind you of something else. A true motivator! I'm not paying you. You fool!" James roared with laughter.

"Not much of the smooth recruiter. I can back out before I start, you know. I'm still not over shooting those poachers."

"I know. But would you rather they kill the animals? How would you feel if your baboon troop got caught in the crossfire and were wiped out?"

"Poachers aren't going after baboons."

"Not the point."

"I know. I'm just not…well, no easy way to say it. A killer. But I want to help."

"Then help! Clearly, you want to, or you wouldn't be on your way with me to help train this anti-poaching force. It's time we got serious, take the war to the poachers. Build a team that will be feared. You've seen what we're up against firsthand and what it takes. So, let's see how today goes. You'll be back with your baboons by nightfall."

"Just as long as this doesn't become a daily thing. I can't neglect my research." Searching for an elusive middle ground, though knowing that was wishful thinking, "Maybe I can just help out with emergencies."

"They're always emergencies," James retorted, an edge to his voice, not wanting Michael to succumb to his fears.

"Well, I mean real emergencies."

"They're always real emergencies."

Shaking his head, Michael said, "I'll do what I can. I'm in. I'm just not sure I can be all in."

Their approach to the training site spared Michael further justification. Ten men were gathered in a clearing, standing to attention when James's car came to a stop. Michael immediately pegged the group as a ragtag force. Maybe that's how militias started? What was this group anyway, he began wondering, looking at a distant shooting range and a small campfire beside a bunkhouse.

Sensing Michael's discomfort, Warden James turned to Michael before getting out of the car. "This isn't easy for any of us. Look at those men closely. We're about to send them into danger. They could be shot or killed. And for what? To save a rhino? I don't want these men developing second thoughts. I need them committed. I'm paying them, but not enough. If you're reluctant, they'll sense it." Pausing and staring directly at Michael, "How are my recruiting skills now? Stay in the car or get out. But if you get out, you have to be all in. At least in the cause. I can't have these men doubting."

Getting out of the car first, James looked back through the open window, softening, "Michael, I need you. We need you. You're the inspirational weapon I've needed for a long time. These men have heard what you've done. You're a hero whether you want to be one or not. Everyone here knows how you've taken things into your own hands to do the right thing. I'm taking a big risk. Hell, we're all taking a big risk. But think about it. Think about how much easier is will be for them to follow someone that's said fuck it, let's stop those bastards. And then picks up his gun to go do it again."

James closed his door, and Michael watched the warden stride over to the men, shaking hands and slapping a couple on the back. "Shit," Michael mumbled, thinking back to his conversation with Caroline and pulling himself out of the car. He began walking to join his new brethren, gaining strength with each step forward, seeing the men staring at him in awe. Michael had been focusing on his own reluctance—to be fair weakness—and further belittled himself as an outsider. As he said to James, he was just a researcher. Worse, an Ivy League brat. What was he doing here? Yet these men viewed him from a radically different perspective. Being regaled with Michael's exploits, he was a brave hero. More than that, he was a warrior who came from a place none of them could fathom, and had come to help, to lead a crusade to protect the animals from wicked men who sought to rape their land of its most precious resource. He sucked inspiration from their gaze. Maybe there was a mythic middle ground.

Their initial exercises were straightforward, if not startling, regarding just how much work there was to transform this unit into an effective force. None of the men had used binoculars before, and James asked Michael to lead a first lesson on surveillance by demonstrating how to adjust the focus. After Michael explained the basics, he walked two hundred paces and held up different fingers, each man in turn identifying his signal with their new magnifying tool. The power to see so clearly into the distance was mind-blowing. By the time they had finished learning rudimentary signals to communicate and take turns with target practice, the men were radiating confidence.

Michael was impressed with the team's transformation in just a few hours. "James, I have to hand it to you. You're an outstanding leader."

"Ha! Don't be fooled. We have a lot of work to do. These men can all track, and the fighting skills will come. The real challenge will be when these men see how much they're out-armed. Some will probably defect. We need to work hard to motivate and train a core group we can trust. That's where I'll lean on you."

"What do you mean?"

"They look up to you. You symbolize the cause. They have to believe they're on a mission. As I said, be willing to do whatever it takes—even if that means sometimes not following the rules."

Michael looked at James and nodded. Fate had handed him this opportunity, and Caroline was right that he now had a choice. He would not let her down. He would not let any of them down—the animals in poachers' sights, his baboons, or his professors. How to pull it all off was for tomorrow.

·   ·   ·   ·   ·

A few weeks later, Caroline convinced her mother to go riding while leaving Michael to trek into town to visit the wildlife office and buy supplies. He was now a regular visitor. She warned him to be careful talking to Ron Easton. Ron and his grotty teeth had pressed himself on her once again at the celebrity fundraiser. She rebuffed him for what she hoped, but doubted, would be the last time. Caroline dreamed that he might act maturely, not taking revenge against her on Michael; yet, she remained wary, stingy with trust. That shield of cloaking intuition enabled her to grow self-assured in such a belittling environment. Once again, her instincts proved correct.

Preparing to meet with Michael, Ron rolled out maps of the zone where Michael was conducting his research. There was nothing like the power of being in charge of permits. At the game lodge bar, James had bragged to Alijah how he and Michael took down a group of poachers. At the time, Alijah pretended delight, though admonishing the Warden to leave enforcement to the proper anti-poaching team. As soon as Alijah was free of James' boasting, he sought Richard's counsel. There were whispers that may not have been the only time Michael was engaged in more than research. A hero in the midst bode danger for business. Kiku and Caroline complicated matters for both men, leaving Ron as the natural choice to carry out any plot compromising Michael. Richard had little doubt Ron would relish the role.

Although he suspected the matter would inevitably arise, Ron was surprised by Richard's urgency in broaching the subject: "Ron, we've got to do something about Michael. He's become a loose cannon."

"Interesting choice of words."

"You know what I mean. Bugger all, I'd like to get my hands on that gun. All his guns."

"I thought you were more worried about his crusading. He's really working with the wardens to train patrols? And if those rumors are true, isn't that Alijah's business? Can't he control it?" Ron asked.

"Alijah's says it's all true. At least that's what he hears. And yes, he could put a stop to it. But for now, it's all just a nuisance. Alijah's taking credit for everything. It's his cover of sorts. Hell, I haven't slept so well as since they accidentally got rid of Blake Roberts. I never trusted that wanker. I'm just worried it might spread. They start patrolling the ports and other parks like that, we've got a real problem."

"Sounds like he's got guts. I wouldn't have guessed it. Too bad we can't turn him to take his guns and come work with us," Ron half-joked, recognizing the value and almost selfishly willing to swallow his pride regarding Caroline.

"Ha! Wish I could float a suggestion, but honestly no chance. He's a crusader to the core, believes in what he's doing. I'll give him that. I'd rather squeeze him a little, keep him in his place. We ought to be able to use him to our advantage. Alijah's son is his guide—well, you know that better than anyone. Anyway, he trusts us. I don't think he has a clue we're on to them. And damn, I think my stepdaughter's in love with him. Thinks he's the bee's knees. It's not like we can just get rid of him or tell him what we're doing. Let's string him out for his permits—that was a good suggestion. Maybe it'll lead to something. We've got to keep him from letting this all go to his head. All we need is some celebrity vigilante knocking-off poachers."

"I'd hardly call him a celebrity," Ron bristled.

"He's a Harvard connected American virtually living with a woman from a titled family and buddies with the warden of an internationally famous game park. He gets invited to the same benefits we do. He's poised to bring us all down. I'm not going to give him that chance."

"Don't you think you're being a little paranoid? I've known him from the day he arrived here. He's just a glorified biologist."

"Good, then let's keep him to that until I can figure out another angle. I've got enough to worry about. Nazuto's upping the take on Alijah again."

"Don't worry. I'll take care of everything. Just play along."

•  •  •  •  •

Oblivious to Ron's scheming, Caroline set out on her ride, coaxing her horse up a nearby ridge to rendezvous with her mother. She knew the destination by heart, finding Julia atop a crest providing a perfect lookout over the distant city. They hitched the horses to a tree and took out a picnic lunch packed into their saddlebags. Smushed sandwiches and black-current teas in hand, they spread out a quilted blanket and looked toward Nairobi Park in the far horizon. Julia never liked these picnics. She sat uncomfortably, not keen on fussing over nature and sitting down to dinner with the ants. Caroline, in contrast, was at home cross-legged on the turf, forcing Julia to acquiesce, seeing her daughter so happy.

Jelly smudged over her lip, Caroline asked, "Mom, what do you think about Michael? I mean, do you like him?"

"Yes, he seems pleasant," articulating each syllable of her few words and then biting into a piece of lettuce with a crisp crackle. "I don't know much about his background."

"Well, he isn't a Keeton if that's what you're implying. But he is very successful. He went to Harvard and even had a scholarship."

"Your father took me to see Harvard row one year. They didn't win, but they did make it exciting. I remember lots of splashing."

Caroline shook her head. "Mommy, you're incredible."

"Whatever makes you happy, dear. Just remember that if you're thinking about something more serious, you're not an ordinary girl. You're a Dunning and a Keeton! That's something. Your stepfather is about to become a member of the House of Lords and your father was the ambassador to Kenya. Oh, I can't bear thinking about what happened to Nigel. Thank goodness Richard came around. He was so kind to me when your father died."

"I know the story," Caroline interrupted in an annoyed tone.

"You shouldn't think so little of your new father. He's quite an important man back in England, you know."

"Mom, we're not in England, and we've been through this a thousand times. He's very kind to me. There's just part of him I don't trust. I have my reasons... What does it matter...As long as you're happy," she said to avoid another silly quarrel.

"I'm just trying to remind you that you're not a typical young woman, and you should think twice before becoming involved with an ordinary researcher, especially one needing a scholarship," Julia said, quietly munching and watching for ants.

"Well, I hope Michael doesn't know as much about genetics as he claims because that's one area I think I want to stay ignorant about." She huffed as she got up, picking up the blanket and heading for her horse. "You know, Mom, I don't even know why I try anymore."

Caroline galloped off, frustration coursing through her as she kicked her horse into another gear, hoping the rush of the air would clear her mind. Her memories of her father were vague. She remembered being so afraid watching him weaken, fighting bouts of malaria and other fevers. When healthy, he always seemed to be away, flying to England to visit people she never met. She tried to suppress the trauma of the one flight from which he never came home. Given distances, hopping from one place to another in a small plane was as routine in Africa as taking a bus; sadly, too, perishing in a plane crash was common enough to be considered a natural cause of death.

When she was a little girl, he would always bring her gifts from his travels. Caroline could vividly remember waiting to hear the noise of his approaching car. Somehow, she could identify it miles away, feline senses on loan. When the car neared their driveway, she would run to the front door, standing at the threshold waiting to see it turn the corner past the bushes. He would have his driver honk the horn as soon as they saw her; then, the moment the car stopped, she would dash full speed and jump into his arms.

He had a grand mustache and adored tickling her with it. One year he returned from a trip with a beard, but it foretold a trick. When she went to pull it, the hairs came off, and she tore crying into the house screaming for her mother. He just stood there laughing. She refused to talk to him until after dinner when he gave her a beautiful gold necklace with a tiny gold pendant. The pendant bore an inscription so small that he took out a magnifying glass, where to her delight she read the words: "To Caroline. Love Daddy." The inscription had faded, now so worn only she could trace the words. She tugged at it, reassuring herself it was still there. She put it on at his funeral and had worn it ever since. It would always be a piece beyond the jeweler's clutches, no matter how high the price of gold may climb.

Why did she cherish his memory so? They never knew each other well. His schedule had always been hectic, and when he spent time at home, guests were inevitably buzzing around. Still, he doted on his children, proud of showing her and Kent off to his friends. Could she be infatuated with him because she now appreciated how famous he was? Ambassador Nigel Dunning. Maybe it was because she struggled with her mother so much. Almost mystically, his presence still hovered, casting a cloud over what Caroline wanted to do and what she ought to do. Reminiscing how he taught her to horseback ride, she hardly noticed a beautiful orange bird emerge from a stand of trees and alight on a branch as she galloped past.

Riding became their magic time. She won all the equestrian trophies in her age bracket growing up. He taught her how to speak to horses, stroke the mare or colt, and kick them with her heel. He always claimed she would become the best polo player at the club because she kicked so well! "Lots of spunk in those heels," he would joke. He was right, she thought. Caroline spied the stables in the distance, slowing to a canter.

He used to love the stables. That was his escape. Whenever she could not find him, he would be out there tending to the horses, talking to them as if they could understand. Sometimes she would sneak up to the door and hide just to listen to what he was saying. Usually, he would advise something silly like: "I'd get you a Kleenex if you were only a person," to a snorting horse, and she could not contain her giggles. He would burst around the corner and pick her up, shaking her about while smiling and making fun of her sneaking up on him. This is where she came to love horses and no doubt where the seeds of her becoming a veterinarian grew. He would be so proud of her career. She smiled and dismounted, stroking her horse's nose as she led him to into the barn.

Her brother worshiped their father. When Kent regaled Nigel Dunning to other people, Caroline would sometimes look at him, wondering whether he was talking about the same person she knew. How can age make such a difference, she thought, stopping in front of the stall. Her brother was five years older and, for most of her life, lived somewhere else. For a while, when he attended Eaton and they lived in London, she saw him frequently - her big brother, always teasing her. There was a lot of chasing, and then suddenly everything changed.

One day her father announced he received Her Majesty's appointment. She was moving with her parents to Africa, leaving Kent behind in England. From that point onwards, she and Kent saw each other infrequently. Gathering only for holidays, the intimacy of family dissipated, relationships becoming forced; just when there was enough time to start bonding again, school breaks ended, and Kent flew back. Phone connections to Kenya were often spotty and sometimes Caroline would go for months only communicating with her brother via letters—which themselves took so long to arrive that any news posted was likely outdated by the time the letters were read. Hence, her horses became young Caroline's best friends.

Leading to more disruption, her local schooling in Africa was mediocre, so her father insisted on sending her to prep school for a year. More flights, more distance, until her mother, in a rare redeeming act, demanded Caroline stay at home. For her part, Caroline was thrilled to be close to her horses.

By the time she matriculated at the Sorbonne, Kent was in his final year of legal training, school a mere stepping stone to a diplomatic post. He was, after all, among the privileged lot. His adult life settled quickly, continuing to date Ann, his college sweetheart. After attending university, Ann began working as an editor for her father's economic journal. Caroline could never remember its name and was lucky to remember Ann's. She had only met her twice before Kent married her. During Caroline's first year in college, they visited her once in France; she returned the favor, making the crossing to see them at Oxford. The meeting was very formal. Caroline always felt Ann was intimidated by her because Caroline was so much prettier. Then there was the ultimate slight. Though she could never prove it, Caroline believed Kent forced Ann to make her maid of honor. In petty revenge, after looking straight at Caroline, Ann tossed her bouquet the other direction.

After their wedding, and in no small part thanks to his last name, Kent gained a junior diplomatic post in New Delhi. The job was an apprenticeship of sorts, the first step on a typical path for those leapfrogging the traditional foreign service training. Apparently, he was doing quite well, continuing to advance. It was over five years now, his most recent letter indicating he planned to stay for another one or two. Kent had two children already, yet she had only met one, the youngest boy, Denholm Scott Dunning.

Caroline walked back to the house, deciding to telephone Kent, the memories jogged at the stables calming her down from the spat with her mother. She did not pause to wonder what time it was in India. That would spoil the impulse. Plus, getting the call placed from Nairobi to New Delhi was miracle enough, regardless of whether it proved inconvenient on the other end. No miracles presently, the operator explaining why she could not make the call. The lines might be free later. They would ring her when the call was ready if she liked. Reluctantly, Caroline assented.

The call never made it through; later, she received a telex from Kent, briefly noting he was off on some mission and would try her on returning. In fact, over a month passed before he was able to reach her, the delay a blessing. By the time he called back, she was engaged. Again.

The day Michael said he was heading to the ministry, he had not met Ron but instead walked around the city thinking about his future. He recalled joking about proposing, but rather than dismissing the idea, let the notion percolate. Carpe diem—why wait months or years? Life is short, and people get shot around here. Michael resolved to press more formally when the time was right. A mere couple of weeks later while visiting in the library, Michael dropped to his knee and told Caroline he was not going back to his camp without her. He rose, nearly knighted, and most definitely betrothed.

Breaking the news to Julia and Richard, they were spared an awkward moment by the ringing of the telephone. Caroline had tried calling Kent before sitting down with Richard and Julia, hoping to reach him first. Once again, she struggled with the lines and was forced to leave a message. This time, though, Kent was home. Upon receiving the message, he convinced the operator to stay on the line and dial straight back. Grabbing the return call, Caroline bubbled the news. Awash in her excitement, Kent congratulated his sister, genuinely happy. His wishes granted Caroline the approval he knew she desperately wanted, intuiting their mother's reluctance. That intangible bond they did share. Michael next took the phone while watching Caroline approach her mother. Julia meekly uttered congratulations, pecking her on the cheek. Richard, uncharacteristically, moved over, giving her an enveloping hug.

"I'm so happy for you. I'd always recommend an academic over a playboy," Richard teased.

Caroline hugged him back, almost overcome. Perhaps this was the moment when he would become a true father to her, when he finally started to care beyond the obligatory. It was not, though, the moment of redemption she relished. In her heart, she still did not unquestionably trust him. Caroline was relieved when she and Michael could retire for the night—together and independent for the first time.

The newly committed couple finally emerged from the guesthouse, week-old errands beckoning. Caroline began sorting through some chemistry notes for her studies, bewildered by the composition of the latest vaccines. Michael, in turn, focused on paperwork for new radio collars to track his baboons.

Sensing the beginnings of a good streak and soon collecting his collars, Michael now drove to pick up the requisite documents from Ron Easton. As he pulled up to the ministry, he was surprised to bump into Jack Whitehead. Rumors about Whitehead losing his job to Easton were circulating, but everyone was close-mouthed about the reasons. Evidently, Jack decided to leave the funding offices for a local advisory post in the ministry itself. He was too valuable a resource to let go, and the government judged he was best on their side. At least for the moment.

Michael could not help noticing Whitehead's weight gain, watching Jack's expression sour as the former minister's cheeks rippled out with a cough. Clearly Whitehead was under stress, Michael thought, as he walked up and said, "Jack, good to see you! It's been forever."

"Too long. Where've you been?"

"You're the first to know. I haven't even gotten through to home. Caroline Dunning and I are engaged!"

"Congratulations, that's great," his enthusiasm somewhat tempered. "So, a noble's marrying a local hero. Sounds almost like a movie."

"What are you talking about, hero?"

"Come on, you don't think I know what you've been up to? You've done what I've been hoping to do for years. The poachers, for God's sake!"

"Jack, none of it's been planned. It all just happened. Anyone would have done the same thing. And I've been trying to keep it quiet. I've killed people! I could be sent to prison for life. Even shot myself."

"Bollocks. I bet you'd do it all over again given another chance. In fact, I hear you have. You have it in you, or you don't."

Michael said, "Maybe. I guess. There wasn't much choice. At least there didn't seem to be."

"Well, it shouldn't be illegal, I'll tell you that. I've never had much inspiration here, never had to work for anything. This job was partly to pass the time. Make me feel important. Maybe do some good. But what you've done. My God! If this were five hundred years ago, you'd become the patron saint of the elephant or something. Keep it up. Let me know how I can help."

"Now you're getting carried away."

"Well, I mean to. I wanted to give you a pep talk 'cause I've also got some bad news."

"What?"

"I take it you don't know?"

"Know what? Let's have it, Jack. You look like a ghost. What's wrong?"

"Michael, I've tried to help you out when I could. And I'll do whatever I can now."

"Come on, already, it can't be that bad."

"It's the permits," Jack began.

"What permits?" Michael asked, growing anxious. Whitehead led him to his office, asking him to sit down, closing the door behind them. That morning the agency had decided to revoke Michael's camping permit in the game park. The decision would effectively put an end to his research since he would not be able to follow his troop. He would be but a tourist. His privileges of camping, carrying a gun, and walking in the preserve would all be eliminated. The inability to leave his rover and observe the troop on foot would cripple his research. Without camping permits he could not even stay in the park! His guns had become suspect, but now he would be tracked. To continue helping James, he would have to go underground, truly underground, and that was asking too much. This was not his country! His days of meting out vigilante justice for the animals would be over.

Even from the most optimistic viewpoint, his research would be kaput. Without a work permit, his visa to stay in the country would lapse. His mind reeled to whether Caroline was a Kenyan citizen and whether that would let him stay. He was engaged to her but had no idea whether she was British or Kenyan. His hunch was the former, and when asking, he would find it to be a good guess. Some, like Jack Whitehead, benefitted from dual citizenship, but being the daughter of a former ambassador made achieving that status challenging.

Michael stared at Whitehead, stunned. "Why?"

"I don't know. Judging from personal experience, it's just one of those things. Rubbed the wrong person the wrong way. Ultimately, we're outsiders, Michael. They've got us by the balls and can do anything they want. You saw where honesty got me. I was demoted, lucky not to be fired."

"Why wasn't I told? Given a chance?"

"I don't know. I didn't even know about it until late this morning. Ron Easton —you know what Ron's like— gave me a call telling me he had just approved some paperwork for your new equipment, plus the next tranche of your grant money, and then regretted it. Said there was a lot of political pressure. Higher-ups weren't keen on tourists shooting people, even if justified. Then he passed it off like it was nothing and asked me about, oh, I don't remember. I wasn't listening too closely after that."

"You think Ron's behind this?"

"That's my bet. Don't underestimate him. He's got powerful friends around here, and at some point, these things now need his stamp. Look at me."

Michael slammed his fist down on the table. "We'll get him back. This is bullshit." His eyes glared, thanking Jack and telling him he would figure out what happened. It must be a mistake. He would talk to Richard and Alijah if that were necessary. Michael promised to keep Jack advised before storming out.

Twenty-five minutes later, he was banging on Ron Easton's office, ready to strangle whoever was behind the door. Unfortunately, a secretary informed Michael that Ron left on a business trip to the coast and would be away for four or five days. Michael began to leave his telephone number, then changed his mind after seeing a copy of the day's paper on the edge of the woman's desk. Ron's smiling mug was just below the fold on the front page, a headline touting his new position. A note was paper-clipped to the side, but Michael was unable to decipher the scribble before Ron's secretary snatched it away. She knew Ron wanted to keep his relationship with the editor private; she had once overheard him offering the man a free safari in return for highlighting Ron in an article. Michael watched the woman place the paper in a drawer, guessing she was somehow complicit in however Ron undermined Jack Whitehead. Frustrated, he pivoted to leave, debating where to go next.

On his way out, the solution hit him: Richard Keeton. Surely his new father-in-law, or at least father-in-law-to-be, would help him. He knew Richard and Easton were friends, plus he would have to side with his daughter. If not, they were gone. Or at least he was gone. Michael now began wondering whether Richard was in on it too. What a perfect plan to get rid of him if they disapproved of the marriage! He knew Julia was not in favor, but everything Richard had done seemed to indicate he approved. On reflection, he thought about Caroline puzzling over why Richard was recently so receptive and caring, being so much kinder, and showering her with money and gifts. Maybe he was just setting her up, deluding her with his favor while laying the blame on Ron Easton. After all, what did Ron care? He got jilted anyway.

Michael turned the ignition: time to search for Richard. His gambit was risky, but if Richard was on Easton's side, it might not matter. Michael could only gain some respect for figuring out the plot. What else could they do to him? On the other hand, if Richard was not involved, he might be the only person who could help. Michael had few high-level contacts. For months, he struggled to get his grant money, then boasted about his new source. Finally, a friend in high places. How could that person have turned out to be Ron Easton?!

Vaguely remembering Richard's mentioning he would be at the Polo Club, Michael decided that was his best bet. If Richard were not there, Michael would drive home and wait for him. Possibly Julia may know something. Michael's adrenaline was pumping hard. His mind racing through what he should say when confronting Richard, the distance evaporated into thought. He was at the gate.

Ron, in fact, had not traveled to the coast. The proud and recently promoted Minister Easton sat alone with Richard on the third bleacher step, chatting while watching a few patrons practice on the field. Ron had been bragging about the flattering articles highlighting his new role, and was surprised when Richard chastised him; seems Richard thought too much publicity could turn a spotlight on their activities. Easy for Richard to turn down press, Ron inwardly fumed. Perhaps he would feel differently if not married to the former Ambassador's wife and about to inherit a lordship. Ron needed to seize his advantage when he could. Best for the moment, though, not to mention the radio interview he set for that evening. The spell of tension between the men was broken by the sound of an approaching car. The club's long driveway called attention to any vehicle driving up, Michael's approach conspicuous.

Michael did not notice Ron until he was already out of his car and in the midst of rehearsing his appeal to Richard. Rattled, pausing to reassess his approach, Michael felt a twinge of pain pull at his stomach. Extra moments, though, could not solve this predicament.

"Good afternoon, Michael," Richard called out, looking ever the part out of an Abercrombie and Kent catalog. "I was just telling Ron the good news about you and Caroline."

"Yes, congratulations," Ron guardedly said. "You're a very lucky man. I'm the first to admit I'm mighty jealous of you." He forced a chuckle, slapping Richard on the back.

Michael wondered whether just one of them or both were lying. He walked up, standing on the ground as they sat on the steps, eye level with him, Easton's feet dangling down close enough for Michael to bite if he wished. Ron's blotchy skin kept Michael from inching closer. He really was a crude animal. And animals should not wear ascots, especially in the burning sun.

"I suppose you've heard the bad news too, then," Michael said, knowing Easton was at fault if he feigned ignorance.

"No, what are you talking about?" Richard asked, looking first to Michael and then to Ron.

When Ron shrugged his shoulders a bit, looking toward Michael, Michael grew angry, bellowing at Ron, "You know what I'm talking about! What the hell do you think you're doing?"

"Michael. Look lad, I think you need to calm down," Ron casually responded.

Michael could barely contain himself. Moving to strike Easton, he held back, backhanding him across the legs to get his attention and vent his outrage. "My research permits. You had them revoked, didn't you? Why?"

"Ah. I just heard about that. I'm sorry. But it wasn't me. That sort of thing is managed at a different section of the ministry. I'm dealing with conservation, park matters, but academic grants go through a different division. I suppose everything eventually crosses my desk, but I'm not in the weeds. I can look into it and try to set this straight. Doesn't seem to make a lot of sense. But please believe me. I didn't have anything to do with that. Gentleman's word."

"The hell you didn't!" Michael could not contain himself.

"I don't need this." Ron rose, gesturing a wave to Richard and turning back to Michael, inwardly enjoying the ruse: "Cheers, Richard. Michael, I'll talk to you when you're rational. Please calm down." Ron turned, climbing up the steps to the clubhouse bar without looking back at Michael.

Richard Keeton glared at his future son-in-law and barked, "What do you think you're doing, insulting one of my friends to my face like that? And a government minister no less."

"I know what you're thinking. Please let me try to explain before you get more upset. All I know is this morning on a routine errand, Jack Whitehead told me that my permits had been revoked. He got a call from Ron the other day asking him why they hadn't told him they were going to do this before he approved my money. He's lying through his teeth. He talked to Whitehead this morning, and to my face, right here in front of you, so you can't deny it, he pretends not to know anything about it!"

Regaining his breath, Michael continued: "I think he set up the whole thing. He's jealous of Caroline and me. It all fits. There's no way they would revoke my license. Whitehead didn't have any idea why, and that type of thing always went through him. He may not have the official position, but he hears things. People still seek his counsel... I haven't offended anyone over there. Someone's setting me up."

"Don't you think you're jumping to conclusions?"

"What am I to him?" Michael asked. "He gets to take something out on Caroline, exercise pent-up spite, I don't know. And maybe he's even trying to retrieve the grant money he gave me. It's his word against mine. If he gets any of that money back, he can just keep it and claim he gave it to me."

"Look, there's obviously some type of misunderstanding, and I don't know what it is. Go home, think about it, try to make more sense out of it. I'll talk to Ron and ...well, we'll see." Richard turned his head toward the field and smirked. His brilliantly white hair glowed in the sun as he shifted his attention to the horses on the field.

•　　•　　•　　•　　•

Michael and Caroline lay snuggled together in his tent, talking about the details of the marriage. Though skeptical whether Richard could straighten out the mess with his permits, he had few alternatives and opted to go back to camp, trying to forget the conversations with Jack and Ron ever happened. They would have to find him to deliver the news. Denial came more freely cloistered as a speck on the savanna.

They told Tad about the engagement and then hustled into their sleeping bags to escape the dropping temperature. Tad had been tending camp alone for a week and had been sitting stoned in front of the fire as usual. Watching Tad add his own smoke to that of the fire's, Michael shook his head, retreating to his tent. His routine had not yet changed much, despite his whipsawed life. Tonight, he discussed the wedding, foregoing his nightly reading and charting. He now had one guest confirmed: Tad. Had Tad even heard him before nodding yes? What did it matter if he understood? Tad would probably never show, even if the wedding was in Nairobi.

He turned to Caroline, jealous of the ease a wedding in Nairobi presented for her. Would any of his family or his friends travel half-way around the world? His best friend Ben would come. Michael thought about all the money Ben was making—he ought to spend it on something. Why not a trip to Africa? Knowing Ben, he would probably try convincing the law firm to let him write off the trip to client development, a pathetically losing proposition. Michael smiled. Absolutely, Ben, his loyal roommate, drinking buddy, would come. Ben had joked about how much he wanted to try some crazy herbs from a real Shaman. Perhaps Michael could arrange something. But the thought made him hesitate. He could just imagine bringing Ben out to a tribal village and slobbering something hideously politically incorrect while gawking at the topless women or warriors drinking blood from a gourd. Maybe an etiquette lesson would need to accompany any invite.

"What about your mom and brother?" Caroline asked. "Did you ask her on the phone yesterday?"

"No. I think I mentioned I was planning to have the ceremony here, but she was so shocked we never got that far. She said my dad would have been happy for me. You know, for once I think I agree with her. I don't know why. I just think he would have looked at me and told me he was proud. He never did that, but I think he would have done it now. He told me he was proud when I won a science trophy in high-school, but I don't think he really meant it. He was just happy he had something new to brag about. He always had to outdo everyone else, and whatever I ever succeeded in, he took credit for. But not this. He never could have comprehended my moving to Africa. My God, I think he probably left Rhode Island twice in his life! I don't think I could have imagined this a couple of years ago. I thought about staying around home for my mom, but then when she started dating, going home was never the same. Do you know what it's like not be able to go home because there isn't one?"

"Yes," Caroline sighed. "I guess we have more in common than we thought. I just hope you last a little longer as a father."

"I'm sorry. I plan to be around a lot longer. You'd never know it from my life the last few months, though. Well, worst case maybe I'll be remembered for my research. There'll be some footnote in a baboon book for posterity. 'Michael Sandburg, who worked and lived with eight hairy baboons for two years...'"

"Oh Michael, stop it..." Caroline snickered.

• • • • •

Richard called Alijah soon after Michael left the club. Everything had worked perfectly. The next step was for Alijah to hand Michael temporary permits: he would appear sympathetic, merely trying to repay the favor for Michael's employing Kiku. In tandem, he would let him know he had heard about his guns—plus other noble but unsanctioned activities—and ask for the weapons to be handed over. They were not in the arms business, but an Uzi was too great a find to ignore. Smuggling guns into the country was much riskier than shipping ivory out. Even Richard had his limits. To him, arms smuggling was a dirty business.

The remaining issue was timing. Permits can be stalled in the bureaucracy for months, and they decided not to rush. They would be better off manipulating him, treating him as a kind of asset. It had dawned on Richard that with Caroline's engagement he inadvertently gained new cover: he was linked to a biology researcher, a true conservationist living among the animals. Why not fund Michael's studies, potentially even donate to bolster that department at Harvard? He could see his name in bold print atop a Harvard zoology bulletin. What a veil! Ron's stupidity shone again. All he saw was dollars. He felt utterly insulated from suspicion. Well, perhaps heading a wildlife agency, he was justified. Known game exporters could use a biologist son-in-law on occasion. None of Julia's begging could convince him not to give away the bride.

# CHAPTER 9

*Nairobi Suburbs (Langata), Kenya*

Richard did not anticipate sending Alijah to fetch Michael's ammunition so soon. The guns would always prove helpful; however, Richard never thought he would actually need them.

There was no way of predicting what Ron stumbled into visiting a store owned by an Indian immigrant. A fortuitous encounter with a group of Indian merchants presented them with a cache large enough to tempt Richard into retirement—or, possibly, with the right weapons, to force the Indians into retirement.

"God damn Asians. We should have figured," Richard stammered, listening to Ron's account.

Most cultures discriminate against some ethnic subclass. In Kenya, that meant the Indians, or in local lingo, the Asians. The fact is that thousands of Indians live in Africa, and every one of those thousands is a potential scapegoat. Ron Easton was astounded by what he inadvertently learned about the Indian population in Nairobi. They were fantastic traders, managing routine corner stores and often dominating the tourist trade at novelty shops. It was Ron's exasperation with his houseboys that unexpectedly led him onto this track.

Ron sent a couple of his boys into town to buy nails and other hardware supplies to fix a few loose boards in his stables. The store they usually frequented was closed, and on a recommendation, they visited another shop on the same street run by a couple of Indians. Staked with enough shillings to cover the purchases and carrying exact instructions on what to buy, the servants were threatened with severe consequences if they returned with ale in their bellies and no nails in hand. What Ron failed to explain to them was quality. A nail is a nail except when a crooked shopkeeper sells you a bucket of bent and rusty ones looking just strong enough not to snap between the thumb and forefinger.

Easton was furious, and after berating his confused staff, deigned to pay the store a personal visit. Finding the shop closed, Ron looked around the neighborhood and was surprised to see the doors open on the store his boys originally planned to visit. Ron walked in, hoping to learn who owned the other shop. The proprietor, a middle-aged man whose young son peeked around the corner, gladly spilled that his competitor's store was owned by a wealthy Indian that lived in an unfamiliar area.

Ron, suspecting he could coax more information from the father and son, bought some sandpaper, chatting at the register. By good fortune, the kids from neighborhood stores played together. They did not harbor the same prejudices as their elders. More importantly, prized information, perhaps gained naively, was always more forthcoming passing time in alleys and playgrounds. "So, you don't expect them to open again this afternoon?" Ron had asked in a disappointing tone, initially oblivious to this underage network.

"No sir," the boy said, his English halting but nevertheless translating for his father whose English was minimal. "If you seeking ivory, I can call and arrange," snapping Ron to attention.

"Excuse me. Do you mean that gentlemen can arrange to sell me ivory? Or is he looking to buy some?" Ron poked back.

"I not sure, sir. I know the man sell if you want to buy. Maybe he buy. I can ask. Do you want more nails too?"

Ron paused, wondering what he had stumbled onto. Probably nothing more than a local trader, making some money on the black market. Quite clever, he acknowledged, never having suspected the Indians previously. Excellent cover. Well, perhaps he should pay them a visit.

"Thank you, I have all the materials I need for now," pocketing his higher quality nails. "But...do you happen to know where the owner of that store lives? I have a good friend who is looking for ivory, and he's leaving tonight! But if the store's closed, I will need to meet him at his house or warehouse." While talking, Ron nonchalantly reached into his wallet, counting out shillings, handing a small wad to the boy, whose eyes widened the breadth of the savanna. "Oh, and I wanted to thank you for your troubles, helping with the store closed and all," trying to dignify the deed. The street-smart boy needed no further translation, shoveling the prize to his father, who until then suspiciously stood listening to the conversation, never uttering a word. At least now, he bore a toothy smile, the language barrier miraculously lowered. In moments, Ron had the address and directions.

The few shillings, plus a pack of cigarettes, loosened all inhibitions, the new friends chatting away for several more minutes. Ron probably met the man before on an errand; there was no recollection, though, as he had never given him a second glance. Like so many merchants, he was there but not there. The shopkeeper remained invisible to a man of a different class and race who fancied completing his errand without the inconvenience of human contact. At least Ron was courteous, a natural by-product of British etiquette that occasionally paid dividends. A touch of politeness, repeat business, and now some kindness to his son—plus of course the few shillings—created a false bond, fleetingly serving both without the need to align motives or shake hands. Ron smiled, thinking, "Money makes the world go 'round," waving goodbye and despite his biases, even nodding slightly in thanks.

●　　●　　●　　●　　●

Soon Ron Easton was miles off main streets, driving through open scrub and then forested land, paved roads a memory. Apparently, a few Indian families built several expensive houses off a secluded dirt road in the hills about forty-five minutes outside of Nairobi. He would probably be the first white man to visit the compound. He wondered whether the government knew about these houses or that these people even existed—

probably not. He only discovered this hidden enclave by probing the man in the nail store via his son.

He throttled his rover into high gear, eventually reaching a bar in the road, an acacia toll gate of sorts. Stopping, perplexed, two men suddenly appeared, one bearing arms. The guard holding a gun surprised Ron, for owning a rifle was no simple task. Paranoid governments fearful of coups kept tight control over firearms, so tight that much of the military was equipped with surplus World War II guns.

"I'm visiting Annad Najiv," Easton said confidently, keenly aware of the stares.

They looked puzzled but relaxed upon searching his car and finding nothing suspicious or even interesting. Ron tried to appear bored. When one of the men demanded he accompany Ron "to show him the direction," Ron realized his aloof tactics had failed.

A canopy of trees hid the sun, and what appeared to be thick forest sheltered whatever lay twenty yards off the path. A trail of dust kicked up to their backs, but as Ron turned his head back toward the gate he managed to glimpse two giraffes nonchalantly strolling off into the trees. Even fifteen minutes outside town, drivers had to be careful. Ron well remembered striking an impala going home one evening, totaling his car. The lush bushes reminded him of his own suburban enclave.

Gazing at a vibrant strawberry-colored tree, he began to wonder why no one knew of this place and how the Indians had come to monopolize it. Soon the trees opened onto an enormous clearing replete with toucan-like colors. A wide oval gravel road adorned with palm trees and flower beds led to three substantial houses. He could spy other parts of the compound in the distance, but Ron's eyes were drawn to the large Indian flag flying over the central pillared house. This was the residence of Annad Najiv, apparently the leader of the mysterious clan.

"Wait here," the guide commanded, hopping out of the car and knocking on the double doors. A squat bearded man emerged, shuffling in his sandals toward the car, gesturing to Ron.

"Jambo. I'm Annad. I understand we need to talk. That, my friend, is good for you. I trust you know how dangerous it is for you to come here? Have you been sent by the government?"

"No. My name's Ron Easton. I work at one of the wildlife funding offices in Nairobi," he said, manipulating the details. "I came to find you after the men in your store sold my houseboys a bucket of rusty nails," Ron lied. He decided to bridge the source of ivory more delicately when hopefully given an opening, not knowing whether the boy managed to send advance word.

An enormous smile covered Annad's face, and unable to contain himself, he burst into a deep belly laugh. "That's why you come to visit me? Remarkable! Come in, come in, let me show you my house."

Annad turned around, clapping his hands. Two men held the doors open for the silk-draped Indian and the astonished intruder to walk into the mahogany parlor. Fine weavings hung down from the walls, resting a foot or two above hand-carved chests. Some animal skins decorated a room off to the right. When they walked past the parlor toward a porch, Easton's eyes widened. Through an open door, he could spy a room where more rhinoceros horns than he could fathom lay on the floor. It was not something that he could easily tally, like sensing the value of a stack of chips at a casino. Could that heap be fifty, one hundred deep? He simply was not sure, his mind simultaneously trying to absorb and count.

"Mr. Najiv," Easton began, barely able to catch his breath.

"Annad, please call me Annad."

"Annad, those horns in that room we just passed. I can't believe..."

Failing to disguise the irritation in his tone, Annad said, "Those are sacred possessions which have been passed down in my family for generations. No one must ever know about them. I fear thieves and especially the government. That's why all the security and your escort."

"How do you know I'm not from the government?"

"Perhaps you are, but that's not why you're here. My store, your visit. Plus, I know you're not here about paperwork or hassling me with some bureaucratic nuisance. The way you clench your hands. You're too nervous to be surprising me with government demands—at least any part of the government that worries me. You are clearly not a tax collector! Besides, I've heard of you. My friend called and told me a white man who bought nails at my store was coming. Of course, he didn't realize it was the same man I heard interviewed on the radio! You're becoming quite the celebrity, Mr. Easton. Welcome, and please, sit down. Would you care for some tea?"

"Yes, thank you," Ron said, thinking back to Richard's warning about too much publicity coming to haunt them. Although thrilled by the recognition, Ron told himself best to downplay his stature, and certainly not mention this tidbit to Richard.

•     •     •     •     •

"And then what happened?" Keeton interrupted.

"Honestly, I couldn't get anything more out of him. He's smooth. A perfect diplomat. I never saw more of the house. I couldn't get him to talk about how he got his money or who else lived there. Always polite, smiling, but stone-faced. Only admitted to moving here from Bombay several years ago. I'm sure that room being open was a mistake. He was angry when I tried to ask about it again. I was forced to play my card and mentioned how the boy at the store suggested I might be able to trade in ivory with him. But he dismissed that with a wave, joking that he had given the boy an ivory carving as a trinket, and he must have misunderstood. Silly children, or something like that. When I left, the door was closed. All I got was a refund on my nails and a pretty clear warning that I better keep my mouth shut. I know he's poaching. They might even be that band that you keep trying to find, Alijah. We're missing an enormous cut. We were just talking about all those rumors about the Indians the other day. I think we stumbled into a bit of luck here."

Silence enveloped the three schemers. Alijah looked at Keeton, who looked at Easton, who nervously reflected on his comrades. The door teased open in front of each of them; all that was required was courage.

The stakes were much higher than they had initially dreamed, the profits beyond what they could project.

"My gut says it's all or nothing. From what I saw, the way Annad evaded my questions, this group is real. We could be crushed," Ron spoke, the most unlikely of the three to break the ice. Richard was their leader and Alijah the pivotal local man. If anyone was dispensable, it was Ron. But he knew that. Greed brought him to this threshold, and greed was what allowed Alijah and Richard to trust him. A flinch, and he was out.

"I think you're right. Seems they're too dangerous. No one has that many rhino horns just lying around. We could even be squeezed out," Richard finally answered.

With the only vote that counted cast, everyone relaxed. Alijah was smug, but he owed too much to Richard Keeton to defy him on such a point. Besides, Alijah was tutored to concede, or at least he was willing to play such part when with his patron.

"That family heirloom line is bollocks," Richard continued. "Let's hope he thinks we bought it, but I think we'd be foolish to count on it. Impossible to tell if he expects us to fall for that explanation. I know somebody at the Polo Club who used to be in India when Mountbatten was Viceroy. Hopefully he still keeps in touch, maybe keeps an eye on the local community. I'll talk to him and try to piece some things together. I just hope they don't already know about us and put you on the whole time, Ron."

"I don't think so, but Annad did know I was coming," Ron said.

Alijah cut in, "They sound like the guys that pulled off that Tsavo raid of ten elephants last month we've been looking for. Not too many people have the guns or planes to pull something like that off. Remember, I had that tip about some Indians? I just passed it off, thinking they wouldn't be able to hire enough hunters who would keep quiet. But maybe they smuggle in guns and do all the hunting themselves. I don't know. It's possible."

Richard nodded in agreement, thinking about the potential for a clash. These Asians could be larger and more professional than his network. The truth would be difficult to uncover. Theirs was not a highly advertised field. Any snooping on the competition would demand stealth. He paused, wondering whether they should consider an alliance.

Richard suggested, "Maybe I should try talking to them. But, however we proceed, I've been thinking it's about time we implement some type of cover in case we get caught. You know, in case, for some reason, we're separated and asked hard questions. How about we call our little plan 'Ostrich?' Lots of people raise Ostriches and sell their eggs. They're worth quite a bit of money. The damn birds aren't endangered, and nobody cares about them. Our ruse is we're selling the eggs to foreign clients, and Ron is working on paperwork to help the shipments and get people licenses to raise and hunt them. Inefficiency just created the general permits to allow ivory shipments as opposed to one restricted to eggs. No one will even blink. If they do, then we'll deal with it, even offer to buy them off. If it gets more serious, we'll do whatever we have to. What do you think?"

"Brilliant," Ron perked up, resolving to keep any records under a file labeled Operation Ostrich. He would need to be discreet, but perhaps a little disinformation or even a black book of sorts may later come in handy.

·　　·　　·　　·　　·

After a crash course on Indian trade and following his hunches, Keeton showed up at Annad Najiv's door. He was unwelcome and treated as an intruder. Several shillings let him pass the guard post, but continuing on to the house, Richard was eerily alone. A man exited the main house while he was pulling into the driveway, motioning Richard to stop, before curtly escorting him inside and leaving him to wait in the parlor. Beautiful weavings and inlaid chests decorated the ornate chamber, yet as Richard soon discovered, there were no chairs. For close to an hour, he stood or paced.

Finally, a short and thickset man with a greying bushy beard came into the room. "Ah, Mr. Ketone, what a pleasure to meet you. I'm very sorry to have kept you waiting."

"The name is Keeton, not Ketone," his disgusted voice cut back. "Doesn't your staff have the decency to offer a guest a chair, Mr. Najiv?"

"Occasionally we indulge our expected guests," Annad's voice now turning cool, his eyes casting a stinging stare.

"Am I really so unexpected?"

"Quite."

"I have my doubts, but that's not important. I ..."

Angrily the Indian cut him off. "What do you think you're doing trespassing on my grounds uninvited and then insulting me? Good day."

Annad clapped his hands, and a servant appeared: "Escort this man back into town." Briskly, he walked toward a far doorway, his steps echoing in the vast parlor off the elegantly creaky wood.

"That's fine," Richard said in a haughty tone, realizing he would have to take the initiative, slowly grasping he might be in more danger than he had anticipated. Despite Richard's activities, he still believed in an orderly and civilized world; successful thieves in his sphere masqueraded as Cary Grant, not underworld thugs or swarthy smugglers. In fact, he even looked a bit the Cary Grant part. "I guess you won't mind my reporting all those rhino horns back in Nairobi. I'm sure none of the ministers will mind learning of the thousands of pounds of sterling in cuts they've missed out on from your smuggling. Or," he hesitated, turning to his pitch, "we could talk about working together. I have connections, could help you with permits. I'm sure some of that *merchandise* could have quite a market in the Orient. Rumor has it that it might be possible to trade with you in ivory too. Mr. Najiv, please think of me as a broker. We can help each other, perhaps expand our mutual trade. I came out here myself, rather than send one of my, let's say, assistants, hoping we could talk directly. Chief Executive to Chief Executive of sorts."

Richard felt good about his entreaty. The bait was cast, Annad at least pausing to listen. The room remained totally silent, the anticipation of a reply suffocating until Annad Najiv marched straight out of the room. He never turned around to face his presumptuous guest. Richard stood dumbfounded in the same room where he had held his bearing for over an hour and only uttered a few sentences. He craned to hear what his would-be host muttered on his way out, unable to understand while watching his escort nod and then follow. The man disappeared, leaving Keeton facing the empty doorway through which Annad Najiv stormed.

Finding his way back outside, Richard started toward his car, baffled, unsure whether to give up and drive away. The vehicle was parked on the gravel about fifty paces away, just beyond a stocky guard who stood, arms crossed, waiting for him to approach. As Richard neared him, the thick-armed man moved to block his way. Swinging wide to avoid an encounter, the scowling figure followed his path, again blocking Richard's way to the car.

"Excuse me, would you please step aside so I can get the hell out of here," Richard ranted.

As he was finishing his sentence, a fist passed through the little space remaining between the two men, thrusting so deeply into Keeton's gut that he lost his breath, crumpling to the ground. A middle-aged man more accustomed to sports where time is marked by bugles, the strike decimated Keeton's body. Searing pain kept him crouching, the guard now grabbing Richard's arm, virtually cutting off circulation. Capitulating, Richard let the man drag him back to the house, collapsing on the same patio where Ron Easton had taken tea.

"What the hell's the meaning of this?" Richard grunted at Najiv seated across from him, each syllable ripping through his chest. He could not contain another groan, clutching his stomach.

"What do you know about my horns? About my business?"

"Enough to have your trade halted, which I would gladly do if I didn't need you."

Forcing a chuckle, Annad indulged Richard. "And what exactly makes you so dangerous and me so valuable?"

In a position more degrading than at any time in his life and suffering from acute pain, Richard cracked. "Listen to me, you fucking WOG," he spat, causing Najiv to exhale vehemently, fuming at the insult. At the bottom of all ethnic slurs rests "Wog," a uniquely British expression referring to any group conquered and ruled by the British Empire. Embodied in this one word were the emotions of ethnic inferiority, humiliation, defeat, and bitterness. Annad Najiv would have preferred Keeton to spit into the Ganges.

"I don't need to listen to this," Najiv scoffed, standing up and glaring at the still bent figure of Keeton. "You won't be missed."

"Oh, you're very wrong. Ron Easton and two of my associates know what I'm doing, where I am, and why I came here. If I'm not back soon, they'll come over and confiscate everything. What will happen to you…I don't take kindly to being beaten. You don't beat a gentleman who comes to make you an offer! You would be wise to let me go. And don't think about running away and pretending this meeting never happened. We have men at the airports too. Blindly loyal to us. I'm walking out of here, and there's no place for you to go. I know you don't have a plane here. I've checked. I can get the horns myself. I don't need those, although I understand you have enough to keep your family unemployed for generations. I came to work out a deal. I want your contacts in the Orient and Malaysia."

Annad had enough of this blowhard, nodding to one of his guards who methodically walked across the room, striking Richard against the shoulder blades with a crude billy club. Richard's body limply slapped the ground. Before he could pick himself up, the guard kicked him in the side. The force cracked a rib. Richard wailed in pain. His body ached everywhere. Only the uniformity of the pain diffusing his attention kept him conscious.

Annad looked down on the writhing figure, rolling him over with his foot to stare at his face. Smashing to the ground had opened a nasty gash above Keeton's left eye, swelling it shut. The beating left his whole face freckled in blood and his usually striking white hair matted with it. Richard kept his good eye closed, struggling to withhold groans, hoping capitulation might prevent urges to drop-kick him in another direction. His defensive mechanisms, together with his stamina, failed. Involuntarily rolling onto his side to alleviate pressure, the move stimulated a shooting pain from his rib. Dry in the throat, struggling to spit, he could not even muster enough saliva to wet his tongue. Nauseated, he passed out.

. . . . .

"How did you get away?" Alijah asked, shocked at the recounting.

"That was easy. When I came to, I had bandages on, and my stomach and ribs were wrapped. They must have shot me up with painkillers. I can't believe they could have done all that to me without my realizing it. There was somebody standing over me. I think the same guy who had been outside before stopping me from getting to my car. When he saw I was awake, he left me. I wasn't going anywhere. I must have passed out again. When I woke up a second time, my side and head hurt like hell. I thought I had a broken nose too," Richard paused before continuing, catching his breath, still wincing.

"Then Annad came in and threatened me. He told me I was alive because he was an ethical person. Can you believe that? What, does he think he is some kind of Indian mafia don? The gall," Richard sneered, oblivious to the irony.

"So, did you thank him, give in?"

"Of course. You think I was going to start calling him a Wog again, get my whole rib cage split open? I thanked him and told him I'd keep my mouth shut. He then threatened to kill me— and Ron—if either of us ever caused him trouble again."

Ron pulled up from his natural slouch, "He said he'd kill me? "

"Oh, don't worry about it, Ron. If he was going to kill us, he would have done it. He had a perfect opportunity which he damn well knows he'll never get again."

"So, what are we going to do?" Ron asked, almost quivering. "I mean, he knows enough about us that he could expose us, even shut us down. He's already got a big operation. Who knows, maybe bigger than ours. And well hidden. They must have great contacts. If we hadn't accidentally run across them... I know there were whispers, but nothing on this scale. And they seem to be well armed, and apparently not afraid of violence..."

"Any more problems you'd like to point out?" Keeton mocked. Alijah fought back laughing into the face of Easton's chagrin. "There's only one option. Annad and his friends are not going to live to see the rains."

"You don't mean," Ron cut in, his cowardice rising into the spotlight.

"I mean we expose them, beat them. We raid the place, take the trophies, let Alijah claim to have found the cache of his life. Nobody cares about the Indians. It will be heroic. Just like before, we'll smuggle away most of it, let Alijah have enough to show off. My god, there was so much that if he takes one-third and claims that's what he found, it would still be the biggest catch ever. No one would ever guess there was double or triple that amount. And then we let those Wogs rot in jail. Hang, whatever, that's not my problem. I just want them gone. It's the same play we've executed before, except this time we'll have to take the goods by force. But that shouldn't be too hard. There is no way after that beating Annad would expect me to be stupid enough to come back."

Alijah, wary, said, "Maybe, but they will be well guarded and on alert. It won't be easy. We have to expect them to put up a fight."

Pulling up his shirt to reveal nasty bruising, Richard said, "Well, if it's war, they brought it on themselves. And, Alijah, don't underestimate your cunning. You could sneak up on a leopard and cut off its balls. They don't know how to play by African rules. The hunters will become the hunted. And just in case, we'll make sure we're better prepared."

Richard reminded Ron and Alijah of their prior conversations concerning Michael, rekindling his lecture on the benefit of rifles with automatic clips. They could not precisely gauge what they would be up against; while still believing Alijah's bush instincts would give them the necessary edge for a successful raid, Richard's beating cautioned him to preach firepower over surprise. He ordered Ron to start looking for ammunition, flares—anything explosive and lethal. Richard then tasked Alijah with setting up a meeting, not-so-magnanimously offering Michael back his permits in exchange for the Uzi and his night-scope rifle. For his part, Richard was heading home to write Caroline and Michael a check and note, congratulating them on their engagement.

• • • • •

It was early morning when Michael looked up from the campfire to see a jeep rolling into camp. The baboons had already moved down from the trees, playing on the log at the camp's fringe. In minutes, they would traipse out into the savanna. Fearful of losing his permits indefinitely, Michael was doing everything feasible to accelerate his research, already tackling the challenge of converting notes into draft reports. Just the night before, he wrote a long letter to his advisor excitedly charting his progress. He had woken up late, now sluggishly boiling water for coffee, watching the troop's morning rituals, formulating a bit of structural tinkering to his thesis.

Unshaven, disheveled, and tired, Michael wiped his eyes, straining to make out who was in the car. The baboons were leaving. This interruption would force him to delay his plans and likely waste time searching for the troop. When the door opened, he was surprised to see Alijah.

Hiding his annoyance, Michael said, "Alijah, this is a surprise. What brings you this way?"

"You, of course. Good morning."

"Like some coffee?"

"Thank you."

Michael rose, taking the pot off the fire. Pouring two cups, then stirring in the grinds, he handed one to Alijah before warming himself with a sip.

"Congratulations. I heard the news about you and Caroline."

"Thanks. I can hardly believe it. I can't wait to go back to the states and introduce her to everyone."

"Where's she now, back in Nairobi?"

"Yeah. I'm only here for a few days. I've been going back and forth regularly since things got serious with Caroline… I'm trying to remember the last time I saw you. Was it at Kiku's initiation? I barely remember seeing you there. God, I didn't see much of anything. They gave me something to drink and it knocked me out. I've never hallucinated like that before."

Alijah laughed: "You're a brave man. It wasn't the drink. You must have smoked something."

"Now that you mention it, I guess I did. I didn't think that was it, though."

"So, tell me about my son. How's he doing?" Looking around, but not seeing Kiku, Alijah continued, "And, where is he? I expected him to be here."

"He took off over a week ago. Said something about needing to go visit a village. Something personal. I thought maybe you'd know."

"No, I haven't heard from him. Probably about some girl and doesn't want either of us to know!"

"Maybe. He seemed restless, a bit off. Anyway, he's doing fine. Except, while you're here, there is something that's been troubling me. At Kiku's initiation I met your wife, his mother. She told me some of the others were picking on him because of me. The contact with whites, foreigners rather, the language and all. And she was definitely not happy about my teaching him."

"They're just jealous. They see how many cows he has, how rich he's become as a young man. He's traveled, can speak English. It's everything I wanted as a young man in the tribe. Most of us thought about getting out. It wasn't that we wanted to leave. Just natural curiosity."

"Your wife threatened me. She told me to leave him alone and not to come back. She thinks you've already left and doesn't want to lose Kiku. I think she wants him to become the next chief."

Michael rose, topping up his mug of coffee. He had debated whether to raise Tza's concerns and now hesitated again before asking, "What do you want him to do?"

"I don't know. Part of me wants him to stay. Not to enter your world. And then part of me wants him to work for me. Leave the flies behind. You know, wear clothes, live in a proper house. Once you leave, it's difficult to go back. I know," privilege blinding him to the fact Tza had done just that.

"I think he'll leave," Michael offered, relaxing having raised the subject. "He loves listening to my radio and is incredibly interested in all the places he hears about. I struggle to get any work done, I'm answering so many questions. Anyway, it's ultimately up to him."

"Yes, he's a man now. He can choose. That's not what initiation is supposed to mean. But that's what it means for Kiku."

Alijah stood up, walking to his car, reaching inside for some papers. He returned to the campfire and sat on a bench across from Michael, rehearsing his speech.

"Michael, I actually didn't come to talk about Kiku. I heard about what happened with your permits and wanted to do something. After everything you've done for Kiku. Here, I've got them issued again. At least temporarily."

Michael took the permits, stunned by the gesture and turn of events. "I don't know what to say. You've saved my career."

"Think of it as a wedding gift." Pausing and then standing up, Alijah added, "Michael, there is one thing, though. It's difficult for me to even bring up."

"I'm not sure I can take any more surprises."

"There is one favor I need to ask. I need your guns. *All of them*, registered and any others—I think you know what I mean. Except you can keep a pistol for self-defense. And I need whatever radio-tracking equipment you have."

"Why?" Michael jumped up. "What makes you think I have a bunch of guns here?"

"Come on. James works for me of sorts. I know what you've got. In fact, it's illegal. I could have you arrested if I wanted... The fact is that you've become an embarrassment to me. I'm supposed to be in charge of the government's anti-poaching division, and all anyone's talking about is you. Let me do my job, and you do your research. You know it's for the best. I don't want this to be difficult."

Michael turned his back, reluctantly acknowledging reality, his tone choking, "I knew I might get caught sooner or later. I guess it's good that it was you." He faked relief. He had long wondered what he would do if caught. With Alijah, he decided not to fight a losing battle. At least not openly. James would surely give him new rifles, secretly ignoring Alijah. It would be far from the first time they dared step over the line. James was intolerant of bureaucratic limits and together with Michael operated their anti-poaching unit with a vigilante zeal; in fact, awkwardly they operated around and in spite of Alijah's instructions. The animals needed protection at all costs and it was not as if the poachers were following rules. Michael would simply fight without the Uzi. He had become too integral a part of the anti-poaching team to just walk away. Michael could barely believe his thoughts. Is this what it was like to be in a street gang? Ditch the made weapon and forage in a back alley for a new piece? Hell, he could probably ask his new father-in-law for a hunting rifle. Richard would be overjoyed if Michael finally joined up for a hunt. He shook his head, thinking if Richard only knew.

Alijah consoled, "You're turning them over to a good cause. They'll be used for the same purpose. I've had a hard time stopping the poachers because I've been so outgunned. They've got planes, the best equipment. Sometimes I don't stand a chance. This will give me a chance at beating them. You don't have to stop them anymore. It's my job. With some of this equipment, I can do it better than ever before. And if I shoot someone, I know the president. I won't go to prison. Michael, you will. What do you say?"

"Do I have a choice?"

"No. But you won't regret it."

"Alijah," Michael began.

"Yes"

"Use them well. Okay? Kill lots of the bastards."

"Let's see what you've got," playing along, though Alijah already knew the inventory.

* * * * *

Neither Alijah nor Michael suspected that Kiku had departed Michael's camp for good, nor that he left to meet an army general. Kiku had heard about General Abo Daniel Oguru from his father, especially how Alijah beat him at a spear-throwing contest at a university party. Now staring at the general, whose power radiated from his six-foot-eight frame, Kiku grasped why his father had pretended to lose. Oguru was a man you wanted on your side and certainly did not want to cross. Kiku was among a group of more than fifty men sitting on log benches in a jungle clearing mesmerized by Oguru's recruiting pitch. Except this was not a government function: Oguru was a secret rebel, enlisting new guerilla fighters to his cause.

Oguru was a bitter man, molded by frustration festering since the injury to his father plunged their family into poverty. Now leading a group of rebels, his anger finally had an outlet. He turned his ire toward the government and non-African minorities alike, seeking to redistribute wealth and opportunity. Kiku was part of the rapt audience, nodding his head, the words affirming much of the Marxist dogma that had come to permeate his thinking. Perhaps the general's goals were not as radical as those Kiku espoused, but Oguru struck enough chords to inspire his new acolyte.

Kiku was welcomed with open arms. The group needed converts, and having men who spoke multiple languages and dialects would enable broader recruiting—and help them keep tabs on those in the city who may suspect the guerillas' plans and try to thwart Oguru's ambitions. However, being discovered by city bureaucrats seemed preposterous when gathering in the bush miles from even the closest dirt road. Oguru had chosen a remote spot on the edge of an escarpment, forcing many of the men to journey for days to attend this meeting. Kiku had left Michael's camp without much explanation, vaguely noting he needed to travel to a village for a personal matter. Without advising Michael, his father, or any family of his intended destination, he had teamed with another recruit and started his new journey.

Kiku knew he did not want to stay in his village and become a tribal chief. He had seen too much of the outside world to spend his life sequestered in such a literally small circle. He was also wary of moving to the city; whether he was rebelling against Alijah's life or merely found it unattractive did not matter. So, when the opportunity came to join the rebel cause, fighting for ideals that first sparked him from over the radio, he decided to leap. Or more aptly walk—which he did for a week until finally reaching the guerillas' campsite. En route, they had passed several checkpoints and been interrogated to ensure their motives were pure. Oguru's nascent force was paranoid about spies and was taking few chances. Kiku suspected there were lookouts throughout the valley below; in fact, he would learn the perimeter extended a safe measure beyond the echoes of rifles shooting at practice targets. The range was quiet now, however, with the whole camp listening to the great man himself, lapping up the rhetoric.

At the end of the speech, Oguru mingled with the men. He knew the importance of being seen, how a simple handshake or word could court years of loyalty. Oguru may have been schooled in the military, but he was a natural politician. Eventually, he came to a stop in front of Kiku.

Switching from Swahili, he said, "One of my men tells me you speak English. Is that right?"

"Yes, General." Kiku swelled with pride.

"That may prove very helpful. I'm glad you've joined our cause."

"Thank you," then hesitating, anxious to question Oguru yet needing to find the courage to plunge ahead. "May I ask you a question? Something tied to your speech."

"Yes, of course."

"When you were talking about how to get the people to rise up, to stand and join us, you said we needed to make them see the faults of the government. What did you mean when you said to make people see the injustice, we might have to make them uncomfortable?"

"That this is war. We need to do whatever it takes."

Kiku had been thinking a lot about class warfare. Weaned observing his father grovel to Richard Keeton, he had become sensitive to the fate of skin color. Michael had been generous to him, yet the relationship had been foisted upon Kiku with Alijah commanding him to display subservience. Kiku had little appreciation for Michael's academic credentials and part of the tribesman's perspective was simply associating the white American with the privilege of being yet another boss. He pushed, "Even pitting black against white?"

Oguru paused, uncharacteristically cautious before responding, "Perhaps. But we have just thrown off the colonial yoke. I'm not sure this is the time. We need to get people's attention, disrupt the status quo. But the actions, what we do, people need to believe it is right. And so do we. We're revolutionaries not monsters and need to be careful. We'll need help and arms, and sometimes it can be surprising who's your friend and who's your enemy. When it's clear who our allies are, then we'll find the right symbols and strike."

"And how do we find the right symbols? Do we look for them? Do we create them?" Kiku asked, eager to push their mission forward.

"Ha," Oguru dismissed the implication. "The excitement of youth. Don't worry. We'll have our victory. Be patient. I am not ready to pit brother against brother —yet."

And then Oguru moved on, not wanting to be dragged further down the incitement slope. Stirring racial tensions would be easy yet also dangerous. He was reluctant to take that path and wondered whether this youngster spoke from naive youth or if this was a broader topic amongst the men. Oguru would have one of his lieutenants listen for chatter. There was little in the wind escaping his ears. Too many of these men thirsted for scapegoats and fights and did not appreciate strategy. Oguru knew that the wrong moves could mean someone else would just come along and try to overthrow what he was set to achieve. He hoped he would not have to become too dirty to win, but win he would.

Still nursing his bruises from Annad's beating, and now in possession of Michael's high-powered arms, Richard was ready to put his plan for revenge against the Indians in motion. To cover for his black-and-blue marks, Richard told Julia and their friends that he had fallen from one of his polo horses. Alijah's seven-member paramilitary force, however, knew better. Training in a remote and isolated field, they experimented day and night with explosives and rifles—oddly honing similar skills as Kiku was learning in his rebel camp. Every man practiced a distinctive piercing call. They were like species of birds blending into the surroundings, yet able to understand each varied trill. Instantly one knew the sound of his brother. A high inflection might signal danger, a staccato pitch meaning they were moving around to the back or the right. They would call while running or slithering forward in the dirt, inching their way stealthily through the tall brush.

Alijah liked being drill sergeant. He mastered several types of whistle intonations, signaling his troops with the precision that modern codes could only hope to duplicate. Subtle nuances shaped each trill, the precise command or expression beckoning this will be tough or hurry up. Alijah choreographed each soldier's actions and movements, weaving the group together in direction and purpose. The emotional bond that lifts men to greater feats than they individually imagine possible added to their strength. Alijah nurtured a collective instinct, whose eyes cut through the shadows and whose ears reached beyond the corners.

With the savvy of a pack of wolves emboldened by the vicious logic of the human mind, seven men set out at dusk down the craggy, volcanic path out of town. The guard at the compound gate who weeks before accepted Richard's bribe lay snoring, his rifle tucked snugly into his crotch, his head bobbing forward nearly snout to snout with his gun. The engines on the two jeeps were cut far enough down the road so as not to rouse any leery sentries, and for about a quarter mile, the men pushed their cars down the path.

An average man would have woken the guard; save for slumping in his spot, he was not visible in the moonlight. But these were tribesmen with keen senses exponentially superior to those of city creatures. In the savanna, each one could pick out a man miles off on top of a hill, indistinguishable to the most expensive hand-ground German lenses. Identifying a snoring Indian would have been likened to stealing candy from a baby if they only knew what candy meant.

Alijah judged an arrow might have merely wounded and a gun would be too loud. Hence, precisely at the moment two men imitated the heckling of scavenging hyenas, Galo clasped his hand over the sentry's mouth and viciously struck him in the head with a large rock. The sentry slumped, still alive but knocked unconscious. Alijah helped Galo quickly tie a gag around the sentry's mouth and bind his hands behind his back with rope. They had been prepared to drive a dagger into the guard's neck, summoning the true cacklers for a leisurely buffet dinner. For now, they were satisfied rendering the sentry incapacitated; however, all the men attacking the compound knew that killing was inevitable despite earlier professing hopes of avoiding slaughter. The overall mission remained straightforward: secure the camp, capture the trophies, and bring Annad and his gang up on poaching charges. They were not bred killers—at least of men posing little threat to their tribe. Still, they were no strangers to violence and each knew his duty. This raid would be messy, Alijah rationalizing that casualties to a few sentries may spare wider carnage. In his heart, though, he knew that was wishful thinking; they would show no mercy if their approach risked being discovered. Poaching was a dirty business.

They reached the edge of the compound without encountering any further sentries, leaving their cars, already-turned around, a safe distance back on the road. Both driver's doors hung wide open, keys ready in the ignition. Slowly they moved toward the beginning of the gravel leading to the courtyard where they planned to fan out and launch the attack. Before they could see their target, though, they spotted two men approaching, about to intersect their path. Alijah bent low down toward the ground, absorbing the faintest whisper. Listening to the men's conversation, he nodded and motioned for Galo.

"They're curious about the hyenas. They haven't seen any hyenas for weeks. They're going to look for them. I'll take the one on the left; you take the other. There're only two. I hear the steps. If they discover us it's over. Knives not rocks—no hesitation."

A quick hoot alerted the rest that men were approaching. Galo and Alijah crouched against the bushes, imperceptible to the Indians and each other. Everything was quiet save the rustling of the night air. The blackness goaded the men's hearts to pound harder, so hard it seemed the noise must be audible to the next. A snap of a twig and the suction of breath made the Indians stand out as if they were wearing neon suits. They drew even with their assassins without a hint of being watched.

Another hoot permeated the evening calm, Alijah and Galo springing in tandem. Unleashing their energy, coiling forward, and piercing their foes in one short stroke, the elegant attack fell their prey instantly. The groans of the Indians barely registered, Alijah and Galo's daggers dripping victoriously from the remains of less greedy hearts. All four lay on the ground under the mimicked chorus of hyenas barking at the blood. Perhaps real hyenas would soon scavenge here too. After a minute's rest, Galo and Alijah made a clicking sound and walked on. In their minds, the killing was necessary, an almost natural act to those raised in the bush and not sentimental about survival—us or them, as the guards surely would not have hesitated.

No one knew how many Indians guarded the compound, but Richard had guessed around twenty. That was a generous estimate, for only three houses appeared large enough for more than a small family. These three substantial homes stood on the perimeter of the gravel circle, the biggest one with a wide porch, Indian flag and central columns matching the description Richard and Ron had given about Annad's home. Behind them and down the hill were scattered modest one-room houses of wood and clay. Alijah and Galo would lead the attack on Annad Najiv's home, others taking the rest of the compound. There was only one acceptable outcome. Everyone had to be taken prisoner or killed (if it came to that). Richard and Ron had both preached caution not to damage or destroy any of the loot in Najiv's house.

Initially, Richard toyed with joining the assault, but the potential bloodshed was unbecoming of his stature. Alijah could carry out instructions; the unit would hardly expect Richard to fight in person. Plus, a whiff of insecurity commanding a group he deemed of less moral standing was enough to dissuade him from leading the raid. Better to wait and arrive once the compound was secured, he thought. He would still have his vengeance, and had few qualms about showing up to survey the spoils. Richard was sure other lords and ladies had compromised themselves with unseemly tasks during ignoble quests to protect and enlarge their positions. Lack of record keeping aids one's conscience, and while the tribesmen may excel at covering their tracks, Richard had designs to ensure there were no tracks at all. Who would believe he stooped to visit such a place, let alone be a party to such hideous acts?

Galo's alias bird chirped the signal to commence. Where single gas lanterns cast enough light to call attention to the presence of people, bright flames suddenly burst. Molotov cocktails struck the two outside houses. Running outside, instead of finding safety, screaming Indians staggered into bullets and bayonets. Alijah and Galo streaked into Najiv's parlor, riddling the surprised and unfortunate sole guard with bullets. Waving in another, Alijah positioned his accomplice to guard the valuables believed stored downstairs. Alijah then began climbing upstairs, ready to shoot again if necessary, with Galo following. At the top of the stairs, they quickly found themselves in front of three closed doors.

Galo kicked in the nearest one, only to find two cowering children huddled on the bed. He pegged them as roughly five years old, maybe even twins. Alijah moved into the room as he saw Galo pausing. He gathered in the silhouette of the two boys cast against the near wall by the glare of the flames from the adjacent building. The innocent eyes of two petrified toddlers spoke back to him through glassy tears. The men walked out, slamming the door.

Two rooms remained, each man putting his ear to one. Alijah motioned he could hear a woman in the room, Galo signaling that behind his door breathed only a dog. Tribesman survive by trusting their senses, so without discussion Alijah drew a knife and kicked open the woman's door, believing that Annad Najiv would eventually come to her aid. When the door flew open, the woman rushed to the window, scrambling to climb outside. Galo stood at the door watching her as Alijah rushed toward the window. Perched on the edge, she slipped and fell to her death, never reaching the sanctity of the eaves and plunging headfirst onto a rock. Alijah's only thought was why she did not sleep with her husband. He had his answer when turning around: he watched a blade pass through his unsuspecting brother. Shrieking at a pitch that instantly numbed his throat, Alijah hurled his knife with all his strength at Annad Najiv. The throw had the force and accuracy which only pure reaction can achieve. Annad collapsed over Galo before his own dagger was even pulled free. A heap of flesh blocked the door.

Alijah dropped to his knees, his body so convulsed he struggled to breathe. He nearly threw up beside the bed, pulling himself up, only shock holding back tears. Sweat staining the sheets and disgust bridling on his lips, he willed himself to step over the soggy bodies, moving to the first room. Ranting, he grabbed one child, shoving him against the bedpost. He did not mean to hurt the boy and stopped before committing a sin he would never forget. Relieved by his restraint, his composure was butchered by what he next witnessed, almost in slow motion: the other panicked child ran toward the window and jumped into the conflagration.

Dazed and carrying the boy from the bed, Alijah made his way down the stairs and onto the front porch. Hoots and whistles filled the air, and on the ground lay several still Indians. The scene was unimaginable. Alijah sat, catatonic, on the porch. Finally, he was roused by the whistle signaling victory. It was all done. There were no more screams, only the whoosh of fires and the chatter of success.

"Alijah, the house is burning!" yelled one of his men. Alijah sat on the porch, oblivious to the flames at his back as the fire spread to Annad's house. They had to haul the horns and tusks out—fast. A couple of men had run back to retrieve a car, the driver now skidding to a stop. He jumped out, reaching in the back and throwing sacks to the men who rushed inside. Alijah remained frozen until someone threw a sack at his face. Mechanically, he trudged inside, soon slinging the bag over his shoulder weighted with rhino horns. Once dumping them in the truck, he sat back down alone, bereft and incapable of hauling another load.

They were lucky. All the horns were carried outside before the fire spread to the storage rooms. The last trip was risky, but they managed to grab every horn before turning to the tusks. The team, minus Alijah, formed a human chain passing tusks out, hand over hand, a river of ivory undulating up and down, man to man, porch to steps, and beyond. Closing in on removing the last few, though, the building erupted in flames; sanity dictated abandoning efforts to move the final group. Four men managed to bring out a couple more, the remaining handful falling victim to the conflagration. Whoever exhumed this grave would find the dead with their treasures and puzzle over what led to their tragic end.

In the car, Alijah wept. Without saying a word, everyone knew the fate of Galo. Paralyzed by shock, Alijah completely forgot to call Richard, but Keeton would learn soon enough.

•　•　•　•　•

Two nights later Richard Keeton stood solemnly amongst the misty-eyed tribesmen. The moon was full, the moment somber. No one noticed the goosebumps on their arms. Everyone absorbed the silence bounding the wails. An ordinary funeral would have focused on the fallen brother, glorifying the spirit and commemorating the corpse. But Galo was consumed in the flames, his soul released without prayer. Nothing remained but memories. Tribesmen have no photographs, no possessions to take with them in an earthen crypt. Galo left only the imprint of his smile and the lore of his spearmanship. Perhaps though, the storytellers would first recall how Galo once brought a white man to their tribe. Not long before, their lives were simple, their goals repetitive. Now Alijah was a government official living in an alien world urging his brethren to leap through time and follow suit.

It was too early to ascertain how future villagers would view Galo. Generations could worship him or remember him as the one who began a downfall. The mourners standing on the circle of dung housing Galo's hut wondered what the following years would bring, everyone commiserating over shared anxieties.

Many of the bereaved villagers furtively stared at Mbobyu, the clan's ostracized warrior and brother of Galo and Alijah, who had boasted of Galo's prowess with a spear to Richard Keeton. Perhaps the transition was inevitable; however, on this day, many of the villagers held Mbodyu and his addiction to game lodge brew responsible. Mbodyu sat alone on a knoll overlooking the village huts, consumed with guilt over the tragedy and leaning gingerly on his walking stick. His staff once balanced his drunken legs but now held the full weight of his grief. His eyes were no longer sharp enough to spot Alijah from a distance. Knowing he would be shunned, Mbodyu still attended the ceremony, determined for Alijah to see him and understand that Mbodyu had no more wanted this fate for Galo than the loneliness now defining his own days.

The first, and one of a handful of white men, ever to visit this village fidgeted with the flies on his nose, oblivious to Mbodyu and the emotions he stirred. One of the tribe's most beloved members lay dead for a reason that only Alijah could comprehend. Brothers wailed, arms-linked, as they danced in a circle. Mothers cried freely. Little children ran about, not understanding what was taking place. Grown men paced around, not understanding what was taking place. Richard Keeton stood stoically, pondering why he had traveled to smear his boots in shit and watch tens of illiterate tribesmen wail through an incoherent ritual.

He, too, was scared. These tribesmen were changing his life. Their lawlessness rubbed off easily. His dependence on them fit less comfortably. At one level, his business had become raping their land for profit. At another, he was educating and equipping them for an inevitable future. The gulf of isolation had shrunk to a sliver of ignorance in the few years he had been in Africa. A generation before, no one in such a tribe would have conversed with a white man. Today, most knew of men like Keeton, but a visit like this remained a novelty. In perhaps ten or twenty years, Keeton thought, the village would be the novelty. He resolutely believed that preparing a few like Alijah for the approaching metamorphosis of culture justified his methods. Galo's death marked the natural sequence of progress. A narrow smile creased his lips. In his mind, he was growing wealthy and making those around him worship him for it.

Around him, though, wails continued to fill the air. The men were now jumping about like manic dancers, stomping the ground with rhythmic kicks that flaked the dung out from the pinwheel of their bodies. Emotion drenched the spot. A stench that was always there yet seldom noticed permeated the air. The wretchedness of life bellowed.

Alijah stared mesmerized before the funeral dancers. His mother and sisters sat hugging each other, rekindling a bond that was too strong for him to resist. Slowly he knelt, joining their world. As the sun beat down against the unprotected savanna, their bodies rhythmically swayed to the chants of those dancing about the circumference of the village. Each one entered that detached state in which their minds were mercifully blank and their bodies wonderfully warm. No eyes remained alert. No faces were dry. Alijah's two sisters had moved from the village years before he met Richard. His oldest sister, Nita, three children older, scarcely recognized him. He never had a chance to ask her how she learned the news. They both cried when meeting the other's eyes.

Their father was spared the agony. He had died, in the white man's measure of time, a few years earlier. His death had not been glamorous, just usual. Some disease, some illness no one understood, grasped him in the midst of winter. Trying to ward off the cold during particularly chilly nights, everyone would sleep huddled around a smoldering campfire. It was commonplace now to use blankets. His father had worn one like a cape during the last weeks of his life. Keeton told Alijah that the same methods exist in most tribal cultures, lecturing about Aborigines in Australia curling up with their dogs on chilly evenings. A four-dog night had seized Alijah's father, an able man who proudly begat three able sons.

Alijah opened his eyes, conscious of his father's absence. He winced thinking about his death, now knowing how easily the white man's drugs may have cured him. The vulnerability of tribal life stared back at him coldly. The world which could have offered his father life had taken it from his brother. Alijah struck his chest with his fist, not bothering to muffle a groan of frustration. He could no longer bear to look at his mother, a disconsolate old woman beaten down from waves of grief; ushering Galo's soul to join her husband, combined with the pain of losing Mbobyu to alcohol and Alijah to an alien world, had crushed her spirit.

His thoughts turned uncomfortably to his son's fate. Kiku had stayed in the village following his initiation before returning briefly to resume his work for Michael. Then he had left, and just when Kiku's excuse for disappearing started to wear thin a message arrived in Michael's camp. Kiku was not coming back. Without further elaboration, the messenger also asked Michael to pass the information on to Alijah, and let him know he would call soon. When they eventually spoke, it was an awkward conversation. Kiku advised his leaving had nothing to do with a girl; instead, he talked mostly about politics and class struggle, causing Alijah to fear he may be under the sway of rebel propaganda. He sent two scouts to try and find him, but they had been unsuccessful so far. That was no surprise given Kiku's tribal training; he could stay hidden indefinitely. Alijah wiped his tears, turning away from the ceremony, coming face to face with a man he did not know—but who seemed to know him.

Zemuani hailed from a neighboring village toward Mt. Kilimanjaro. Years ago, Galo became betrothed to Zemuani's sister; now that she had reached puberty, Galo was almost through raising the twenty cattle needed to consummate the marriage. Alijah had offered to help, but Galo scoffed, too proud to accept brotherly charity. Alijah suddenly found himself heir to the cattle and Nina, Zemuani's baby sister. Zemuani extended greetings, Alijah shooting back a petrified stare. Alijah would have to marry her. He also knew the only connection they were likely to build would be lying together; perhaps an emotionally baron marriage could yet spawn other fulfillment. The prospects were hollow. Theoretically, he could bring her to Nairobi; but he never would, her destiny sealed before starting. The last thing he would be able to explain to Sara was yet another wife. Any marriage to Nina would have to stay in the shadows.

Explaining how he would be forced to live most of his life away from her, but that he would provide for her and their children, appeared to assuage Zemuani. Alijah then said, "I won't bring her to the people who took Galo. She's already old enough to understand. Perhaps my son... I have a different wife in Nairobi. I don't want them to meet. They'll never understand each other."

Zemuani reluctantly nodded his head. He was a contemporary of Galo's who had lost his own father to alcohol. The wonder of bigamy just might allow the marriage to work. Wealthy men often had many wives, and he recognized Alijah might be one of the richest men their tribe had ever known. It would be an honor to have him as a relative, even if his sister spent but the few hours with him necessary to bear children. If she were lucky, he might grow fond of her, elevating her to be his primary wife. He knew that was unlikely. Probably, she would never understand him; and, from their brief conversation, Zemuani recognized Alijah would probably never give her the chance. Still, he was happy. His sister would marry a rich and famous man, and as her brother, he would benefit from both the bridewealth and the friendship. They embraced, and Zemuani began his three-day walk home to inform his sister about her husband-to-be.

Alone at the edge of the circle framing the village's center, Tza dolefully watched the future brothers-in-law separate. What role she would now play was uncertain. She hoped affection would weigh more heavily in her favor than the payment of cattle. She wanted to remain Alijah's primary wife— at least in the village. This was not a moment to make demands, though, for she sensed Alijah's confusion and despair could only be soothed through the solitude of prayer. She was at once a crutch and a complication. Tza would endure the misery of not being needed until she could once again feel loved. Watching Alijah, she trembled with the thought she might never see him again. Since his marriage to Sara, his visits had become sporadic, even painful. Whatever

Tza's longings, she would have to settle for bittersweet memories and lonely nights.

Dusk loomed as Richard Keeton made his way over to Alijah, who now stood alone, his back to his village watching the sun fall from the sky. When he reached him, the enormous orange ball fit perfectly within the outstretched arms of a wishbone-shaped tree in the distance. To those watching them from the village, they appeared as lonely sticks against an orange backdrop. Uncomfortable, Richard woodenly reminded him how sorry he was but then backed away. He desperately wanted to relinquish the role of surrogate father. Best if they move on, he encouraged; and drained of emotion, Alijah simply nodded, following silently.

Behind him, Alijah's family stood as silhouettes until the dust rising from the tires gave way to darkness.

# CHAPTER 10

*Lugano, Switzerland*

Jacques Frankel tweaked his son's cheek, telling him to button up his coat or else he would catch cold. They were outside the Lugano train station fighting the bitter drafts surging up the tracks. Jacques boy, Yves, crumpled up his scarf, pushing it against his ribs so he could pull his collar tight and fasten the last button. With the extra warmth secured, he crooked his neck lazily skywards, then back down, squinting into the distance. After puzzling over the crisscross ties flowing to a vanishing point, he leveled his gaze back out over the tracks in the hopes of being the first to spot Uncle Richard's train. Yves put his hands in his pockets and asked his father how it could be so cold inside the protection of the station. The boy had inherited Jacques's thin frame, not much meat under his coat to protect against the chill. Fortunately, Yves had his mother's eyes and tender features, spared the gargoyle beak of a nose trying to peck free of his father's face.

It was 10:52 on the big station clock on a Saturday morning that promised an equally bitter afternoon. Richard's train was due in from Zurich at 10:57, which in Swiss time meant the train would pull in at 10:57. Indeed, within a minute of the scheduled arrival time, the train slowed to a stop. Jacques took Yves' hand, thwarting his wandering away in the crowd looking for Richard. Richard had left Kenya three weeks before, stopping in Hong Kong before flying to New Delhi to visit his stepson, and then finally continuing on to Zurich. He expected the flight to be an ordeal and was quite content to stay overnight by the airport and continue by train in the morning. He dissuaded Julia from accompanying him by telling her he would be conducting business most of the time. She still wanted to tag along but changed her mind when presented with his itinerary. Seven cities in three weeks—three of which he actually planned to visit. He claimed Alijah and Ron had put together a funding drive, and he was their goodwill ambassador. Before leaving, he privately joked to Ron that his wife's most endearing quality was her willingness to acquiesce.

One bag over his shoulder, and another pulling his arm to his knees, Richard glanced between bodies before setting down his luggage and waving. Yves broke loose, dodging several passengers before jumping into Richard's arms. Richard always stopped in Switzerland whenever in Europe to visit Jacques and Lana, and delighted in watching Yves grow. He was now eight years old and beginning to develop his father's slight frame and mother's wavy blond hair. Jacques and Richard's parents had been close friends, and growing up, Jacques and Richard followed suit. Jacques parents wanted him to learn proper English, and sent Jacques to boarding school with Richard in England. The boys then joined their families to holiday together over Christmas and again in August. By the time they were finishing secondary school, though, and especially once university age, their fathers started directing their careers. Not surprisingly, the boys drifted apart, separated by countries, language, studies, and family legacies.

Richard's father was a member of the House of Lords, a successor to a family seat first awarded to Harold Keeton in the late 1800s. Harold had run a small garment factory that sourced its cotton for fabric from America until the outbreak of the Civil War. When the South ceased meeting all their demands, Harold decided to quit his job and sail off to Africa in search of new raw materials. A friend boasted about their colonies' cotton production, and he decided to take orders from local merchants and charter a boat. His business turned out to be enormously successful as he arranged regular charters from Lagos on the African West Coast to supply British manufacturers. Not only were his supplies more dependable, but he could undersell any importer from the United States. By the time he was thirty-five, he was a rich man hungry for growing richer. He expanded his imports from Africa and became an intermediary for a South African gold merchant. He also strove to break into the diamond market yet never made much of a profit. Strong monopolies already controlled the most lucrative mines, and he never succeeded in obtaining an exclusive contract. He once invested in a mine that turned a modest profit, but made the bulk of his fortune from cotton, gold, and other raw materials.

Lord Harold Keeton's first wife died from a disease she caught somewhere in Africa that doctors could never diagnose. On a voyage back home, she started sweating terribly, the medicine on board providing no relief. They were too far out to sea to find her any quick help. She died before they touched land. An enormously rich man at this point, he settled in the countryside near Salisbury, eventually marrying a much younger woman from a titled Dutch family. Richard remembered visiting his grandmother's home near Leiden, sailing amidst the pretty canals and drinking wonderfully rich local beer.

Richard's father, Lord Winthrop Keeton, spent his life draining the money that Harold had first made. He managed a plantation in Nigeria left to him for a while, but eventually sold that to free himself of all distant responsibilities. By the time Richard was born, there was little left of Harold's mini-empire and not much more of the fortune than the lands represented. The houses, furniture, and possessions rivaled those of the best estates, but the bank accounts were no longer blinking green. Richard grew up watching his father squander what was to be his inheritance and hated him ever after.

His father pushed his boys to work hard in school. Even though Graham was the oldest and therefore destined to take over the family holdings, Lord Winthrop always expected Richard to bear his part in helping build back some of the old business. Richard took his mission to heart, blinding himself to reality, not truly believing he would be cut out as his second living son. He excelled by ignoring the likely outcome, convinced he was more capable and worthy than his partying brother Graham; moreover, he felt destined to inherit, believing that fate would somehow leapfrog him over the accident of a slightly later birth.

Spurred on by Harold's lore, Richard worked doggedly to learn everything he could and grasp what was surely his eventually to claim. Harold left many long letters behind, which Richard used to read for inspiration, keeping them in a box on his desk. He was always amazed at the detail and passion embodied in the yellowing scrawls. The letters seemed to read as if their author intended them for an audience rather than a friend. The missives were a chronicle of a style and time that he coveted experiencing and always believed he would find in Africa. He fanaticized that when he could afford it, he would take a merchant ship the whole way to recapture the aura of the letters. The journey was his destiny. His oldest brother, Alistair, had been killed in World War II when Richard was thankfully too young to comprehend the soot that stained their church. The duty fell to him and Graham to save the remnants of what the name Keeton once represented.

He believed his father's credo that it could be done. Unfortunately, though, the businesses were virtually nonexistent, and the routes, ships, and trading rights now possessed by others or canceled. There was little hope, and after years of toiling, he lapsed into the malaise he watched growing up. At first, he thought Graham's car crash was the fulfillment of the fate he had intuited, soon to make him the proper heir. But then Graham simply hung on, a vegetable waiting for a title, with no hope of ever restoring glory. Richard was unwed, untitled, and lost when his father died. Those now seemed like halcyon days next to the resentment and bitterness filling his blank diary after the title passed. He was left suddenly to care for a brother who did not even have the faculties to appreciate the injustice. Compounding Richard's grievances, the cost of Graham's care was eating away at what was left of the estate. Thirsting for a way to pass the time until Graham's inevitable decline, Richard, as custodian, decided to sell off most of their remaining land, keeping only the house in Salisbury built by Harold. He sold some pieces to Jacques and visited him before sailing to Africa. He made up his mind to sail the long way, taking Harold's letters along with him. He knew no one on the trip and continued around the Cape to Kenya, rumored to be the most civilized place on the continent.

A few years later, providence shined on him when he seduced the newly widowed Julia Dunning, securing enough money to begin his climb back, desperate that the Lordship be a fitting crown to the legacy he was rebuilding. After marrying Julia, an equal partner in coveting a proper title, he seldom left Africa. Richard used to travel back to Europe once a year, visiting Jacques in Switzerland and some friends and his mother in England. When his mother died, he came even less frequently. Now seeing Jacques, Richard was reminded of one the few things he looked forward to when returning.

Jacques and Lana had an even more pampered life. Jacques' father was a genuine banking baron, grooming his son to follow his path. Jacques never questioned his direction, studying finance at university before joining his father in business. Several years ago, he had taken over full responsibility and thrived once in control. He knew the business better than anyone else. Though perhaps not as dominating as his father had been, Jacques had a sixth sense for timing. He always attributed it to his knowledge of history and, in particular, his reserve of patience, a quality his father never possessed.

To some, the description of a Swiss banker can sound cliché, but to Jacques, it was a duty to fulfill the part. With connections the world round like Richard, Jacques leveraged the history of his vaults, the tentacles of his privileged network, the rock of the Swiss Franc, and the nuclear shield of Swiss privacy to enlarge his holdings. His father had initially built the bank in Zurich. Jacques expanded branches to Lugano and Zug, choosing benevolent quieter cities on pristine lakes to shelter fortunes both dirty and genuine. In the end, he converted it all to gold.

He modeled his empire on better-known Swiss paragons of banking, renting rich marbled spaces with modest engravings by the entrance. A customer would first caress the buzzer, the door monitored by a hidden guard watching the security camera. Once the guard deemed it likely whoever beckoned could buy a Mercedes as easily as a ballpoint pen, the door would click open. Passports would be checked and signatures stored; however, it was all about a simple number. The Germans and Swiss and their numbers. Jacques was careful to take personal care of his clients, engaging with just enough aloofness to ensure the mystique remained. For those wanting vaults, he maintained properly sealed rooms as if James Bond himself were set to saunter in and retrieve mysterious papers stuffed in an aging metallic drawer. Of course, he would deduct a measured fee for the kindness of his services and the rental of the less than square foot condominiums. No statements were maintained or mailed, and administration kept to a minimum.

Jacques' accounts were like IP addresses before their time, denoting a place and access, but devoid of tracing actual locations. Ah, like the Internet before hacking or accountability or even search. It was a blissful arrangement if you maintained the only access. Who cared if the ante were more than a proper sized apartment on a nearby lake? A big box leading to a little box, leading to a discreet number. It was all such a clever little game, save for the fact it was real and that some boxes were so black it took the loss of a soul to look inside.

Who knew what lay inside some of those boxes that Jacques' father Rolfe first hid? Jacques may have turned a blind eye, but he doubted he could be absolved of the sins lying behind what his father likely abetted. He occasionally shuddered at the thought but then morally cleansed himself, cocksure that he should not bear responsibility for the sins of the father. His father was still alive, somehow having absolved his soul of guilt, living on an estate overlooking Lake Como and the Alps. His parent's villa was beside the real Bellagio, not some fake casino owner's Disneyland version. Old money, dirty money, quiet privilege, boxes best left unopened.

Rolfe always wanted Richard to visit, treating him like a second son. This time, Richard made Jacques promise not to leak he was in town, but now he was stuck. He looked up at Jacques, smiling as he put Yves back down, knowing that the boy would tell his grandfather. Jacques had won. After lunch, Jacques and Richard took a stroll along the winding road leading up the mountain to Jacques' house. He lived above the town, a few kilometers away, the rustic yet immaculately maintained roads winding up the mountains dotted with pines and even olive trees in the benign climate that managed a touch of Alpine with an ode to the

Mediterranean. His living room afforded a panoramic view over the town and its steeples sprawling from the edge of the lake. Across from their reflection loomed snow-capped mountains making the view equal to that from warming huts on the distant slopes. Richard joked that Jacques and Lana's living room rivaled the best of Switzerland's gondolas for scenic tours. Their walk took them along a road offering the same views, subjecting them to the cold quiet for the price of admission.

"So, you want to buy a chalet?" Jacques confirmed.

"Absolutely! I've always wanted one, and I thought it would be a perfect place for Caroline and Michael to honeymoon."

"I don't know where you're getting all this money, but we'll look tomorrow. Actually, I do know where you're getting all the money..."

Richard looked sheepish, "What do you mean?"

"I mean this deal. The money you're having me launder."

"I'm not laundering anything. I'm just exporting a bit more than I have before. We stumbled onto a big cache."

"Come on, Richard. Don't patronize me. I'm sticking my neck out for you, and I don't even know what's going on. If you can't tell me, you've got to be in a lot of trouble." Jacques looked at Richard sympathetically, pausing a moment, and then continuing up the hill. It felt colder now that they had been walking a few minutes, and he pulled a ski cap out of his pocket. Richard was already wearing a Russian hat Lana had lent him.

Jacques rarely inquired into his clients' deals, but Richard was different. They had grown up almost as family; that bond, however, rather than drawing them closer, caused Jacques deep anxiety. Though irrational, he feared he could be tainted by whatever Richard was meddling in, an assumed witness or collaborator. Nobody would believe he did not know. Jacques himself would hardly find his own denials credible, regardless of actual facts.

"No, no I'm not in trouble. Yet!" Richard laughed. "The less you know, the less risk you're taking. I'll tell you if you really want, or if byzantine documentation requires you need to know more. Why don't you look at the new invoices? I brought them with me. Let's see if there's a problem first."

Uncomfortably keeping his distance, eager to know and not know, Jacques cowardly demurred, "I'm sure I won't need to know anything more. I was just asking. I thought you might want to talk about it."

"No. I'm sure you've guessed half of it anyway from what I've told you the last few times I've been here. It's not as if the invoices are coming from London."

Jacques coughed quietly, his visible breath clinging to the cold and seeming to trail his words, "I suppose I've known for a while. When you first asked me, I had no idea we were talking about this much money. I hope you know what you're doing. I've got to tell you, I really don't approve."

"I didn't think you would. I just hope you understand."

"Keep on hoping, Richard. Take this last one as a favor and forget the fee. But I can't promise I can keep this up forever."

"No reason to be anxious…And however you want to handle the fees is fine. I appreciate everything. The money's there. The deposits won't be this big in the future. I think we might be slowing down after this one."

"Well, you'll have the new account opened and a record of deposits. Everything should flow through smoothly if you keep the amounts down. I'll keep an eye on it, but I want to limit any direct involvement. Everything just goes regularly through the bank, okay? We'll use the Zug branch. Better not the town I live in."

"Of course. Look, I get it, and as I said, I'm grateful. I'll give you these invoices, and after you set things up and wire the correspondent banks that the bank has these, you should be almost through. I'm sure they'll wire the money once they know you've got these. They always have," Richard crowed.

"I'll put everything through Monday morning. If your customers, or whatever you want to call them, put up the money as you claim, it should be on deposit by next weekend. If in a few weeks you walk in with proof of delivery the money's all yours. No questions asked. The documents will speak to each other."

"There won't be any problems, don't worry. The captain assured me the ship wouldn't sink!"

"I hope not. I'm not sure how careful you're being about everything else. I mean taking the invoices to India before coming here. Do you realize the risk you were taking of having them stolen?"

"Don't worry. I've thought everything through. My partner has access to the documents and permits and all that stuff in Kenya. We had the invoices made out in quadruplets rather than the normal pair. I've got an identical set in a safe at home. Anyway, I never let them out of my sight, and if anyone ever stole them, we'd be there waiting for them when the ship came in."

"What do you say we head back? I'm getting cold," Jacques said, looking out over the lake and away from Richard. He rubbed his hands together hard, tugging his hat down further. Soon they traded gifts. Richard gave Jacques a briefcase made from impala skin stuffed with papers to be opened in private. For Lana, he had a silk scarf from India, and for Yves, a turban. Yves had become besotted after spying the odd head tourniquet in a book and ran around the room as if ready to rise with the rugs. Little Aladdin wore himself out, succumbing to the couch and falling asleep during Uncle Richard's story about chasing lions.

The adults had dinner with Rolfe, who asked Richard why he was staying an extra few days. He answered that he was trying to buy a chalet. To make good on the story, Richard closed a deal Tuesday morning. In a secluded spot about an hour away, on the gentle slopes above Lake Maggiore, stood a twenty-year-old, three-bedroom cottage. The wooden roof sloped like the rest, but what sold Richard were the three fireplaces, one in the living room plus another two warming the large bedrooms.

Isolated by a dirt road, the cabin appeared unattended but for cords of wood piled up almost to the roof. It was only a short hike from a private train crossing and conveniently nestled between the access road and a private dock. With binoculars, the quaint square's clock tower just up from the lake could be seen in the distance, but today clouds ominously rolled in to protect their privacy. Richard explained that it made the perfect honeymoon spot. Jacques smiled, wondering why Richard went so far as to buy it. He knew he would never visit, and the only one he could impress was Julia, who would love it to "placedrop."

None of it made much sense to him. Not then when he helped Richard sign the papers, nor several days later when Richard was back home, the money deposited, and the ships docked in their ports. Jacques thought about taking his initial twenty-five thousand dollars and giving it to Yves for a future Safari but decided to decline the fee. It was the type of money he suspected first made his father rich. It was not the type of money he now needed to keep.

Periodically, he would drive by the chalet only to see the stack of wood untouched. He hoped he would finally have a chance to meet the next generation, but Michael and Caroline had still not visited. The cottage stood empty, surrounded by some of the most breathtaking views on earth. No one besides Jacques ever came to look. Practically no one but he knew the house existed at all. Richard paid in cash, so there was no mortgage and no paperwork save a filed title. An independent account generated just enough interest yearly to pay the taxes.

Jacques heard that Richard was negotiating to buy one of Harold's old estates in Scotland but was having trouble with an owner who had bought it to capture the same sentimentality for which Richard now bid. When he probed further, Richard passed it off, denigrating the opportunities and claiming there were only so many properties for sale in Kenya. He nevertheless promised Jacques great deals if he ever felt like venturing overseas. Just hop on a plane and remember his passport and account numbers. Always papers, documents, titles. That captured Richard's visits in a nutshell—except for all the other unspeakable stuff best kept at a distance.

·     ·     ·     ·     ·

Kent Dunning found his stepfather's trip puzzling, deciding to call Caroline to make sense of the visit and his requests. Richard wanted to try shipping some trinkets into the state of Gujarat and had asked Kent if he could arrange permits. Kent refused to help when sniffing what Richard was really peddling. Powdered rhinoceros horn was used as an aphrodisiac in certain provinces in India. In Malaysia, where it was touted as a medicinal panacea, the contraband sold for an incredible $150 per ounce. Kent presumed Richard's stop in Hong Kong was to distribute the horns for future sales and that the sojourn to India meant that sales to Malaysia were already set.

Julia answered the phone, and after catching up a bit told him he had just missed his sister. "Caroline's working at the vet clinic. No, wait, maybe she's at the large animal rescue center. She volunteers there one day a week. I can't keep her schedule straight. I'll just tell her to call you back. And to make sure she catches you before leaving. She's going to the US with Michael. He has a paper to deliver and needs to meet with his advisor or something like that. Caroline said they decided it would be a perfect opportunity to take a side trip and meet Michael's family."

"I would have thought she'd be trying to get out of meeting the in-laws!"

"Kent, that's not very diplomatic. Especially for a diplomat."

"Very funny mother. Look, I'd rather not wait weeks to talk to Caroline. Can you please make sure to pass along the message? It's not critical, but I'm anxious to talk to her about something."

Unfortunately, Caroline was not able to reach Kent before departing on her trip. It would be weeks before they were able to speak.

•     •     •     •     •

Caroline was so excited she kept her face pressed against the window as their plane began its final descent into John F. Kennedy airport in New York. Despite having promised to visit several people in her college days, she had never been to the United States. The commitments had waned with time, but not her desire. She had fought with Michael about the trip because she wanted to play tourist. He longed to relax with his brother and tie up his dissertation, convincing her they would return soon.

For his part, Michael would be through with his Ph.D. shortly, and if she liked the States, as she called them, they could move there for a couple of years or permanently. Michael tried to ignore the genuine possibility that a near-titled British lady and free spirit of Africa might not like—nay, could even loathe—the bustle, gaudy commercialism and different tribal prejudices which defined many corners of America. Segregating insecurities, Michael retreated to focusing on his chances of being offered an assistant professor post and not so secretly praying for a move back to hallowed academic grounds in Boston.

Caroline knew Michael had his heart set on a position at Harvard and could not deny him his professorial fantasy—at least for the moment. Compromising for this trip, she settled for a brief taste of New York, Boston, and Washington, D.C. Let him yearn for his dream, she yielded; it was easy to wall off as if an existential thought the possibility of actually living in the United States. Anyone coming to their senses would recognize the superior prestige held by dons of Cambridge. Good heavens, St. Andrews was even highly acceptable, and the lush hills of Scotland could house a comfortable horse farm despite its bone-chilling weather.

Keep an open mind, Caroline thought, excited about the United States' possibilities, trying to coax a pioneer spirit from a life carpeted with the ease of narrow expectations and challenges alike. She had made an appointment to visit a budding veterinary school at Tufts. To her, the name had a silly similarity to Tusks, so she deemed it Tusks U and assumed she could find a way via malapropism and fine academics to concoct the next steppingstone in her veterinary journey. If they did not encourage specialization into large animals, by will or stepfather she would sort a way to endow her studies. And maybe she could discover a wonderful horse farm in the nearby rolling hills; Michael was eager for her to see the famed countryside that in autumn painted a gumdrop-like collage of leafs. Perhaps this was just a mind game to keep her options open.

The reality was she was not American and would likely end up back at the Royal Veterinary College specializing in horses. Hopefully, too, she would soon be back in the bush aiding the next victim of a poacher's snare. She missed the savanna already. How could she be happy in a land where elephants barely roamed in hundred-meter pens or where people associated riding more with westerns than Ascot?

England or Africa, it didn't matter, she resigned, and a sampling of America could be fun before the throes of a continental debate. They would visit Michael's mother and her beau, Jack, in New York first, staying a few days before flying to Boston. They would see Michael's brother JJ, and stay in New England either a week or perhaps ten days depending upon how his advisor received his work. From Boston, they would then fly south to Washington for a few days and stay with Michael's friend Ben. If everything went smoothly in Boston, they could leave for Washington earlier and have some extra time back in New York before flying back. The entire trip would take around three weeks; undoubtedly, they agreed, it would be too short. Nevertheless, Michael insisted on the time frame. He needed to return to finish his research; plus, he argued, if they stayed longer it would only make it that much more difficult to trek back to the equator.

Caroline knew his rationalizations merely covered up repressed paranoia from his first arrival in Africa. The reentry would not be as difficult this time. She could not hope to convince him of that, though, nor rationally discuss the matter. So, she agreed on the timeframe, knowing the next itinerary would be up to her. These were memorable weeks in their lives, and the urgency applied to his thesis was ludicrous for a subject matter identifying patterns over generations.

None of their bickering mattered once the plane touched down and the passengers spontaneously burst into applause. Caroline looked to Michael, who instinctively joined in the clapping. It was an outburst of patriotism that could perhaps best be appreciated by a visitor from Britain. Karen, his mother, and Jack were supposed to meet their flight. In anticipation of an awkward greeting, Michael spent the entire wait through customs reiterating his pleas not to prejudge them on appearance. Caroline no longer had any idea what to expect but sensed Michael growing tenser with every step towards the exit.

There was no missing them around the corner. As soon as Michael saw Jack in his burgundy leisure suit with his arm around his mother in her mangy raccoon coat, he made up his mind to stay in New York only two days. Mercifully, one of those days, he would sleep. His mother, Karen, had become a blond while he was gone. Bleached was more tolerable than Jack's change. He opted for the look of hair, donning a new mat like a strung beanie. Michael told Caroline in private that he would not be surprised if he had it made from some of his mother's hair. He tallied the number of people to whom he could dare make such a remark, narrowing the field to one. He was so glad they were going to be married.

Michael was more embarrassed by his mother than he originally feared, not sure how to converse. Short answers punctuated long pauses. Feigning interest in their lives, Karen asked whether they planned to settle in Kenya or Europe, or possibly back in America. Michael responded they were not sure. Caroline tried to interrupt and carry on the conversation, but Karen seemed uninterested, the earlier question a mere formality. She did not want their lives to merge, ardently denying the tie. When her husband died, she relied on her two sons and sulked, depressed about having to go through the motions for the rest of her life. Michael left for college, and she was utterly alone, primed for snapping. When he returned, she was slipping, the distance increasing with each visit. Severing all ties, she moved to New York and reemerged, unconnected and unconcerned with her past.

Karen now approached life with an abandoned selfishness that Michael could no longer comprehend. To her, he did not matter; his brother JJ did not matter; his father never even existed. Karen's sons were now nuisances to be tolerated out of an obligation remote and ever waning. So, Michael adapted. Embittered and resentful, he pushed on. By excelling in school, Michael's life became earlier marked by his achievements and goals than befell most other sons. Nothing was scripted, and nothing was asked. Escaping from a vacuum of support, he had crawled out to overcome abandonment and pressure alike. Finally, he had a partner, someone to lessen the task of scripted isolation. And his mother still did not care. Michael wondered whether this family jettisoning steeled him for the encounters with poachers, his ability to compartmentalize and fight back well honed.

In a hollow effort to salvage a bit of dignity, Michael told Caroline that deep down Karen was happy for him. His words sounded forced. More tellingly, his mother had become Karen to him, just another woman with another name. Seeing Michael's wrecked family bonds broke Caroline's heart. As she reflected on her own life, she thought how lucky she was to have a new father so accepting of her and so welcoming to her family.

•    •    •    •    •

Michael sat nervously with Caroline in one of Harvard Square's half intellectual, half boho coffee houses. In a few minutes, he would know about his Ph.D. chances. Michael tapped his fingers on the table until one stuck to some old jam. He wiped the top furiously with his napkin, only managing to smear grape around a larger area. If he could stop a waitress, he might plead for help cleaning his mess with a consolation refill of his coffee. He looked at Caroline and smiled. Her face was nearly obliterated by a huge muffin dripping melted butter the color of her hair as she tried to wrestle it to her mouth.

A man with a feather earring and a ponytail dangling down over his shoulder pulled on a Harris Tweed coat and walked past, bumping Michael's elbow. Caroline watched the man moving to the register. He waited his turn to pay behind a redhead with a backpack over her shoulder. It was cold outside, and woman wore a heavy scarf stretching to the floor. The restaurant was too loud to hear what she said to the clerk. Several people in line eagerly watched her gather up change and then looked to see if anyone had gone to sponge the table. It was snowing lightly, and while moments before they were grateful for the drafty warmth of the entrance, they now wanted a seat. Two men in the middle of the line went around the wait-to-be-seated rope and sat at an uncleaned booth, causing some commotion.

Caroline was soaking up the atmosphere, so bohemian next to her Paris and London experiences. Michael's anxiety over his pending meeting, though, made it difficult to immerse herself fully. She had told him not to worry and that his advisor would be overwhelmed by his work. Finally, after frustrating everyone who counted the empty plates as a signal, Michael stood up to leave. The crush to take their still dirty table reminded Caroline of a pack of hyenas rushing in for the spoils.

Michael left a tip, sick of debating and shaking his head, thinking Caroline could never comprehend the rigors of the ivy-covered laboratories. Great was expected, not appreciated. The standards were intentionally insurmountable on a first try. Yet, he dreamed of walking in and being stroked with the adulation of a Nobel laureate. He had done real fieldwork, after all, that deed revered by crusty blackboard academics. They spoke of the times not as paying dues but rather as the period in their lives when they so immersed themselves in the grit of the profession that they emerged with the virtue of authority. Those were the noble enlightening years making the pursuit both tangible and fulfilling. A couple of years packed a lifetime of lecture stories.

Michael was tired, fighting a flu caught between climates. He did not hold his present life so dearly. Every morning in camp he had to check his shoes for scorpions and the edge of his tent for scorpions. He had fought off a mild case of malaria, ate cabbage for a week when he was delayed picking up supplies, and even killed a few men. There were at least two stories there. He kissed Caroline goodbye and checked their rendezvous point with her again, fearful that she would become lost in the chaos of Harvard Square.

Michael set off determined: he would be damned if they criticized him now after what he had been through! It had been over a year since he walked through "the yard" as it was locally known. Michael reminisced past each tree on his way past bronzed John Harvard and the gates leading towards the old museums. When he neared Divinity Avenue, the snow began to fall harder, and he pulled out the Celtics hat JJ made him stick in his pocket that morning. He coveted Steve's office. Overlooking the courtyard from the fifth floor of the Museum of Comparative Zoology, Professor Barton's view bespoke of tenure. He could watch his students picnicking on the grass below or spin around to see the rows of cabinets and books lining his office.

Michael would never forget their first meeting. He had made an appointment and two days later received a shorthand jotted note with directions on how to reach the office. The note told him to enter through the front door and ignore the guard taking admission tickets to the museum. If he walked in looking serious and carrying a briefcase, he could push back the iron bar and enter freely. Next, he was supposed to wind through a few exhibits until he found the skeletons of man and apes displayed together. Behind them would lie a staircase, and by the shoulder of the sperm whale suspended from the ceiling, a camouflaged door with a buzzer would be revealed. Shaking free of his daydream, he now pushed the same rusty button, listening for Steve Barton's footsteps coming down the corridor past the green cabinets and their formaldehyde treasures.

"Michael! I can't believe you're back already. I can remember when you were just leaving and bitching about all those shots over at UHS," Professor Barton, alias pal-of-the-PhD-candidate Steve, greeted him.

"Yeah. I can hardly believe it too. Only it seems a lot longer. My mother always told me that time went slower when you're exposed to new things. Like going to camp. Every year I went back, the summer seemed to go faster. I don't know if that will ever work with Africa though."

"Well, for your sake, I hope not. You should enjoy it while you can. I'm jealous. I sit here every day in this cubby hole and stare out the window."

Michael looked over the old office and sat. Nothing had changed. The same torn map of the world was tacked to the wall across from Steve's window and desk, pins stuck in the places either he or his students had studied. Darwin's *The Origin of Species* lay beside the New Testament on a shelf otherwise holding volumes of Scientific Americans. A picture of Steve in Tanzania with Mary Leakey stood propped against the windowpane. Photos of Professor Barton's family were fitted around a cube on the front of his desk. Michael once kidded him that he ought to take up smoking a pipe to fill out the ambiance, but the crazy old academic preferred munching on orange tic-tacs.

"So, what do you think," Michael began, his sentence trailing off. "Will I get a window?" knowing his advisor's reaction would be more than a telltale of his Ph.D. chances.

About one year before, he set out to study the social behavior of the yellow baboon, Papio cynocephalus, one of man's closest relatives. Genetically the species is frightfully close, but those yearning for safe distance can find solace partly in their behavior and mostly in the presence of a tail. Michael's troop ranged during the study from a low of twenty-two when he began his research to thirty when he left for the States. Out of this thirty, all of whom he named and could distinguish readily from a distance, seven were adult males, eleven adult females, and the rest infants and, for lack of a better term, adolescents. His research, when summarized, sounded quite mundane, but at the time, it was groundbreaking.

Michael focused on the dominance hierarchy in the troop, keeping careful track of rank and mating opportunities. Popular theory suggested that the top male exclusively mated with all the adult females and that the males fought their way towards the top. In fact, Michael found that virtually all males mated occasionally and that the ratings shifted. Most males never made it to the top, but as he stated in his summary, all males did get on top.

During his observations, three different males held the champion slot, but two different times the number one and two contenders took over the title for a month or two at a time. Those that started at the bottom seemed destined to stay near the bottom. Michael tried to give them appropriate names, calling the perennially bottom male Dopey and the top two Studly and Poobah (Thor had fallen off). Steve Barton warned him that for publication, the names had to go.

While the research confirmed existent data about general behavior patterns, diet, and body size, Michael's findings regarding reproduction were innovative. Not only was he able to chronicle that certain males held their place atop the dominance hierarchy, but more importantly, that these same males mated more frequently near the time of the females' ovulation. In other words, Poohbah's copulatory frequency was much greater than Dopey's during the times when the chances of fathering Poohbah Jr. were highest. He was able to show that there was differential success among males in such a troop; most importantly, he could document that success was related to the dominance hierarchy and would be reflected in the next generation.

Sex is always a hot topic in evolutionary circles, and it was particularly hot at Harvard when Michael set out on his research. The more sex you had, the more kids you have was the socio-biologists' motto. By studying humping, scientists felt sure they were discovering the missing link to behavioral studies and evolutionary physiology. The only important goal to the socio-biologists as far as the animal was concerned was reproductive success. How many genes any individual could pass on to the next generation was the sole yardstick of that individual's worth. Because relatives also carry many of the same genes, it was important to keep track of relatedness and how successful each relative was in their own right.

Animals that did not seem to reproduce as much as others may be doing the best they can, efficiently investing some of their energy to ensure the survival of their offspring as well as their sisters. Altruism, the perennial thorn in the theories of reproduction, could be justified on such grounds. Genetics, behavior, and evolution could be reconciled in neat equations multiplying genes from close family members and tabulating who won.

Michael's research was significant because it provided the empirical data to back up the emerging classroom theories. The entire field was relatively new, and the pioneers of the new science were his current teachers and even colleagues. Pushing his findings to the limit, Michael's examples could become case studies vindicating controversial theories, perhaps winning him fame in his own time. A Nobel was surely not in sight, but being recognized like a Watson or Crick within his sociobiological niche was possible.

"What about parental investment," Steve asked. "Have you got anything for the soap opera theory?"

"Huh?"

"Never heard of the soap opera approach?" Steve mocked.

"No. I have no idea what you're talking about."

"Parental investment. Generally, a male will only spend time nurturing a pregnant female if he is sure the baby is his. The more a male thinks the female might have mated with others, the less time he's likely to spend with the female and the less likely they are to form a monogamous pair bond. Then..."

"Yeah, I know all this. I still don't follow you," Michael interrupted.

"Well, the soap opera theory is just that. Every soap opera revolves around paternity uncertainty. After about ten episodes, you find out that Jack isn't Tony's son, but is Cliff's son because Cliff was having an affair with Jack's mother, and because they're now sleeping together again, the truth comes out."

"Oh."

"So, paternity certainty is important. It regulates all social behavior. How close is Poobah to the different females? Does he know he's humping them at the right time?"

"I don't know, I'll ask...Jesus, Steve. I've been keeping data on bonding and care. I don't know. I'll try to correlate it. I'm not sure what I can draw right now, but I've got the relevant information down."

"Good. Now, what about pictures, films?"

"I don't have any with me, is that what you mean? All I've got is some snapshots back in camp."

"You ought to leverage those, you know. For a book, we probably want pictures of Poobah flashing his fangs or something. Films, documentaries are hot. A good movie can cover up a lot of bad writing."

"You thought my writing was..."

"No, no, it's fine. But the decision isn't mine. Just cover all the angles. We may never use it."

"You think the whole thing's in trouble," Michael panicked. "I mean, I thought things went pretty well. You don't think the other profs will buy it?"

"No. I didn't mean that. I just meant you now need to do a better job writing the research up. I realize this was thrown together for me now. But I've got to be an asshole. This isn't just a thesis you're writing. If this is approved, you might be offered an assistant professorship at Yale, or here, god forbid. Now, go back and get me some pictures, and I'll work on the ratings..."

Michael relaxed, absorbing that Steve lauded the research and there was a damn good chance he would be offered a position. He knew how Steve's mind worked and what specific hints meant. Nothing uttered ever turned out to be irrelevant. Years of dreams, hours of hard work, months of sickness, and minutes of dread culminated in his smile. Success had been acknowledged, and its trappings were but patient weeks away. He shook Steve's hand, extending his thorn-scabbed fingers in a gesture of both confidence and appreciation.

He wanted to tell Steve about his relationship with Caroline but calculated their relationship best be kept secret; at least until his readers issued an irrevocable stamp of approval. Their wedding plans might give one of the readers the wrong idea about his round-the-clock dedication to the research while in Africa. Steve's advice was to deny him the truth.

•    •    •    •    •

Michael's brother, JJ, and Caroline toasted the academic star in the gigantic pier-front bar at one of Boston's most famous seafood restaurants. Watching the twinkling city lights through the low fog, they drank with abandon. Neither reunions like this nor assurances like those in the afternoon came often. The seaside booth they waited over an hour for was finally reset and vacant. "Lobsters for three." No need for a menu. Caroline excused herself, and JJ looked up at Michael.

In a slightly slurred tone, he said, "God, Mike, she's beautiful. A fucking noble too! I can't believe it."

Michael beamed. While petrified to introduce Caroline to his mother, he had been looking forward to this moment for weeks. He fantasized about showing her off to JJ, never worried about his brother proving an embarrassment. He always figured Harvard had elevated them a social notch, catapulting them into the American elite. There was no past to be ashamed of, given Michael's fiction that the past began when they seized control over their lives. Based solely on achievement and looks, it was hardly possible to associate Michael and JJ with their formative years. Hurdling odds, they each preternaturally drifted to the top. Academically gifted, they were both surpassing goals that less capable dreamers set as their pinnacles.

Just shy of six feet, and more red-headed than Michael, JJ eschewed Michael's scraggly machismo look. In stark contrast, he parted his hair cleanly, often sporting designer clothes meant to exude status. This evening he was wearing an Italian silk and wool sweater, understated and showy at the same time. He could afford it: JJ earned more money in the last year than either of his parents made in their lifetimes. Perhaps it was time Michael joined the family's march toward more conspicuous success. After all, Michael sat with his arm wrapped around a woman who was to commoners like them a princess. Further raising his stock, soon he would be offered a post teaching at an institution where he once felt privileged merely to be a student.

Regardless of achievements and accolades, Michael struggled with an inferiority complex, worried that he was not on par with Caroline. If he could only understand that petty mutual insecurities strengthened their bond, he would have less to fear. No matter how jealous Michael grew of Caroline's birthright, and no matter how hard he tried to deny the feeling as being ludicrous, he basked in his association with her. He thrived in her presence and lived vicariously in a world without the pressures of achievement.

The delusion was mutual. Caroline longed for the opportunity to carve her own world, unguided by expectations, unshackled of tradition. Her life was an assumption from which Michael teased an escape.

Caroline unfolded her napkin when she sat back down, placing it on her lap as she spoke to JJ, "Michael tells me you're thinking about politics."

"Well, that's about it: thinking. You know, consulting is just solving everyone's problems without getting publicity for it. It would be nice to be doing something where you tried to solve the problems you care about rather than whatever bullshit case a client pays you to muse over. I don't know. I was just complaining to Michael and said that's what I'd do if I could afford it."

"Well, I think that's a great pursuit. My brother is sort of in politics, working as a diplomat. Following in my Dad's footsteps a bit."

"That's right, Michael told me about your father. He was an ambassador. That's amazing."

"Yeah," Caroline said, melancholy, thinking about her father. "I wish I could go back in time and discuss it with him. I was so little. I didn't appreciate what he did or how lucky I was."

Michael could sense the conversation becoming awkward for her, interrupting, "Well, be grateful you revered your father and have happy memories. And that you can be proud of your family. God, I'm still so embarrassed by Jack. JJ, I don't know how I made it through introducing Caroline to Jack and Mom. She keeps on changing every time I see her—and for the worse."

"Can we not go there?" JJ said, now finding that turn of conversation equally awkward. "If you want to talk about change, how about you? Couple of years ago, you're a scrawny kid fixing up junk cars and trying to impress girls, then get a perfect score on your admissions test and win that scholarship. Now listen to you. It's like you're moving at light speed."

Michael paused to crack a claw, spewing juice all over his bib. "You think I'm that different because of Africa?"

"I don't know. But yes. Tougher. Hard to put my finger on it. There's a certain swagger, but also something underneath it. Something you're not telling me. Give me time. I'll get it out of Caroline." He held his glass up in a toasting challenge.

Now sucking strands of lobster from the claw, Michael said, "No need. I think tougher may be a good way to put it. I was a scared little wimp when I first traveled there. Now I don't think I'll ever be shocked by anything. I guess today was just a reward for the battle. Oh, and by the way, I've become pretty good with a gun."

Michael wanted to recount the trauma of killing Gamala and his naïveté when meeting Susan Bennet in camp, but the experience was still too raw, and he was just beginning to catch up with JJ. Another day, and yes, he would confide in him, hoping he would find some solace in creating a triumvirate of witnesses, virtual and real, to his deed. He had lost touch with Susan—well, he had never really been in touch, paralyzed how to respond whenever he thought of replying to her letter—and rarely broached the subject with Caroline. Perhaps JJ would prove the additional confidant he craved. For now, he mentioned surviving a grisly event at his campsite, where a local was accidentally shot, and almost coming home immediately. He credited meeting Caroline and her pulling him through, having grown up understanding the savanna's capricious violence. He never expected to stare the meaning of survival of the fittest in the face, as if the theory only applied to lesser species.

After deciding to hide the truth about Gamala, he felt obligated to be candid about more recent exploits. He plunged ahead, describing the first poachers he gunned down with Warden James. It became apparent this was not his only kill, in fact, only the beginning. Caroline and JJ could feel the scars through his voice. Michael bemoaned the continent's seductive evils; beauty and isolation lured even the most principled away from their moral roots. As if transported to the Garden of Eden, temptation to newcomers like Michael was irresistible. Decisions could no longer be moral deep in thickets where butterflies disguised themselves as scorpions. Fighting back was instinctual.

Michael lamented that he never helped a baboon or aided a life. Arriving as an innocent observer, hoping to add knowledge, he left only taking, using, ruining. All the white men thought they were improving the natives' lives, teaching the so-called savage to read and write. But no savage grew richer. Only the white men grew richer off the thrill, off what they could pillage, off what they could sell. Michael knew he had become a minor legend protecting the animals and was destined to be a well-known professor; it was all, though, at the expense of what he took from the land. And he would violate Africa again. Its images, its deceptive tranquility would draw him back. And he would kill again if he must. It was the cost of being an outsider for the benefit of stepping back in time. That was the trivial piece he had to take, so short of the temptations obsessing the poachers. And now Caroline would help keep him centered, ensuring he stays on a righteous path. He needed to fight growing numb and pretending he could hide consequences in the bush.

"Yea, Mike, you're right. You've changed a lot. I'd like to see the slides sometime," JJ said, looking to Caroline, who though pained, had been prepared for Michael's cathartic outpouring. She truly believed that by confessing to his brother, he would unburden himself and start accepting that he had bravely reacted to circumstances—showing true mettle in having acted more than once—and that pride should start drowning out self-doubt. There is a brutality in the wild that one simply must accept. Like war, kill or be killed. Michael had proven his courage, and she loved his reflective remorse, demonstrating that he acted out of necessity and defending the animals. He was anything but a killer. JJ, though, could absorb but a fraction of these contradictions and definitions, and still bewildered, sought refuge, "I think I'd like another drink. No, make that a triple."

· · · · ·

Michael slouched back in his chair, wondering if his life would come to read better than it lived. He had gone so far as to call Susan Bennett's number but then hung up the instant she answered the phone. He knew it was her, chickening out—no need for further catharsis, already reliving the first week in camp too many times.

He stared at Caroline, questioning why she was interested in a man like him. Michael feared she would inevitably become bored with his everyday life, making it critical for Caroline to cultivate her career as a veterinarian. Should he take a professorship near where she could launch her practice? What if she ran a horse farm or insisted on moving back to Africa? Most of the exotic animals in Cambridge were stuffed in museums, and he could not condemn her to a research lab when he had witnessed her heroics saving the last of the animals that were future generations bridge to the past. He marveled at her abilities and the greater contributions she could make to the preservation of species than his footnotes on understanding their baser instincts. In Africa, perhaps he could play as an equal, but in what was posturing as the real world, what would transpire? She met him at his most exotic, and he worried the romance might falter with the mundane. Fortunately for Michael, such bursts of self-pity and insecurity tended to wear off with his hangovers. Why did he persistently fail to acknowledge the simple fact they were in love, smitten beyond logic?

Prone to introspection on long flights, borderline delusional at times, Michael woke up from the first leg of the journey back. The whirlwind trip to America was a jet-stream memory, and he was for the first time consciously leaving the ivy halls to step into his Indiana Jones-like quest. Could adventure be tempered, he wondered, or was it an all-in pursuit? Not long ago, living in a jungle tent, staring in wonder at the baboons shooing away the monkeys in the trees, hearing lions puffing in the distance, was more of an adventure than he dared to fantasize. He hoped that daily magic would still suffice, praying the adrenaline rush of the wrong kind of hunt would not prove too tempting.

·　　·　　·　　·　　·

Back in Heathrow, waiting for a flight to Africa, Michael sat reading brochures that came with their new camera equipment. They were carrying-on a new lightweight movie camera along with a few accessories, checking the rest. Caroline was the expert. She kept talking about the filters they were able to buy. The sun in Kenya is so intense that a marginal variance in filters could make an enormous difference in the final film quality. They bought the best and paid for it too—thousands of dollars.

"I still can't believe Richard told you to buy all this stuff and didn't tell me," Caroline said.

"I'm not making it up. He said the first question when we came back would be what did we buy."

"I don't understand why he's suddenly spending all this money. Telling me to buy a whole new wardrobe on Park Avenue!"

"So, what? I mean, this is everything I've ever dreamed of."

"Because this is everything I was always made to feel I had. My mom inherited a decent amount of money when my dad died, and I know Richard's family had fallen on some rough times. He tried to hide it, and didn't want me to realize he was living a bit off my mom. But I knew. In fact, more than she did—or would admit. If I ever suggest he's taking advantage of her, she gets offended and changes the subject. Anyway, now, I don't know, I'm taking advantage too. Which is weird, because it was mine to begin with. But for Richard, it's like something happened, and he's trying to show off all of a sudden. So, I'm...just suspicious."

"I don't know. He's Richard Keeton. I always thought he was rich. My god, look at your house! House isn't even the right word. Manor. Estate. When I first met you, I thought about where I was from and thought you'd never talk to me."

"Well, it's mom's house too. But, maybe you're right. Either way, you're getting a pretty good deal out of this, aren't you?"

"You're damn right I am!" Michael played along, kissing her in the middle of the busy waiting lounge before the people watchers.

Soon they were airborne, en route to Kenya to tidy up their affairs before the wedding. Michael knew what he needed to complete for his research, already envisioning the day when he could pack up his tent for good and start teaching. But then he thought about the poachers, an angry resolve cloaking him. It would not be easy to leave.

Caroline, too, was now lost in thoughts about her future career. Blankly gazing out at the light clouds, she reflected on how much her life was about to change. She liked Tufts more than expected, the pretty quad on the hilltop. Continuing veterinary studies there would be fine. That heralded the problem, though; she was not content with fine, or even what may be lauded as high achievement.

The conversation with Michael, and thinking about Richard's sudden largesse, reminded her that she always had more, without effort or greed. She did not picture herself as a snob. She loved playing polo— was it her fault the game happened to be her favorite childhood sport, and she was a natural? Why chastise herself for the luxury of growing up with a pet giraffe? Of course, she should be at a top veterinary school. Was she supposed to worry about which one and some silly ranking system? If she wanted to go to Oxford, she would go to Oxford. If Tufts was fated, then Tufts. By the benevolence of birth, she was free from the need to prove herself. She should attend whatever school proved convenient, of course assuming within at least the top echelons. No matter, the degrees all conferred the same status of a veterinarian. Raised in exotic surroundings, and so apart from the frenzy of competitive academics that she could not even see the quest lest appreciate it, Caroline tried sizing up the cadence of what others deemed normal. Despite certain oddities, ultimately, the United States did not seem particularly foreign to her. Was that normal?

Michael intuited her thoughts: "Well, what did you think of America after all? Was it what you were expecting?"

"It looked like what I was expecting. New, very clean, but there are so many weird things. Little things. I don't understand why they add tax to everything. How are you supposed to know the price when it says one thing and then when you go to buy it, the price is something else? How can people tolerate that?"

"I agree. I like the value-added tax."

"What do you mean? You can't agree. Defend your stupid system."

"No, I won't. That's like saying that because I'm American, I've got to defend the whole Watergate mess."

"Okay. Defend Watergate."

"Jesus, I'm not going there."

"Michael, why so apathetic all of a sudden? What about all those stories about marching in college, about how stupid this or that war was? I'd say something, and you'd tell me I was wrong. No one challenged me like that before."

Sighing, "Yeah, I lost my *Free Mandela* t-shirt a while ago. I was pretty gung-ho about so many causes in school. But then you wonder if you can ever make a difference. What good is that shirt or marching going to do? I just came back from Africa and see the futility. Like my marching is going to change something. What's the chance he'll be free, or anyone would even hear from him again? Sorry, I'm getting off track. I don't know what any of this has to do with defending my country. I'm not apathetic, but I can't march and I'm not going to waste my time defending things I don't believe in. I have enough of my own problems now.…. All I care about is finishing my research and helping James and the team nail some more poachers…And I don't want to lose you."

Caroline looked at Michael, wishing she could close the wound. "I didn't mean to make you so angry. I just don't like your taxes. I didn't think that meant we'd have to be afraid of discussing anything…I can understand wanting to be selfish though. Being white and privileged in Africa can make you feel that. That's what my dad used to say. Everyone either wants something from you or is suspicious of you. So, you isolate yourself. You become selfish, lose perspective. It's beyond wrong. He told me to fight that feeling. I was so young, but I remember that." She began to choke up, clutching her necklace. "Michael, I don't want that to happen with us."

"Neither do I. I just don't know what's in-between camp and the club. I think it's everything I'm used to and nothing you've ever seen."

"I think you're right. Maybe that's how I felt about the United States."

# CHAPTER 11

---

*Nairobi Suburbs (Langata), Kenya*

Caroline puzzled over the second message from Kent beckoning her to call as soon as she was back home. They seldom spoke. Her brother had two little boys Caroline did not know. She had a fiancé he had never met. When Caroline began describing Kent to Michael, recalling silly tales of growing up, she realized how much she missed him. Kent always seemed far away. First, he went off to school; then, when Caroline grew old enough to follow, he still lived in another country. Anywhere in Europe used to be close. Now, somehow, they were living on different continents, neither of which was home.

Nairobi and New Delhi rhymed a bit in name once put into English, a language alien to those hailing from local tribes and castes. To foreigners, they were exotic cities known more for their place on maps than the people who inhabited them. In geography class, Caroline's teacher would call on her and ask what the capital of India was. She was supposed to give a name, that was all. The stricter teachers might force her to name the leading export or perhaps the predominant religion. Daddy would ask her if they taught who was the last viceroy. Lord Louis Mountbatten, she now giggled, thinking back to days of quizzes and pencils. Most of the people are Hindu, her exam began. It waxed on about the people, Gandhi and Pakistan, before betraying appropriate labels with inappropriate questions: "Why do they put dots on their foreheads?" Caroline came home with a magic marker dot, fighting Julia petulantly, declaring she would only wash it off when she met a real Hindu. Caroline smiled, remembering those innocent times while waiting for her brother to pick up the phone.

"Hello, Hello, is Kent Dunning home?" Caroline burst into the receiver, forgetting her voice's pitch would have little effect on being heard in Delhi.

"Caroline! I've been waiting for you to call. Mom told me you went off to the States with Michael."

"Yes. We just came back, and I found your message. Sorry, I'd been rushing off when I received the first one, and couldn't get a line through. Mom said it wasn't urgent so I thought I'd call when I returned. Is there something wrong? This new message made it sound like it was important I call right way. I was worried."

"No, nothing's wrong with me. Hey, I want to hear about your trip, but first I'm anxious to talk to you about Richard. That's why I called originally. I had an incredibly strange visit from him, and I can't figure some things, actually most things out. I'm worried I'm being suckered into one of his schemes. I thought you might be able to help."

"I didn't know you saw Richard," Caroline said, now as confused as Kent. "He didn't mention he was going to India. He was in Delhi?"

"Yeah. A few weeks ago. I guess he left Nairobi not long after you. Didn't you know that?"

"No, I didn't. But he's away a lot. He doesn't always tell me where he's going. I can't believe he would visit you and not mention it, though."

"Well, anyway, that's not the point itself. He said he had come from Hong Kong and had a friend who's interested in shipping rhino horns into India. They use them here in one of the western provinces, Gujarat, as an aphrodisiac. I don't know exactly what they do with them. I keep getting an image of some guy with a turban sticking a horn up his ass."

"Jesus, Kent!"

"Look. He started going on about how he had some contact with access to stockpiles from when the government caught poachers; they were trying to get rid of elephant tusks and rhino horns mostly. He said the whole thing made him a bit sick. But then he told me, better to take advantage of the situation as long as they were laying around. Claimed maybe it would do some good and earn the government money to fund efforts to stop the whole mess. He realized he could help out through the network he uses to ship an odd trophy or two. Apparently, there's a lot of demand from Singapore, and I think in Malaysia the ground powder from a rhino horn can go for a ton of money. Thousands per kilogram. I checked it out after he left. His information is basically correct. You can buy the powder, and it's very expensive."

"So, what did he want from you?"

"I'm not exactly sure. He said he wanted me to help a friend of his in Hong Kong ship rhino horns into India. He said the whole thing was harmless. I asked him if he was involved, and he hedged, just saying indirectly, helping out this friend. He said he still likes to hunt, and he'll ship off a trophy here and there. So why not make a bit of money along the way? And I think he's still a member of the Naturalist Society. I don't get it. What a hypocrite! I don't believe half the story. It's obvious he's dealing in this stuff. He claimed that in Hong Kong, when he mentioned he was flying to visit me in India, he had this proposition put to him. He said not to worry about it. It was just a proposal, and he thought mine as well tell me since it was sort of a good deed, and there was a lot of money involved," Kent paused.

Moral condemnation in his tone, he continued, "A good deed. Can you believe it? Whole thing's a cockamamie story. I'm not sure he even went to Hong Kong, and no way he just happened to mention it. I think this was the only reason he visited. For god's sake, I started to ask myself, do I even know this man?"

"What are you going to do?" Caroline asked, the question somewhat rhetorical.

"I don't know. Do you know anything about all this? I mean, am I dreaming things, or is what I think might be going on really happening?"

"I don't know. I don't talk to Richard about his business. Funny you should bring this up, though. I was just talking to Michael about how, lately, Richard's been unusually generous. It's made me suspicious. I know he used to indulge us, doing small things to make us like him. Often felt as if he was trying too hard and didn't realize we could tell. But I used to chalk that up to the insecurity of being our stepfather. Now with Michael, ever since we became engaged, he's been especially solicitous. I never thought he'd like him, and well, you know Mom. Richard's been a buffer, really surprised me, made her accept him. Maybe I'm being naive and have been taking it for granted. I guess because I needed his help and didn't have to fight. I'm getting along with him better than I ever have."

"Okay. I'm glad he's at least being so good to you and Michael. But also sounds like your gut's telling you something is strange too. Come on, selling horns and ivory in Asia? Who does he spend time with?" Kent turned the conversation back to his immediate dilemma.

"I don't know. It's not like I see him dragging tusks into the house with anyone. He seems to be spending a lot of time with this creepy guy that kept asking me out, Ron Easton. He's the new head of a wildlife organization here. And then there's a former tribesman he put through school named Alijah, related to one of his hunting guides. I think Alijah helps run the anti-poaching division for the government. I think that's right. Maybe he's heading something within the anti-poaching unit? That could be where this stockpile of horns is from. It's plausible. If anyone had access, then Alijah would make sense."

"Or it would be the world's greatest cover," he scoffed.

Kent pressured Caroline to describe Ron and Alijah in detail. Parrying his insinuations at every instance, she began to wilt under the logic of his hypotheticals. Suggestion after suggestion, which she could not refute, unnerved her until she could not talk any longer. Caroline pledged to call him back after investigating whether Richard had indeed gone to Hong Kong and whether he would cop to the balance of his itinerary. They agreed she should not confront him directly until they had more than circumstantial evidence. After all, they were coming to defend their mother, and there was no need to alarm her without solid proof. Kent and Caroline had already questioned whether Richard had been too freely delving into their mother's accounts; they were loath to accuse him of trading in contraband before solidifying facts.

Caroline decided to confide in Michael. She would tell him everything Kent insinuated, trusting Michael's opinion as the only insider and outsider. He was supposed to meet her at the clinic that afternoon and then go to lunch.

.     .     .     .     .

Caroline loved practicing as a veterinarian, finding a sense of peace even amidst squeals, bleats, and neighs. As he walked toward the clinic's door, Michael breathed relief that today he would not be startled by a roar or trumpet; those calls were reserved for Thursdays and emergencies when she volunteered at the large animal rescue center. Being a veterinarian in Kenya often brought adventure. Usually when he arrived he had to wait. Sometimes she was in surgery with an animal he knew nothing about, but when not at the rescue center she tended to be mired in sorting out a new test or treatment for her beloved horses. Today, though, Caroline opened the door and was ready before he stepped inside. Michael instantly knew something was out of the ordinary.

"It's about time," she chided.

"I'm early! What are you talking about?"

"Never mind. Here, let's walk outside where we can talk privately. I had a really disturbing call from Kent." She proceeded to relay every detail of her conversation, finally stopping after taking a seat on a bench by an empty corral.

Michael remained standing, pacing next to the fencing, wanting to break free of the circle much like its frequent occupants must feel. He unconsciously scratched his neck, just another animal working out a bit of anxiety. After a pause, he looked at Caroline and said, "You know, it all makes sense. It's possible. Maybe even likely."

"You mean you agree with Kent?" Caroline asked hesitantly, not wanting the apparent truth confirmed.

"Add it up. That big check out of the blue when we got engaged. The money for the camera equipment so I can make a short film to top off my research. We were just talking about how, all of a sudden, he was doing everything so lavishly. He could be using us to launder his money! I know it's pretty hard to believe, but when you start piecing things together..."

"We don't have any proof, really," Caroline hedged.

"Even so. Just suppose it's true. I'm wondering who else is involved. He can't be doing this alone."

They both looked at each other and blurted, "Ron!"

· · · · ·

There was no mention of conspiracy theories in the banter at Alijah's house in Nairobi. Nor was there ever any discussion about Tza, the two choosing to ignore Alijah's other family as if they were artifacts that could be hidden for later study. In fact, life at home had become remarkably routine. Sara was teaching at the best private secondary school in the city. She was enjoying the spoils of her star husband's rise. Their newest purchase was a phonograph player.

It was a German model with two speeds. The songs crackled from the inconsistent current running through the speakers and a less than sharp needle; nevertheless, they were fortunate to have even these inferior luxuries. Spare parts for automobiles were an owner's nightmare. It was too much to expect a replacement for something as unusual as a phonograph needle. Sara decided to put her energy into finding records.

Like so many, she discovered The Beatles after the band had broken up. She hummed the themes repetitively. Sara loved the song "Michelle." It made her feel proficient in French. Lyrics from most of the songs were confusing and meaningless. She had no idea what a Walrus was.

"I am the Walrus?" she said to Alijah, repeating the phrase as the song filled the room. "What is it?"

"An animal with tusks. Just like elephants. They swim. Like a swimming pig with whiskers and tusks. They live on the ice. Don't you teach the kids about this stuff?"

"No. Just about the African animals."

"That doesn't sound fair. What else do you teach them then?"

"Oh, about you," she said, humming the song. "I had a student today who wanted to be just like you when he grows up. I told the class about your job the other day."

"So, I'm a celebrity," Alijah preened.

"Don't let it go to your head. You know what I told him?"

"What?"

"He's too honest. He can't work for the government."

"Sara," Alijah moaned.

"So, what's a yellow submarine?"

"Oh god."

There was a knock on the door. Alijah turned his head, happy for the diversion but confused because they were not expecting anyone. Pulling the door open, he was stunned to be staring at Kiku. He had not seen him in a while and was struck by how much his son had grown to resemble both Galo and Tza. A lump came to his throat looking at the familial sharp-arrow jaw coupled with a masculine version of Tza's enchanting almond eyes.

"Can I come in?" Kiku asked, pleased with his surprise.

"No." Alijah reacted, shelving his sentimentality and reminding himself to remain cautious. "I told you never to come here. How did you find me here?"

"It is your house, isn't it?"

Kiku curiously peered inside, seeing Sara in the distance. Their eyes briefly locked before Alijah shut the door and walked outside.

"Come on, let's walk. I heard a rumor you joined the rebels. Is that true?"

"Yes. I actually came to warn you. And wanted some help. Will you help?"

"Wait a minute," Alijah said, looking at his son with an equal measure of love and suspicion. When Alijah visited Michael in camp to coax the permits-for-guns bargain, Michael had told him that Kiku left without providing much reason. He vaguely recalled something about visiting another village, and Alijah had joked it was probably about some girl. Since then, though, Kiku had not returned. After receiving a message relayed via Michael, his only contact was the brief phone call during which Kiku advised Alijah he was fine and taking some time away—asking Alijah not to look for him, he was living in a distant village. During the conversation, Kiku described how he had loved learning about different political systems over the radio and wanted to do something to change the world. Alijah implored him to return to Michael's camp, warning his son not to take the political propaganda spewed over the airwaves to heart. Alijah recalled even offering Kiku a job in his ministry; arguing the best way to learn about politics would be to spend time working in the government. That had been their last conversation, Alijah's subsequent efforts to track down his son proving futile. Now confronted by Kiku's announcement that he had become a rebel, Alijah realized how badly he had misjudged the signals.

"Kiku, so that's why you left Michael's camp? At first, I thought it was over a girl. Then you said no." Casting his eyes down, "Now I wish it was over a girl...You know, I tried to give you the chance to learn about other cultures, about America and England. To learn English is a privilege. I arranged this opportunity as a kind of school, for you to learn what others in the village will never comprehend. Not to join some rebel group! Don't throw everything away. Take a different path than me, fine. But working with Lord Keeton, learning English, it's what got me my position. I even know the President. Think of that! Why are you doing this, wasting your advantages?"

"Father, I'm not wasting anything, or throwing anything away. I've learned a lot. I speak their language as well as you. Maybe better. That's helped get me noticed. And I have studied—which is why I joined. And it's time."

"Time for what?"

"To move on, to start my life, to fight for what I believe," Kiku said, flush with the arrogant wisdom of youth.

"That's what you mean by joining the rebels? Do you have any idea what you're doing? Did they recruit you?"

"No, I joined them. Proudly. Our government is corrupt. I want to free the people."

"Kiku, I'm the government. Do you see me oppressing people? Do you think of me as corrupt?"

Hesitating, but then looking back at Alijah's lavish house, the accouterments of success draping the walls and rooms that Sara had turned into a comfortable manor, Kiku continued, "Money had to come from somewhere to pay for all this." He swept his hand back toward the house in a grand gesture.

Shaking his head, Alijah defended, "Yes, I did need money for this. But I work for it. Hard! And so does Sara, teaching. I've been promoted at the ministry, and I have an important position. This and more can be yours with hard work. I'm not stealing from people to live like this."

Alijah paused, knowing he was speaking half-truths, wondering if he should let down his guard and bring Kiku into his confidence. How could he not? This was his son! And yet, how could he? This was his son! Is not the father supposed to be a role model, a paragon? How could he turn to this disillusioned youth that he had left in the bush and tell him the truth? That seductive, enriching, and yet criminal truth. Exacerbating his dilemma, Alijah was looking Kiku in the eye while standing outside his modern house, a house Alijah shared with a city wife who looked down on his tribal roots. In time, he deferred, he could do it. But not now, not when Kiku was carried on the wave of a cause, blinded to the subtleties of survival. Kiku was still fleeing tribalism, looking for meaning in a socialist paradigm or some other utopia. Being part of the next coup was an escape, but not an escape that would provide fulfilment. He was incapable of seeing beyond the cause and grasping the more complex challenges of ruling, governing, and surviving long-term.

Protests for privileged like Michael were manifest by wearing *Free-Mandela* t-shirts. For Kiku, protests were dangerous, the opportunity for change thrust upon him in the form of an AK-47, a uniform, and a march more likely stained with blood than bar-b-que sauce. And as if this were all elective! Boy soldiers were brainwashed, recruited, bullied, bred every day in some areas. Fortunately, they were not in the heartland of barbarity. Most joining today, like Kiku, were those swept along by the verve of inspiration. Still, they were far from the 9th green, the hail of "good shot" grounded in a different reverence.

Alijah fought Kiku's blank stare, and in that instant, he peered into his soul. He shivered, seeing he had lost him. Alijah realized that in their conversation Kiku was no longer listening but looking through him, spouting dogma, believing dogma, dripping dogma. Alijah's heart broke. There would be time. Today was hardly the moment for didactic lectures; he needed to maintain a bond, simple father to son, nothing more. Whatever Kiku asked, Alijah would do his bidding.

"Kiku, you asked for help. What can I do? I don't know what you're talking about."

"We need a diversion."

"For what?"

"Papa, don't ask so many questions. It's complicated. We need a diversion, okay? We think stirring up racial trouble may work. We're trying to figure out who to hit. I wanted to know if you'd object to..."

Alijah cut him off: "Don't give me the name. I don't want to know."

"Okay. I'll just say he's the perfect symbol. And if you're willing to help..."

"If you're talking about someone I know, keep me out of it," Alijah interrupted him again, now quite anxious. "My life is complicated enough. I can't take more risks right now," pausing, wondering if he would be willing to take a considerable risk— even put his life on the line—for some crusade he would never truly be privy to nor understand. Would he go that far to rehabilitate his relationship and prove his loyalty as a father? No, the role reversal was too significant. He should be the one giving orders, issuing challenges.

He saw Sara sneaking a look in their direction, behind the window and too far to hear the debate, but sensing the tension. It was as if an eye was cast from another world, luring him back to the city equilibrium he was carving daily, wary that he would slip back. Alijah thought about when he had broached the subject of Tza and Kiku with Sara, and how they had managed to live for so long as if Alijah's tribal family were a mere mirage. Kiku showing up now was the last thing he needed.

Alijah willed himself to compartmentalize his problems with Sara, and focus on Kiku. His son was standing right before him, forcing Alijah to grapple with a different basket of secrets and emotions. He admitted he could no longer protect Kiku. That was not his world. It was about which raid to defend or battle to pitch. No luxury of *Free-Mandela* t-shirts and asking for sauce on the side.

"Kiku, do you know what you're doing?"

"I think so. I believe in it."

"You believe in it. Great!" Alijah said pejoratively, calming down as they walked briskly and silently. Yet falling back into his yearning to steer him to a safer path, he added, "You know I can get you a job if you want it. Anything. School. Just let me know."

"I know, Papa. But that's not what I came about."

Alijah now wondered if he had made the wrong decision, and should have left him with Tza, never brought him to Michael, never exposed him to the white man's ways, to *his* ways. Wistfully, he said, "I thought you'd be our next chief, you know."

"Your father probably thought that about you."

Alijah chuckled, "Yes, perhaps. I think he dreamed that for Galo." Turning to Kiku, as the father he had never been, Alijah asked, "Are you going to be okay?"

"Yeah. I'm fine. I'll call you soon and let you know how things turn out. Don't worry about me." He then whispered something about exploiting racial tensions into Alijah's ear that paralyzed Alijah's thoughts. Before he could respond, Kiku took off on a motorcycle. It was the same motorcycle Alijah had won years before in the contest when he first met Sara.

"Crazy boy," he muttered, then called, "Be careful!"

Alijah had never given much credence to the opposition or Kiku's involvement. He assumed this would be a passing phase, and in a few months, he would beseech him for a job, perhaps even join the legitimate military. Kiku's visit this time, though, made him uneasy. Racial tension. What the hell did that mean? A symbol?

Alijah was frightened enough that he would quickly send a confidential note to Nazuto telling him a messenger had warned of trouble; of course, he would omit a few details, wary not to be viewed as a conspirator. Alijah loved his son, but he was also loyal to the president. One day he hoped the two plotters would meet. They had so much in common, Alijah willed, as he turned around and headed back inside. It all made as much sense as a yellow submarine. He could not manage to rid the melody from his head.

·   ·   ·   ·   ·

Michael and Caroline were still mustering the courage to confront Richard when Julia burst onto the porch, interrupting their plotting.

"Ron Easton's been murdered!"

"What?" They both gasped before recognizing the truth of it written across Julia's face.

"Oh my god." Michael's mind raced for answers. He despised Ron but never wished Ron dead. What the hell happened? Paranoid, thinking what a small community it was and how overtly Ron managed to offend people, Michael's mind drifted to whether he might know someone culpable. Had Ron yanked someone else's permits? Could he be dragged in? Was he in danger?

"How did it happen?" Caroline asked, getting up to comfort her shaking mother.

"They don't know. Someone just found him. They think he may have been lying in his house dead for a couple days. Shot in the head. They said Ron's body was then...Oh my god... mutilated. They cut his head off! They cut his head off!"

"Jesus!" Michael staggered. "Why? Do the police have any ideas?"

"Not yet. I don't know. Who would want to kill Ron? I think it was a racial killing. These blacks never liked us here. I always feared something like this happening."

"Mom, calm down. You know that's crazy. Let's not make this even worse," Caroline pleaded, turning to Michael and mouthing, "Fucking prejudices! I'm sorry."

The phone rang in the other room. Michael left to answer it, leaving Caroline and Julia hugging each other. It was Jack Whitehead calling for

Richard. Michael seized the opportunity, taking the call as he closed the study door.

"Jack, it's me, Michael. Richard's not here."

"Michael," pausing a moment, his voice quivering, "Have you heard about Ron?"

"A minute ago."

"You don't sound...very overwhelmed. Guess you haven't heard the details," Jack said, still reeling from the news.

"No, I have. It's unimaginable. What do you want me to say? I'm just absorbing it. Julia told us he was decapitated. Jesus. What the hell's happening, Jack?" Pausing, almost speaking out loud, "Then again, you're probably not shedding too many tears either. I know there was no love lost between you."

"Wait a minute. What are you implying? This is barbaric," then becoming defensive, "You don't suspect me, do you? Come on, Michael. I wouldn't do something like that. Do you think I'd hack off his head? Really."

"No, of course, I didn't mean that. It would never cross my mind. Come on, Jack, I was just thinking he'd been an asshole to you, probably behind getting you kicked out. I'm not thinking straight right now. I haven't processed it. We're all in shock over here. As I said, we literally just heard. Anyway, what do you know?"

"Nothing. The police are stymied from what I hear."

"Fuck the police, what do you suspect? What does Alijah think? He knew him pretty well. Have you talked to him?"

"I heard he came into work but locked himself in his office and isn't talking to anybody. He's probably left by now. I tried to call, thinking the same thing. Maybe he'd have some idea. But he didn't answer. I was hoping Richard might know something. That's why I was calling. Ask him to call me. Look, I've got to go. This type of killing stirs up a lot of tension. People can even start suggesting it's some racial thing. I was planning to go over to his office, snoop around. I can only imagine the types of files he's got. I'd bet that'll turn up something. You want to meet me there?"

"Interesting you should say that about the racial tension," thinking about Julia's outburst and then deciding to put those aspersions aside. "Never mind. What was I saying...," Michael hesitated, but then thought about his earlier conversation with Caroline. There was a real possibility clues lurked in Ron's papers, and he could get to the bottom of their suspicions about Richard. "Probably a good idea about checking his office. Sure, why not? After jerking me around with my permits and all, I'd like to see what's there."

Michael hung up the phone and returned to find Caroline consoling her mother, both of their eyes red. He could not understand why Caroline was so distraught over Ron but then began to fight off a lump swelling in his throat. Thinking of the grotesque scene in Ron's house made him shiver. He sat down and hugged Caroline. He whispered to her that Jack Whitehead called for Richard, but he didn't seem to know anything more.

Caroline wiped her eyes and gave Michael an unsettling, penetrating stare. He could read her thoughts: when would Richard come home?

Michael said, "Look, I know we have to talk to Richard, but I'm going over to Ron's office. Maybe the police haven't been there yet, and we'll find some clues. And selfishly, I'd like to see whatever dirt he's concocted about me before it falls into someone else's hands." Michael grumbled, his sense of self-preservation now keenly honed, "I may never get another chance. When Jack offered, I told him I'd meet him there. I suspect he feels the same. God only knows what Ron had on him."

"Don't you think we should wait and confront Richard first? Especially if there's a chance he was in on something dirty with Ron?"

"In theory yes, but there's not enough time. I've got to meet Jack. And let's not assume there is more to this. Ron pissed off a lot of people. It's probably a case of someone taking revenge."

"Let me come with you."

"No, it's crazy my going. I'm not risking your getting caught up in this too. Anyway, you should stay here to take care of your mom and talk to Richard when he gets back. I'll wait a bit in case he shows up soon, but it might be better if you talk to him alone."

• • • • •

Richard conspicuously did not come home, nor did he call. Michael and Caroline patiently waited a bit, and then Michael left to meet up with Jack Whitehead. Whatever files Ron kept at home were probably already confiscated by the police. They hoped they would at least be the first to rummage through Ron's office. The building was closed when they arrived, forcing Jack to break in through the rear door. Ron had changed the locks. Jack glanced around before breaking the pane while Michael revved his car's engine to muffle the sound.

In the office, they found a series of locked filing cabinets that Michael jerked open with a crowbar he grabbed from his trunk. They were familiar with the office and had anticipated the difficulties of their search. The first two cabinets they sifted through seemed to hold only official records of permits together with statistics about species in the area, geography of the country, and tribes in the region. The next cabinet contained financial statements along with information relevant to fund drives. Finally, in the last cabinet, they found individual dossiers on people receiving grant money and key government figures.

Ron had a file on both Richard and Alijah, as well as Jack and Michael! Jack quickly pulled them and stuck the files haphazardly in his briefcase. Hurriedly he flipped through the rest of the names but found nothing interesting. Michael asked him if he could take a look, hoping to recognize something Jack might have missed. He would wait to read his own file later.

He glanced at several files before stopping and pulling out a folder marked "Operation Ostrich: O. Aguru." Rifling through the folder, he saw the full name Omondi Aguru, recognition filtering through the haze. Omondi Aguru had once stopped by Caroline's house. Michael remembered Omondi helping him with his car the first time he visited. Omondi had also been with Alijah once when he had run into him at the game park lodge. Finding the name here seemed odd, and he burrowed into the notes. The information indicated that Omondi served as a truck driver for Richard and Ron between Nairobi and Mombasa. But driver for what? The records first only showed that Ron bought a truck in Omondi's name. On the third page of notes he stopped, calling for Jack to look at the dossier.

While they would need to decipher all the details, the surface implication was that Omondi regularly drove a customized truck to transport elephant tusks and rhinoceros horns. It seemed there was some type of sophisticated poaching ring, and this was the ledger of profits. Equally startling, it appeared that Ron put all the information about his own finances from the ring's sales under Omondi's name. Too anal not to keep records yet sly enough to avoid keeping them under his own name, Ron was apparently chronicling data under Omondi's name in case he was ever caught. Omondi would be the perfect person to frame. Title to the warehouse had been put in Omondi's name to conceal the true ownership. Technically, he owned the truck as well. No goods were ever sold without passing before Omondi's eyes. A straw man.

Jack gazed over the figures in amazement. Richard and Alijah would have been equally stunned had they been looking over his shoulder; neither man knew of the ledger's existence. They both distrusted Ron, but never suspected that he was recording items—information that should never be written down. The notations included tracing where different goods were sourced, how many animals of different species were poached in charted regions, the month-to-month price fluctuations in the mid-east and Hong Kong for ivory and rhino horns, the various ships used to export the goods, and the profits made. On a following page, Ron had begun to chart density areas for elephants and rhinoceroses based upon these figures and general government census reports. He labeled the regions by letter, trying to pinpoint which locations would be the most productive for hunting. In a legal business, these figures would be an indispensable tool for the efficient exploitation of the area.

While the notes tried to disguise the members of the group, Jack and Michael immediately believed these figures linked more than Omondi and Ron. In fact, Michael thought back to his conversation with Caroline, and now feared the worst about Richard.

Jack interrupted his thoughts. "Michael, let's get out of here. We've found enough. I recognize Ron's handwriting, but all these notes seem to have a code. Shouldn't be hard to figure it out. I've got to spread everything out and put it together."

"Can you tell anything more?"

"Just that it appears to be chronicling inventory and sales from some type of poaching ring. Looks like three or four key people. Ron's got to be one of them. And it looks like he's framing this Aguru guy. The others, I don't know. But I'd say Richard's an odds-on bet."

Jack placed the file in his briefcase along with the others. A final frantic search through the drawers revealed no other startling documents. Everything was put back in place. Michael even bolted the back door from the inside. Leaving through the front door, locking it behind them, there was no tangible sign of their visit beyond the smashed window in back. Lots of windows in this town were cracked, though, and the lock made it appear that perhaps no one had entered.

$$\bullet \quad \bullet \quad \bullet \quad \bullet \quad \bullet$$

Meanwhile, Richard arrived home to find Julia alone. She was stretched out on the divan in the living room blankly staring out the picture window. He tried to comfort her before betraying his loyalties once again.

"Julia, I want you to go back to England for a while."

"Why? What are you going to do?"

"There's been unrest in the city in addition to Ron's murder. And rumors about the military are starting to spread, people worried about a coup. Whether there's some military lockdown, racial unrest, hell I don't know…none of it is good. Meaning it could get risky for foreigners, especially someone prominent like you. Because of Nigel, you're an easy target. Nobody knows what's going to happen. Sometimes I feel like there's a fuse just waiting to be lit, and this might be the time."

About an hour later, Michael returned, briefing Caroline on the paperwork stash he and Jack discovered. Still trying to digest everything, while faintly holding out hope they had not in fact solved the puzzle, the pair sequestered Richard in his study. When Richard closed the door and asked them to sit down, proudly pointing to his hand-crafted ebony chairs, they accepted. They both felt downright uncomfortable, but it had nothing to do with the hard seats.

There had been insufficient time to parse through all the notations with certainty; Michael and Caroline remained armed with only suspicions. Well, at least suspicions on Caroline's part. Michael felt certain of the truth having processed what he had seen. He viewed the details Jack was pouring over hardly worth reconciling. Perfect footnotes were for his thesis, but once crossing the equator he had become accustomed to shooting first and untangling nuances later. It would be merely a couple of days before they pieced together links evidencing that the triumvirate was in fact Richard, Ron, and Alijah, and that Omondi was being framed. Ron wrote everything in shorthand, but the code took only time, not a professional, to crack.

Caroline began, "We think there's more to Ron's death than you're telling us. I got a call from Kent the other day telling me about how you wanted him to help sell rhinoceros horns and ivory in India. I've been wondering for weeks how you've come up with all this money lately. Then, when I thought about Ron, there was the same pattern. I don't know what the two of you have been up to, but it stinks of poaching."

Richard raised his eyebrows, moving to take a seat on the couch, buying time, though, in truth, he had rehearsed his story. Wryly smiling at Michael, he rebuffed the accusation, "Well, that's quite a story. I don't know where you concocted it." Turning to Caroline: "I think your fiancé has something to do with this. He came ranting to me and Ron at the club with another far-fetched notion before we sent him packing."

Now looking at Michael, Richard barked: "And you. Where the hell do you get these ideas! What gives you the god damn right to accuse others without the slightest bit of proof! I've been selling skins and trophies through a friend in the Orient for years. I've not tried to conceal it." Turning toward Caroline, "On my latest trip, I thought it would be a good time to visit Kent. I happened to mention I was on my way to Delhi, and my friend Roland Weathers asked me if I could do him a favor.

They've been having trouble getting certain things into India, and I told him I'd see what I could do. That's it. And if I could get my hands on some inventory Alijah has stockpiled from confiscated goods, I could do the government a favor and make a tidy profit. The ministry's earmarked to sell those items anyway, and with the prices they pay over there, everybody wins. Christ! The whole trip was motivated because I wanted to surprise the two of you by buying a chalet in Switzerland for your honeymoon. I even did it! Lake Maggiore. Go call up Jacques if you don't believe me. And don't thank me now."

Caroline hesitated, realizing how circumstantial the rest of their evidence would likewise appear. She looked over at Michael, but his face was set and determined. Focusing again on Richard, she further pressed, "I don't know what to say. A chalet? That's unbelievable, and if what you're saying is true, unbelievably generous… but also, out of character. All this money. You're a Lord, or virtually one, but this is almost nouveau riche the way you're spending lately. Always going away hunting." She paused, aware that she was rambling, but how could she not? Her confidence rebounded when she recalled the damning documents in Ron's office. "How do you explain Ron's murder then. This wasn't an accident! I don't believe you have no idea what's going on."

"I'm sorry. I don't. You're being irrational. And if you want to know crazy, I hear people are beginning to suggest there could be racial motives. Rumors are already starting to fly. And maybe it isn't all that crazy. Ron would be a perfect symbol—maybe he was. If he hadn't been such a publicity hound… Always in the paper, smiling on the front page, on the radio. Remember that celebrity fundraiser with the Hollywood stars? He took all the credit, but looking back, think about it. There wasn't one black in the whole crowd. Colonial rule, whites, exploitation. Name it. I don't know. I don't really buy it." Little did Richard realize the newspapers would soon be suggesting the same links.

Richard continued, "I've got to make some phone calls, think about it a while. I think you're just upset—everyone's upset— and are jumping to rash conclusions." He stormed out, slamming the door behind him.

In the wake of defeat, Caroline now sat, emotionally drained and confused. Richard sounded absolutely convincing, his story even lining up with the tales and excuses obfuscating the facts for Kent; still, he said nothing which would directly refute any of their accusations.

"Michael, he's lying."

"Let's wait for Jack to finish going through the files," Michael said, equally unconvinced. "There's got to be something there to nail him," pausing, realizing his predicament. "Sorry, I don't mean to be callous. I know you don't want him to be behind this. But you better prepare yourself."

•    •    •    •    •

An unusual calm hovered over Nairobi as Richard and Alijah drove to their rendezvous at the warehouse. Men with green berets and gaudy pins stood with rifles on street-corners. The President did not come by, nor did new batches of anxious tourists wait with their cameras for a glimpse of the motorcade. Fewer people seemed to be crowding usually impenetrable intersections. Street vendors squat by their wares, others sheltering in shadows against adjacent walls in the midday heat. Caroline's veterinary clinic was one of the few venues remaining open, an emergency clinic for those most innocent of victims. The atmosphere was grim, and if wounded animals could prophesy, they would likely opt for another ark and a fresh start.

At the warehouse, Omondi Aguru pulled the sliding door back down to conceal the truck inside. Only a few lights were on, swinging from the ceiling in the breeze from the ever-spinning fans. The doors were all bolted. The absence of signs and people made the building appear deserted. Typically, it would be. But now, as Richard asked Omondi to leave them alone, Alijah paced around the room, trying to devise a plan. He passed in and out of long shadows formed by the sun streaming through the dirty windows high above his head. He could hide in the dark corners here as well as anywhere else in the city. Hard as he tried, he could not keep his mind from returning to Kiku's warnings of racial tension; no, he pushed the worst fears away, incomprehensible, but sadly not wholly far-fetched.

Richard joined him, pensive, fidgeting with his hands. There still was every chance that tensions would pass, but normalcy had unfortunately become a contingency. Two men, implausibly partnered, sat silently reading the other's mind. They had already discussed Ron's gruesome death, anxious to move on and put the image out of mind. Neither man was particularly close to Ron, their partnership sustained more by convenience than loyalty or love. Yet, the loss was hard to absorb—at least on a personal level. Fortunately, the business implications were not dire.

"I guess it was smart to start thinking of cutting out Ron," Alijah said, their earlier conversations about jettisoning Ron now proving providential. "Dealing with all the permits will be difficult, but I think I can handle it at the ministry."

"Have you talked to Nazuto?" Richard asked, hoping their countless payoffs to the President would at least grant them information.

"No. He's shut himself off. I'm sure I can get to him if we have to. But I think we'll be OK for the moment. Things aren't that bad yet. Anonymous threats, reports of unrest, looting, fears of a potential coup attempt," Alijah hesitated. He pondered whether they were blowing things out of proportion; and yet, the tension on the streets was palpable. Ron's murder was real. Equally ominous, Kiku's showing up was a testament to the rebel's imminent threat of a coup. He thought about conveying Kiku's warning to Richard but kept quiet. No need to reveal that he might have had some notice. "You'd better be careful. Everyone knows you knew Ron. I don't buy a lot of the rumors, but I'd rather be black today. And Kenyan. Foreigners make convenient scapegoats."

"I know that. I've got Julia packing already."

"Good idea. What about Michael and Caroline?"

"I don't know. I just told you about our conversation. I don't know if they bought the story about selling off ivory that the government had confiscated. Hard to disprove. That's what makes it so good. And we've even done it a fair share of times, mixing in some stock when we were short. Doesn't matter. They're not going to listen to me now. I'm going to suggest they think about going to America for a while, but I don't know..."

Alijah began listing different alternatives for Richard, suggesting everything from departing that evening to meeting with Nazuto to staying near Alijah's village. If Richard's house would not be safe, there were limited places to seek refuge. Anyone smart who had a particular vendetta against Richard would trace their relationship and ferret out Alijah's relatives. With the implications grim for all of them, Alijah pondered moving Sara; she was the most vulnerable among his wives. She was pregnant with their first child, and he was worried about her health if they were forced to move quickly. Tza and his new wife Nina, who had been betrothed to Galo, would be safe in the villages. He had not heard from Kiku since his admonition.

Richard could listen no more, restless to continue with their plans despite the change in events, greed trumping fear. They were scheduled in a few weeks to fly across to the Mara region in Tanzania for what they hoped would be their greatest slaughter. The wildebeest migrations would be hitting stride, millions of animals helplessly sprawling across the plains, herds of elephants joining the mix. The season promised the spectacle as surely as the Nile to the north would flood. Perhaps they should leave early, leave the chaos behind, and hide out in the savanna, oblivious to what was going on in the capital. They would be virtually untraceable, and on return, after disappearing for a month or more, feign complete ignorance. They could isolate themselves from the city chaos and live by the migrations instead of calendars. Alijah tried to point out the practical problems involved. He was a government minister and could hardly disappear now without it looking like an escape.

Richard, though, ranted on, obsessed with the notion. He would consider going on a run to Uganda instead, limiting the safari to a last trip if they then surmised it was too dangerous to return. They would journey to Uganda or Tanzania and leave from there. But only after one last hunt.

Alijah interrupted the nonsense, "Richard, you're crazy. Get out while you can! When things settle down, you can come back. We'll start up again."

"I'm not bailing out. Things are apt to calm down. Ron wasn't exactly loved. We'll make one last run, an epic take. We can do it. Then I'll get out if we have to." Subliminally Richard recognized his plan was foolhardy, but so close to obtaining his dreams, he was obstinate about not leaving before he could fulfill what he had come to believe was his destiny. Reading those hallowed letters of Harold Keeton, vicariously traveling by sea with him to Africa, the title about to be bestowed, restoring the Salisbury estate to its grandeur—he had come too close to abandon the quest. Richard could not fathom quitting just shy of securing the fortune that was already maturing and the bloat of which was so tantalizingly close. No modest retirement plans here. Twenty more rhinos.

For the first time since they had known each other, Alijah overtly defied Richard's command. Several times before, he challenged him and ignored instructions only to follow the leader in the end. But now, Alijah was powerful enough to be selfish. Richard was running, not he. This was his country, and he sat at its top. He was already one of the wealthiest men in the capital, and he knew he could afford to wait. There was no reason to risk everything on a desperation run, only to flee to a white land where his friendship would be denied. Nazuto's preaching swelled within his head as he watched Richard pathetically beg, unaware of his apprentice's savvy.

"I won't go with you, Richard. I'm going to see Nazuto. If he thinks things are too dangerous, maybe I'll get out. But I am not going with you. Not right now, at least."

Feeling betrayed, Richard soon found himself in the dank room with only the truck and a couple of chipped tusks. This was no time to wallow, he resolved, and bolted the door behind him.

•　　•　　•　　•　　•

While Richard headed home, Michael and Caroline were downtown hoping to withdraw the remainder of Michael's funds in case they were forced to leave. With Ron Easton dead, there was no one to vouch for

Michael's accounts. Should violence break out, any records could be destroyed. The bank was closed and had no sign posted as to when it might reopen. The bulk of Caroline's money had always been kept in a London account, with a local Nairobi branch holding enough for day-to-day expenses. She at least felt secure. They decided to wait an hour in a hotel restaurant, hoping that someone would come by and open the branch. Schedules sometimes functioned this way on normal days; the stores would open and close randomly, leaving customers to the proprietors' whims. They found themselves conspicuously alone in a once bustling restaurant, a waiter looking at them suspiciously when they entered and asked if the restaurant was open.

"Michael, when you said you'd finished collecting everything you needed, were you telling the truth?" Caroline asked, fidgeting in her seat.

"Yeah. I've got enough. Not ideal, but enough. You can keep a study going forever, but there's no reason I can't cut it off here. I've got the new videos and everything."

"Good, I want to get out of here. I already have everything I need from the clinic. I could use a few more things, supplies, a couple of books, but if I have to leave for some time, I'm okay. I'll talk to Jomno at the house and make sure he takes care of the horses. I'm more worried about them than anything, but we can't exactly take them with us. He'll watch over them...Let's go check the bank again. I'm scared. I've lived here for a long time, and I've never felt this level of tension."

"What do you mean?"

"It's eerie. Stores are closed, I can't reach people. Phone lines are down. Nobody's on the street. The military's staring at you everywhere."

"I think you're exaggerating."

"Michael, didn't you see the paper this morning? The International Tribune quoted General Oguru criticizing Nazuto for patronizing the white natives and letting them control the country. He called Nazuto a puppet!"

"Politics as usual. But, okay, I get the message. I can't believe some major change is going to be touched off by a freak murder and some looting."

"Damn it, Michael. This is exactly the type of thing I can remember my father talking about. He lived through these things. He knew the people who managed the transition to independence over here—which thankfully went peacefully. But it didn't have to go that way or stay that way. I can remember him telling my mother, when he thought I was too young to understand, to watch for the little things. If a houseboy doesn't show up, if mail doesn't get through, if more guards are on the street than usual, if the banks close. It's all happening! This has all the makings of a pending coup attempt."

"Okay. Listen, let's give the bank one last try and then go over to the Polo Club. People seem to congregate there. Natural place to retreat to. Maybe Jack will be there. Let's see what others are doing and what they've heard. There's no point in guessing and going it alone."

· · · · ·

Traffic leaving town was stalled for miles, a distinct contrast to driving within the city's radius. Horns were blaring, and hundreds of people were walking, swarming the edge of the streets and blocking the car's path. Michael and Caroline left the main roads toward the suburbs, instead following dirt backroads around towards the club. They had to climb a hill and then head down the other side to see the polo field. When they reached its zenith, and began winding down through the trees, they began to smell smoke but saw no flames.

Around the last bend, the smoke grew stronger and choked their view. The club was in flames, and in the distance, they could hear people screaming.

"Let's get the hell out of here," Michael urged. With no opposition from Caroline, they raced back to the house.

Richard had returned too, fuming about Alijah to Julia without being specific as to why he was so upset. When Michael and Caroline walked in, he launched into another incoherent tirade. With a scotch in hand, he ascended the flight of stairs to pass out in dignity. Caroline asked Julia what was wrong before realizing the rhetorical nature of her question.

Julia said, "I don't know. Richard was swearing when he came home. Oh, and by the way," turning to Michael, "There's a message for you."

"From whom?"

"Jack Whitehead."

"Thanks," Michael said, his heart pounding.

The note read, "Call immediately!" Michael showed the note to Caroline then picked up the phone to call. It was dead.

# CHAPTER 12

*Nairobi, Kenya*

Suddenly the streets were full of bullets and broken glass rather than people. On a corner near where Michael and Caroline previously waited for their bank to open, a stern army rebel held his AK-47 machine gun to his hip. His eyes flickering from side to side, he watched for anything to move. When a shadow from a flag across the street waved in a storefront window, the youngster mercilessly opened fire. Glass instantly shattered, but the rebel heard no screams. Either the store was empty, or those inside were instantly killed. He suppressed even a flinch of curiosity. With the gun taut against his hip, he stared out with a cold-blooded glare, waiting for something else to happen.

Alijah had been downtown when the first rounds were fired. A trickle of traffic continued to flow, and vendors still stood by their stands during a non-existent morning rush hour. Most people stayed home in fear, but foolhardy skeptics ventured downtown to carry on in the face of what they called absurd paranoia. Threats of coups were commonplace. The more hearty boasted they would hang out in a favorite local bar waiting for the government to quell the insurgency. But today, no one was crying wolf.

Rebel troops descended on Nairobi with unaccustomed efficiency. Distinguishing their jeeps with red flags and wearing red armbands around their sleeves, the rebels drove in guns first. Armed with several Russian-made machine guns and walkie-talkies, they had a significant technical advantage over Nazuto's regime. The incumbent military was outfitted primarily with Browning machine guns; still lethal, but nevertheless surplus weapons from World War II. A rebel-manned jeep with a machine gunner scanning side-to-side sped onto a street, spewing more bullets every ten seconds than the government defenders could fire back in over a minute. The defenders ran. Taking up ground to mount a new defense on the next block, they found themselves ambushed, cut off. The lead rebel jeep radioed to another group to reconnoiter from behind. Moments later, a different machine-gun-led jeep sped into an intersection, isolating the block. Reinforcements fired from every direction. Those defenders not dropping their cumbersome rifles and fleeing, left the streets to climb buildings for a sniper's advantage.

Upon reaching their new high position, they paused, surprisingly finding the streets below deserted. Frantically, they kept searching for something to shoot at from their perch. Seconds later, the grenades and mortar shells exploded, the buildings crumbling under them. Soldiers leapt from windows and rooftops, hoping only to break a leg or arm in the fall. Few were so lucky. They jumped into dense smoke, landing on quick forming rubble of twisted cement and glass. Some tried escaping down the stairs, only to be choked by smoke, tripping over those succumbing before them. Those not panicking sought fire escapes if they were fortunate enough to have taken refuge in buildings sporting them; others scrambled up to rooftops hoping the gutted buildings would smolder but not fall. Many of these men survived, but could not help their cause, the rising smoke cutting off their view and preventing them from returning fire.

Battling street to street, the insurgents swarmed from varied angles, using machine guns backed-up by regular troops to cluster their foes within discreet blocks of deadly holdouts. No sooner than the defenders felt they were amassing enough strength to strike out and retaliate, the rebels would back off and watch the block blow up in flames.

By mid-day the rebels controlled most of the city, machine-gunners stationed in front of key buildings volleying shots to keep doubters at bay. The law courts, city hall, and Parliament had all fallen. No radio stations were working. The wire stations were deliberately left open and guarded as a refuge for foreign journalists. This was where a stolid rebel waited with his machine gun, shooting at anything that moved. Any government offensive to retake the city would have to come from the outside and proceed down a few specific streets. The city was not that large, and it was easy once taken to seal off the main roads. If successful, siege was their only remaining fear. The rebel generals scoffed that executing a siege, though, would be more of a miracle than their takeover.

The rebel soldier guarding the newswire station, flanked by two compatriots, reloaded by stuffing a new clip into his machine gun during the longest lull of the day. Ready again, he glanced around before suddenly clutching his shoulder and falling back against the wall. Two men sneaking around the corner had managed the shots before ducking behind a barricade. Simultaneously, a jeep roared into the avenue bearing down on the rebels at full speed. The rebel soldier, now soaked in blood, limp against the wall, dropped his gun where he had been standing. One of his compatriots grabbed the weapon and fired directly into the oncoming jeep. Thirty yards shy of careening into them, the jeep uncontrollably swerved into the sidewalk, crashing into a newsstand. The already torn bodies of the driver and gunners flew through the air. Other deadly cartwheels spun in front of Parliament for the next three hours until, finally, most signs of resistance appeared quelled.

Alijah, by instinct, had left the city just before the vanguard shot its way toward the government buildings. He was still in earshot of the shooting when he pulled away, heading towards where he guessed Nazuto would be hiding. The phone lines had been down since the evening before, and all his attempts to find out where the President hid proved futile. He placed his bets on a compound near Nairobi Park, which Nazuto always referred to as the shelter. Long before reaching the access road, a roadblock stopped his car. After checking his papers and expression carefully, the soldier let him pass.

He hoped his luck would continue throughout the day. Bedecked with medals granted him by Nazuto, Alijah cruised through the remaining checkpoints with relative ease until he reached the gate to Nazuto's house. There, several guards sat with rifles in front of a tank physically blocking the entrance.

The guard in charge cocked his rifle as Alijah slowed his car to a stop, stepping out with his hands up. Holding up his identification, Alijah implored, "I'm a friend of the President's."

"Stop right there," the guard said.

"I'm not moving." Alijah slowly lowered his free hand to turn his pockets inside out. Another guard came up behind him, frisking his body, then nodding that he was clean. All guns were lowered. Nevertheless, they refused to allow him through despite his credentials and official pass signed by the President.

"I can't let you in. Absolute orders."

"Is President Nazuto here?" Alijah pleaded. "I tried to call and couldn't get through. Look, I'm Assistant Minister of Wildlife!" Stretching the truth, he said: "I'm a cabinet member. I've just come from the city and escaped the shooting... I can give him the latest reports. Come on! Let me inside to talk to him. At least let him know I'm here...Just ask him. Please!!"

While pretending to fumble with his identification and fix his pockets, Alijah not so subtly let his money fall to the ground. The tangible cash moved the commander enough to come forward, now less skeptical. He gathered in all of Alijah's papers, handing them back after crossly looking them over again. Scooping up the cash and stuffing it into his own pockets, he escorted Alijah around to the gate, walking him inside.

Alijah was left in a guarded room of the mansion and instructed to wait. He looked out the window, feeling numb. He could see over the trees towards the city buildings in the distance from the house's high ground. A cloud of black smoke rose from the town, making the buildings look like they were swaying in the haze. Perhaps they were. He shook his head, wondering whether the symbols of civilization were toppling before his eyes. The concept of being several stories high and looking down was something Tza had never been able to grasp, no matter the effort. How could she ever comprehend this? Alijah leaned against the side of the window, staring out, wondering about his families. He never had time to contact anyone except Sara, their brief chat via radiophone painfully insufficient. That morning he told her he would be back after stopping downtown. In the turmoil of the day, he had not managed to swing by home, now regretting his hasty choices. He should have prioritized Sara. By the time he attempted phoning again, even his last lines of communication were down. Now Alijah was left cursing what would appear as callousness, but in reality, was navigating the quagmire of what had become civil war.

Out the window, a dog ran around the grounds, confused and barking. It could sense something in the air—a new danger posed by even more sensitive noses pent up in Nairobi Park. The lion population could sniff the carnage miles off as cubs not yet versed in hunting moved towards the park fences. Some were leaping up against them, scraping at the wire, desperate in their scavenging quest. Should they spring loose, they would find hundreds of bodies strewn throughout the city. Blood from the human carcasses dampened the littered streets. The developing stench mixed with the smoke and dust to asphyxiate the breeze.

Beleaguered, Nazuto burst into the room and began talking before Alijah could pick himself off the wall. "You've come from the city? What's happening? Our communications have been cut."

"Well, I didn't actually see much. I headed out just after I heard the shooting get near. There didn't seem to be much resistance. Minutes after I first heard shooting, it seemed to get pretty close."

"That's what we've heard. We received a report a while ago that Parliament is about to fall. As soon as that happens, I'm leaving," Nazuto declared, emphatic about his retreat.

Alijah stood stunned, the severity of the situation exceeding any of his fears. He presumed the coup attempt to be routine, the type fought off every few years. This was his first time witnessing such an assault, and he had mistakenly categorized it as threatening but not fatal. There had been no signs to gauge why this attack was so cataclysmic. The collapse of the government seemed an impossibility. When driving out to the compound, he obsessed about how long Nazuto would seclude himself before restoring order. He even dared to consider the purge that would ensue. A tremor shook through his body. He was a target.

"Are you sure?" he asked in disbelief. "You can't mount a counterattack?"

"Alijah, I don't think you understand. If I don't leave within the next hour or two, I'll be publicly flogged."

"Where? Where are you going? ...How?"

Alijah froze as Nazuto pulled a gun and pointed it directly at him.

"Sorry, Alijah. I don't have much choice."

"What are you doing?" now almost apoplectic in his tone.

"How did you know to warn me a couple of weeks ago? When you told me there might be some terrorist act trying to stir up racial violence, huh?"

"I was warned myself."

"By who?"

"Someone in the rebel forces," he answered, not wanting to admit his son may have been responsible for the overthrow. "I wasn't quite sure," his only desire now to protect Kiku.

"I'm sorry. I don't believe you."

"But, that's..."

"You betrayed me!" Nazuto yelled, pulling the trigger. Alijah slumped to the floor, mortally wounded, struggling for his last breaths. "It was my son. I couldn't tell," the balance of his sentence dying with him. Nazuto dropped the gun where he stood, and somewhat shaken himself, strode out of the room to escape in a waiting jet.

The Nairobi airport had been closed since nine o'clock the previous evening, and though not on his presidential plane, Nazuto was still bound for safe refuge. By dark, he would be in Kampala, Uganda.

·    ·    ·    ·    ·

Michael, Caroline, and Julia had hoped to be similarly airborne when they headed in the dark for the airport. Richard's friend Edmund had come by the house, having been at the Polo Club when it went up in flames. He promised them seats on a British embassy plane that evening if they wanted to go. Richard refused for himself but just as ardently insisted that

Julia leave with Caroline and Michael. Caroline and Michael's interactions with Richard remained strained, in fact in Michael's case frosty; however, without any discussion everyone naturally put castigations aside to focus on the imminent threat.

There seemed no good reason for staying, believing when calm was restored, they could return at will. At eight, Edmund came by, relaying he had been in touch with the airport. The plane waited on the runway and would take off near midnight. They had to leave early to beat the roadblocks rumored to be springing up by the moment. Because leaving a car at the airport was tantamount to forfeiting the car, Edmund arranged to have his driver bring it back to his house after they departed; taking two cars risked more inspections and was out of the question. With no room to spare, Julia's houseboy Jomno struggled to tie extra bags onto the roof of the rover. Richard calmly stood to the side, arm around his distraught wife. He pledged to join them shortly, embracing Julia and pecking Caroline on the cheek. Looking around for Michael, he spied him in the car, wedged in by luggage, and merely waved goodbye.

Their fears of perhaps not making it came true, encountering a roadblock halfway to the airport. Handing over British and American passports to the inspector in silence, the pending refugees held a collective breath until the flashlight was shut off and their documents returned. Miraculously, they were waived on without a question. Abetted by reckless driving, they soon reached the airport. Although they glimpsed their plane in the distance, the group never managed to board. A curfew had been declared, and no planes took off to leave the country—except for the one carrying Nazuto.

While Nazuto jetted towards safety, Julia, Caroline, and Michael waited in the Keeton's house, having managed to run the gauntlet of checkpoints and rejoin Richard. Between Richard's hunting guns and Michael's remaining research equipment (plus a high-powered rifle he had managed to sequester, gratefully donated from Warden James), they were well-armed. Blocking off the house's entrance, they stationed their houseboys as guards at the gate and around the perimeter. They could fend off any ambush, but not a current of the full-scale revolt. No news reached them, nor did the gunshots draw close. Only the cloud of smoke drifting out over the suburbs and dissipating over the savanna brought word of any resolution. The quiet, plush suburb stayed mute, harboring the type of isolation that the residents vainly hoped for when they first segregated themselves.

The next day passed in slow motion, all quiet until Michael burst into the living room. He was carrying a radio. "The government just announced it's broadcasting a message to the nation at five o'clock." Debating what happened, everyone rose, clustering together, waiting for the news.

Caroline suggested letting the staff guarding the gate come inside to listen with them, but Richard nixed the proposal. This was no time to let prudence give way to hope, he declared. With fear evident in his listeners' eyes, there were no objections.

Soon, the radio blared the national anthem. The crescendo caused even the strong-hearted to pause.

"Citizens of Kenya, this is General Abo Daniel Oguru. I am in command of the government forces which today have taken control of the country. We are in control of Government House and the Parliament. Former President Nazuto and his family have reportedly left the country in search of asylum.

"I am declaring martial law for the next seventy-two hours until calm is restored in the country. There was no fighting on the coast in Mombasa and minimal bloodshed here in the capital of Nairobi. Repairs will begin tonight, and services should resume normally the day after tomorrow.

"President Nazuto corrupted the government and has left the country deeply in debt. The new government pledges its support to eradicate these evils and restore the country to the prosperity of its first days of independence.

"To achieve these goals, we seek support from Western allies for new loans to educate our people, equip our depleted army to fend off rebellion spreading from our neighbors, and modernize our most basic public services. We seek to build more housing, build roads to connect our great cities, and most importantly, better feed our people.

"We encourage the foreign population not to leave but to stay and help us rebuild Kenya. We want to work in cooperation, not as puppets like Nazuto.

"We hope to hold elections in the near future. To prove our desire to reunite the Kenyan people and provide jobs, we plan to start constructing a road linking the interior to the coast by the end of the week. Anyone wanting a construction job on the project should come to the square in front of Parliament on Friday to sign up. Whoever works on the project will receive fair wages, plus free food and clothing.

"In an address tomorrow at this same time, I will announce the new Cabinet and Parliament members. Membership will be roughly apportioned according to tribal populations in census areas. The current justices will be retained except for the high court whose appointees served to apportion cruel penalties at the behest of the dictator Nazuto.

"We have peace tonight in the capital and have freed ourselves of the men who were driving us into ruin. I beg you not to take to the streets, but rather to support the new Kenya. Together we will prosper and reach the potential that we all dreamed about when granted independence such a short time ago. We have acted today because it is too late only to dream. Tomorrow we can wake up proud, new, strong, truly independent for the first time.

"This is General Abo Daniel Oguru. I have served our country loyally my whole life and look forward to serving you in the days ahead. From Government House, goodnight."

The radio launched into the national anthem again, but Michael killed the song after the first few notes. The news itself was broadly consistent with expectations, all evidence pointing to a coup. What no one seriously anticipated was the government falling so quickly, virtually without a fight. Now reconciling to the reality of a new regime, they prayed the junta would remain welcoming to the expat community. Interpreting Nazuto's overture to foreigners as a euphemism for tempering racial tensions, Michael and Caroline took comfort in this small token of security. Words might mean little given their predicament, but it was all they had as members of a privileged white minority. Perhaps the ramifications would be limited, and they could all merrily resume their lives. The question of the moment, though, was clear: did they want to stick around and speculate?

Trying to lighten the mood, Caroline put on a positive spin, "I guess we can stay. How about a toast? To the resiliency of the British!"

Richard looked up, sarcastically retorting, "How about to the death of Alijah?"

"What do you mean?" Michael joined in, his tone with Richard ever bitter.

"You know what happens to ex-cabinet officials or high-ranking ministers. When a new rebel government takes over: if they find him, he's dead."

"When was the last time you talked to him?" Caroline asked.

"The day before the shooting started. I was supposed to talk to him last night, but the phones are down. And, you know, it was too dangerous to go out. I don't know if he thought the same thing and stayed home, whether he went into the country, maybe took off in his plane. He mentioned trying to get in touch with Nazuto, but I doubt he got very close to him. I don't see how he could without knowing where he was staying. He would have had to guess and get lucky. I hope he either took off in his plane or fled to a village to be with one of his wives. The government won't check there. No census in the villages, they'll have no idea and doubt they care."

"Do you know how to find his village, where he would go?" Michael asked, unsure he could track his way to Kiku's village again without help.

"Yes, yes I do. I guess when things calm down, if there's still no word I could head out and see if he's hiding. But I'd have to be careful, make sure I'm not being followed. We've all got to watch what we do the next few days."

By the next morning, relative calm was restored in the city but not in the Keeton manor. Caroline and Michael stayed up nearly all night discussing what they should do. The options were clear-cut: leave immediately or play wait and see out at the campsite. Then there was the issue of their impending marriage. They had accelerated the date anticipating Michael being offered a professorship, and now they had to reverse course and push it back. Who would fly into the country in just a few weeks to attend? Realistically, friends would be scared to travel. They agreed to postpone the ceremony.

"What about your research?" Caroline asked, turning the conversation back to other logistics, not ready to delve into the challenge of how to deal with Richard.

"It's done. Or done enough. I can leave whenever we can find a flight." A bit testy, he said, "I told you that before."

"I was just asking! I didn't know if you said that earlier because we had no choice."

"No, I meant it. I'm really done. I've applied for the professorships, filmed everything I want. I already had my key research complete when I met with Steve at Harvard. As soon as I tweak the writing, they'll hand me the Ph.D. on a platter, honors a la mode. I've already written a strong draft—that's what Steve basically blessed. I just need to sit down, put all the numbers together, and pull together some charts in the appendix. You know, all those calculations of gene fitness. Then clean it up a bit, and hand it in."

"That simple? And then you'll get an appointment?" Caroline mocked the ease.

"Don't jinx it. Okay? I hope it goes that smoothly. With any luck, I should get an offer when we get back. I still have to nail a couple of interviews. A lot of the time, they'll grant the position contingent on your Ph.D. being awarded. That's what happened with one of my tutors when I was an undergraduate. She was working on her Ph.D. and was supposed to be done with it that spring, but in April, Berkeley already had an offer outstanding to her. If Steve wasn't lying, I'm pretty sure I'll have a job within a few weeks of our getting there. I'd just as soon get the hell out of here right now and come back when things have calmed down. And you're rich, so we've got plenty to live on." He winked.

"I knew you were marrying me for my money. Finally, it comes out," she played along.

"Enough."

"Okay. I told you I've dealt with the horses. I couldn't leave without making sure they're taken care of. Everything else is set. The clinic can go on. It all breaks my heart…" Their planning and rationalizing easing the tension, Caroline and Michael looked at each other and embraced. The research, the clinic, the marriage were all important concerns. What trumped everything else, though, was that they were petrified and wanted to flee. Together.

· · · · ·

Julia and Richard less playfully wrestled with their own decision. Julia was emphatic about leaving, and Richard resolute about staying. Julia had spent too much of her life living in outposts reminiscing about the antiques she so seldom could enjoy. Her daily routine was exotic, her life a romanticist's vision. But she wanted to stop, to relax in ordinary elegance, to be pampered in her waning years. Those goals remained a pipedream in Nairobi, even with the restoration of calm. Life was too difficult living amongst snakes and dinosaur-like creatures. Nigel had dragged her to the bush, and when he was Ambassador, it was wonderful, parties, safaris as living zoos. Monkeys and canapés galore—until he died. Then she married Richard, eager to become the next Lady Keeton, waiting out Graham's damn decline, stalking her silverware-to-be at the grand house in Salisbury. For years she longingly waited, knowing one day they would go home. Now came the shove. She was damned if she was going to do anything but grab hold of the momentum. It might never come back.

Mustering every ounce of his hereditary stubbornness, Richard dismissed Julia's thirst for flight. He knew that someday he would leave. After all, that was the only reason he came initially. Perched at the threshold of realizing his dreams, becoming the reincarnated Lord Keeton, the coup jeopardized his final steps— Julia's hysteria even threatening to stop him altogether. He would not be so manipulated. Victory was too close. He would return like a king to one-up or at very least equal Harold.

"Julia, I just can't go. Soon. I promise you, soon."

"Always soon! I've let all my possessions tarnish. My friendships have faded away. I can't go to the symphony, shop, or drive alone with peace of mind. What else do you want from me, Richard? I want to go back home to England. Is that so terrible? Don't you ever long for that?"

"Yes, and I want to go too. Just not immediately. Not like this. Will you deny me trying to find Alijah? Let me look for him in one of the villages. Then when I find him, go on one more hunt, knowing it will be my last. That's all I want. Space to withdraw properly. Then I can leave, knowing I won't yearn to come back. It's not that far away. It isn't."

"I won't fall for it this time. You're just stalling, and I refuse to swoon to your fantasy visions!"

"What if we set a date? An actual date. Say four weeks from now—absolute. Would that satisfy you? Will you compromise at all? Will you let me look for Alijah before we rush off?"

Julia stood defeated, unable to parry Richard's appeal. In the stark face of prejudice, she had watched Richard grow dependent on Alijah. She believed he truly cared and could not force him to leave without learning Alijah's fate. Her sympathy turned icy, however, on the subject of hunting. Three weeks she compromised. That would let them stay through the wedding. She, too, had an argument Richard could hardly fight. Unfortunately, she would soon learn about its postponement.

In the middle of the night, both the house and city were finally quiet. Smoke from intermittent blasts quashing any remnants of resistance still cast a haze for miles, obscuring the usually vivid stars. Low clouds radiated heat close to the ground making it hard to breathe. Thick humidity further amplified the miserable mix, choking downtown and the surrounding suburbs. Sweat hung ready to masquerade as morning dew. Another tainted day rose to the shrill shattering of glass in storefronts already littered with bits of corpses.

Peace lingered in the wake of isolated outbursts of indiscriminate revenge. Angry mobs vented their frustrations, throwing rocks and bottles wantonly, lighting fires, and ransacking businesses. As innocents fled the masses, howls of joy faded down littered and deserted streets. An occasional gunshot struck back, but few people owned weapons. All most could do was wait, the next morning's light benevolently bringing an end to the horror.

Former President Nazuto woke early to listen to the radio broadcasts, hoping for news of a holdout. Instead, his fears were confirmed, his new life in exile beginning. Besides the dead, he and his family were the primary victims. The new government made no pretense of ousting any groups: not tribes, not whites, not Asians. In a few days, the country would be running as it had been for all Nazuto's life, but he would never be allowed back to watch the normal bustle. His wife, now a refugee too, looked sadly at the deposed benefactor. The day was unimaginable. Enraged, he swung a chair at the window, breaking the pane and thinking about jumping. If he were on a floor higher than the first, he might have tried. But to die an alien is no nobler than to live in exile. Decimated, he vowed to struggle on. In his heart, though, he knew his reign was over.

·　　·　　·　　·　　·

Meanwhile, Richard snored soundly, content that he had put Julia off and dreaming of finding a herd of elephants in a clearing. It would be his last peaceful slumber before the police came for him just past dawn.

# CHAPTER 13

---

*Nairobi Suburbs (Langata), Kenya*

Ever since the coup, Oguru had been rounding up scapegoats and so-called subversives. Former government officials and those who had profited from their ties to Nazuto's regime were high on the list. Any evidence of corruption or disloyalty was sufficient to justify immediate incarceration; being in a minority group cast a further target. The search was hardly systematic or public, but fear began spreading through the expatriate community within a couple of days. For former "official" advisors, the panic began with the first bullet and would never cease. Richard had never been a government official or even tied to an agency and mistakenly felt immune. He did not know if Alijah had gone to find Nazuto or opted to go into hiding, patiently waiting out the storm.

Caroline answered the door, waking Richard when she learned it was the police. Richard wondered what they could want at such an early hour, grumbling his way downstairs, cinching his bathrobe as he walked. He had anticipated some inquiry about Ron's murder, but also expected recent events might delay if not indefinitely bury the case. Two men were waiting in the foyer as Richard gingerly made his way down the banister. It was still early, and he used every moment to clear the haze of sleep tugging at his lids. Richard would need to be alert.

"Good morning, gentlemen. How can I help you?" Richard strived to be cheery. Even he was wary about direct encounters with the police. Based on recent events, he was not even sure if they were regular police or from a military unit aligned with the new government.

"Richard Keeton?" the senior-most officer asked.

"Yes, that's me."

"You're under arrest. You'll have to come with us."

"What? What for? I haven't done anything," Richard barked in the haughtiest voice he could muster.

The younger man took out a pair of handcuffs, and Richard backed up, moving above them onto the stairs. As soon as he retreated, the officer drew his gun and pointed it at Richard. His glare made it quite obvious he would not hesitate to shoot.

"Okay. Okay," Richard's voice quivering as he moved back into the entryway, surrendering and confused.

The officer spun him around, handcuffing his wrists behind his back, pushing him toward the door.

"Can I get some clothes?" Richard pleaded.

"No. Your wife can bring some."

"Julia!" Richard screamed.

In an instant, Julia and Michael joined Caroline in the foyer, the bleary triumvirate standing together in shock. Numbed by the sight, they all paused to register the improbable image of Richard in his bathrobe, hands cuffed, stubbly and frightened. Even his usually gleaming white hair appeared muted.

"Oh my god!" Julia stammered, Caroline then echoing her words.

"They're arresting me. Go to the embassy. Julia, you go with Caroline. Michael, get some money and try to follow me. God knows where I'm going."

"What are the charges?" Michael asked, uneasy about aiding Richard, yet alarmed by the sudden intrusion.

"They won't tell me."

"They've got to tell you. I demand to know what's going on. I'm an American citizen, and you're arresting a British citizen. You can't just do this!"

The senior officer looked nervous for the first time, deciding it was wise to reply, "There are many counts. Poaching. Bribing government officials. You will be provided the list at the station. The orders came directly from General Oguru."

The officer pulled out some papers, showing Richard and Michael the warrant. Richard's head dropped, "He's telling the truth. It's from Oguru directly. Shit. Julia, go to the embassy. Now! Tell them to have a seat on a plane today and come get me. And bring me some clothes. The wankers. Who do they think they're dealing with?!"

The policeman shoved Richard forward, hitting him in the back hard enough to make him stumble. Julia started reaching for him, but the other officer, still wielding a gun, blocked her path. With Richard outside, the officer spun around and closed the door behind him. Once out of view, the younger man crunched Richard's back with the butt of his gun. Thinking back to Annad Najiv, Richard stopped his cursing.

Meanwhile, Julia rushed upstairs to grab clothes for Richard and throw on some herself. Alone, Michael pulled Caroline away to a quiet spot in the study.

"What are we going to do?"

"You better go down to headquarters. You heard him. I'll go with Mom to the embassy and try to straighten things out."

Michael looked at her incredulously. "Straighten what out? The police must have been on the same trail we were. He's guilty! What the hell can we do? Christ, we were probably gonna turn him in."

"We were going to stop him, and we still weren't sure," Caroline corrected. "Whatever. We didn't know what we were going to do," trailing off, reflective, before snapping back, realizing there was scant time to muse about the predicament. "Whatever we were thinking about, I don't want him beaten. You know what jails are like here! And this is the military. One of those guys was wearing a red hat. Come on. We better hurry. Leave a message when you find out anything."

"Okay." Michael threw up his hands. "I'm going. But I don't know whose side I'm on."

"Fuck you," Caroline blasted, hysterical with emotion.

"I won't let them hurt him. Calm down. He's too well connected. It's probably just to scare the shit out of him."

"Well, it's working pretty well."

"Yeah, I know."

Michael grabbed some fresh clothes and ran to the car, putting on his shirt as he went. He tried to piece the evidence together in his mind. How had they found out? What did they know? The morning sun rose as he sped toward the city, the glare a fleeting relief blinding his thoughts. Michael considered whether they were even taking Richard to the police. Nothing made sense. The men wore police uniforms, but one of them was wearing a rebel-red hat plus Oguru was the military. Not much difference under martial law, he supposed, all branches already subdued. There was no transparent chain of command except Oguru claiming to be in charge. Maybe he should have sped after the police car and trailed them, but somehow a chase seemed futile. He would be better off showing up dressed and composed. Michael was confident they would not beat Richard. He saw the flash of hesitation, indeed fear, in the cop's eyes when he threatened embassy reprisal and the might of the U.S. heaped on top of the U.K. No, they would not harm him, at least not yet. He just damn well better be there, he now swore to himself.

Three impalas sprung across the road and made Michael swerve to miss their path. A majestic buck hesitated, staring back at Michael's car before disappearing into the morning's mist. Whose land was this? Michael tried to fight the sense he was an intruder, trespassing on the animals' domain and meddling in politics of the absurd. Regardless, he could not escape, doomed yet again to sort through a crisis neither of his initiation nor within his control. He was speeding toward town to help rescue the very man he wanted to see arrested! Richard was the embodiment of what he had pledged to fight, the very master poacher he swore to stop! Still, his foot pressed the pedal, unmoved by the irony. In his gut, he hoped he had the courage to let Richard rot. He had not made up his mind. Whether he could cover that up from Caroline or whether she would ultimately agree was another matter, which would simply have to resolve itself later.

On his way into town, Michael thought about the papers, Kent's call, and Richard's denial. What a masterful liar, he thought. There was an art to being so unabashed. Either Richard was a pathological liar and did not know the difference, or else he was so cold as to lie with dispassionate ease. He wished he could reach Jack. There must be something more in those papers. Cursing at the down telephone lines and halfway to town, he plotted a detour to Jack's house. Richard could wait. Chances were he could be waiting an awfully long time! As Michael headed toward Jack Whitehead's house, what he did not know was that Jack had been arrested too; in fact, more than a day earlier.

·     ·     ·     ·     ·

"What have I done?!" Jack Whitehead screeched at his arrestors.

"Shut up" was the last thing he remembered when he awoke alone in a cell. He had no idea where he was, but of one thing, he was confident: there were no positive signs around.

Four dank cement walls and a dirt floor granted no clues. At least there is a window, he thought, standing up and peering through the bars. There was a small courtyard outside, and he spied a couple of men in military fatigues smoking and playing cards. Jack turned around, banging on his door to no avail. He could hear muffled groans, but no one acknowledged his own. His bladder hurt. The cell was ten feet wide at best, and he surveyed the ground for where to relieve himself. He decided to piss on the foot of the door. Perhaps a trickle of urine would seep through and rouse a guard's attention.

His calculations were correct. He wondered, however, if it was worth the price when the billy-club struck his gut. Unlike Richard, he had been given five minutes to change when he was arrested. He took the opportunity to jam some valuables and cash into his pockets. Jack had been relieved he could easily hide a wad of bills, an unintended benefit from a diet and newly baggy pants. When he got to the cell, he buried the stash. He had now retrieved most of the money and let a couple of hundred shillings fall to the ground. Jack enticed the guard with promises of more if he could speak to whoever was in charge.

Jack assumed the money saved his life. The prison's military leader agreed to see him, and during their discussion Jack let another bunch of dirty notes fall to the ground. By the end of the day, Jack would miraculously be waiting to see General Oguru himself. But he would need more than money to secure that audience.

"Why was I arrested? That's all I ask," Jack began, wanting to beg but mustering an air of dignity to talk to the prison's leader.

"You worked with the ministries. Everyone linked to Nazuto's been arrested. General Oguru is determined to wipe out each link of the former corruption."

"But I didn't side with Nazuto. I had the most honest damn reputation around here. They fired me! I lost my job because I wouldn't take the bribes!"

The lieutenant looked at the ground to the money Whitehead had sprinkled at his feet. "You expect me to believe that! Get this liar out of here," he said to the guard.

"Wait. Look, just hear me out—one minute. I, I know it's hard to believe, but I didn't bribe, and I didn't take bribes. I gave the guard some money to try and talk to you because I didn't know what else to do. I was desperate. I just urinated in my own cell! Someone knocked me out and I don't even know why I'm here."

"What do you want from me?" the lieutenant said.

"What if I could give you proof? Documents of Nazuto's corruption. Papers that would show what some of his ministers were doing and proved that he knew about it. Things you could print in the papers, show the press."

"Where would you get such papers?"

"After the coup, I went over to my old office. The man who fired me had been murdered. I thought I might find something. I knew the type of things they were up to and wanted to try to clear my name. That's when I found them."

Slowly, Jack Whitehead convinced the lieutenant that he could be a hero. By bringing Jack to Oguru, Jack could give the general the hard evidence Oguru needed to denounce Nazuto to those who thought Oguru merely another military tyrant. This was credibility! And he could have a respected white Kenyan tell it to the West, praising Oguru for having stepped in and set things straight! It was a brilliant plan—if it worked.

· · · · ·

Waiting to see General Oguru, his emphysema-induced cough back with a zeal, Jack sifted through the papers he had found with Michael at Ron's office. Ron's office, he thought. What a travesty! That was his office, should still be his office! When he had gone home and studied the notes, the puzzle finally became clear. All the details of what Ron, Richard, and Alijah masterminded were there. Ron had to be a fool to keep these notes. Jack assumed it must have been extreme paranoia that drove such record keeping. He wondered whether Ron realized just how incriminating the ledgers were. Then again, the information was not exactly putting Ron away. If he had lived, though, Ron likely could have framed the others.

"The General will see you now," the guard interrupted Jack's thoughts.

At six-foot-eight tall, Oguru was an imposing figure. His brawn further distinguished his appearance, but he also bore an air of self-assuredness nurtured from years of success. The passion that flickered in his eyes when he out-tossed Alijah at the university dinner now manifest as raw power. One word, and he could have Jack Whitehead decapitated or castrated or whatever he chose to have done to him. One word!

That an individual can wield such power over other men is no less remarkable a slice of nature than the ability of a lion to chase down its prey. There was an inevitability about this man. Jack felt nauseous in his presence. Jack could come off the hero or a sniveling tattletale groveling for his life. Jack bowed slightly and did not bother to extend his hand.

"Thank you for seeing me," he said, with an equal mix of fear and gratitude.

"I'm told I will soon be thanking you. You have some papers which show Nazuto taking bribes?"

"Better than that, General. I have documents that show Nazuto actively encouraged and supported a poaching ring. One of his top ministers, who was supposed to be protecting the animals, was, instead, slaughtering them at record numbers, illegally selling the trophies to foreigners, and then paying Nazuto a cut with the profits. Nazuto must have known everything. It's all here," Jack emphasized, placing the papers on the desk in front of the General. Thank goodness, the lieutenant had taken him home to clean up and fetch the documents before meeting the General.

Jack Whitehead's heart skipped a beat as he prayed for a favorable reaction. There was no way of knowing whether Oguru was a supporter of the poachers himself and envied Nazuto for his clever scheme and cut. He prayed he was honest. Or, if not honest, he prayed Oguru would be grateful for the information that he could use to discredit Nazuto.

General Ogugu asked, "Who else was involved?"

"Alijah, I don't know his last name, Ron Easton and Richard Keeton were the principals. Ron Easton is dead. I presume you've heard all about his murder," his question hanging in the air, Jack waiting to see if Oguru would claim culpability or feign ignorance.

"Yes, I heard of his murder. I don't see how that's relevant here," Oguru skirted the question.

"It's because he was partnered with Richard Keeton. Keeton's a white Brit who has a house in Langata. And married to the widow of Britain's former Ambassador to Kenya, Nigel Dunning," he emphasized, punctuating the size of the fish he was dangling, the racial and political overtones implied. In fact, he thought to himself, it would be quite a coup for Oguru to arrest Keeton and parade him as the hypocrite he was. He would make the perfect scapegoat if he were not the real thing. The not-so-subtle trade laid out, he continued, "I don't know where Alijah is. I would expect he is trying to escape with Nazuto or something. I really don't know."

"He's dead," Oguru said, stunning Jack. "His body was found at Nazuto's compound. I once met him. I didn't think he was the type. He was in a position to do so much, you know. At least that's what I thought. Now I see why he was in the position at all."

Whitehead sensed a melancholy tone in the General's voice and decided to gamble, "I tried to devote myself to saving the wildlife. I preached the glory of this country to foreign tourists and investors. It killed me to see what the people in power were doing. These men had my job taken away to exploit it and kill the animals. I knew they couldn't be trusted, but I had no idea just how bad it was until I found these papers last week. I only hope the world learns how important your victory is. It's not too late. I swear on my life, everything I've said is true."

Jack shook with fear when he finished his soliloquy. His life was on the line and at the mercy of one man. He could believe him or have him shot, or both. Jack knew too much simply to be let go. He stuck out his chin, clearing his throat confidently, standing ramrod straight as if back in boarding school line having the knot of his necktie inspected. If Oguru were to sentence him, he wanted him to be laden with the moral guilt of condemning a gentleman, and a gentleman who devoted his life to bettering the country he was now ruling.

"I believe you. We'll look over the papers to have the rest arrested."

Jack could hardly believe his ears and strained to keep a smile from creasing his lips. The moment was fantastic. Justice. A symbol of hope. Whatever you wanted to call it.

"Would you accept your old position back? Minister of Wildlife," Oguru's voice broke in to halt his free fall of relief.

"I'd be honored. Of course! You should know, however, that I'm a dual citizen. I still hold a British passport."

"No matter. Come back and see me in one week. I'll issue a press announcement. Then I want you to go to the West and tell them what kind of man I am. I don't want to be labeled a dictator. I may have to run the country that way for a while to keep it going. But I believe in what I'm doing. Do you understand?"

"Very much so. I look forward to working for you."

"Good. And Mr. Whitehead, if I ever learn that you were part of this ring or ever hear that you've accepted a bribe, I'll have you shot."

Inhaling a deep breath and deciding to ride his good luck, Jack concurred: "That would only be fair. May I then have the authority to have poachers shot, General?" Jack somewhat impetuously asked, forgetting at the moment that his thoughts were rooted in the goals Michael and he had discussed.

"Of course. Good day Minister Whitehead. I thank you for your patriotism."

●　　　●　　　●　　　●　　　●

Jack Whitehead was still dizzy from celebrating when Michael Sandburg came crashing to his door.

"Jack. Thank god, you're here. We need some help, but before I explain, I need your phone." Michael hoped to find a live line. En route, it dawned on him he was still unsure which station Richard was being taken to—if to a station, now feeling guilty about not immediately following the police hauling him away. Jack's phone was dead. What was happening to their lives!

"Jack, Richard's been arrested. They're taking him in right now. Poaching, the whole book."

"I know. I turned him in."

"What?"

"The papers. Here, I kept a copy in the other room. I sorted the rest of the notations and the picture became clear. Richard was the mastermind. Richard, Ron, and Alijah. It's as we thought."

"What do you mean you turned him in?"

"I didn't have a choice. I probably would have done it anyway, but I had no choice. Sit down. You're not going to believe this one."

Jack recounted the vicissitudes of the last day, from pissing in jail to his new post. It seemed incredible. It was incredible.

Now knowing thanks to Jack where Richard was shackled, Michael headed to speak with the military police. Not surprisingly, they would not consider bail for Richard, nor would they tell him much of anything. Michael returned home confused and tired, eager to talk things over with

Caroline. Catching each other up, Michael recounted his conversation with Jack. She could hardly believe it, the confirmation of Richard working with Ron to poach almost a footnote. In a daze, Caroline told Michael that she and Julia had filed a protest at the embassy; sadly, the staff could do little more than offer comfort. The new government was still forming, and they did not even have a contact with whom to lodge a complaint. "We'll do everything in our power," they had feebly promised.

And so, Michael and Caroline hugged each other while Richard rotted. In fact, by coincidence, Richard rotted in Jack Whitehead's urine. They were keeping all the society whites who were arrested at one jail that had fast filled to capacity. That was, of course, until Jack Whitehead vacated a cell. Now Richard watched the same guards play cards and take slow drags on their cigarettes.

•   •   •   •   •

Michael woke early, anxiously driving into town searching for the day's edition of the International Tribune. He found one at the Hilton and began devouring the news. Nazuto had made it safely to Uganda but had been denied asylum by most of the western countries. The press predicted that he would leave Uganda soon since it was precariously close to home and not likely to remain safe for an extended stay. So far, Nazuto's only options seemed to be Morocco and Saudi Arabia. He had an estimated fortune of thirty-eight million dollars, most of which was believed embezzled over the years from government coffers. Exile from the Kingdom would at least be comfortable; not exactly the existentialist horror reviled by Camus.

Reports from the capital tallied the number of followers not so mysteriously found dead during the past days. Their ranks included everyone from Nazuto's relatives to missionaries suspected of laundering funds. Atop the list, however, were Nazuto's crack troop of bodyguards. Brutish enforcers who had terrorized the populous for years, they were doomed from the moment the capital fell. There was too little time to hide and too many victims who knew their homes and buddies. Once a guard was spotted, it was hard to stave off a public flogging. The scenes were repeated in grotesque similarity throughout the country but finally appeared to be tapering off. The paper suggested the only reason for the decline was the shrinking number of potential victims, not the hunger to continue the pace.

That mobs formed lusting for revenge was not much of a surprise. Innately cunning, the master of the carrot and stick, Nazuto for years had subdued those not quaking in his presence with promises of loyalty. It was one thing not to capitulate and quite another to court him as an enemy. Common goals and passions would not temper a man who acted capriciously, and at times cruelly, and treated each moment of life as a temporary passing unconnected to the rest. Time was on his side, Nazuto used to brag; blinded by youth and dismissing consequences, there were few constraints. Guilt was anathema. All that remained was the momentum of megalomania, which grew exponentially until finally, it knew no bounds.

In contrast, Ogugu was a little-known figure both in his own country and to the outside world. The papers were speculating, but some theorists argued he was strongly influenced by Marxist philosophy. Others pointed to his university training and the disillusionment suffered by his father, a one-time Olympic hopeful. He had succeeded by recruiting talented young lieutenants and preying on racial tensions. As always, there was also a healthy measure of luck.

Michael looked up, weary of the conjectures. No one knew the truth. Oguru had not granted interviews to the press, yet the pages needed filling. The public's appetite for behind-the-scenes coverage was voracious. Michael left the paper in the hotel lobby, heading home. A brief stop at the American embassy assured him he was safe and could focus on packing up, even tinkering with his research notes.

What he was really thinking about, however, was Caroline. Richard's predicament was putting a severe strain on their relationship. Michael grimaced, pondering his choices. With the world around him crumbling, he craved stability. Caroline was his new world. He could face the future, no matter how bleak, so long as she was there. That sense of grounding steadied him as he gathered in the chaos of streets strewn with broken glass, anxiety permeating every man's stare. Amid this omnipresent tension, Michael felt peaceful. He could die knowing that she knew how much he cared, how much he loved her. It felt corny, but as he drove, he composed a poem to her in his head. He would rush home and kiss her gently on the lips, waking her up, and telling her he loved her.

Yes, he had to make their relationship work and somehow resolve the complications Richard posed. Back home, he could never find someone who would understand the adventure his life had become. The local politics would be so stale. The conversations! The semi-annual men's sale would be going on this weekend. Did he need a new belt? Michael shook his head and crushed the accelerator. It was a dirt road. He shuddered at the claustrophobic thought of pavement: pavement everywhere, closing in, curbs of prosperity.

•    •    •    •    •

When Michael arrived at the Keeton manor, a pregnant black woman was waiting at the gate. She seemed familiar, but straining his memory, he could not recall who she was. Nevertheless, he was positive he knew her. She was pretty, curvaceous even while carrying a child, dressed casually in a black dress. Sara, wife number one or two of Alijah, depending on how one counted, immediately remembered Michael.

"You're Michael, aren't you?" Sara began.

"Yes, Michael Sandburg. I'm sorry, I can't remember your name. I know we've met."

"Sara. Alijah's wife. I think we met at one of those embassy parties."

"Oh yes. Hi," Michael perked up, then finding himself awkwardly staring at her stomach. "And I see you are expecting. Congratulations."

"Thank you. The doctor said it's a boy."

With the conversation turning to Alijah, Michael flinched, his mind starting to race. Did she know? Michael had learned of Alijah's fate from Jack Whitehead. Unsure how to handle the news, or whether she was aware, he softly asked, "Have you heard from Alijah? Is there any news?"

"He's dead. Shot." Sara had done her crying, but the words still made her lips tremble. "I loved him. He was never all mine, but I loved him."

"I'm so sorry," Michael said, putting his hand on her shoulder, unsure of how else to respond. He thought about the papers Jack Whitehead translated and realized Alijah's fate was for the best. Alijah would have been dead shortly in any event, perhaps even tortured. Should he tell Sara, he wondered. Did she know? How could she not know? He and Caroline had not been sure.

"I'm looking for Richard. Do you know if he's home," Sara asked, her tone still somber. Something in her voice told Michael she did not trust Richard. This was not a social call.

"No. I guess you haven't heard. Richard was arrested. They have him in a military prison. I just found out the details of where he's being held."

"Prison?"

"Yes. I suspect the same might have happened to Alijah had he lived. They're rounding up Nazuto's supporters, you know."

"Yes, I've heard. I was hoping Richard would come to the funeral."

Michael thought about the implications, wondering about Kiku and Tza. Did they know? He wanted to ask Sara whether she had consulted them. Did Sara even know about them? Had Alijah ever discussed possible funeral arrangements with her? Maybe he would prefer to be cremated with the tribe. The thoughts danced in his head as he suppressed the urge to ask Sara. Sara's pregnancy only complicated matters further and he decided it best to avoid any discussion of Tza.

She continued, "I think he left a will. Richard was in charge. He always said there was a lot of money. I don't know. I haven't seen it. I just remember his telling me to talk to Richard if anything ever happened to him."

"I'm sure it's all taken care of," Michael tried to comfort her, knowing he would have to talk to Jack again to unravel Alijah's end of the finances. "Look, I'm supposed to visit Richard. Let me talk to him. It's difficult now. I'll try to reach you in the next couple of days and let you know."

"But the funeral..."

Ashen, "I'm sorry. I wasn't thinking. I'll call you by tomorrow morning. Is that Okay?"

"Yes. Let me give you my address. The phones are not very reliable lately. Maybe you can come in Richard's place…I'll give you the address for the funeral too."

·　　·　　·　　·　　·

Michael was denied access to Richard and decided to accept Sara's invitation and attend Alijah's funeral. He was hoping Kiku would be there.

Caroline held Michael's hand as they walked into the church. It seemed strange being in a church, but Sara's family had lived in the city for three generations. The missionaries had taught her grandmother, and she had attended one of their schools before university. Sara was seated in the front row, her pregnant tummy apparent. Michael wondered if Kiku knew he was about to have a half-brother.

The preacher talked about Alijah as a hero. He had known him, though not well, and viewed him as a pillar of his generation. Michael thought about the irony of Alijah's fame. If the men and women in the room had only read the papers he and Jack discovered. Maybe they did know, Michael speculated. Alijah was emotional and cocky. Could he have kept such riches, such a scheme secret?

Sara looked down at her stomach and cried. Once the eulogy was over, she collected herself and rose. The minister was still leading the ceremony, but all eyes were on the widow walking the wrong way down the aisle. Her eyes met Michael's, and she then cast her gaze down and rubbed her belly.

"You'll grow up to be a better man than your father. I hope you never know what kind of a man your father became," he could almost hear her whisper. That was when Michael realized Alijah could be a hero to the children. On paper, in the stories, he was indeed a great man. His eyes followed Sara to the door, and in the light stood Kiku.

Outfitted in his military uniform and broadened by its epaulets, Kiku looked larger than Michael remembered. Had it dawned on Michael, he would have realized that it was the first time he had seen Kiku in western clothes, to the extent rebel uniforms counted as such. Sara walked past, uncomfortably pausing to nod with the formality of a stranger paying respects; they were no strangers, though, even if perhaps Sara wished the relationship away. Kiku was a complication she had never known how to handle; a tie to Alijah's past not cut with the ease of an umbilical cord but rather tied with the strength of an unbreakable bond still coursing with common blood. Kiku rebuffed the slight, moving to embrace her, no stepmother but still family of sorts. Michael pulled out a handkerchief to wipe the tears from his eyes. Somehow, he knew it was their first embrace and that Kiku understood she carried his kin.

When the ceremony was over, Michael walked outside and brought Caroline to say hello to Kiku. After conveying his sympathies, Michael asked whether there would also be a ceremony in the village. If so, he wanted to attend. Kiku shook his head no, and in his eyes, Michael knew that Tza disapproved. In the end, he had abandoned her, unable to face his past. There was no spirit of revenge. Galo's funeral had emotionally crippled the village, and bringing back Alijah's ashes would only reopen the wound. Caroline sensed the emotions that were stirred, asking Kiku if he wanted to be alone with Michael. He nodded yes, coveting the privacy.

Kiku had become a lieutenant in Oguru's forces, lapping up the dogma like a thirsty lion at the watering hole. He had helped plan the coup, even seeking Alijah's help to stir up racial tensions as a cover. They recruited the outcasts for help, preaching Marxist class equality. They even reached out to the Asian community, and many of the Indians, resentful of their treatment, agreed to act as lookouts. Converts were given food, clothing, and rifles; quite a loot for those living in the streets. Kiku believed in the words he spoke. He always had, Michael thought. What a pity he had never understood the context.

The brutality of Ron's murder was not part of the plan Kiku helped foster, and throughout his life, Kiku would feel guilty about the grotesque means that tainted the rebels' otherwise lofty goals. He had never appreciated—still could not—the embers and angst of racial violence, nor the wanton brutality it could unleash. Had he done so, he never would have asked for his father to become complicit. Staring at the ground solemnly, Kiku bid thanks that Alijah had been smart enough to reject involvement. He wondered if, in his shoes, he would have had the foresight or courage to do the same. What had he, what had they all unleashed, he wondered, wiping tears from his eyes and walking away. Mercifully, at least, his agony was not compounded with the guilt of knowing he had contributed to Alijah's death. He would never learn that Alijah's rejection was an inadequate shield and, that cruelly, the vaguest taint from the bond of father to son had doomed Alijah, unwittingly casting him as a traitor.

"So, what's he doing now," Caroline asked Michael, who had now rejoined her.

"Interestingly, he's been put on military patrol overseeing part of the round-up. Guess he speaks pretty good English and they've collected lots of people like Richard."

"Do you think he can help with Richard?"

"Maybe. I think so."

"Well, did you ask him?" Caroline's tone sharper than she intended.

"No, I didn't ask him. It's a little difficult seeing Richard's been charged with having worked with and probably used his father to slaughter animals for profit. I've got to think about the best angle. Anyway, over at the embassy, they told me they hoped he'd be set free soon. No idea if they have inside information or that was just wishful thinking. I wouldn't be surprised if they were trying to get rid of me. It was chaos over there."

"Well, there are worse things than wishful thinking right now."

"What do you want to say to him if he gets out?" Michael probed. "We know he lied to us. Do you still want to confront him?"

"I suppose. I'd like to make him promise he's done with all that. Just admit it. Then I want him to move back to England. That's what mom wants. Maybe I can force him to make some kind of amends. Maybe work in a rehab clinic for wounded animals that I can help supervise as a vet. I know, it will never happen. But indulge my fantasies."

"Fantasies," Michael raised an eyebrow, trying to lighten the mood briefly. "In that case, what about the money? I could use a fortune."

"You're kidding, right? I haven't even thought about whatever he's stashed. I bet there's a lot. Maybe we can convince him to give it to a good cause."

"Like wildlife research," Michael snickered.

"Yeah, like animal conservation," Caroline half-heartedly laughed to herself, stoking the fantasy.

The stakes were too high to keep up diversionary conversation and they drove home from Alijah's funeral in reflective silence. Soon their car pulled up to the sprawling mansion. The same giraffe that Michael had seen months before in his stupor when joining Richard for breakfast stood at the well taking a drink. The giraffe was majestic, turning to run when it saw the car coming toward the house. Its legs seemed to suspend in mid-air as it loped away toward the bush. It disappeared at the same moment Julia burst through the front door, screaming hysterically.

Richard was now also being charged with treason: the penalty death. The military could sentence him on a whim. Jack and Michael's evidence made him the perfect sacrifice. Jarring wisdom!

# CHAPTER 14

*Nairobi Suburbs (Langata), Kenya*

The morning paper splashed Jack Whitehead's appointment across the bottom of the front page. Michael Sandburg dignified the news by spilling his coffee and obliterating the picture. He had arisen early again, having slept fitfully, still used to rising at sunrise in his tent. His mind futilely spun schemes to free Richard without exonerating him. Michael was ready to capitulate, no more enlightened than when he vainly cycled ideas in the middle of the night pacing the halls. Even Michael now feared for Richard. Michael looked down at the stained paper hailing Jack's resurrection. Jack Whitehead had managed to manipulate the events to his advantage. "Maybe he's the damn cause," Michael mumbled to himself, thinking about how they plotted to ensnare Richard. In truth, Michael knew Jack was a good person. Nevertheless, struggling against his will, his mind relentlessly searched for a scapegoat. A chill shook him; he, too, was at fault. It was, of course, not fault, but Michael was lured into feeling guilty if not responsible.

Michael had killed people intentionally. A lot of them. On enough reflection, he could justify each one. This was different, however; in his gut and his heart, he knew this was wrong. It had to be stopped, and relying on the embassy to take care of its subject was too risky an option. Michael toyed with notion of a prison escape, but the daunting logistics quickly halted those thoughts. He grimaced and picked up the paper, Jack Whitehead and his puffy cheeks virtually beckoning from the page. Michael resolved to pay him a visit for advice. Jack must be grappling with guilt, too, Michael hoped. He would not want Richard executed. What did they want for Richard?

The solution appeared to Michael instantly, so obvious. He finally had his opportunity and the grace of time to turn events his way. Michael felt smug as he rushed to get dressed. He was on his way to make Richard a deal.

· · · · ·

Before meeting Richard, Michael had one critical visit to pay—or, as it turned out, call to make upon learning the lines were back working. He phoned Sara to let her know he hoped to see Richard that afternoon. Michael would bear the news about Alijah, then address the will. She thanked him and was nearly hanging up when he asked if she knew where he could find Kiku. He knew they were not close, but with the funeral still fresh, Michael hoped Sara might be able to confirm Kiku's whereabouts. She could not, but then Michael remembered something Kiku mentioned about his posting as part of the military patrol. Within a couple of hours Michael was able to track him down.

By early afternoon Michael sat with Kiku in an empty café. "Your English has improved," Michael said, waiting to seize his opportunity.

"Yes. I think I now speak like my father. He always had his accent, you know."

"I think you're right. Not surprising, you look like him too," nodding with a confirming smile before turning to business. "You know there's a couple of things about your father I wanted to talk to you about. I spoke to Sara today."

"Yes." Kiku grew serious.

"She said he had a will, but she doesn't have it. Richard Keeton apparently knows everything. Probably controls everything. Or at least most of everything. Sara suspects there's a lot of money. I assume you know about Richard?"

"Of course."

"Of course, what? Did you know he and your father were partners?"

"No. Well, I thought, maybe. But I really never knew."

Michael hesitated, realizing the delicacy of the conversation. He did not want to bury Kiku's reverence for his father along with the body. "Well," Michael said, "the facts aren't all clear. But it appears Richard was poaching animals. He's been arrested. He could even face execution for some of the charges."

"That sounds... extreme," Kiku interrupted, choosing his words carefully, not letting on how privy he may be to the machinations.

"Anyway, it seems that he may have been working with your father. Now I don't know how much Alijah knew. No one does. But I do know that Richard paid for his education, took him under his wing, treated him almost like his own son. I'd be shocked if Alijah didn't grant him a little latitude. You know, grant him extra hunting permits."

Michael emphasized the word "permits," trying to keep the story credible without tainting Alijah more than necessary. It could even be possible, he thought. "Alijah loved Richard. He'd have done anything for him. He owed him his life."

Michael paused and stared at Kiku, who was listening intently but not saying a word. He continued, "I suspect that Alijah had a lot of money, and I was hoping to go to Richard and ask about it. I was also hoping that you might be able to help me get him out of jail."

Michael leaned back and sighed. The bait was there. He had debated whether to emphasize the moral obligation, the friendship with his father, or focus on the money. He could not decide, and not knowing how Kiku would react, pushed them all.

"Is this a bribe?" Kiku began. "I'd be getting the money anyway, wouldn't I?"

"I don't know. Maybe it all goes to Sara," Michael hypothesized. "She did come to me about it. If it was all going to you, I doubt she would have raised it. Honestly, I was surprised he had a will. And then there's the baby," he let the intimation hang before continuing. "In your village wouldn't you just automatically inherit as the oldest? This might be all Sara's doing."

Kiku now shifted uncomfortably, the doubt and anger clear in his expression. "Maybe."

"I don't have any stake in the money," Michael took his cue. "I just want to get Richard out. I'm engaged to his stepdaughter. He was your father's lifelong friend, his mentor. I thought we had the same interests. I only brought up the money because Sara called me, and I thought I should let you know."

Kiku sighed, "What do you want me to do?"

"I want you to get him out. Legally or illegally. I can put him on a plane out of the country. I just need to get him out of jail." Pleading, "I don't want him to die. I can't let that happen to Caroline. Can you help get him out? Please."

"I'll try." Kiku nodded soberly, conflicted by his current cause, personally not feeling any loyalty to Richard but still acknowledging how much Richard had done for his father. Without that path, he would not speak English, would not have met Michael and listened to the radio waves, would not be who he was. "What about Sara? And the money?" he then asked, the quid pro quo evident. Fealty to Marxism had its limits.

"I'll do whatever you want. If I tell Richard we're getting him out, I'm sure he'll do whatever we want. He has a penchant for acting self-interestedly," Michael grinned. He knew he had won, but suddenly felt a bit hollow. His intention had never been to cut off Sara completely, yet he needed to play all his cards to convince Kiku. Michael parked that dilemma for the moment, thinking Caroline might be able to help him sort out a way to protect Sara while keeping Kiku in the dark. "Can you get me in to see him quickly?"

Kiku nodded yes. "If you don't hear from me, be there tomorrow morning at eight."

•   •   •   •   •

Richard looked and smelled wretched as he rose from the bare floor of his cell to greet Michael. His white hair was caked with dirt, now a speckled Oreo-colored mop. He had only been in prison a few days, but the time had broken him. The words Richard Keeton and weakling fit uncomfortably in the same sentence, yet nothing had prepared him for this level of degradation. Unshaven, disheveled, and with a rasp in his voice, Richard looked old. More than old, Richard looked defeated.

They stopped beating him after the first two days. The embassy officials demanded a visit, and the jailors were forced to clean him up. He had been fed, brought fresh clothes, allowed to wash, and even jogged around the courtyard. He had not ventured outside since. The food was rancid, and Richard barely ate. The guards made a point of always giving him the food and reminding him it was his choice not to eat. The live insects crawling around the bowl were not their problem.

"Michael! Oh, what a relief. How did you get in?"

"Never mind. How are you holding up?" He looked around, aghast, "It looks pretty… rough."

"I'm no martyr. It's hell. What's happening? The guys from the embassy couldn't tell me anything. Can you get me out of here?"

"I think so. I've got a plan."

"What? Tell me! They're acting fast. No one will ever know. They can cover it up. They can accuse me of whatever they want. No one will ever believe my side."

Michael was pleased with Richard's tone: he was desperate. Grimacing and tugging at the back of his neck, Michael began. It was going to be a rough speech, but he had made up his mind. He had the leverage and was going to use it. Today's message was not about right or wrong or even fairness. Wasn't that how the game works, he thought to himself? He could do the proper thing, the moral thing, or he could, in one act, turn everything to his advantage. Bringing down Richard and his ilk, memories flashing back to the baby elephant streaked with blood, had driven him to kill; here, he could press his ultimate victory. Is vengeance truly a worthy goal? There is no right course, he thundered to himself. He had been taken advantage of since the day he arrived. The opportunity would never be there again. He could still change everything even after striking a deal. His heart pounded.

"There's a cost," he began. "Ron Easton kept a record of everything. Ledgers on you, Alijah. You haven't been framed. You're guilty as hell, and you know it."

Richard backed against the wall in shock, "What?"

"Do I really need to repeat it? Ron kept a book. Every sale, every transaction from your poaching. Probably to protect himself. Jack Whitehead and I found it when we searched his office."

Richard knew he was defeated. "God damn bastard," he muttered, unclear whether he was talking to himself or back to Michael. He looked at the ceiling hoping for inspiration, a next move, though he knew he was facing checkmate.

"You're in here for good reason. They could kill you and flaunt it to the press. Totally justified. I have a copy of Ron's notes. I know."

Michael paused, looking at Richard, now thoroughly in command. He pressed on: "There's more. Sara, Alijah's wife, called me. Alijah was shot during the coup. She thought you had his will. She wanted you to come to the funeral. It was a couple days ago."

The cumulative news was more than Richard could bear. He squat in the corner, fully overcome. Ron hacked to death, Alijah killed, the great and soon-to-be Lord Richard Keeton decrepit in a dank jail cell in the middle of Africa. How had it come down to this? Out of moves, just when he was to be kinged. It really was checkmate. Choked up, he asked, "Alijah was shot?"

"Yes, I don't know the details…. Does it matter? I went to the funeral. Caroline and I both went."

Richard thought back to the day he first met Alijah, seeking to replace his guide Colonoso, and how Galo's spear whistled through the air and struck more truly than the best knight could have boasted with a lance. Cocky Alijah, brilliant Alijah. Yes, he had taken advantage of him, groomed him, even used him. But he needed him and never would have been so successful without his bravado. Despite the rock of aristocratic upbringing and years shielding emotions, Richard cracked. He started weeping like a child. Michael was not sure whether Richard was crying for himself or Alijah. It hardly mattered. Richard was responsible for both.

"What do you want from me?" Richard capitulated.

"If you want to get out of here, I want all the money. Some of it I'll need to help get you out. The rest, well, you shouldn't care too much about that. I'm marrying Caroline anyway. You can think of it as an early inheritance."

"You. Fucking. Bastard," Richard stated, resigned, equal weight on each syllable.

"I think that's what you just called Ron. Go ahead, use all the names you want. Ron's dead. Alijah's dead. You can be too. Your choice."

Richard lost his temper, abandoning all gentlemanly decorum, lunging at Michael. Michael was caught off guard but quickly regained his composure. He was in prime shape and decades younger. In Richard's weakened condition, it was not much of a struggle. Michael easily threw him to the ground. He held Richard down until he began to choke. Michael let up, pushing him back against the wall.

"I came here to help you, you know," Michael rubbed in the insult.

Richard, raised a proper British subject, had never spat in front of another man, let alone at another man. This time he could not resist. Unfortunately, his mouth was dry, and he could only muster a weak sound. Dribble clung to his lip—an indignity beyond his imagination. Richard knew this was the lowest he could ever fall, the nadir of his bearing. He wanted to die. But he was not willing to die.

"Okay. You win. Just get me the hell out of here."

"Remember, I have Ron's notes. Don't think about getting out of here and double-crossing me. Anything happens to me before the money clears, they're released, and you're back in here or worse. You understand? Complete cooperation."

"I'm following, Mr. Sandburg. Never thought you had it in you."

"Neither did I..." Michael paused, as if his moral compass would knock him off balance. With time, he might debate slippery slopes, but time was now precious, and he continued, "Look, we've got a lot of details to work out. I need to know everything."

Richard began by shading the truth about his accounts, but when Michael presented him with a page from Ron's records, the evasion became futile. Richard told him everything. The money, the accounts, the code words with Jacques Frankel in Switzerland. Michael even had him write out a letter to Jacques authorizing the transfer. Richard asked to keep enough to live on with Julia back in England, and Michael pledged to think about a fair sum. In fact, he had not worked out precisely what to do with all the money once he took possession. It all hinged on the amount. Thirteen and a half million dollars, he added! Michael could hardly believe his ears.

After tallying the plunder, the conversation turned to the coup and what people were saying. Michael was eager to learn more about how Ron's killing fit in, and was hoping Richard knew something the papers were omitting. Somehow even in prison, Richard had his sources. Between what they had both learned, a clearer picture started to emerge.

Apparently, Oguru headed an extremist schism, which aligned itself with other minorities, including the Asian population. Both outcasts of sorts, they joined forces in hopes of a chance to strike. They were backed by some groups close to Russia, who supplied them with better weapons than standard army troops carried, comrades in arms in yet another proxy struggle. Everything was couched in class jargon, wrapped conveniently in Marxist banter. "Christ, what's become of this continent," Richard mumbled.

The plan was to stir up racial trouble in the cities as a pretext for the invasion. The Indians did all the early work since presumably they would be the least visible. Nobody would link any attacks upon the whites to the Indians. They were both small minorities, largely indifferent to the other's presence except to the possible extent of inadvertent camaraderie being dependent on the mood of the black majority. "So, they murdered Ron, stirred up some looting of white businesses and everything worked perfectly," Richard surmised, noting the weakness of certain assumptions again.

"After the murder, everyone pointed fingers. Ron was a perfect target. Highly visible, always being in the press. I told him he was an idiot for being in the papers. Plus, he was living with a black woman. Tensions were stirred. Didn't matter whose side you were on. The insurgents had a pretext or rallying call, whites were scared, those in power or seeking power flexing their muscles. Saviors or savages depending on your perspective or prejudices."

Richard, beset with his own set of prejudices and paranoia, mulled whether the coup had anything to do with revenge against them. The raid on Annad —could someone have tied Ron to the assault? What if they found out we were smuggling contraband across Asia under their noses? Richard puzzled over the possibilities. Would he ever be safe even if Michael got him out of prison?

·　　·　　·　　·　　·

The guards came for Richard in the middle of the night several hours after Michael received a return cable from Zug, Switzerland. Michael's call with Jacques Frankel had gone smoothly: twelve million six hundred thousand dollars had been transferred into a new account. The account was under Michael's name, password rhinocerostusks. Michael puzzled over the missing nine hundred or so thousand dollars; Richard had promised upwards of thirteen and a half million. Before arranging for Richard's release, he confronted him one more time.

Apparently, Richard had donated $500,000 to the Royal Naturalist's Society in England. The Society had always been a good cover, and somewhat amazingly, Richard had kept his word to Andrew Harrington. The balance of just under half a million dollars was Alijah's share, which had been set up in a local account. Less than five percent of the loot had gone to Alijah, a miserly amount given his instrumental if not paramount role. Faced with the evidence against him, Richard still had the audacity to tell Michael he had intended to donate one million dollars to Harvard's sociobiology research center when Michael became a professor. Michael did not believe a word of the lie and pledged to donate twice that amount the day he drew up a will.

Divvying up the fortune to fairly compensate both Sara and Kiku proved easier than he had imagined. Since Michael was de facto trustee of the fortune, Caroline suggested simply leaving Alijah's local account for

Sara. It would be as if the account was joint from the beginning. Michael would tell Kiku there was one and a half million dollars and that he would give him one million, two-thirds of the share from the will. It was such a large amount of money that neither Kiku nor Sara would complain. They would each be rich beyond their expectations.

When Michael delivered the news—to each of them separately of course— the only price he extracted was absolute silence. The money came from questionable sources, and Michael threatened to reveal the sums to taxing authorities if he ever learned Kiku spoke to Sara, or anyone else; Sara was similarly warned. Michael also promised both of them that he was trying to seize control of Richard's share. Diplomatically, he failed to reveal the amount, instead pledging if he obtained the money, he would donate a sizable amount to funding wildlife research and the local anti-poaching efforts. Additionally, he promised Kiku that he would set up a land trust enabling his tribe to buy its current land, tribal areas becoming a subject of debate in the government.

Michael further weighed what to give Tza directly, concerned that the money had little value to her or Alijah's other relatives. At some point, future generations would likely become assimilated into the rest of the country. Michael hoped, though, that that day would be far off and that they could retain their tribal character and dignity into the next century. Putting the money toward the land, and allowing them to maintain their current way of life, was the best gift he could bequeath. But Michael also wanted to earmark something meaningful for those like Alijah who looked beyond the tribe and wanted an education. He reckoned he could establish a trust and set certain educational thresholds—for which the funds would pay— to draw any principal. Without that type of governance, Michael feared money might be squandered, harkening back to the first day he had seen a drunken warrior passed out on the grounds of the game lodge bar. There were no easy answers—the proverb no good deed goes unpunished coming to mind.

After these grants, Michael estimated upwards of five million dollars would remain. The final tally would depend upon the land costs, the educational trust and a small amount he would set aside in trust for Tza.

Michael breathed a sigh of contentment as he drove with a guard to wait outside the military compound for Richard. Haggard, Richard was led outside, spirited away quietly, unbeknownst to the commander. Michael was not privy to the precise details, having decided it was best to let Kiku coordinate the "release." At first, they hoped to have the charges dropped. When Kiku encountered resistance, though, Michael agreed to an escape plan. Every day they waited could be dangerous. Michael also feared that eventually Kiku could be linked to Alijah, and he would lose favor. Sadly, he believed it was inevitable. Well, if he needed to bribe his way to safety, he would have plenty of resources.

Richard walked to the open car door, and Michael motioned for him to jump inside, "Hurry up. Get in."

"Where are we going?" Richard asked, confused but elated to be free, or at least escaping.

"To the embassy. There's a plane waiting at the airport. Julia's already there. Caroline's going to go too. They'll take off as soon as we board, but we thought it would be safer to transport you in a diplomatic car. The airport can be tough at this hour. They've still got roadblocks up."

"What about the house, my accounts? I can't just go."

"Sorry. There was no way to get the charges dropped. Oguru really did know about you. And with Alijah apparently paying off Nazuto…we were lucky to get you out. It was a hell of a lot tougher than we thought. Hell's gonna break loose when they see you're gone."

"Did you have trouble with the embassy?" Richard asked, now keenly aware that he was a fugitive.

"No. You know the guys over there. They think you're being set up, and I didn't tell them anything else. There was little concrete proof, and it was pretty easy to pass off Oguru's accusations as trumped up charges. The dust'll clear soon enough."

Richard was nervous, but he accepted the story. It was plausible. Strangely, what worried him most were the British authorities. He had just escaped from prison for a crime he had actually committed! His heart rushed, and he stared out the car's window silently, lowering it halfway. The fresh breeze was soothing. By the time they neared the embassy, his confidence had come back. Richard could not believe Her Majesty's government would turn over a loyal subject, a man descended from the revered Lord Harold Keeton, to such a charade of justice!

•    •    •    •    •

Richard relaxed for the first time in weeks as the plane took off, arcing north toward Europe. Michael had neglected to ask him about his personal accounts in Jersey, an independent isle jurisdiction tied to Great Britain often used for offshore payments. Richard reclined in his seat, confident that he had enough money to be comfortable. His dreams of the type of wealth that would have restored his estate and reputation to the bygone levels of Harold Keeton were gone. He could accept that fate. Harold had written that only gentleman gamblers accumulated vast riches. He had won and lost and maybe would win again one day. Richard never imagined that the press had discovered his plight, and reporters would besiege him upon landing at Heathrow. This flight would be his last moment of peace.

Richard looked over at Caroline, who was asleep across the aisle. Julia had reminded him about Caroline's wedding plans with Michael and then their likely move to the US. First, Caroline hoped to make arrangements for a recommendation from the Veterinary Society to a school in New England. Sounded something like an elephant's tusk. She always struggled to remember the name Tufts.

In a few weeks, Caroline planned to rendezvous with Michael in America. Richard was appalled at the thought of Caroline marrying Michael. "The blackmailing bastard," he thought. Then suddenly, and seemingly beyond his control, Richard began to laugh. He realized he would have done the same thing! Quite clever in fact, Richard mused, disgusted at the outcome but paying homage to the victor. By the end of the flight, Richard came to applaud the marriage. The recent jumbling of their lives hardly served as a telltale for settling down. He dared not predict whether halting the chaos with an isolated pledge of permanency would augur well for Caroline and Michael. Better hail, though, than begrudge a bold move.

Richard envied their action, consoling Julia with words speaking of jealousy rather than shock. This was precisely the time when each of them must seize control over their lives. Would such exciting choices arise again? Richard talked about needing to grasp his fortune before the present reprieve expired, speaking almost as if the apocalypse was before him. Whatever else lay ahead, stability probably did not. His two closest compatriots were dead, and survival could be his alone if he acted swiftly. Michael and Caroline must feel the same way, he urged; the temporariness of their position made impulse irresistible. Like newsreels of babies born in the midst of war, marriage plucked from the turmoil of parliamentary roulette can only inspire hope.

Julia did not feel similarly inspired, staring out the plane's window catatonically. The horror of the bodies lying in makeshift ditches after the coup was hard to erase. She made the mistake of taking a back route into town to reach the western union lines. Phone service had been erratic, and she wanted to let Kent know they were fine. She brought one of the houseboys with her, and at the sight, she made him take over driving. She now wished she had made him turn around. Julia also thought about Nigel, recalling when they first traveled to Kenya with Caroline after his appointment, and bemoaning how it had all gone wrong. What would he have thought of all this? Her mind then took her to Richard, and how he convinced her to travel back to Africa. She glanced over at him and then back out the window, the continent slipping away. She never wanted to go back.

· · · · ·

Within months Michael finished polishing his dissertation and was offered an assistant professorship at the University of Virginia and Harvard. He admitted to be overconfident about the positions and now rejoiced at avoiding the humbling his brother JJ warned might be coming his way.

Barging into Steve Barton's office, his secretary letting him in at the unexpected sting of the buzzer, Michael trumpeted, "Steve, have you heard the news?"

"Of course, I've heard! Congratulations! Who do you think makes these decisions anyway? I've been trying to call you for the last two days. If you accept here, you better damn well get an answering machine."

"Sorry. It's been beyond hectic. And I wanted to see you in person."

"I assume you're going to take it?"

"Of course! I just first needed to convince Caroline. When I got the offer at UVA, well, you know, it's near horse country, and that's her first love. Pretty tempting. And a lot cheaper to live out on a farm in Virginia."

"So, what did the trick?"

"Well, it was pretty simple. Caroline was offered a research position at Tufts at their new veterinary school. They want to expand into large animals, and she has more experience than anyone there. I can guarantee you she's the only one in Medford that's ever looked up an elephant's ass!"

Steve laughed, no idea how to one-up that one.

"Anyway, we're now looking for a place nearby to live. I want to be close, at least at first. We're making an offer on a house on Brattle Street."

"Is this the same student who kept bitching about not getting grant money every time I heard from him?" Steve half kidded, pausing for a response.

"Well, rich in-laws never hurt," Michael smirked, not wanting to reveal more than was necessary.

"What, did you marry a Wedgwood or something? Brattle Street isn't exactly your typical Cambridge suburb. They're all blue blood historical mansions over there."

"What do you want me to say? I married her for her money. Okay?"

"Just so long as I could hear you admit it."

Michael started a retort but then thought better of revealing that Caroline fell in love with Lexington, out in the countryside, and that living in Cambridge —even if it was an unaffordable mansion to an average professor— was a compromise. They had found a beautiful old estate in Lexington with a vintage barn, large enough for a stable. They were closing on the property the next day, planning to spend weekends in the country, even if it was still under an hour away.

Michael was unexpectedly rich, and while he would not flaunt it, he was not beyond taking advantage of his new privilege. Caroline was already wealthy, and had resisted taking any of Richard's tainted money. Still, he viewed the share he convinced her and Kent to accept as compensation for the toll Richard had exacted on their family; or, they could consider it an advance on inheritance. As far as he knew, estate laws rarely looked at the sins of the father—or in this case, stepfather. The upshot was most of Richard's money would be funneled back to help those in need in Kenya, and Michael was moving into an estate with enough land to build a polo field. He might need quite a while, though, to drop that last tidbit in conversation with his professor.

"Now, about the job. You're serious, you're definitely going to accept?" Steve interrupted his musings, Michael's mind having drifted back to the dust flying up in the chukker where he had first cast his eyes on the daughter of the notorious and future Lord Richard Keeton.

"I dropped my letter off at the department office on my way over here. I thought about this day every time I didn't think I would make it. Every time I found a leech in my shoe, or was stuck eating cabbage for a week, or my car broke down and I couldn't get a ride into a lodge for food, I thought about typing that letter. It's the first thing I've ever typed without even thinking about a rough draft. I can't believe it."

"Oh, don't get too carried away. It won't be long before you're stuck grading your first exam."

Michael smiled, rising to leave. As he extended his hand, he winked while chiding, "Got to get to the realtor's before three to firm things up for the house. Thanks." Prudently, he decided to omit which house.

·    ·    ·    ·    ·

Richard's life, though putatively free, resembled a self-proclaimed exile. Nervous at the sight of blacks and Indians whenever traveling into London, he opted to rest in seclusion. Time had already overcome the scrutiny originally suffocating his return; perhaps, so he prayed, it would overcome his nerves. Oguru proclaimed that neither Richard nor Nazuto could ever walk freely, and Richard deemed it wise to heed the warning. At least temporarily, Michael and Caroline appeared safe and happy: someone in the family escaped unscathed, Richard joked to Julia. She went along with his mockery, still suspicious of the poaching rumors which he continued to deny even to her. The trappings of their remaining wealth stood hidden for private enjoyment, defeating the very purpose, as far as she was concerned. They infrequently entertained and now rarely ventured the two hours to London for a show or dinner. Cooped up again, Julia begged Richard to let her at least subscribe to the Royal Ballet. "Why did we move back then?" she barbed, of course having no interest in returning to Africa.

"To stay alive," he quipped back, shutting her up until she could muster the spirit of insolence again.

Michael and Caroline were coming to visit, a diversion worthy of postponing their growing restlessness. Wary of airports, Richard waited at home while Julia struggled to peer above the crowd waiting outside Heathrow customs.

·   ·   ·   ·   ·

As the plane reached the isle of Britain, Caroline's homesickness peaked, "Michael, I can't wait to see Salisbury. It's been so long. We've got to do this more."

"Do what more?"

"Come to England, get out, you know," she said. "I'm just not used to America yet, and I still wonder if we made the right decision. Remember, I'm the alien now, and that's a lot for someone that grew up with diplomatic immunity," she kidded.

"Ouch. I can't top that. But, come on. I've got a dream job now. And so do you, might I add. We can't just pick up whenever you feel like it. And what about the opening of the Polo Club of Lexington & Concord? I thought it was a brilliant idea for you to affiliate it with the Nairobi club and the Royal whatever…The place is already fully subscribed. It's unbelievable. In the heart of the Tea Party and Revolution, people still fawn over anyone they think is linked to nobility. Such hypocrites. As much as I'd hate it, we should have your parents over just to fulfill the lure of schmoozing with a real Lord and Lady. God, are the people going to be disappointed! And you're a pretty hot commodity now, too, people gossiping how the owner of the club comes from a titled family. If I told them you'd slayed a dragon rather than stitched up an elephant's ass, and concocted a family crest, they'd probably build you a shrine. Soon I'm going to have to make an appointment just to see you."

"Oh, Michael, you almost sound jealous. Just because you're a lousy rider, and you don't have a family crest," she teased.

"What, you have a crest?" Michael paused, a bit dumbstruck. "You mean my kids could have a real family crest?" he played along, yet with a hint of genuine intrigue.

"We'll talk about that later. I thought you were just talking about how content you were, and now you're fawning over the trappings you were ridiculing."

"Holding his hands up in defeat, Michael admitted, "I am happy. Everything I could have ever dreamed of. Plus setting up an endowment for James's anti-poaching force was a brilliant idea. And incredibly selfless of you and Kent."

"Well, I couldn't keep all those millions. Sort of blood money."

"Still, it's a lot of money. You could have kept more—it's not like you're keeping the lion's share, to use a bad pun."

"Oh Michael."

"Look, really, I'm very grateful. What do you want me to say? I get to sit by the pool, take the dogs out in the woods, and tinker with how I'm going to offer a bunch of scholarships. And don't deny it. You're happy too. You'd go crazy if you were back here being dragged to pretentious cocktail parties by your mom, desperate to get out because Richard's scared of his shadow. And damn well should be. You wouldn't last the month."

"That's not what I meant when I brought up the whole thing. It's just...I don't know, a big transition. From England. From Africa. Its supermarkets, that's it, supermarkets. I'm used to eating in tents or having something cooked for me. I can't get used to the whole concept of these enormous supermarkets. I don't care if it's Sainsbury's or Safeway, and I don't know whether I ever will."

By now, Michael was laughing and put his arm around her. Impishly looking up, she continued, "I'm serious. I'm anxious about it."

The pilot interrupted them with his message of final descent. Seemingly instants after re-buckling, they were clearing customs, looking through the crowd for Julia or Richard. Caroline hoped Kent would come in time for the holidays. He told her he would do everything he could to make the trip.

Spotting Julia, Caroline broke free from Michael and their luggage, running up to her like she used to when she was a little girl. Despite criticizing her incessantly, Caroline loved her mother. Not exactly an expert on salvaging parental relationships, Michael did not question Caroline's fidelity, chalking it up to losing her father so young. Her real father's replacement, Richard, had not come to greet them. Julia told them he was waiting at the house with Kent and Ann. Michael marveled at her ignorance.

During the following days of reunion, everyone managed to forget most of the past year's turbulence, easing into the contentment of being together as a new family in England for the very first time. Even Michael and Ann, Kent's wife, felt oddly bonded to the spot as if this too were their childhood home. Only Richard had grown up there, dreaming that one day he would be able to usher a group of strangers into the glory of his past. Unfortunately, all he could offer was the disgrace of his present.

· · · · ·

The week before the family gathering in Salisbury, Richard and Julia were shopping in London when they heard an explosion outside. Someone had set off a car bomb. Joining the curious onlookers, they realized they were slowly approaching where they last left their car. Richard grew agitated and began scouring the crowd for Indians and Blacks. He no longer knew whom to trust, categorizing the world into safe and suspect groups. People in the streets were muttering something about Ireland. A woman with a Gucci bag and a stylish navy hat replete with plume poked her way toward Julia, trying to fight her way out of the crowd, muttering, "Terrorists, Terrorists everywhere."

There were rumors of Oguru hit squads roaming about the world, hunting down defectors and rebel schemers. There was no method to confirm whether the reports were accurate or merely bluffs. When speaking with Richard, Michael did little to dispel them, although he was sure the rumors were false. Urging prudence, he warned Richard to keep a low profile, avoid newspapers, and never comment on African politics. In time, perhaps already, he would be forgotten.

Richard devoured the warnings, structuring his life to avoid all confrontations and public exposure. Linked to famous landed families and having returned to Britain in a flourish of media attention, the daily rags initially camped by his door. He could not walk outside to gather a newspaper without tripping over unctuous reporters relentlessly lusting after details of the saga that had become his life. An invalid Lord, his corrupt younger brother relegated to stalking Lord Graham's bedside in an unseemly vigil waiting for the coveted title, a fugitive fleeing Africa with the wife of Her Majesty's former ambassador, a great hunter sequestered in a mansion holding trophies reminding him of glories now all in the past—how lurid!

The media's attention was stoked by Jack Whitehead, who fulfilled his pledge to General Oguru by denouncing Richard in the international press. He exposed him as a poacher, an embarrassment to the British Empire. He derided Richard as hailing from a family that had gained fortune as trading pioneers on the continent, but now brought disgrace and lack of dignity to the family name. The evidence was damning. However, Richard, the mastermind that he was, realized that he could squelch the indictments as the mere ravings of an old man collaborating with a thuggish dictator who had usurped power in a coup. Jack's accusations could be dismissed as a ranting and insignificant voice from a distant shore. Communication was not yet connected at dizzying speed, missteps harder to expose in an analog world, secrets immeasurably easier to bury. Richard's ultimate trump card was that a true gentlemen's word, and more than that a Lord's word (!), commanded a measure of uncompromising respect. What crazy crony of some African rebel should be fabricating untoward tales and besmirching his name!

Richard defiantly waited out the storm, steadfast in his belief that while the sensational travails would remain bait for a while, his stature would prevail, and the media voyeurism would wane. Patience, Richard kept consoling himself, clinging to the vision that he would be The Lord Keeton one day. And what funds he had managed to hide from the pending Lord's tusks, horns, and assorted other contraband would help restore a bit of the Salisbury estate to its grandeur. Yes, one day, he had to believe, he would restore his honor.

While Richard waited, attention gradually dwindled—as, frankly, it should have, as his attempted self-deprecating avowal that he was not all that interesting happened to be true—until finally the presumptive Lord and Lady began to feel secure in venturing out beyond the front door. Julia no longer felt watched because Richard stopped mentioning the possibility daily. But he never forgot. The torment was palpable. On occasion, he would close his eyes and picture himself shackled, back in the cell.

Except for Richard's paranoia, there was no reason to link Trafalgar Square with past horrors on a continent no longer loyal to the civility of a crown. The pedestrian walking beside Richard to the scene of the car bombing cared only of family life's daily vicissitudes, drawn to the diversion as a mere spectator. Richard's heart, however, thumped uncontrollably. He could not help pondering whether by some fortuitous stroke of luck his life had been spared or whether he had just been warned. Julia huddled close, asking him if he could see anything above the mob when he stretched up high. Finally hopping for a view, he came down to earth a relieved man: the car blown up was across the street from theirs.

"When we get complacent, it will come for us," he predicted. "One day, I'm going to have a heart attack, just from anticipation." That would be the ultimate injustice, he thought, dying before Graham. His hands still trembling, Richard backed away from the crowd to finish shopping for some new shoes. He bought the most expensive pair. He could not really afford them, but it made him feel better.

·  ·  ·  ·  ·

Michael only stayed the weekend, rushing back to Boston to edit an article and polish his lecture notes. His work was already being cited, and his teaching performance the first quarter swelled the ranks of his new class. "Michael received such great evaluations," Caroline boasted at dinner when all he could think about was leaving. Michael smiled: the evaluations were generally favorable, only a few socio-biological curmudgeons in the lot. It was a small notice posted on kiosks around the school that took the campus by storm. He would pick five students from the class to accompany him as research assistants in Africa over the summer, all expenses paid. Anyone receiving a B or better in the course would be eligible to apply for the position. Final selections would be based on interviews, not grades.

The opening lecture attracted so many students that even the three hundred seat hall's aisles were packed. Michael began, "I didn't realize this course already had a reputation as a gut," and received a huge ovation. He continued, "I suppose most of you are interested in the travel section of this class, so let me say a few words about that. The poster is not a fraud. I've established a fund to take students of this class with me for as long as they'll let me teach around here. I have three criteria.

"First, I expect some degree of academic standards to be met, but I'm intentionally setting them at an attainable level. Everyone who does the work and is interested will qualify, not just those at the very top. Second, I'm paying for this out of my own pocket, so I reserve the right to be arbitrary. Finally, I hope to choose people who want to give something of themselves to Africa, who might be motivated by something more than slideshows and resumes. For the students I take —and the number is flexible, I may take as many as I like and can swing visas for—everything is included. You just owe me the duty of being conservation missionaries during your slideshows when you come back. Let me just tell you one story, and then I'll get to the subject of this class.

"I was reading a book the other day about a researcher—let's call him a biologist— that was having an affair in his tent with a native woman he employed as a cook. One day the native's husband unexpectedly visited camp, having walked from his village for two weeks to reach the spot. When he caught his wife with the foreign biologist, he challenged him to a duel which the biologist had to accept. There were no phones around, no law to govern. The biologist, facing imminent death, grabbed a rifle he always kept loaded in his tent, just in case lions or leopards should stray through camp, and shot the tribesmen when he raised his spear and seemed to be bringing it forward. It was a pure case of self-defense.

"No one else was in camp, and the biologist and the woman quickly realized they had to hide the body. While she stood in shock, not knowing exactly how to react, he dragged the body out to a clearing not far from the camp where he knew lions frequently roamed. He heard them roar every night in the bushes. It was dusk, and the biologist hurried to set up floodlights, and with his rifle and camera waited for the lions. About an hour later, they came, and as a female scavenged on the carcass of the tribesman he turned on the lights and snapped two pictures. Quickly he dropped his camera and shot the lion, scaring the rest off. He then set the camera up on a tripod, positioned the shot, and took a picture of himself standing above the dead lion and man.

"The biologist immediately contacted the local and international press, conveying a story of the lion attack and how he had escaped but come to the rescue a moment too late. Lion attacks are rare, and the biologist immediately became a folk hero and international celebrity. Hollywood rushed to make a movie, publishers drooled over him for the rights.

"I tell this story to illustrate the type of person I'm looking for. Anyone who could ever think up a story like this I don't want on the trip or in my class. But I do want someone who is interested in explaining the biological reasons why the female lion, not the male, came hunting that night, and also someone who could keep their wits about them and shoot in self-defense if they had to. This class will teach you about the brutal reality of genes and death. It will never teach anyone to shoot, but I hope to convey something about the nuance of instinct.

"All right, let's take a look at the syllabus."

## THE END

# AUTHOR'S NOTE & ACKNOWLEDGEMENTS

I was inspired to write this novel from an experience volunteering in Kenya on a rhino rescue project. Many years ago, I was lucky enough to spend a summer in Kenya's Amboseli Game Park helping train a government unit to capture and move endangered rhinoceroses to sanctuary areas (helping is a stretch- I was a piddly volunteer fresh out of an anthropology program). It was shocking to learn about the scourge of poaching animals, a tragedy that has sadly only grown worse over time.

I remain inspired by the work of evolutionary biologists and researchers studying animal behavior. I was fortunate to study under some of the field's luminaries like Steven J. Gould and E.O. Wilson and later in life spend time discussing conservation efforts with Jane Goodall. I could never have imagined when conceiving this novel that it would be published in the wake of a global pandemic and amidst alarming climate shifts—dystopian charting forces that have put a new and urgent spotlight on the loss of natural habitats and survival challenges confronting beloved species.

*This is a pure work of fiction.* And yet, there really are people who will slaughter some of the most majestic animals gracing the earth in order to sell their parts for profit. In many cases, the professed reason is a pure myth or fraud—such as the belief that powder from a rhinoceros horn has magical medicinal value or can serve as an aphrodisiac. Equally tragic is the fact that neither a rhino nor elephant need die to take its horn or tusk (not that I am suggesting that the act of hacking off a tusk or horn is defensible in any event). I have had the immense privilege of seeing countless rhinos and elephants in the wild, both in Africa and Asia, and hope that generations to come will also have the opportunity. I am in awe of these animals and heartbroken that their survival is threatened.

Beyond thanking the animals – for just being themselves—there are a lot of people I'd like to thank. First, I want to thank Black Rose Writing, my publisher, for believing in *The Lord's Tusks*. I also want to thank my agent, Kirsten Schuder, for sticking with me, prodding me when appropriate, and championing the story. Along the way, I also had one particular editor who was incredibly helpful in providing story consistency and other notes—thank you again, you know who you are! Also, thank you to Ugna, Ali, and Charles at Holland Park Media for assistance with my cover design, and to Sara Ayers for her photography skills. Finally, I could never have completed this book without the support of my family, whose inspiration is limitless.

# ABOUT THE AUTHOR

After majoring in anthropology at Harvard, Jeff Ulin traveled to Africa volunteering with a unit capturing endangered rhinos and moving them to sanctuary areas. He jokes that stint prepared him for working on *Indiana Jones*, but it was his training in entertainment law that landed him on Skywalker Ranch working for George Lucas. After managing global sales/distribution for *Star Wars*, Jeff co-founded and ran animation studio Wild Brain where he created Disney's hit *Higglytown Heroes*. Raised in Kansas City and Boston, Jeff spent many years working in California and has also lived as an expat in London, The Hague and Mallorca. In addition to writing fiction, Jeff is the author of *The Business of Media Distribution*.

# NOTE FROM THE AUTHOR

Word-of-mouth is crucial for any author to succeed. If you enjoyed *The Lord's Tusks*, please leave a review online—anywhere you are able. Even if it's just a sentence or two. It would make all the difference and would be very much appreciated.

Thanks!
Jeffrey Ulin

We hope you enjoyed reading this title from:

# BLACK ROSE
## writing™

www.blackrosewriting.com

Subscribe to our mailing list – *The Rosevine* – and receive **FREE** books, daily deals, and stay current with news about upcoming
releases and our hottest authors.
Scan the QR code below to sign up.

Already a subscriber? Please accept a sincere thank you for being a fan of Black Rose Writing authors.

View other Black Rose Writing titles at
www.blackrosewriting.com/books and use promo code
**PRINT** to receive a **20% discount** when purchasing.

Lightning Source UK Ltd.
Milton Keynes UK
UKHW040154080922
408474UK00001B/38

9 781685 130688